The Heart of The Actuary

K T BOWES

Would you like to join my In-crowd?

I'm a believer in 'try before you buy.'
Unless it's underwear because that's super dodgy.
There's nothing worse than forking out your hard-earned
cash on a doozy and regretting it.
I want you to love my work and feel like you got value for
money.
Three of my novels are free series starters.
One is free only to subscribers.
If you'd like the free ebooks and to hear about others direct
from me, then join my mailing list at ktbowes.com

Acknowledgments

This novel is for all those readers who have demanded the
fourth book since I shelved it back in 2017.
My excuse was homesickness. It's hard to write about a place
you love when describing it makes you miss it more.
But here it is.
And I've loved writing it.
Rohan Andreyev has grown on me much more than in that
first meeting when he told me his story.
And Emma has taken her fire and learned to wield it.
Thank you for keeping your faith in me, my friend.
I hope you feel it's been worth the wait.

Minus

Emma Andreyev clutched her daughter tighter, fearing her trembling hands might drop the tiny body to smash on the hard floor. "I need to fetch my son from school." A mistimed swallow cut her sentence in half.

"Then you'd better organise something." The security guard folded his arms and spread his legs, the stance intended to intimidate Emma. "Because the cops are on their way. This store doesn't tolerate thieving, lady."

Humiliation sent an unhealthy flush spreading from her chest to the roots of her hair. She'd stolen nothing since the sandwich which fed her starving belly on her sixteenth birthday. The sympathetic shop owner caught her and compounded her shame by offering her a chocolate bar to add to her meagre meal. The items clung like ash to her throat, and she vowed to starve in the future.

Her gaze flicked to the doorway and the guard turned his body to study whatever caught her interest. He shifted enough to block the open door, and the flash of determination in his gimlet eyes removed it as a viable escape. Emma backed up further in the tiny office. Her spine hit a filing cabinet and the dull clang sent papers spewing sideways from an unwieldy pile teetering behind her head. They floated to the brown carpet like flakes of snow. The scent of cheese and onion crisps wafted around the room as a haze. Stephie murmured and bumped her forehead against Emma's shoulder. Dread filled her heart, and she cringed as her breasts tingled and then ached in a simultaneous warning. Feed time.

The two security guards had approached her as she exited the store. At first, she hadn't acknowledged their shouts, her mind occupied with her next task. Emma had bought the craft items required to turn her son into a book character overnight, the plan both genius and achievable. She'd intended to feed her daughter in the car park before fetching Nicky from school. When the guards took her by surprise in the blinding sunlight, all common sense deserted her. She allowed them to cup their palms beneath her elbows and frog march her through the aisles. Other customers turned to stare, and shock struck her dumb.

"You won't let me check your bags, but the cops will make you." The security guard postured, a wide grin splitting his face almost in half. Enjoyment flickered behind his muddy brown irises. His shirt buttons strained against a torso which arced from his collar to his waistband. He formed a human grenade stuffed into a uniform. "You're the second one today." He rocked back and forth on his heels as though expecting Emma to congratulate him. She pressed her spine against the filing cabinet and it tipped enough to hit the wall. Stephie grumbled again, bopping Emma's ear with her tiny head. Panic heightened the blue buzz in Emma's ears and prevented her from rational thought.

"I need to sit down," she rasped. She blew out a breath between pursed lips. "I don't feel well."

"She doesn't look good, Pete." The guard's sidekick stepped through the office door in time to hear Emma's plea. The antithesis of his colleague, he walked on beanstalk legs and his wrist bones protruded from the cuffs of his sleeve. "You need to let her sit down. The cop earlier said you can't be mean to them."

With a grunt of irritation, the overweight guard shoved a chair towards Emma. Its wheels splayed beneath it as it juddered across the worn carpet. Emma stared at it for a moment before sinking into the blue fabric. She rested her shopping bag on the floor between her feet, wincing as her handbag plunged south from her shoulder and landed on top of it. An unhealthy clunk told her it squashed one of the craft items. She prayed it wasn't the paint.

A vibration from the phone in her pocket acted as a starter motor. Emma shifted Stephie to lie with her head in the crook of her elbow and gazed down at her baby daughter. The child blinked her long lashes, wide blue eyes peering out at her from a state of perpetual curiosity. Her crown bounced against Emma's arm as she swivelled to drink in as much of the scene as her brain could process. Her gaze settled on the two guards and she frowned. At not yet six weeks old, her eye muscles and developing retinas would only discern the blurry shapes in the distance. But Emma's reaction to them communicated fear.

Stephie's rosebud lips parted in a wail and her forehead creased. Emma groaned in misery as her body responded and the pads in her bra soaked up the first of her milk leakage. She looked up at the guards. "I need to feed my baby." Panic added a note of aggression to her tone, galvanised by Stephie's discomfort. "Get out."

The heavier guard glanced at his colleague and rolled his eyes. Then he scowled. "No way, lady."

Stephie squirmed in her arms and drew her legs into her chest. Turning her face towards Emma, she scented the milk and urgency infused her cry. Responsibility and hormones cauterised the vying emotions of humiliation and fear. The child's needs dominated everything, and Emma slipped her hand into her blouse and released the catch on her maternity bra.

The security guard's eyes bulged like boiled eggs as Emma's knuckles showed through the fabric. He saw no flesh, but his brain ran riot with ideas and suggestions. She pushed Stephie inside her oversize blouse and winced as her daughter latched on to her nipple. Her toes curled in her plimsolls with the effect of the first strong sucks. The child quieted, her tiny fingers fretting at Emma's blouse as she got busy filling her stomach.

Maternal instincts lit a fire in Emma's belly, and rational thought returned. In a pretence of shifting position on the chair, she slipped her right hand into the pocket of her sweatpants and caressed the hard edges of her phone. The skinny guard nudged his colleague. "We should give her some privacy, Pete. She might report us for human rights or something."

"I won't do that." Emma's voice sounded stronger. Her phone buzzed against her fingers. "But you will be sorry." She pressed the longest button on the right of the screen. Three presses in quick succession. The action seemed to suck the energy and life from her. Putting her faith in someone else to bring rescue and consolation presented a risk. She tried not to consider what might happen if no one came. Because he would this time. He would come for her.

Plus

Emma glanced at the feed from the security cameras. He strode across the store, his back ramrod straight and his features hard and angular. A ball of unnamed emotion rose into her throat and sat there, blocking her next breath. Her chest tightened with its weight. She tried to swallow but it stuck. He'd responded to the SOS she sent from her mobile phone, not hesitating to seek her out and weigh into her mess. Her eyelashes blinked while her brain clamoured for explanations. She'd coped alone for so long, raising her son without hope of ever escaping her self-made poverty trap. Emma gulped, understanding what she'd missed until that moment.

Her heart gave a painful stab of fanfare as her rescuer moved with speed and determination across the store. He disappeared from the monitor as he moved beneath the camera.

The security guards relaxed while she fed the baby. She'd managed it with such discretion, the fat one seemed a little disappointed. The men still blocked the doorway, but they'd turned their bodies towards each other to chat. With their backs to the security monitors and their jaws occupied with gossip, they didn't realise a tsunami of pain headed their way in a few short seconds. Pete waved his arms as he mentioned the name of the store twice in his eagerness to impart irrelevant titbits.

Emma latched her daughter off the second breast and let Stephie's body flop across her thighs. An efficient feeder, she'd nursed herself to sleep within fifteen minutes, unlike her older brother who'd messed around for hours and given himself regular bouts of colic. Emma fastened her bra and lifted Stephie over her shoulder. Gentle pats to the baby's back sent the air bubbles gurgling through her digestive system as she snuggled against Emma's neck.

Five. Four. Three. Two. One.

Rohan Andreyev appeared in the doorway. His tall, muscular frame occupied the space, cutting out the fluorescent lighting from the corridor. His silent approach sent the security guards scrambling.

"You can't come back here!" Pete flapped his arms in front of him. "The cashier can help you, out there."

"We've got a bit of an incident." The skinny guard took a more reasonable stance.

Rohan balled his fists and his entire body tensed. He walked through the guards as though they didn't exist. They parted before the wall of hard muscle like leaves resisting a waterfall, closing behind him.

"The cops are coming." Pete raised his voice, all authority gone from it. "We did a citizen's arrest. For shoplifting."

Rohan ignored them. His facial muscles relaxed as he stared down at his wife. "Well done." He gave her a nod of approval. "You remembered to press the button."

Emma nodded. Rohan's presence negated her need to assert herself. She must hold it together until she reached her car. Then she could cry like a baby. She cleared her throat. "They mentioned the store name. I hoped you'd know where to come."

"Da." Rohan replied with the Russian affirmative. "I heard." He lifted his hand and gentle fingers coasted over his daughter's round head. Her downy hair moved beneath his touch. His nose wrinkled and his jaw hardened as he spun to face the two men. He directed his next question to them. "Why are you holding my wife here? Tell me." Authority dripped from his tone and the guards baulked against the force of it.

The skinny guard pointed towards Emma's shopping bag. "We're not sure what she stole." The words stammered from his lips. "Someone saw her put something in there, but she didn't pay for it at the checkout. We arrested her just outside the store as per the legal requirements."

Emma's heart sank, and she released a groan with her next exhale. Gratitude flooded her senses when Rohan didn't turn to question her or doubt her integrity. She tutted and leaned her head back against the brick wall behind the seat. The rough texture snagged at her curls.

Rohan bent and seized the shopping bag. He upended it on the floor and craft items scattered around his feet in a wide arc. Red paint dribbled from its cracked plastic container, staining the carpet with the last few spots it hadn't already spread throughout Emma's bag. Rohan held the fabric by one corner and jerked his head at the two guards. "Well!" he demanded. "Talk duraki!"

Idiots. He'd insulted them in Russian. Though the word might have sounded nonsensical, they understood his meaning.

"We need the receipt!" Pete sounded less sure. He shifted from foot to foot and glanced backwards at the doorway. Emma's gaze flicked to the security feed, and she saw a police officer walk through the automatic front doors.

"Emma?" Rohan's tone sounded tender. His faith in her sent tears prickling against her eyelids.

"My handbag," she whispered. "I stole nothing, Ro."

"I know." Leaning down, he grasped the handles of Emma's bag and hauled it against his chest. He fumbled the clasp and zippers before withdrawing a length of greying receipt. Grunting, he shoved it back inside and withdrew another. "Bargains for Everyone," he announced, his tone confident as he read the header displaying the store name. "I will read things to you."

"No." Pete shook his head and his voice became a whine. "That's not how it works. We take the receipt. There's a process."

"Not today." The Slavic undertones of Rohan's accent induced a sense of threat where none existed.

"What's happening?" The cop arrived in the doorway and the guards took turns to fix identical snarls of victory on their faces. Pete gave a slow nod and rubbed his hands together. His muddy irises lit with a peculiar sparkle.

He jabbed his index finger first at Emma and then Rohan. "This woman stole from the store and wouldn't let us check her bag. Then this guy turned up and started breaking stuff." He pointed to the red stain on the carpet. The cop stiffened and his eyes widened.

"Not blood!" Rohan's tone dripped with disdain. "It's paint for our son's costume. My wife nipped to the shop, and these clowns detained her. For no reason!" He turned his blue-eyed glare on the two security guards and they both swallowed.

Emma cleared her throat. A hard birth followed by a blood transfusion, surgery, and weeks of recovery had sapped her energy. It also benched her self-confidence. She'd relied on her husband enough for one day. "Take Stephie," she said to Rohan. "I'll sort it out now." Their fingers brushed as Emma lay the child in her husband's arms. "Thank you," she whispered, the word communicating more gratitude than the action warranted.

Rohan took his daughter, handed the fluttering receipt to Emma, and stepped away from the mess on the floor. Seeing his hands busy and no longer bunched into fists, the guards heaved a collective sigh of relief. Emma spotted a glimmer of disappointment in Pete's flaccid features. She sensed he'd enjoy a few good work stories, although he'd always tell it from the hero's perspective.

Emma held the receipt out to the police officer. "Please, can you read the items? I'll match it to what came from my bag."

Pete tried to complain, but the cop silenced him with a frown. He stepped in front of the guards and obscured their view. Fresh faced and pleasant, he seemed keen to get to his next job. Between them, they matched everything from the till receipt to the items scattered on the carpet. Red paint stained Emma's fingers as she handled the objects with which she'd intended to heal her strained relationship with her son. Rohan made a phone call while she worked, asking a friend to collect Nicky from school.

"He'll be disappointed with me." Emma looked up at Rohan and watched the blue of his irises darken. Tears welled in her eyes. "I promised."

Rohan's lips twisted, and he gave a definitive nod. "Will be okay," he assured her. "I'll make sure of it."

"There's nothing extra in this lady's possession." The cop turned to the security guards, his tone terse and his movements jerky. He squatted next to Emma, his Kevlar vest obscuring the outline of his torso. "So, what's the issue here?"

"Her handbag." Pete jabbed a chubby index finger at Emma's bag. Discarded at Rohan's feet, it remained open, old receipts still spewing from its bowels. Emma looked at the evidence from a lifetime ago that she once ventured out alone and without fear of her body's inadequacy.

The police officer released a sigh of exasperation. He jerked his head at Emma. "Do you mind, miss?"

"No." Emma sat back on her heels, exhaustion dragging her muscles towards the earth. Her plans hadn't seemed over ambitious as she made them with Nicky that morning. Yet the day's events robbed her of her dwindling energy as though she'd already swum in rapids. She stared at the office carpet and wondered how she'd survive until bedtime.

The police officer dug through Emma's handbag. His radio crackled on his vest. He shuffled the old receipts into a pile and sat them on the desk, his actions conveying care and respect. Emma's red purse sat on top of them and he lifted out a book. "*The Cock with the Crimson Comb*." His lips quirked upwards into a smirk. "Victor?"

He faltered on the surname and Rohan finished it for him. "Victor Vazhdayev. It was my brother's favourite book. My syn wishes to dress as the character. For my brother on the anniversary of his birthday." Rohan's jaw showed through his cheek. He didn't elaborate on Anton's current status, his brother's ashes scattered in the gardens of Wingate Hall. Instead, he jerked his head towards the packets of feathers covering the floor. Red paint stained the plastic and obscured the labels. Rohan's eyes narrowed as he turned to face the guards. "I suspect my wife pulled the book from her bag to check the colours. That's what you saw."

Emma swallowed and stared at her ruined project. Misery shrouded her like a cloak. She'd wanted to fetch Nicky from school herself and show him the feathers and paint. She'd used Stephie's nap time to cut out a cardboard crest and find an old jumper suitable for attaching the coloured feathers. But she'd failed. Again. Allaine would greet him from class and the disappointment would further damage their tenuous connection.

"She could have stolen it from the children's section." The skinny guard reached for an explanation, though his guilt laden gaze flicked to the battered story book. "Someone saw her do it."

The police officer set the book inside Emma's handbag with care. Then he turned to the guards. "Get the manager," he demanded. "Why isn't he here?"

Pete fluffed his chest and his buttons strained enough to create gaps of hairy pink flesh between the edges of his shirt. "Off sick today," he announced. Assumed authority glowed from his eyes and he straightened his spine. "We're in charge."

The officer's shoulders slumped. "Right," he replied, his tone brusque. His index finger jabbed to within centimetres of Pete's bursting shirt. "Then I suggest you replace every single item from this lady's bag and apologise." His teeth ground in his jaw.

Multiplied By

The short walk across the car park passed in a blur. Emma kept her gaze lowered to the pavement, concentrating on her feet padding one in front of the other. The ruined cloth bag flapped at her legs. Someone bumped against her as she followed Rohan. She winced at the pain jarring her stomach and lifted a hand to protect herself. The bag strap twisted over her wrist and spread red paint over her sweatpants. Emma didn't glance up at the culprit, humiliation shrouding her as she imagined scandalised shoppers whispering behind their hands. She stopped at the curb before following Rohan. To her surprise, no one showed any interest in her progress. Trolleys wheeled through the car park as people unloaded their shopping into their vehicles. An air of busyness tingled around her. Emma heaved out a breath laced with relief and the residue of fear.

Rohan stopped to wait for her. He balanced Stephie over his shoulder and carried Emma's belongings in his other hand. Her tan leather handbag bumped against the new cloth shopping bag containing the replenished supplies for Nicky's transformation. They beat a tattoo against Rohan's trouser leg. Emma sighed again, and he turned towards her. "You okay?"

"Just shocked," she admitted. "It's not how I expected my afternoon to end." She flapped the empty bag in her left hand. Paint seeped through the lining. The security guard had insisted she take it away with her.

Rohan shifted Stephie on his shoulder and handed Emma her handbag. "Find the key?" he asked, his tone gentle.

Emma's fingers shook as they dug beneath the receipts and closed around her car keys. The familiar jangling tightened her chest again and the fearful lump returned to her throat to obstruct her voice. Relief tinged with terror. Emma lifted the key attached to a bunch of others and held them out to Rohan. His brow knitted for a fraction of a second as he assessed her before deactivating the central locking and hauling open the passenger door. Stephie's head lolled as he slid her into the baby seat.

Emma leaned her spine against the yellow paintwork and closed her eyes. The sunshine reflected off its bright surface, turning it into a blazing orb which glowed behind her eyelids. She'd waited for weeks to drive it after her surgery.

Her shoulders slumped at how the trip turned out so far. "What a disaster," she breathed.

Rohan pressed a kiss against his tiny daughter's fluffy head and withdrew from the vehicle. He shut the door with a click. His arms infused Emma with security and tenderness as they enfolded her and crushed her cheek against his shirt. She released another sigh.

"Are you really okay? You can stop pretending now." His voice rumbled through his chest and Emma gave an unconvincing nod. Her fingers traced the line of his jacket. The starchiness of the fabric jarred something in her understanding.

"Where are you going?" She hated how needy and demanding she sounded. "Why are you wearing this?" Her hand tipped palm upwards as suspicion loaded her tone with angst.

"Easy," Rohan soothed. His fingers smoothed across her shoulders. "I need to work, Emma." His lips quirked on one side. "I can't live off my brother's money and my wife's goodwill forever, vozlyublennaya."

"You can!" Emma gripped the cuff of his jacket, desperation in her voice. The fabric creased beneath her fingers, Rohan's favourite knife absent from its hidden seam. "Please, don't leave me now." Begging stripped her emotions raw, and she recognised the ball of fear in her throat. Her subconscious had registered his clothing and tried to warn her. It hadn't been relief at seeing him after all.

"I have a job."

"But you promised." Emma's voice held a faint whine. "No more jobs."

Rohan's fingers stroked the line of her jaw. She searched his expression for deception. "I agreed not to accept any until after the baby arrived. I kept my word." His irises glittered in the sunlight. "One of my old clients ran into difficulty. They need me to retrieve stolen data from a disgruntled employee. It's an easy fix. Shouldn't take me more than a few hours. The hardest part is finding him. I've got Dolan onto it already."

"So, what's the catch?" Emma's eyes narrowed in suspicion. "If I hadn't needed you, would I have got home and found you'd gone?"

Rohan threw his head back and laughed. His reaction unsettled Emma even more. "You still don't trust me?" He placed his right hand over his heart and feigned sadness. "But I've worked so hard to give you full disclosure," he said. "I made promises and honoured all of them."

Emma grumbled and her fingers gripped the sill above Stephie's window. "You say you've kept them, but how am I to know?"

Rohan's nose wrinkled and the light dusting of freckles over his cheeks shifted with the movement. "What else can I tell you? I haven't worked since Stephie arrived. This is an old client and I've hunted risks for them before. It's a routine actuarial job and nothing dangerous. You don't need to worry."

"When will you be home?"

Rohan ran a hand through his hair and sighed. "I'm waiting for Dolan to give me the details and then I promise to tell you more."

Emma walked her fingers over the sleeve of his jacket. "But you're armed, aren't you?" The absence of the knife in its hidden pocket meant nothing. There were other places he kept weapons. Her gaze flicked to his knees, wondering if he'd fastened the blade to the shin of his prosthetic leg instead. Her brain locked, making it impossible for her to decide if that was a good or a bad sign.

Rohan cocked his head. "You needn't worry, Em." His long fingers slid his phone from his back pocket and he dialled a number. Emma searched his face, studying the myriad tiny battle scars in case he disappeared like she imagined he might. Like he had once before when the army took him and made him a captain.

A movement in Emma's peripheral vision sent a jolt of fear ricocheting up her spine. The overweight security guard lumbered into the car park, a packet of cigarettes clutched in his fingers. He concentrated on lighting his fix, and Emma resisted the urge to yank the driver's door open and dive into the seat.

"Hey, Allaine." Rohan's call connected. Emma frowned. "Please, can you bring Nicky to the supermarket to meet us? His mother wants to take him to a coffee shop. Yes, tell him she bought the stuff for his costume." He listened to Allaine's reply. Nicky's voice sounded through the speaker, a high, irritated tone. "Five minutes then." Rohan killed the call and pushed the phone into his pocket. He smiled at Emma. "Allaine will leave my car here for you. I'll drive them home. Spend time with our syn and come back when you're ready."

Gratitude flooded Emma's chest. She glanced at the sleeping baby in the passenger seat, her mind already performing calculations between feeds. She pressed her hands against her cheeks and scrubbed as though to rid herself of the afternoon's events. Nerves tickled the pit of her stomach. She released a ragged breath. "Thank you, Rohan," she whispered. "He's finding it difficult. It used to just be him and me. Our house is so busy now."

Rohan nodded in agreement. "I know," he replied with a sigh. "Ray said he's almost finished the rooms over the stables. Allaine and Kaylee already moved in most of their gear." His eyes crinkled at the corners. "Then there's only Freda to send home and it will be just us again. Moya sem'ya. My own little family."

Emma blinked and nodded at the thought of the elderly lady who'd taken up residence in their spare room. Despite owning an apartment at a local seniors' community, Freda showed no sign of leaving. A smile cracked the serious expression marring Emma's features. "She got her bloomers stuck in the washing machine yesterday. Ray had to remove the drum."

Rohan waggled his blond eyebrows, and the humour sent sparkles skidding across his blue irises. Light heartedness shrouded them both for a moment. Then Rohan's Mercedes drew up alongside them and Allaine reversed the enormous car into the next space. Nicky's sullen face glowered at Emma from the rear seat.

"Here we go," Emma breathed. "Operation Make Amends, phase two."

Greater Than

"You said you'd meet me from school with the new baby today." Nicky slouched next to her, his shoulders rounded and his gaze on the pavement. "I told everyone. You made me look a liar."

Emma gritted her teeth and fixed a smile onto her lips. She reached out to take her son's hand and noticed the ruined cloth bag still in her fingers. "Damn!" she hissed. Paint stained her thumb and the back of her wrist. She cast around for a dustbin.

"What's that?" Alarm drew Nicky's blond brows into a furrow. "You're bleeding?"

"No." Emma blew out a breath. "It's a long story."

Nicky paused on the path and settled his hands over his hips. The action gave the appearance of a much older man demanding answers. Rohan. "Tell me the story," he demanded. His features softened. "I'm desperate to forgive you. The story might help."

"Okay." Emma spun around on the street. "Just let me find a bin first. I think there's one outside Sainsbury's."

"No." Nicky shook his head. "I need to see the evidence."

Emma released a groan and balled the bag into her hand. Something dug into her palm and she rearranged the seam of the strap to dangle beneath her wrist. "Right," she said, checking her pocket for the cash Rohan gave her before leaving. "Baptist coffee shop? I think it's open late today."

"Yeah!" Nicky punched the air with his fist. "I wanna cuppa tea in a special cup and saucer. And I'm pouring it from the pot myself."

"Okay." Emma relented, relief sliding through her nerve endings. The trip to the church cafe run by senior citizens became a favourite treat leading up to Stephie's birth. Staffed by volunteers, the cafe kept the prices affordable. Nicky had developed a penchant for the tea cakes and as food loosened his tongue, Emma found out all his secrets for the price of half an hour and a couple of pounds.

Nicky switched sides and held his mother's fingers. Emma's muscles relaxed with each step through the centre of the small market town. Nicky's pace increased as they turned onto Manor Walk, his jubilation emerging as skips and bounces. His feet slid to a halt outside the door. Lifting one hand, he pinched his thumb and forefinger together. "Please, may I have the tiniest little tea cake?" His eyes grew round, and he dropped the fingers to pat his stomach. "It might help me concentrate if your story is a bit boring."

Emma pursed her lips to avoid reacting. Her instinct drove irritation, but his honesty encouraged humour. She checked the wad of notes Rohan shoved into her pocket and saw with gratitude he'd anticipated his son's persuasiveness. "Yeah," she replied. "Daddy gave me enough for that." He'd given her enough for a night at the Hilton hotel, but she kept that to herself.

Nicky struggled with the door and bounced into the cafe with enthusiasm. He held out his arms like a televangelist and announced their arrival. "I'm back!"

An old lady waved from behind the counter. She propped herself up on a stool and fed cash into the register with a smile. "Bill!" she called over the hubbub of chatter. "Bill!" Her wavering voice summoned an elderly man waiting tables. He wore a chequered pinafore tied around his torso to protect his formal shirt. He jerked his chin upwards in recognition and his wife jabbed a crooked index finger at Nicky. "Our boy's back!"

"Hooray!" Bill threw his arms into the air in exaggerated delight. Though as Emma watched, she sensed the sincerity in his movements. "And how's our Nikolai?" Bill bent his body in half to speak at Nicky's level. "We've missed our little helper. How's that new sister of yours?"

Nicky tapped his chest with importance. "Stepanovich cries all the time. And she poops a lot." He clamped his fingers over Bill's wrist. "I wanted to call her Svetlana. It means lumin... lumin... bright light." He fumbled over luminescent. "But Uncle Anton didn't get kids, so my dad pinched one of his names."

"We'd love to see her." Bill's rheumy gaze flicked up to Emma and back to Nicky. Emma swallowed, relieved when he didn't press the point. She figured her weight loss and pale complexion told him part of why they'd been absent.

"Bill, do you have a tea cake for me?" Nicky glanced at Emma, responding to her frown. "Please."

"Pardon?" Bill dipped lower, his precarious balance digging the soles of his sensible shoes into the carpet. Nicky edged closer, positioning himself next to the old man's hearing aid. Bill cupped his right hand behind his ear as the filter snapped free between Nicky's brain and mouth. Instead of repeating his request, Emma's son regaled the whole cafe with the source of the sadness dogging her bones.

"Mum can't have no more babies," he announced. "Something broke when Stephie popped out." He winced and glanced back at Emma. "She's been a bit sad because of her hystericalectomy." A second glance caused his eyes to widen at what he saw in Emma's face. "Oops," he whispered. His lips twisted and guilt radiated from his cerulean irises.

"Take a seat." A feather light touch on Emma's shoulder made her jump. A horrible hush descended over the customers. Emma sensed their collective pity wrap around her psyche like a damp blanket.

"This was a mistake," she breathed. Her arms squeezed her torso, gripping with the intensity of a strait jacket.

"No, it wasn't." Freda's exotic floral perfume worked her affection into Emma's senses. She squeezed the ball of Emma's shoulder with increased pressure. "Take a seat in the corner. I'll fetch your order and sit with you a while." Freda's knotty fingers pushed her towards the table where her son busied himself clambering into a chair. Someone had encased her feet in concrete and her trainers dragged against the carpet as she moved. The effort of sinking into the cushioned chair cost her everything, leaving nothing in the tank for scolding Nicky.

Emma's son stared at the embroidered tablecloth. When he looked up, tears filled his eyes. "Sorry, Mummy," he whispered. "I can't help it. Things can only sit in my chest for so long before they pop out." He patted the space over his heart. "They get too heavy for me."

Emma nodded. The blockage in her throat seemed to shift enough to admit a faint croak to escape. "Know how you feel."

Nicky frowned. He slid from his chair and edged it closer to hers. The metal legs dug into the carpet and left drag marks. "Don't cry, Mummy," he pleaded. His lips twisted, and he rested his small fingers over the bunched fists in her lap. "Let's not tell Daddy about this." Abandoning his chair, he climbed into her lap and stretched his arm around her shoulders.

"How did you find out?" Emma pursed her lips and imagined her wily son playing in the many secret tunnels which ran through the manor house. But before she could summon a rebuke, he pressed a slender index finger over her mouth.

"Daddy said." He bobbed his head to force eye contact. "But don't be cross with him. I missed you so I got into your bed without Daddy seeing me. He didn't turn on the light while he made a phone call to Ray. Then he sat on the bed and cried."

Emma inhaled and a palm pressed over her heart. "He cried?" The notion sounded ridiculous. She'd never seen Rohan Andreyev cry, not even as a boy. His stoic, blank, Slav expression formed the backdrop of their shared childhood.

Nicky nodded, the action exaggerated enough to jog the chair. "Yes. About babies."

Emma swallowed and released the held breath. She'd spent the last six weeks wallowing in self-pity and forgotten the horror for Rohan. She remembered seeing him hold their daughter as the midwife wheeled her away. Blood coated her from the waist down and the images winked out after that. As she sat in the seat in the warm cafe, the fabric of her sweatpants dug into the fresh scar tissue across her abdomen. The surgeons hadn't wasted time on keyhole surgery. They'd slit her open and repaired the damage. No more babies.

Freda appeared at the table, a plate of tea cakes in her gnarled fingers. She placed them in front of Nicky's chair with a flourish. Bill appeared with a tea tray. Three mismatched cups and saucers sat next to a china pot. With his shaking hands, he set them in the centre of the tablecloth. Brown tea dripped onto the fabric to join the other indelible stains.

"I'll pour!" Nicky bounced off Emma's knee and she winced at the twinge of pain which bloomed outward from her groin. Freda pulled out the chair on her other side.

"You look like someone kicked you in the guts," she announced. She bobbed her head of white curls to reveal a hair clip adorned with sparkling gems. The light caressed them like kisses, a testament to their status as genuine diamonds.

"That's how it feels." Emma pursed her lips. She lifted her left hand, the cloth bag still squashed into her fist. Red paint spread from her wrist to stain the cuff of her sweater. She groaned and unfurled her fist.

"Is that blood?" Freda leaned closer.

"No." Nicky interrupted. He stood on his tiptoes and hoisted the teapot with a grunt. His jaw flexed with the effort and he dribbled tea into the nearest cup. "It's a long story. Wait for me, please?"

The Freda Fraction

E mma's story sounded far less dramatic in its retelling, but Nicky hung on every word. Butter added a sheen to his rosebud lips, teacake crumbs dotting his chin and cheeks. He paused, his hand lifted halfway to his mouth and his eyes wide. "Tell it again," he insisted. "What did Dad say to the men?"

Freda leaned forward, tea dripping down the dainty china cup in her fingers and splashing into the saucer. Both members of the audience held their breath. Emma pushed out her bottom lip. Her shoulders slumped, tiredness filtering back into her muscles. "I've told you twice." She reached for her teacup and it clanged against the mismatched saucer. "He said, 'Why are you holding my wife here? Tell me.' And then the guards kinda fell to pieces."

"Why are you holding my wife here? Tell me." Nicky's lips split into a wide grin as he repeated the sentence in a gruff voice. A crumb plunged from the end of his nose and landed in the yellow slick on his plate. "Isn't he wonderful?"

"Fantastic." Emma spoke through gritted teeth. "I hoped you'd be pleased about the items I bought to make your book character."

"I am." Nicky's blue eyes widened with sincerity. Then his blond brows furrowed into a line. "But I'd quite like to go as Daddy."

A gargantuan exhale whooshed from Emma's lungs and her body sagged in the chair. She kept her tone level. "Daddy isn't a book character. *The Cock with the Crimson Comb* is a book character. I bought the stuff to make that one for you."

"Yeah." He twisted his lips into a grimace. "Okay then." He pushed another section of teacake between his teeth and the conversation halted. Freda lifted a manicured eyebrow and observed him. Her lips parted and Emma sensed her waiting to censure Nicky if he dared to speak with his mouth full. He didn't and she closed her eyes, letting the warmth of the cafe and the mixed scents of food comforted her.

She jumped as Freda's cup clinked against its saucer. "Will I put that dirty bag in the rubbish for you?" she asked, her tone gentle.

"Thanks." Emma wrinkled her nose as she inspected the remnants of red paint staining her nails and the back of her left wrist. A rumpled paper napkin had removed the worst of it. She reached sideways and lifted the bag from the carpet, careful to hold it by its strap. Freda hauled herself upright and took it between her finger and thumb.

"Craft paint is like Baileys Irish Cream," she declared. "It looks a small amount but it goes absolutely everywhere."

Emma allowed herself a lopsided grin. "I've never seen you spill it." Since claiming the spare bedroom a few weeks earlier, Freda had supped her way through four entire bottles. Emma hadn't noticed a single drop wasted.

"Where's the stuff then?" Nicky cocked his head and a pink tongue poked out to lick the butter from around his lips. "Please can I see it?"

"Dad took it home." Emma's blunt reply induced a furrowed brow, and her son gave a definitive nod.

"Can we go home soon? I want to know how you'll make me into *The Cock with the Crimson Comb*."

Emma peered at the dregs in her cup. Her body's reluctance to move warned her how much the altercation with the guards had sapped her meagre energy. But she forced her head to nod and pushed her chair back from the table.

"Stop!" Nicky commanded. His tone of voice mimicked Rohan's with such accuracy, it caused both her and Freda to halt like marionettes. He pointed a delicate index finger at the bag swinging from Freda's hand. "There's something in the bottom of there."

Emma shook her head. "There isn't. The security guard pulled the broken carton out and threw it in the dustbin." She wrinkled her nose and tried not to relish the red smear which stained his white shirt cuff. Freda gave the bag a wiggle and it swung from side to side.

"I think he's right. There's something in here." She let the bag unfurl itself and pulled the neck open to peer inside. Then she involved her other hand, hauling it apart by both straps and pushing her face inside it. Red paint transferred itself to both hands and added a pink hue to a snowy white curl.

"No!" Emma forced herself into a standing position. She unglued her feet from the floor with a massive effort. "Just chuck it in the bin, Freda. You're getting covered in paint."

"But there's definitely something in the bottom." She withdrew her face and before Emma could object, upended the bag onto the white tablecloth. Flakes of dried paint littered the space like bloodied confetti. A soaked tissue plunged south and bounced twice before resting next to the pepper shaker. A thin piece of black plastic landed with a clatter, freed from the folds of fabric in the very bottom of the bag where the seam had frayed. Freda blinked, Emma frowned, but Nicky pounced.

"Got it," he announced. Red paint spread across his fingers. Emma gaped as he wiped the case on his school jumper.

"Nicky! No!"

"It'll come off," he promised. His cerulean irises glimmered, and he closed his fist around his find.

"What is it?" Emma held out her hand, her brows knitting in confusion.

Nicky's slow-motion movements displayed his reluctance as he took his time laying it in Emma's palm. Red paint transferred from his fingers to hers. "It's a flash drive." His lips pursed into a scowl. "Finder's keepers, loser's weepers."

Emma gave a slow shake of her head and watched her son's face crumple. "It doesn't work like that, buddy," she informed him. "I think it belongs to Daddy. Perhaps he dropped it when he rescued me from the guards."

Freda gave a relieved nod. "Yes, it's one of Rohan's little gee-gaws. I'll just throw this bag in the dustbin and then finish my shift here." She fixed a winning smile on her lips and cocked her head at Emma. "Could you be a dear and swing by the front of the cafe with the car? It'll save me getting a taxi home."

"Home?" Emma narrowed her eyes. "Your apartment?"

Freda squeezed the bridge of her nose and turned her head to avoid Emma's scrutiny. "No dear, the manor house. I'll just have one more night there."

Nicky hauled his school coat over his shoulders and flipped the hood over his white-blond hair. "You keep saying that." He giggled, the sound emanating from his stomach as though she'd made a joke. "But then you stay for another week."

Emma's muscles tightened into a cringe. She adored Freda but hadn't factored in the ninety-six-year-old moving in at the most chaotic time of her life. She widened her eyes at Nicky's tactlessness and stuffed the flash drive into the pocket of her sweatpants. Oblivious, her son swiped a last covetous index finger across his empty plate and licked up the butter. Emma put a palm on his head and steered him towards the outer door. "I'll wait in the Commons car park next door," she said, "give us about fifteen minutes."

Freda pursed her lips and dipped her head just once. "Thank you," she replied, her tone soft. Her breathing sped up, her thin, birdlike chest rising and falling with more frequency. Emma frowned, regretting her inhospitable thoughts.

"You're welcome." Emma turned. "See you soon."

Nicky bounced through the door, his coat rustling against Emma's palm. He tipped his face up towards her when they reached the street, the paleness of his complexion as the hue of a delicate flower beneath the navy hood. "Something's up with Freda." He confirmed Emma's fears like an oracle. "I saw her crying in the library at home." He released an exaggerated sigh and pushed out his bottom lip. "Crying, crying, everybody's bloody crying."

Heart Calculations

"What's wrong? What happened?" Emma glanced at the empty hallway behind her and then clicked the bedroom door shut. Nicky's voice echoed downstairs as he ran to the kitchen. "Where's Stephie?" She kept her fingers fixed around the worn brass doorknob.

Rohan sat on the mattress of their four-poster bed. He'd discarded his outer clothes and only a pair of boxer shorts covered his nakedness. An eerie paleness had sapped the usual tan from his complexion. His hand trembled as he dipped forward to retrieve the crutch leaned against the nearest post. The other metal rod had fallen backwards and lay just out of reach. "Stephie is downstairs with Allaine." His voice sounded flat and toneless.

Emma stepped away from the door. A strange aura shrouded Rohan, creating a barrier between them. The scarred remains of his knee appeared jarring in the normality of their bedroom, as though an artist had smudged it from the picture with a careless thumb. "Do you want me to fetch your prosthesis?" She bit down on her tongue, regretting the question as soon as she'd released it.

Rohan nodded, his response taking Emma by surprise. He guarded his independence with ferocity, refusing help with the simple tasks he could perform himself. She strode to the wardrobe and hauled open the door. The prosthetic leg stood where he left it as he'd exchanged it for the crutches. Rohan's neat shoe and sock encased the foot. Emma gritted her teeth and seized the ghoulish reminder of what her husband had lost in Afghanistan. The prosthesis creaked beneath her touch, the plastic housing the mechanical parts reacting to her clumsiness. She walked towards Rohan, forcing a feigned blankness onto her expression. She didn't know whether to cradle it like a child or hold it out in front of her as something distasteful. Rohan watched her movements, his perceptive gaze reading her most private thoughts as though she had scrawled them over the floral wallpaper.

"Are you taking a shower?" Emma leaned the prosthetic leg against the mattress next to Rohan. The worn cuff designed to encase his stump sagged against the bedspread. She paused in front of him, her fingers twitching as she itched to stroke his cheek and connect with him.

"I already did." His answer sounded brusque. Emma frowned at the dryness of his hair and the absence of a towel. She fought the desire to challenge him when she looked down and saw the graze marring the knuckles of his left hand.

"Rohan?"

The instinct to meet her gaze revealed a cut nestled beneath his fringe. Blood had trickled into his blond eyebrow and left a pink stain over his skin. Rohan's pupils dilated as he watched her confusion, and he waved his right hand to dismiss her concern. "It's nothing."

"You fell?" Emma pushed her hands into her pockets to stop her mothering him and jeopardising the fragile remains of his dignity. "It's my fault," she stated. "I noticed the rubber mat had worn and intended to replace it this afternoon." She paused, wondering if he would allow her to mitigate the situation or resent her interference. She walked a tightrope with Rohan's injuries, never knowing whether to ignore his difficulties or commiserate over them.

A narrow line appeared between his eyebrows. For a fraction of a second, he looked as though he might reject her attempt to minimise his disability. Then he pursed his lips and frowned. "The crutch slipped against the tiles."

Emma risked pushing her luck. He so rarely accepted her help she craved his need for her like a long since relinquished addiction. "Should I hang around while you start again?"

She stared at the rug to avoid meeting his gaze, watching him in her peripheral vision.

To her surprise, he nodded. But as gratitude and delight flooded Emma's senses, she saw a wicked twinkle fire in Rohan's blue irises. He cocked his head and snatched control of the moment, attempting to salvage what he'd lost. "Come in with me?" he whispered.

They didn't make it as far as the shower. Six weeks of avoiding anything more than a kiss had left them both ragged. Emma's emotions soared with relief as she sat across his thighs while he removed her shirt and bra. Her dread that the surgery had stolen her passion along with her womb proved unfounded. Rohan's knuckles pressed against her spine as he released her bra and she leaned down and brushed her lips over his jaw.

"I've missed you so much," he breathed. His touch coasted along her neck and he dug his fingers into her hair. In seconds, he had tipped her sideways onto the mattress. Kisses filled with heat left burning trails on her skin. Mischief sparkled in his eyes as he released the cord on Emma's pants. He maintained eye contact with her, slipping the fabric over her hips. Emma sensed him waiting for her to tell him to stop. A depressing monotone in her brain echoed warnings and admonishments, urging her to protect herself against disappointment. She silenced it by hauling down her underwear and revealing the hasty scar drawn across her abdomen.

Rohan trailed his index finger above the angry red line, though he didn't touch the wound. Emma held her breath as though expecting him to reject her. His irises sparkled as he looked up with a smile. "Mine is still worse." His lips quirked upwards and crow's feet creased the corners of his eyes into laugh lines.

Emma exhaled in a whoosh. It had frightened her more than she dared to admit. Perhaps she didn't need to speak to him about Nicky's revelation. Not yet. She tilted her chin and accepted her husband's kisses, drawing a temporary line in the sand of her life and stepping over it.

Octogenarian Intruders

Rohan left on his hunt before the sun woke, and Emma battled through the day. He phoned her after lunch to inform her of his delayed return. Exhaustion dogged her steps as she dealt with Nicky and the baby, falling into bed after reading Nicky a story. She planned to enjoy her own book, but sleep claimed her and the novel slid to the mattress and closed with a hollow thud.

Emma's eyelids flicked open, and she lay still in the empty bed. Her head had slipped off her pillow and caused pain to bloom up the side of her neck when she moved. She'd woken with a start and yet no reason presented itself. Stephie snuffled in her crib on Emma's side of the bed. Her tiny lips smacked as she searched for her thumb, the sucking accompanied by a satisfied sigh as she found it. Emma knitted her brows in the darkness. The silence of the house shrouded her in its embrace, the peace interspersed by an occasional click of the gravity fed water system.

Rohan's absences affected her deepest after dark when her mind gained space to roam across their shared history. She sifted through the memories as a floorboard near the doorway settled with a dull clunk.

The mattress shifted as though someone else in the bed had altered position. Emma held her breath. She hadn't moved.

Fear drew a line along her spine with a hooked fingernail. Her brain scrambled for logical explanations until she settled on the likeliest. "Nicky?" she whispered. She edged her fingers onto the empty side which Rohan favoured. The cool sheets reinforced her aloneness.

Emma pushed herself up in the bed. The thud of her own heartbeat obscured all other sounds. She sensed the presence in the room, an aura which oozed a silent threat. It sent her scrambling to stand next to her daughter, the sheets tumbling to the ground in her wake.

"Easy." The male voice held a familiar calmness, its serenity washing over her panic like cold water dousing a fire. "I just want to talk."

Emma's body shook from the shot of adrenaline coursing through her veins. Unsteadiness plagued her reply and a gulp of air cut her sentence in half. "Go away," she growled. "Get out of my house. Now!" Stephie sighed next to her, and she pushed her fingers through the darkness to clasp the wicker edge of the crib. The rough weave scratched against her skin.

"We need to talk." His voice held determination, daring her to disobey. Like father, like son.

Emma scrabbled on the floor for the blankets Stephie always discarded. She pulled them over the crib's hood to soften the glow from her bedside lamp. When she flicked the switch, it bathed the room with light. Stephie's bare feet protruded from the bottom of the blanket. Tiny toes splayed and relaxed as she settled. Emma left a gap to allow cool air to filter into the tent she'd created, then she scooted back onto her mattress and hauled the sheet up to her chin. "Two minutes, Winston," she bit. "If you won't leave, I'll call in the cavalry."

The tall man stretched out his legs and eased onto the mattress where Rohan's right foot would once have laid. Emma's skin prickled at his effrontery. His expression remained impassive, and she wondered if he even registered what crime he'd committed. Winston rubbed his eyes and gave a nod of acceptance. "Where is Alexei?"

She glanced at her husband's empty pillow and hauled the sheet higher before folding it over her stomach like a flimsy ward of protection. "Rohan." She corrected him with a bite in her tone.

Winston breathed out through his nose. "My son answers to Alexei Oskar in my presence, Emma. Don't test my patience. I've indulged you so far."

Emma's gaze flicked towards the closed bedroom door and the loose floorboard which had alerted her to Winston's movements. "What do you want? Why are you here?"

"I'm always here, Emma. Watching over you."

"Well, don't!"

Winston frowned at the ingratitude in her tone. He chose to ignore it. "Your husband rented his London apartment and sold the manor house in Falkirk."

Emma's heart pitched into her stomach. She braced herself for more secrets and pushed away a spark of disappointment in Rohan's neglect to communicate the changes in his finances. "And?" she bit. "What do you want me to do about it?"

"Why is he consolidating his assets?" Winston leaned on his right hip and faced her. White stubble dusted his cheeks and chin where he'd missed shaving. Dark circles underlined his azure irises.

"I don't know and I don't care." Emma turned her head to see Stephie lift a perfectly shaped foot and kick the blanket. "Please leave." A pop betrayed the thumb leaving her daughter's mouth. A familiar grunt accompanied her nappy filling.

Winston rose. Still straight backed and tall for his age, he dipped his head in a bow of acknowledgement. "It's ill advised to live such a passive existence." He raised an eyebrow as though to drive home his judgement. "You don't ask enough questions, girl. Why do you show so little inquisitiveness? Don't you wonder why Alexei became a captain in the British army after only a few short years? Do you not ponder on the work he does without your knowledge? Talk to your husband," he demanded. "Find out what he's doing." His long legs carried him to the bedroom door, and he paused. "I want something else from you." His gaze coasted across the crib and back to Emma's face. He tapped the architraves with a bent finger. "No matter. Another time will suffice." Then he let himself out, closing the door behind him. Only a dent in the bedspread's surface showed he'd ever disturbed her. Emma stared at it as Stephie's grunts turned to heated complaints.

"What's your father up to?" she breathed. Winston's questions had roused her curiosity, creating an itch she needed to scratch.

Stephie fed for a while before the dirty nappy distracted her. Emma paused the feed to peel the rubber pants and fabric from her daughter's pink bottom. Stephie lay on a plastic mat on the four poster bed. She blew bubbles, beating her arms like a windmill as Emma replaced the nappy with another from the stack in a drawer. "All clean." She wrinkled her nose and blew a raspberry on her daughter's rounded tummy. After fastening the poppers of the tiny vest, she hoisted Stephie over her shoulder. "Let's put this nappy to soak and we'll deal with it tomorrow."

She rinsed the soiled terry cloth and dumped it in a bucket of soaking solution. Stephie kicked her arms and legs on the bathmat and sucked her fingers. The baby's happy gurgling changed to whimpers of protest as Emma bent to retrieve her. She still hadn't satiated her bottomless stomach, condemning her mother to another hour of sitting up in bed. "At least you feed faster than your brother." She kissed the side of Stephie's soft face, rewarded by her tiny mouth rooting against her shoulder.

The digital clock on Rohan's bedside table showed the time as after midnight. Emma reached for her phone and turned it over in her fingers. "Do you think it's too late to ring Daddy?" she asked. Her brow furrowed at her mistake as the baby stopped feeding. "It's okay," Emma soothed. She let the phone drop onto the mattress and stroked Stephie's fingers until her feeding resumed its steady rhythm. She fed herself to sleep and Emma held her against her shoulder to bring up the gentle burps which threatened to her settling. An hour later, she put Stephie in her crib. She turned the child on her side and wedged blankets around her to prevent her rolling. Then she sneaked into the bathroom and closed the door behind her.

Two Plus One

"Chris?" Emma sighed. "I'm glad you're still awake."

"What's wrong?" Sounds issued from the room he sat in, muted gunshots and explosions. "Hang on, let me stop this game before you get me killed." A series of clicks followed and then Christopher's slow exhale. "Why are you still awake? You wanting some company?"

Emma tightened her jaw against his attempt at a joke. She heard the seriousness behind it, sensing she only needed to invite him over to start something they would both regret. "I had a visitor." She glossed over the emotional issue and jumped straight into the security breach. "How?"

"I'm not sure." He sounded confused and his tone changed as he rose. Footsteps betrayed his movements, the squeak of trainers on the tiled floor of the renovated folly. "Let me check the monitors." Emma waited as Christopher reviewed the security footage. He tutted twice before inhaling into the phone. Emma yanked it away from her ear. "Who was it?" he demanded. "I can't see anything."

"Rohan's father." She made poor work of keeping the bite from her tone. "Sitting on the end of my bed."

"What? Are you okay? What did he do?"

"Asked some questions about Rohan's finances and left." Emma caught sight of herself in the bathroom mirror. She wrinkled her nose at the tired woman staring back at her. The harsh bulb above her head accentuated the shadows beneath her eyes. She dropped the lid on the toilet seat and slumped onto it. "When is Rohan due home?"

"Driving back as we speak. Mission not accomplished. So, he's got a wasp up his ass. I have warned you." Christopher slurped something and swallowed, turning the call into a conversation with a washing machine.

"Yuk!" Emma hissed. "Poor Rohan. So, does that mean he'll get home in half an hour or half a day? Where's he driving from?"

"Half a day." Christopher added a food item to the mixture in his mouth and continued speaking. "Make that half the night, actually. He should arrive mid morning. Do you want me to wake Ray and ask him to patrol the property?"

Emma sighed, her chest caving as she expelled all her air. "No. I'll check on Nicky and go back to bed. Rohan's convinced Winston means no harm, so I must trust him."

She cleared her throat and realised her mouth felt dry. "Can I change my mind?"

"On which part?"

"I'm thirsty. Please, can you ask Ray to meet me in the kitchen? It sounds wimpy, but I don't like wandering around in the dark by myself."

"Will do." Christopher's voice softened. "Give it a couple of minutes and then go downstairs."

"Thanks." Emma killed the call and forced herself to stand. Her stomach sent a sharp twinge across the healing tissue, and she added painkillers to her mental list of reasons to venture downstairs. In the bedroom, she pulled her dressing gown over her pyjamas and stuffed the baby monitor into the pocket. Pausing at the closed bedroom door, her fingers twitched on the ornate key sitting in the lock. She debated locking Stephie into the room and dismissed the idea. Winston had shown no hostility towards her children.

Emma stepped into the hallway and pulled the door almost shut behind her. She padded across to Nicky's room and breathed in her son's familiar scent, the aroma of grass and toothpaste. Stepping across his bedroom floor, she trod on a rectangular piece of Lego. Two of the sharp corners dug into the arch of her foot and she hopped around on one leg until the pain subsided.

"Mum?" The sheets rustled as Nicky propped himself up in his bed. "What you doing?"

Emma sank onto his mattress with a sigh. "Falling over your toys."

"Oh." Nicky threw himself back against his pillow. "I thought you were dancing."

Emma rolled her eyes in the darkness and didn't trust herself to reply. She allowed two decent inhales before she answered him. "I came to check on you but stood on some Lego."

"Ouch. Sorry." Nicky yawned. "I thought I picked them all up."

"You missed one." Emma couldn't keep the sarcasm from her tone. She rubbed a hand across her face. "Sorry for waking you."

"It's okay. Can I sleep with you?" Kicking off his sheets, he rose onto his knees.

Emma nodded in the darkness, sighing as her son wrapped his arms around her neck. "I'd like that," she admitted. "Hop into my bed and don't wake Stephie. I'm nipping to the kitchen for a drink. It won't take long."

"Okay. I love you Mummy." Nicky pressed a kiss to her temple and clambered off the mattress. His footsteps padded across the hall and into her bedroom. She hated to admit that having Nicky in the same room as Stephie brought her comfort. Her wily son would protect his sister with his life. Or at least raise the alarm.

Emma rose and picked her way across the floorboards, careful to kick out her toes to avoid another tussle with stray

Lego pieces. She stuck her head around her bedroom door and waved at Nicky in the light cast from the bathroom. "I won't be long," she promised.

He nodded and snuggled into Rohan's pillow. Emma closed the door behind her and descended the stairs to the ground floor. She used the back steps, rounding the doglegs and listening for signs of Winston. Crockery clanked from the kitchen and she exhaled a tight breath. She prepared her apology as she padded across the cold tiles, expecting to see Ray as she opened the kitchen door.

"I warmed some milk." Christopher half turned, a sultry look in his brown eyes.

"Weren't you in the folly?" Emma pushed the door closed behind her. "You got across here fast." She leaned down to fondle Farrell's black ears as he lumbered off his bed to greet her.

Christopher smirked and poured hot milk from a saucepan into two mugs. "I got meself one of them electric scooters," he said. "It goes great along the tunnel until it narrows. It's halved the time needed to get across here." Creases showed at the outer corners of his eyes. "I'm awake, anyway. Didn't seem worth disturbing Ray."

Emma's nod appeared half hearted. "It's not really why we employ him, is it? That would make for a strange one liner in his job description; wait while the missus makes herself cocoa."

"You'd rather have cocoa?" Christopher paused on his way towards the table. He held the two mugs in front of him in the same way she'd seen him wield handguns.

"No, no. Hot milk is the less fattening option." She offered a wary smile to bolster the claim, regretting it as his gaze roved across her dressing gown. She found painkillers in a high cupboard near the door and slumped into a chair. The tablets skittered from their foil wrappers and Emma held them in her palm and stared at them, wondering how many she would need to take before she became addicted to their numbing effect.

Christopher placed the mug in front of her and took the adjacent seat. His knee touched hers as he sat and Emma tensed. Pain and stress sapped her energy and made her reluctant to embark on their familiar, circuitous conversation about boundaries. To her relief, Farrell nosed his way between them and laid his chest across her bare feet. His heartbeat thudded against her toes, drawing Emma out of her own problems enough to clear a little head space. She pushed the tablets into her mouth and spoke around them. "Did you see how Winston got onto the property without triggering our security?" Emma lifted the mug and took a fortifying sip of her drink. A thin film stuck to her lip, and she wrinkled her nose and used her thumb and forefinger to pull it free. She draped it over the side of the mug and avoided that section of the rim.

Christopher seemed not to notice as he pulled his mobile phone from his jeans pocket and peered at the screen. Brown shadow coated his cheeks and chin and added a rugged appearance to his already stunning looks. Emma looked away as he gazed up and caught her watching him. "I think he's cracked our codes." Christopher's chocolate irises became gimlet hard. "I know he's Rohan's father, but he's twisted as hell. He does nothing without a reason. It also means there's a back door in our security somewhere that anyone else could find and exploit." Christopher spun his phone around and held it up for Emma's benefit. Her eyes widened at the grainy black-and-white image of a man walking straight through the front gate and sauntering up the long driveway.

"Damn!" She placed her mug on the table and maternal instinct made her tug the baby monitor from her pocket and increase the volume. Her fingers twitched against the buttons. When she lifted it to her ear, she recognised the subtle notes of Nicky's snoring. Emma placed the monitor on the table next to her mug. "I'm not sure whether or not to be afraid of him," she admitted. "He's never done me any harm, and although he underestimated Rohan, he tried to protect him with his antics a few months ago." Emma rubbed her knuckles across her eyes. "I'm too tired to think straight."

Christopher's smile conveyed sympathy. He flicked the cover over the screen and laid his phone face down on the table. "You look tired, Em. Is there anything I can do to help?"

Emma replied with a slow shake of her head. She reached for her mug and her hand trembled. "Not unless you can go back in time on your electric scooter and switch a few things around for me." She let her other fingers coast across the fluffy fabric of her dressing gown as though soothing where her womb once lay.

"Did you want more babies?" Christopher's question detonated sparks behind Emma's eyes. She gave a sharp inhale at the realisation he'd asked the one question everyone else avoided.

She leaned back in her seat, wiggling her toes against the comforting warmth of Farrell's chest. "I don't know," she admitted. "But I would have liked the choice." She swallowed and stared down at her fingers. "I feel traumatised at the way everything happened. One minute I was staring at my daughter and the next I woke up in agony. There's a massive gap where the hours in between should be."

"If anyone understands how you feel, I'm sure it's Rohan."

Emma's head reared back in shock and her lips parted. "It's hardly the same thing. Losing a leg in the middle of a war zone is quite different to a hysterectomy." Emma heard Nicky's clear voice in her memory as he informed everyone in the Baptist coffee shop about her hysticalectomy. Her shoulders slumped, and she released a sigh.

"It seems pretty similar to me." Christopher raised a dark eyebrow and cocked his head. "Rohan needed to grieve his future as an army captain with two legs. He didn't start living again until he accepted that life had robbed him and it wasn't fair. Perhaps that's where you're at now."

He tipped back his head and finished the last of his hot milk. It left a sheen around his full lips, which he wiped on the back of his hand. "I'll take a walk around and check all the entry points, but I watched Winston leave through the front door. I don't believe there's anyone else here."

"Thanks." Emma extracted her feet from beneath Farrell and padded across to the sink to rinse her mug. Then she dumped it into the dishwasher and leaned against the counter. "Do you know what's going on with Freda?" she asked. "I can't understand it." She tapped her fingers against her lips. "Do you think she gave Winston the gate and alarm codes under duress? I'm not sure if he still has an apartment in her building, but it might explain her strange behaviour and her reluctance to go home."

"Nah." Christopher shook his head. "Freda can't remember her own phone number. I don't see her digging around to find alarm codes to give to a man she doesn't like. Besides, she's become part of the family. She wouldn't risk that."

Emma folded her arms and leaned back, the hard edge of the counter pressing against her spine. She raised an eyebrow and shook her head. "Allaine's husband did."

Christopher made a sound like a growl. "And he earned himself some cash and lost his wife and youngest daughter in the process. Freda is not Will, not even close. Shame on you, Em."

Emma released a sigh and padded back to the table. She lifted the baby monitor and shoved it into her pocket. "I know," she conceded. "Please don't mention this conversation to her."

Christopher made a zipping motion across his lips with his thumb and middle finger. "Get some sleep." He lifted his arms into a stretch, causing his tee shirt to ride up above his waistband. Tanned abdominal muscles peeked from beneath the white fabric. He flexed his biceps before releasing the pose with an exhale. "Before you go, do you want to tell me the secret that's burning your conscience?"

Emma froze, one hand on the monitor in her pocket and the other raised to grasp the door knob. "What secret?" Natural irritation crept into her tone and she ground her teeth in frustration. Long shadows flitted across the ceiling as Christopher leaned back against his chair and folded his arms.

"I knew it!" he hissed. "I spent too many years watching your every move to miss the little stress tells. Come on, what did you do?"

Emma formulated the lie as she turned, fixing a blank expression over her face and working hard to keep it there. She sacrificed the knowledge of the flash drive to protect her real secret. He was right. It burned her insides with the ruthlessness of lava. "Someone planted a flash drive on me in the store yesterday afternoon. I need you to look at it."

Christopher's left eyebrow quirked up and his brow knitted. It looked as though an invisible hand had taken a black pen and marked a tick across his forehead. "Nicky told me about that. But it's not what I'm talking about, Em. Tell me the truth. Don't make me hunt for it."

"I just told you." Emma flooded her voice with a lightness she didn't feel. "I'll give you the flash drive tomorrow. It got covered in red paint. I've wiped the casing with nail polish remover." She cocked her head. "That was the right thing to do, wasn't it?"

Christopher narrowed eyes the hue of burnt sienna. Emma held her breath. When he waved his hand in dismissal, her eyelashes fluttered as though expecting a physical blow despite the distance between them. "Whatever," he growled. "But don't come crying to me when it blows up in yer face." His Irish accent spread like honey over Emma's guilt, and she turned away without answering. The door clicked shut between them and she pursed her lips and stared at the ceiling.

Factor

Emma woke to a text from Rohan the next morning. He confirmed he'd get home around midday but didn't confide in her regarding his failed risk elimination. The familiar secrecy crept between them and pushed it aside in her mind. She hadn't plucked up the courage to ask him about the night he'd cried after her surgery. She promised herself she'd ask him later and kidded herself that he'd tell her the truth. Their marriage began amid subterfuge, and her own guilt made her powerless to change it.

Freda shuffled downstairs as Emma strapped Stephie into her baby seat in the front lobby. "Are you coming straight home?" she asked. A hair net and curlers adorned her snowy head like a crown. She'd missed most of her fringe in the laborious process, and it stuck out at right angles from her face. A fluffy dressing gown covered her from chin to floor.

"I just need to nip somewhere after dropping the children at school." Emma stood and gave her a smile. "It shouldn't take long. Why?"

Freda waved a gnarled hand. "Never mind. I've taken a shift at the cafe. I'll ask Ray to drop me in town if he wouldn't mind."

Emma shrugged. "I'm going to the store next to Sainsbury's. Do you want me to come back for you?"

"No, no." Freda patted her hair net and wrinkled her nose. "I'll sort myself out, dear. You carry on." She shuffled towards the kitchen, her mind switching to breakfast as she followed the scent of the toast Ray had just browned for himself.

Emma studied Freda's lumbering gait for clues, squeaking as Christopher spoke from behind her. "And where are you going dressed to kill, Mrs Andreyev?" His silky timbre gave her goose pimples.

She hadn't considered making up an excuse for her glamorous attire. She'd dressed to impress in a light summer frock and high heels, keen to distance herself from the cowed woman of the previous day. Christopher's irises glinted, and she suspected he read the truth in her face. As if to send him a visual confirmation, the skin over her heart heated, and a flush blossomed up her neck and into her cheeks. "I'm fed up of wearing sweatpants." She stuck as close to the truth as possible.

Christopher jerked his head upwards and stuck his tongue against the corner of his lip. Emma tried to ignore the seductiveness of that single action. Then he grinned. "I know you're up to something. Don't call me if you get arrested again."

Emma's forehead puckered. "They did not arrest me!" she bit. "They weren't police."

Christopher ignored her, holding out his hand. "Have you forgotten something?"

Emma hauled the flash drive from her bag and placed it into his palm. She pursed her lips as he sauntered along the corridor to the kitchen. Her fingers rested over her hips and readied herself for battle, acknowledging the futility of it before she even opened her mouth. Let Ray deal with the scroungers hankering after his toast. She turned towards the stairs and yelled again for Nicky. His footsteps padded overhead as he obeyed. Emma shook her head at the sudden realisation. It wasn't Ray's toast, but hers. Ray, Freda and Christopher had kitchens of their own, but ate her food instead. She rolled her eyes and shelved each of the battles for another time.

After dropping Nicky and Kaylee at school, Emma pushed the pram through the familiar automatic doors and paused. Her fingers shook on the handle and she distracted herself by tweaking the fly netting over the hood. Stephie lifted a foot and five perfect toes pressed through the flimsy fabric. "Go to sleep, baby," Emma soothed. She stroked the tiny foot with her index finger and kept her shoulders squared in a show of fake bravado. Christopher suspected her of having a plan, but she doubted he'd guessed the ridiculousness of it. She lifted her chin. "Here goes nothing. Stuff you Dolan," she breathed.

Feigning an outward appearance of confidence, she steered the pram towards the counter. The woman behind the register gave her a forced smile. "How can I help you?" she asked. Her badge hung at a jaunty angle, as though representative of her lack of commitment to her employer. Emma had noticed the day before that her name, Sandra, was taped over the previous owner's.

She swallowed a ball of fear. "I'd like to speak to a security guard please, Sandra." She kept her tone light. Her fingers gripped the pram handle until her knuckles showed white. "I'd rather see the younger one if possible."

"Oh." The woman wrinkled her nose. She swivelled her head on her neck before giving a shrug. "He's around here somewhere. Unless he went out the back for a smoke. Why do you want him?" Her gaze dropped to the baby and her eyes widened. "If it's a paternity thing, he denied the last kid." She gulped and pursed her lips before adding, "Apparently."

"It's not a paternity thing." Emma gave a ragged inhale. Another customer lined up behind her, pushing a trolley overflowing with dented cans of fizzy drink. Sandra glanced at the newcomer and switched gum from the left side of her mouth to the right. "I won't be a minute, me duck."

Emma took a fortifying breath and fixed a pleasant smile on her lips. "So, please can I see him?"

Sandra's eyes narrowed to dark slits in her face. She appeared older than Emma, but the gum chewing suggested otherwise. An air of teenage insolence shrouded her. Then her jaw dropped as though a hinge had broken. A blob of white chewing gum rested against the back of her lower teeth. "Ohhhh!" She dragged out the syllable with obvious enjoyment. "You're that woman from yesterday. The one who nicked the craft stuff."

Emma's head shot up and indignation filled her face. "I stole nothing!" she snapped. She clamped her tongue between her teeth to avoid the urge to defend herself against someone who couldn't care less.

"I'm in a hurry." The customer behind gave her trolley a shove, and it rolled to within a few inches of Stephie's pram. Emma glared at her and turned her attention back to Sandra.

"Please call the security guard," she demanded. Tilting her head, she channelled Rohan's brand of determination. "I have all day. I don't mind waiting here until he comes. Other customers might find it interesting to hear what happened to me yesterday." Emma lifted the fingers of one hand from the pram and inspected her nails. She fixed a serene expression on her face. "I'm thinking of taking legal action against the store." Her eyelashes fluttered, softening the hardness of the glare she gave Sandra. "It would be a shame if the publicity caused financial hardship. And redundancies."

Sandra dipped sideways as though falling. The long tresses of her greasy hair slithered across her forearm as she reached for a microphone next to her on the counter. She flicked a switch and static crackled through the speakers. "Security to front counter. Security to front counter. That woman is here. The one who nicked all that stuff yesterday." Sandra released her finger from the button and turned to Emma with a smile. "He'll be here any second." Fixing her hands on her hips, she gave her an expectant glare. The customer with the trolley bumped it against the hood of the pram, forcing Emma to move backwards at speed. Adrenaline pumped through her veins and her muscles twitched with a reflex of wanting to flee.

The guard proved Sandra right. As Emma waited to the side, running feet heralded the man on duty. She heaved a sigh of relief as good fortune brought the younger of the two. He skidded to a halt in front of Sandra and shoved the customer's trolley out of the way. The woman yelped in pain as the wheel rolled over her foot. "Where is she?" Unbridled enthusiasm glinted in his eyes.

Sandra ran a can of fizzy drink across the scanner until it produced a satisfied beep. Then she rolled it down the slope to clatter against its mates as they waited for the customer to limp around and pack them. She lifted an accusatory index finger and jabbed it in Emma's direction. The skinny guard's head swivelled and a mask of dread settled over his angular features. He turned his body as though with great effort, the enthusiasm draining through an invisible plug hole in the universe. The soles of his sensible black shoes squeaked across the tiles to where she waited. "What do you want?" His tone held aggression, and he lifted his chin to peer behind her. "Where's that scary husband of yours? I already apologised."

"It's not about that." Emma gazed down at her feet, angling the toes of her stilettos so they met in a neat triangle. Her dress accentuated her curves, but Sandra's recognition meant it didn't differentiate her from the traumatised woman of the previous day. Glancing up, she met the security guard's worried gaze and softened her expression. "I wanted you to help me with something," she said. "And I can pay."

At the mention of money, the guard appeared even more suspicious. He backed away, shaking his head. "I like this job. I'm not gonna risk losing it for a couple of quid, lady." He continued backing away until his feet got caught up in the mat in front of the automatic doors. His cheeks reddened as he waved his arms to save himself.

Emma gave a feigned nonchalant shrug. She lifted her purse from her forearm and popped open the clasp. "Pity," she mused. Her fingers plucked out the fifty pound note, and she inspected it before replacing it and closing the purse with a snap. "Thanks for your help. My lawyer will get in touch about the damage to my property." Placing both hands on the pram, she steered towards the automatic front doors, standing aside to let another customer pass.

"Wait. What?" The security guard took a step towards her. His gaze remained on her purse and naked hunger glowed from behind his blue irises. He raised his hand to stop her from leaving. "What damage?" He gulped and wrangled with an internal decision. "What help?"

Probability

"Pete's off sick today." The guard led Emma to the back of the shop and into the same office as yesterday. She cast a cursory glance over the chair she'd slumped in while feeding Stephie. A familiar wave of hopelessness sank its teeth into her psyche. She straightened her spine and shrugged it off with grim determination.

"So, you're in charge?"

The skinny guard wrinkled his nose before shaking his head. "No. The manager is here today. He just nipped out to grab a coffee." He glanced into the corridor and pursed his lips. "Let's make this quick."

Emma pushed the pram into the corner and clicked the brake over the rear wheel. She slipped her purse off her wrist and left it sitting on the hood. Then she turned to face the security guard. "What's your name?"

He splayed his legs and folded his arms. "That depends what you want me to do for fifty pounds," he replied. "It might be best you didn't know my name."

Emma waved her hand in an affectation of nonchalance. "It's a hundred pounds, actually. In return for a little peek at your security footage."

The guard's eyes widened, and he gave a slow nod. "A hundred pounds?" His posture stiffened. "I can't delete anything. That will get me fired."

"I just need to check the camera for something that happened outside." Emma's gaze flicked to a screen in the corner as the view divided into four. It displayed the store's interior from a vantage point near the ceiling and from four different angles. After a few seconds, the image changed, showing the lobby, the car park, the street and the loading bay behind the shop. It cut back to a single view of the cash register and Sandra retrieving her underwear from her crack. Emma folded her arms. "Something happened after we left here yesterday. Someone bumped into me outside the front door. I need to see their face. Please can you show me the footage?"

The security guard gnawed on his bottom lip for a moment. Then he cocked his head. "That's not worth a hundred quid. What are you planning to do with the information? If that Russian husband of yours goes after someone, I don't want it traced back to me."

"You have my word." Emma injected sincerity into her voice. "I just need to see who did it."

"But why?" The guard fixed his hands over his hips.

She shrugged. "Perhaps it's best you don't know."

"Fine! A hundred quid. Up front. And I'm not telling you my name." He held out his palm.

Emma turned away to extract the notes from her purse. She laboured over the action much longer than she needed to, working on hiding the smile burgeoning on her lips. When she held out the two crisp fifty pound notes in her fingers, she avoided staring at the identical coffee mugs on the filing cabinet next to the computer. One bore the name *Pete* written on it in a cursive font. The other had squiggly writing betraying its owner as *Matt*.

The guard snatched the money like a bird pecking seed. He crumpled the notes against his palm but kept them in his fist. "Five minutes," he hissed. "That's all you're getting."

Dropping into the chair in front of the computer screen, he shot Emma a glare filled with suspicion. He stuffed the money into his top pocket and hammered the keyboard with his bony fingers. "What time did you leave yesterday?" he demanded.

"Twenty past three in the afternoon." Emma's brows knitted as she remembered the taste of disappointment in her mouth. The foolish guards had robbed her of the opportunity to fetch Nicky from school, and the time had become etched on her brain.

Matt's fingers flew over the keyboard as he searched the software for the correct time. Then, using the mouse, he dragged a pointer backwards on the timeline along the bottom of the screen. Emma watched over his shoulder as the sky outside the shop darkened and lightened in reverse, creating a black and white grainy image which morphed into the previous sunny afternoon. She held her breath and watched herself leave through the front doors of the store. The cloth bag hung over her forearm, filled with craft items for Nicky's costume. Stephie nestled against her neck, winding her hands through her mother's lank ponytail.

Emma balked at the sense of defeat shrouding her slumped shoulders. The shapeless sweatpants hid her figure and helped her to disappear against her surroundings. The guards appeared behind her and she watched herself turn.

"Oops. Too far." Matt drew the cursor forward along the timeline, concentrating his efforts on the camera feed over the front door.

Emma experienced a wave of gratitude. "I don't want to see inside the shop." She didn't need to witness a replay of the parallel drama unfolding just inside the doors as they led her crestfallen figure to their office.

The timer on the screen fast-forwarded as Matt searched for the relevant moment. As his fingers hovered over the mouse, Rohan strode beneath the camera. His long gait carried him into the car park, a list throwing his right leg sideways before hitting the ground. He appeared tall and imposing even from the camera's high view. Emma remembered watching the back of his head moving away from her, Stephie peering at her from over his shoulder. She saw herself appear, the epitome of despair following in his wake like a stricken boat towed by a tug.

It happened so fast, she almost missed it. "Stop! There!" She jabbed her finger at the screen. "Go back about two seconds." Matt's fingers twitched on the mouse and Emma's body reversed at speed like a comic strip character. Matt winced as in her excitement, Emma slapped his shoulder. "Can you slow it down more?" she demanded. Matt performed his magic and she watched a slowed down version of herself reverse into the shop. It pained her to watch the misery oozing from her body language and face expression. She slouched as though the weight of the world rested on her shoulders. Emma gritted her teeth and steeled her resolve. She'd wallowed for long enough in the unfairness of her circumstances. This event would provide her catalyst for change.

The figure on the screen looked taller than she remembered. Matt played the feed forward in slow-motion, his brows knitting as the man appeared from beyond the camera's view. He altered his trajectory to avoid Rohan's line of sight before making a direct line for Emma. With her shoulders hunched and her head down, she didn't notice him. Her body rocked as he bumped her from the side.

"There!" She touched the screen with her index finger. "Back up just a little more. Is it possible to zoom closer?"

Matt pressed keys on the keyboard and the view grew large enough for a close-up of her right breast. The grainy quality of the pixelated image salvaged her modesty. "Oops. Sorry." Matt used the mouse to drag the picture sideways. He pressed more keys, and the image zoomed out to show Emma's entire body. Her movements reversed frame by frame, but the defeat in her face remained constant. The man appeared to her right, lifting his arm as he approached her. The cloth bag swung from her wrist and a light breeze caused it to flap against her leg. With an incredible sleight of hand, he touched the lip of the bag. A small misjudgement caused him to catch Emma's elbow with his. It rattled him enough that he altered his course, looking over his shoulder at Rohan. It created the slight bump she remembered. The fragile, video version of herself wobbled before righting and continuing her slouching walk. Her hand rose to protect her vulnerable stomach. Using the dexterity of a magician, the man replaced his arm by his side and continued his journey. Emma frowned as he glanced back at her, revealing his identity. He pursed his lips at the Emma on screen and she saw concern and regret in his familiar features. She shook her head and released her held breath.

Matt clicked a button, and the screen blinked. The feed returned to its four split images of the inside of the store, the date stamp from each camera showing the real-time. "You know him?" He squinted up at her from his seat.

"Yeah." Emma licked her lips and ran a hand over her forehead. Sweat beaded there, the aftermath of the stress knotting her stomach.

Matt pushed back his chair and rose. His fingers patted the notes in his top pocket and he frowned, the cash burning a hole in his integrity. "I don't see how that was worth a hundred quid." A shadow crossed his face as though he regretted his honesty.

Emma hid her reaction by turning aside to her pram. She fitted the strap of her purse over her forearm and used the toe of her stiletto to release the brake. Lifting a quizzical eyebrow, she stared at the security guard. "Fifty pounds to show me the footage and fifty pounds to forget. Matt." Her eyes flashed with a dangerous intensity and he took a step away from her. His heel bumped against the filing cabinet and the mugs clunked together.

Emma's heels clicked along the corridor, their echo loud and jarring. She didn't stop until she reached her car, blowing out a breath laden with confusion. "Why?" she demanded of the azure sky. "And why him?"

Division

She'd intended to find out who put the flash drive into her bag and tell Rohan. But Emma's discovery made it impossible to do that without first finding out why her friend's husband had done such a ludicrous thing. "I don't get it, Stephie," she confessed as her daughter sat in her baby seat sucking her fingers. "Why is Frederik in Market Harborough?" After a moment of thinking up plausible scenarios, she slipped her phone from her handbag. Unlocking the screen, she searched through her contacts and pressed the call button over the familiar number.

"Emma!" Susan's delight at hearing her voice infused her with guilt at the time lapse since their last conversation.

She left an awkward moment of silence before replying. "How are you? It's been too long." She wound down her window and inhaled the scent of a fading English summer.

The edifying aroma of cut grass mingled with blossom and exhaust fumes. Stephie turned her head to the side and her eyes drifted closed. Her rosebud lips rooted against her thumb until she settled and the constant motion of her fingers and toes stilled.

"Busy as usual." Susan chuckled, and Emma pictured her friend fondling the ears of the golden retriever who stood in the gap for her sight deficit. "Jay says hello and to tell you he misses you."

Emma closed her eyes and her fingers twitched at the memory of the dog's soft fur. Part of her longed for the simplicity of her old life in Aberystwyth, for the thrill of studying and the comfort of Lucya's little council house on the outskirts of town. She released a sigh. "I miss it," she confessed, "Professor Lindley explaining the origins of the Dewey Decimal system and Jay chewing the eraser from my pencil case."

"But you've gone on to bigger and better things." Susan gave her characteristic good-natured giggle. "Did I tell you we were moving?"

"No. Where are you going?" Emma crossed the fingers of her left hand and prayed it would provide at least one answer to her questions. Frederik might have a legitimate reason for being in Harborough instead of miles away in Durham. She pursed her lips and pushed aside the flash drive's presence for the moment. "Did you or Frederik get a new job?"

"It's all been a little sad." Susan cleared her throat. The sound of footsteps on a tiled floor broke the silence. "Let me find somewhere to sit and we'll have a natter. There's stuff piled everywhere. Frederik is great about not leaving things on the floor for me to trip over, but I keep trying to sit down and discovering he's piled it on the chairs instead." She grunted and something clattered in the background as it fell. "Damn! I'll pick that up in a minute." She released a sigh and moved the telephone closer to her mouth. Her voice became clearer.

"I needed to stop work. It was only a matter of time before my vision failed me. And Jay is getting older. He found it hard to take me up and down the steps to the archives. The library manager showed more kindness and patience than the rest of the staff, but it became obvious I couldn't stay for much longer. Someone complained about getting dog hair in their tea when Jay walked past the coffee table. My poor boy's tail wags. I can't stop it any more than he can. In the end, I retired. I can't expect Frederik to keep me in the style to which I've become accustomed without a second income." Susan released a fake laugh which masked the sense of defeat resonating through her words. "So, we're downsizing and moving further south. Frederik landed a wonderful job as a security manager at Lincoln university. I'm following you around the country."

"You are. At least you're getting nearer. But Lincoln is still a good two hours away from Market Harborough." Emma studied an ant as it crawled along the edge of the glass before marching across the car's yellow paintwork. She searched for another reason for Frederik to visit Harborough. "Has the new job started already?"

"Not officially." Susan's ambiguous answer told Emma nothing. "He's worked a few days to learn the security systems. Lincoln seems quite a leading-edge university from what he's heard. He's rather excited about getting to play with all their technology. He's spent the rest of the time finding us somewhere to live."

"I saw someone who looked like him in a store yesterday." Emma waited. Two hours from Lincoln to Harborough and then back again would eat into a day. It couldn't be passed off as a lunch break. She waited for Susan to offer an explanation for Frederik's visit, frowning as she fired it down like a missile.

"No, it wasn't him. He must have a doppelgänger."

"So, when do you move?" Emma drummed her fingers on the sill of her window and changed the subject. She twisted her lips in thought.

"The house here sold within a week. The university gave us some helpful suggestions of places in Lincolnshire to live. Frederik sorted it all out by himself to save me the stress. He stayed at a motel and viewed over a hundred houses for sale. Then, he found the perfect little bungalow in a village outside the city. There are paths for Jay and me to walk on, and he says there's a bus stop right outside the front door.

I'm looking forward to a fresh start. I can't imagine staying here and not working. Every time I leave the house, Jay turns towards the library. He doesn't understand."

"Poor darling." Emma imagined Jay's blond brows furrowed into a line of confusion as Susan resisted his gentle direction. "Lincoln city is beautiful. You'll love it."

"Enough about me and all my woes. Did you get the card I sent to congratulate you on the new baby?"

Emma closed her eyes against the blur of confusion and misery which had surrounded Stephie's birth. She couldn't picture the card, but it came as no surprise. "It was beautiful." She acknowledged Susan's generosity with a lie. "The whole episode has been quite chaotic, but I'm finding my feet again now."

"Isn't it extraordinary that Rohan and Frederik knew each other in the army?" Susan chortled at her own thoughts. "You think we'd see more of each other, wouldn't you?"

Emma narrowed her eyes against the glare of the sun, not sure if Susan intended to level criticism at her. She wrinkled her nose. "I'm happy to drive to Lincoln to see you once you're settled. I could bring Stephie while Nicky is at school."

Susan laughed, and she sounded more like her old self. "I don't think you'll get away with that." She giggled. "Nicky and Jay were partners in crime. I imagine you must all come one weekend. Let's make it when the men are available. I'm sure they'd love to catch up and gossip about their army days."

"Definitely." Emma kept the sarcasm from her tone. Once she told Rohan about the flash drive, she imagined he'd have rather a lot of catching up to do with Frederik. She said goodbye to Susan and ended the call, no nearer to discovering the reason for yet more subterfuge, or the fact she'd found herself sucked into it.

Variable

Emma left Stephie in her pram in the darkened corridor and stepped into the kitchen. Sunshine bathed the south facing room, intensifying the aroma of burnt toast and coffee. Christopher looked up from the laptop he'd opened on the table. Emma's heart sank. "Don't you have a home to go to?" she asked, her tone half joking and half serious. "You set the folly up like mission control, but crouch over a laptop in here."

He ignored the veiled barb and linked his fingers behind his head. His biceps bulged through his tee shirt. He watched her stride across the kitchen and touch the kettle. Finding it only warm, she flicked the switch and grabbed mugs and instant coffee powder while she waited. "Where's Ray?" she asked, her gaze flicking up at the antique wall clock. "Is he coming in for morning tea?"

Christopher exhaled and dropped his arms. He straightened his rumpled tee shirt on the way down in a casual movement. "Ray is mowing the grass behind the house. He just started."

"So, not for him, then?" Emma raised an eyebrow and put the third mug back into the cupboard. She fixed coffee for herself and Christopher without needing to ask how he wanted it. Her fingers performed the reflex actions while her mind returned to the grainy image on the security feed at the store.

"You're not equipped to run your own investigation." The sternness in Christopher's voice shocked her. Emma jumped and spread sugar crystals over the counter. He continued, his tone acerbic. "That's Rohan's department." As she glanced back at him, he shook his head and mirth bloomed in his eyes. She flexed her fingers and fought the urge to slap the smugness off his handsome Irish face.

"Don't tell me what I can and can't do." She ground out the words through gritted teeth, but only fuelled his amusement. She realised too late she'd confirmed his guess. For a fleeting moment, she imagined he'd followed a location signal from her phone to the store. But he didn't need to when she gave up her secrets under the first sign of pressure.

"Talk to your husband. Maybe he knows more about the flash drive than you realise. Don't go back to that store. You won't find out anything."

"Yeah, right!" Sarcasm laced every syllable of the brief sentence. Emma drew her features into a sneer as she mopped up her spill. "So, you believe Rohan pretended not to notice someone he trusts planting a flash drive on his wife! He rescued me from a shoplifting accusation. I can't imagine him accepting a friend using me as an unwitting courier."

"A friend?" Christopher snorted. "This is new." He cocked his head and frowned. "Someone he trusts?" He spread his fingers across his chin. "I didn't leave the folly and Ray took Freda to the cafe, so that leaves Frederik. How is he involved with this? He lives five hours north of here."

Emma tapped her forehead with an index finger. It amused her he'd included himself in Rohan's list of friends. She doubted her husband shared his sentiment. "Not anymore. He's taken a new job in Lincoln." She faced the window, leaning across the draining board to study the cloudless azure sky. The threat of autumn hung over her like a shroud. Her shoulders sank. "Okay genius, work this out for me. Even if Frederik drove the two hours here, how did he know I'd walk through the front doors of that store at that moment? It was my first trip out and I should have been at school fetching Nicky." Emma's eyes narrowed. "He followed me. Or Rohan." Her lips creased into a grimace and she stamped her stiletto heel on the kitchen tiles. "He must have waited outside the store." She clicked her fingers. "I wish I'd thought about it before I got the security guard to show me the footage. I saw Frederik bump into me, but not where he came from." Emma wrinkled her nose. "Matt won't let me have another look. That whole episode cost me a hundred pounds." She dumped Christopher's mug of coffee on the table in front of him and reached for hers.

"A hundred quid? Cash?" His head jerked back and his eyes widened. "Where did you get a hundred quid?"

Emma ran her bottom lip over her teeth in a replica of her son's distress tell. "Rohan had a stash of notes. I borrowed a couple."

Christopher swore and covered his mouth. "Please tell me you didn't take it from a black briefcase he's hidden somewhere in the house?"

"Why?" She shifted her feet and her heels scraped against the tiles. "I didn't take it out of the briefcase. I borrowed it from a pile on the floor next to it."

"Emma! You just paid someone in counterfeit fifties! You'd better hope it doesn't track right back here."

Her jaw dropped. "Why does my husband have funny money in our house?" Scenarios tumbled through her mind.

"Because he confiscated it from someone else two jobs ago! The risk was dodgy cash. He destroyed the software and printer but kept evidence for the client. You went into labour and they're waiting for him to take it to them." Christopher tilted his head and stared at the ceiling. "The client is the Bank of England, by the way. This gets better by the minute. You need to get it back from the security guard. And fast."

Emma groaned. "Please don't make me. His name is Matt, and he's an asshole."

Christopher made a sound like a growl. "I can't believe you did that, Em." His lips curved upwards into a reluctant grin and he cocked his head. "I have to admit I'm a little impressed, although taking the baby on surveillance isn't a grand idea."

She sighed and spun on her heel, enjoying the pivot of the stiletto tip and deciding to wear them again. Her sweatpant days were over forever. She abandoned her mug on the counter and turned to face him. "I needed to know who put the flash drive into my bag. Have you found out what's on it yet?"

"Nope." Christopher rose and hauled a biscuit tin from a nearby cupboard. He turned it in his hands and set it on the table. "Want one?"

Emma's eyes narrowed. "No thank you, I don't want one of my own biscuits. And why do I feel there's something you're not telling me?" She edged nearer, trying to read guilt in his eyes and failing. He'd been at the secrecy game a long while and never revealed something unless it suited him.

Christopher shrugged. "Look who's talking! But yes, there's a lot I can't tell you." He shot her a smile over his shoulder. His slender fingers plucked a gingernut from the tin and he placed it between his teeth while he closed the lid. Taking a bite, he spoke with his mouth full. "Because then I'd have to kill you."

"You and whose army?" Emma grumbled under her breath.

"I don't need an army, babe." He chuckled deep in his chest like a freaky Father Christmas. He finished the biscuit and his fingers stroked the lid. Distraction glazed his mahogany irises as he considered taking another. Emma's pulse ticked higher, and she ground her teeth together at his arrogance. Rohan's voice in her head told her to ignore the Irishman in the same way he did. But the pervading sense of failure nipped at her psyche and introduced thoughts of vengeance. She imagined Rohan leaving the security guard, a hundred pounds lighter and with only half the information. It wouldn't happen.

Lines appeared across Christopher's forehead as he turned and noticed the wave of anger heightening Emma's colour. "Hey, I didn't mean it." The feigned light-heartedness disappeared, and he met her in the centre of the room. "I'd never hurt you. With or without an army." He bent his knees to bring his face level with hers. "And I'll do some shopping and replace all the food I've eaten." The fingers of his left hand twitched as he reached for an escaped curl next to her cheek and twisted it with exaggerated gentleness. He dared to rest his right hand against her collar bone. His irises sparkled as the edge of his palm touched the softness of her breast beneath it. He swallowed and Emma sensed him debating if he should kiss her. Time seemed to halt and leave them in limbo.

Rage bubbled in the space beneath his hand, stoking Emma's temper. She pressed her right hand over his wrist and for a second of pure delight, Christopher's eyes widened as he imagined her accepting his advance. Her fingers closed, and she forced his hand harder against her chest. A dart of pain shot through her left breast. Emma spun her body in a sharp movement, pivoting on her right foot like a dancer. She took Christopher's arm with her, catching his ulna against her hard ribcage as she lifted her left arm and twisted his elbow. He released a gasp as he lost his footing on the smooth tiles and collapsed to his right knee. Emma kept his arm raised high and gave it another painful twist before releasing him. "Don't touch me again," she snapped. "You promised. If you can't handle being around me, leave."

Christopher remained on the floor as though bowing. He drew his arm against his body with exaggerated care. The wrenching action had tugged at the wound across Emma's abdomen and she masked her discomfort. The blank expression she fixed over her face covered the wave of guilt she experienced as Christopher stayed on his knees. Her physical assault had barely touched him, but her emotional rejection had cut deep into an old wound. "Sorry." He sounded cowed, and she paused at the unexpected apology. It wasn't his usual pattern of behaviour.

Emma swallowed. She dipped her body and offered him her hand to help him stand. Christopher glanced sideways at her outstretched fingers before accepting a concession he didn't need. He sprung upright with the grace of a boxer and released her fingers as though fearful of contamination. He narrowed his eyes at Emma's wince of pain and the cursory palm she laid over her stomach. "You hurt yourself?"

"No." Emma turned away to mask the lie. "I need to feed Stephie. Please can you find some time to examine the flash drive?" Her stiletto heels clicked against the tiles as she strode towards the door.

"Em!" Christopher's voice sounded husky and carried sadness. "Did he teach you Krav Maga to defend yourself against me?"

Her shoulders relaxed, and she exhaled as she turned. Christopher dug his hands into his jeans pockets and he resembled a chastened schoolboy. She shook her head. "No, Chris." Her voice softened. "He taught me self-defence but hoped I'd never need it. Out there." Her teeth gnawed at her lower lip. "I know he's working again, but I didn't know about the counterfeit job. He doesn't realise I worry less when he tells me the truth."

Christopher wrinkled his nose and stared at the red quarry tiles beneath his feet. "I don't understand you and Rohan. It makes no sense to me."

Emma inhaled and watched him struggle. His eyes appeared dark and fathomless. She took a step forward before correcting herself. "It doesn't need to," she whispered. "You have to accept I'm another man's wife. My love for you has its root in friendship. I can't give you what you want."

Christopher raised his head and focused on the scene through the window. Moss covered the stone wall at the back of the stable yard. Smooth rolling hills rode the horizon. "I thought about taking him out once," he admitted. Emma closed her eyes against the endless possibilities at his fingertips as he trawled the dark web for contacts and clues. Common sense told her not to interrupt him. "But you still wouldn't have me, would ya?"

Emma's subconscious commanded her fingers to move across the smooth fabric of her dress and cover the space where her womb had failed her. She shook her head, the answer certain. "No." But not for the reasons he imagined. She couldn't give him the children she knew he wanted and besides, she'd never trust him.

"Okay." Christopher dragged out the word and hauled his hands from his pockets. His spine straightened through a sheer act of will and he reached again for the biscuit tin. "I'll look at the flash drive this afternoon."

"Thanks." A pitiful wail from the hallway signified Emma's rescue. She twisted the brass knob and pulled open the door, affording herself one last glance over her shoulder at Christopher. His chocolate irises sparkled with a glassy quality, and she steeled herself against his misery. She had enough of her own to carry. "And find out how Winston got through our security, please? It's urgent."

Stephie blinked from the hooded darkness of the pram and her lips stretched into a line of unhappiness. Seizing the handle, Emma steered her towards the open door of the comfortable lounge and stepped into her favourite room. She closed the door behind her with a resounding click and leaned against it. Her heart pounded in her chest as Stephie's protests lifted into a hearty wail. And she wondered how much longer she could walk the line between her husband and the persuasive Irishman.

Equivalent

Emma settled on the window seat to feed Stephie. Turning sideways against the cushions, she drew up her knees and got comfortable. As she released the buttons of her bodice, she held her breath and the baby latched onto her nipple. It hurt less, the child's feeding tugging at her scar to contract a womb that no longer existed. She relaxed and Stephie fed with enthusiasm, her tiny fingers clenching and releasing.

Emma changed her dirty nappy half way through, playing with the baby's toes and smiling at her enthusiastic kicks. She folded the soiled fabric into a reusable carrier and stuffed it beneath the pram. Grabbing her phone from her purse, she checked her emails while Stephie fed herself to sleep on the other breast. With a quick glance towards the closed door, she used her settings tab to take the device off the Wi-Fi which Christopher had installed in the house. Then she opened the secret email account she'd set up a few weeks ago. Cradling Stephie limited her to scrolling one handed and Emma frowned as she peered at the screen. She'd done her best to secure the account, ensuring not even their resident hacker would stumble across it. Using the authenticator app meant flicking from one window to another, and she fumbled over the keys. She sensed it was only a matter of time before Christopher discovered her subterfuge. She didn't intend to make it easy for him and using her phone data instead of the Wi-Fi network helped. Logging into the account via an incognito internet browser removed her search history, but she knew she walked a fine line. Christopher snooped for a living and he already suspected her of keeping something from him. He'd threatened to start hunting, which meant he hadn't yet. She'd share everything in her own time, starting with Rohan. But first, she needed something to tell them.

Hope burgeoned in her chest, but disappointment flared instead at the sight of the empty inbox. Emma tutted and tried refreshing the screen a few times, but without success. "I should have heard some news by now," she breathed. "They asked for a week." Her mood deflated, she closed the email account and reconnected the phone to the house Wi-Fi. A familiar emptiness spread out from her abdomen and leeched into her soul. Tears threatened, stinging the tender membranes of her eyelids. Crying achieved nothing, changed nothing. The last six weeks had taught her that.

Emma let her phone slide onto the window seat and rested her head against the cushion. A mower fired up in the distance and grew nearer, the sound of the engine changing as its driver engaged the sharp blades beneath it. She tilted her head and opened one eye, watching Ray's outline as he steered the heavy machine across the front lawn. Dust hung around his head like an aura, kicked up by the rotary motion of the blades against the dry grass. The scent of hay filtered through the cracks in the joinery and filled the lounge with the essence of summer. The azure sky soared overhead without the marring of a single cloud. It looked like perfection after a shaky start to Britain's most coveted season, but Emma's gaze focused on the dust and the ease with which it choked the scene. It spat from the back of the mower with every turn, showering the lawn which Ray had manicured like a putting green. An ex-soldier, makeshift medic and crack shooter, he'd once told her he felt happiest on the lawn mower. He said the cutting process satisfied him, offering redemption through slicing the unruly tufts into order. He claimed it made a sharp contrast to the army where there were no do-overs. Error led to injury or death, not nice even stripes and submissive grass.

Stephie's head lolled. Her lips parted and a line of milk trickled from the corner of her mouth and disappeared into the collar of her cardigan. Emma dabbed it away with a soft cloth from the change bag and used it to protect the shoulder of her dress as she winded the baby with gentle pats to her fragile back. The roar of the mower stopped with an abruptness which left an echo of its engine in the silence. She turned to gaze through the window.

Ray clambered from the bucket seat and lifted his baseball cap from his head. He ran a hand through his greying hair before setting it back down again. His long stride took him across the wide lawn to the driveway, and Emma leaned sideways to follow his trajectory. Rohan's Mercedes idled at the fork which led either to the main house or to the stable yard. Sleek and black, its paintwork glinted in the sunlight. Emma imagined the smell of its newness and the smoothness of its walnut dashboard beneath her fingers. Rohan had bought it just before Stephie's birth, getting rid of the one which Emma had dented too frequently to count. She'd driven the new one back from the coffee shop, the experience blurred by an emotional fog. It was too big for her. Christopher had fitted it with high spec tracking devices and other technology she didn't understand. It represented Rohan's other life as the Actuary, a persona which had pre-existed their reunion and acted as the unwelcome third person in their marriage.

Emma's warm breath fogged up the window despite the heat of the day. Stephie grumbled as the acute angle of her lean constricted her stomach. Rohan exited the car and closed the driver's door behind him. He waited for Ray to reach him, his posture casual and relaxed. Leaning against the car took the weight off his damaged limb, and he folded his arms like a man with infinite patience. A shiver of anticipation snaked along Emma's spine and she tried to identify it. Desire? Security? Or just a meeting of lost souls on a wavering path to nowhere?

A gentle breeze carried from the south whipped Rohan's fringe into a haze of white hay before dropping it into a sexy tumble over his eyes. Emma sighed and sent telepathic messages of urgency, hoping he'd hurry and come to her. She imagined his arms around her, the story of his Russian heritage retold through his familiar scent of pine, cedar and juniper.

Emma placed her right palm against the glass and spread out her fingers. "Look at me," she whispered as Rohan chatted with Ray. "Notice me."

Rohan shook hands with Ray as though making a covert deal and not meeting an old friend on a lawn in south Leicestershire. Emma wrinkled her nose and tried not to dwell on the weight of the information she lived beneath but couldn't understand. They all agreed it was better that way. But for who? She trod an unsteady path like a blindfolded tightrope walker, testing for the cord with her toes and expecting nothing but mid-air at every forward movement. "Better for them," she whispered to her sleeping daughter.

Emma placed Stephie into her pram, tilting her onto her right side to stop air bubbles forming in her tiny stomach.

Her fingers expressed their love in the care with which she fitted the rolled blankets either side of her to stop her rolling and covered her with a light sheet. When Stephie yelped in her sleep, Emma freed her tiny fist and prised the thumb free. She lifted it to the baby's rosebud lips and her daughter sucked it into her mouth with enthusiasm. Stephie settled with a rapidity which appeared almost supernatural. Emma wished she could do likewise.

She rose and stared through the sash window, in time to watch Rohan get back into his car. His movements appeared fluid and easy, though she sensed his tiredness in the set of his shoulders. The driver's door clicked shut, and the vehicle slid along the driveway like a knife through butter. Emma inhaled through her nose and released a slow exhale through her lips, ridding herself of the melancholy which the empty inbox had brought down on her head once again. Rohan drew his car alongside her and wound down the passenger window. He smiled at her and blew her a kiss.

Emma waved, her lips stretching into a smile. She'd wanted him to look at her, but he didn't need to see her to confirm her presence. He already knew she was there, informed by that strange sixth sense which arced between them like a rainbow. Rohan slid the Mercedes behind Emma's bright yellow car and cut the engine. He lifted his overnight bag from the boot and walked towards the front door. A sense of rightness filled the void in the pit of her stomach.

She strode across the oriental rug which Anton had picked out for her months before she knew the house existed. Both Andreyev boys had lived beneath the shadow of damaging family secrets. Emma's shoulders relaxed. "You keep yours," she whispered, "and I'll keep mine."

Expression

Tiredness shrouded Rohan like a cloak, mussing his hair and drawing dark circles beneath his eyes. Emma met him in the lobby as he sat on the reclaimed church pew to remove his shoes. The toes of his left foot arched upwards as he inspected a hole in his sole. The synthetic outline of his right remained still and lifeless, its ridged silhouette showing through the fabric of his sock as an artist's illusion.

Emma cupped her hands either side of his head and lifted his face like a flower she wished to admire. She touched a kiss to the furrow marring his forehead. "Welcome home," she said, her tone soothing. Rohan's shoulders sagged, and he dropped the shoe to the hard floor tiles. It hit with a dull thud and tipped sideways onto its mate.

"Well, that was a disaster." He reached up and stroked Emma's forearms. She closed her eyes and enjoyed the solidity of his touch and the sense of safety which poured through the front door after him.

"Why?"

Rohan's sniff sounded disdainful, and he shook his head. "I got a hole in my shoe." His irises sparkled with the richness of gems and he blinked. A strand of his white, blond fringe bounced against his eyelashes, adding an air of vulnerability. Emma responded to the momentary lapse in his armour, dipping at the waist to press a kiss against his cheek. Stubble scratched her soft lips, and he smelled of yesterday's faded aftershave. He'd removed his jacket, but creases dug valleys in the back of his shirt from the driver's seat. Some hidden trigger in his despondency tugged on his emotional link with Emma, and she sensed the shard of failure buried deep. It didn't seem enough to kiss away his ails. She needed more. She wanted to lock Rohan and her children in a hidden vacuum and just take the time to exist and to breathe without interruption. Perhaps she could deal with her barrenness there and come to a resolution.

Emma threaded her fingers through his and tugged his right hand. Rohan's brow knitted for a moment before he read and comprehended the intention in her eyes. He rose in a single fluid motion, padding along the corridor behind her in his socks. They skirted the kitchen door and Emma glanced back, lifting her finger and pressing it over her lips. She led Rohan into the lounge with its high ceilings and ornate sconces. His irises darkened as she lifted the key from its hiding place above the architrave and fitted it into the lock.

Calm accompanied the decisive click, and Rohan exhaled. He pulled his tie from around his neck and loosened the top button of his shirt. The limp on his right side appeared more pronounced as he released his cuff links one at a time and dropped them into his trouser pocket. A long stride carried him across the oriental rug to the pram parked next to the window seat. His eyes crinkled at the corners as he gazed at his sleeping daughter. He dipped forward to stroke Stephie's forehead with his index finger, the motion soft and yet conveying strength and adoration. "She's so beautiful," he whispered. Rohan glanced up at Emma, his irises sparkling with hues of azure and cerulean. His face held an unusual peace, so raw it caused her to hold her breath. A voice in Emma's mind told her it wouldn't be sufficient. That she wouldn't be enough. It robbed her of the happy yellow colours which had produced a momentary respite amid the grey. Doubt set up its insistent clamouring in her head.

When Rohan held out his hand to her, the staccato beat of her footsteps caused her to stumble over the edge of the rug. "I'm sorry," she breathed, her voice growing in pitch.

Rohan caught her and pulled her against him, his powerful body a rock in a flooding river. "You have nothing to apologise for," he whispered. He tilted her chin with his thumb and kissed her, his lips tasting of soda and warmth. His biceps strained against his shirt as he led her from the edge of the rug, and Emma sensed he'd misunderstood. She anchored herself in his love, pinning her arms around his waist and locking her fingers as though fearing he might wash away like flotsam.

Rohan's fingers dug into Emma's hair, his touch tender as he held her still and teased her lips with his. He gave her no chance to correct him on the origins of her apology, leaving her breathless and desperate. Her brain addled beneath the force of his passion, and she was sixteen again and swept away in the enigma of Rohan Andreyev. She forgot to close the curtains against the buzz of the lawn mower or the gaze of the high sun straddling cumulus clouds. Her knees obeyed the silent command of Rohan's tug on her hands, and she sank onto the patterned rug with a sigh. Hand knotted from Mashwani kilim, decades before she was born, the rug cushioned her and absorbed her sadness. She waited while Rohan eased himself to the floor and forced his right leg to bend. Breath snuffed from his lips as he snickered and Emma saw his flicker of fear that his ungainliness had ruined the moment. She furrowed her brow and reached for him, snuggling against him as they stretched in front of the empty fireplace. "I love you," she whispered. "I'm glad you're home."

"Me too." He held out his left arm as a pillow for Emma's head and tilted her chin with his index finger. "I become centred here with you. This place lets me orbit, but I must always return."

Emma smiled as a lightness entered her heart. She fortified its walls against distraction and future misery, providing herself with a temporary haven to shelter behind with her husband. Her kisses silenced them both, banishing her immediate problems and allowing her to focus. Rohan's fingers fumbled with her bodice, his movements making her ticklish and giggly. When he growled in frustration, she hauled at the delicate fabric and spread the seed buttons far and wide. The popping of stitches accompanied a terminal tearing sound and the floral fabric's susurrations whispered over the silence as it fluttered open. Rohan gasped and his eyes widened at the disastrous effect of her impatience. He pursed his lips and froze, waiting for Emma's reaction. The tinkling of her laughter filled the room and he shook his head. "You are one crazy zhenshchina," he breathed. His fingers caressed the lacy edge as it crossed her thigh.

"I know." Emma's eyes narrowed in challenge and she added a defiant tilt to her chin. Rohan sighed, and the hardships and failure of the previous twenty-four hours relinquished their hold on his mind. He kissed her again, his hand straying beneath the hem of the ruined dress. The distant strains of the lawn mower serenaded them as it subdued the landscape into regimented lines.

Less Than

"Christopher said you didn't succeed." Emma poured tea from the pot. Rohan's mug clunked against the oak kitchen table as she sat it in front of him.

"He talks too much." The milk slopped as his long fingers fumbled the tiny handle of the jug.

"What went wrong?" Emma used his pause to pour herself a cup and ignore Rohan's easy dismissal. "Didn't you secure the risk?"

He gave a slow blink, but it didn't mask his irritation. "Da." He nodded and twisted his lips into a grimace. "At least, I thought so." His azure eyes glazed into a faraway look and Emma sighed. She imagined the complicated computations running on a program in her husband's intelligent mind as he weighed ratio and outcomes.

"It's like getting blood out of a stone." She reached for the sugar bowl, her spoon already poised and her taste buds anticipating the heady influx of carbohydrates. She let out a growl of irritation as Rohan shifted it out of reach.

"What?" He frowned, and his expression mirrored her indignation. "You asked me to stop you gaining extra weight. This is me stopping you."

"But I want it." Her voice took on a childish whine. She regretted it when he winced.

"Fine." He pushed the sugar bowl towards her. "Then don't ask for my help."

Emma lifted the tea to her lips and sipped the tan liquid. Rohan hadn't wanted the role of calorie gatekeeper, but she'd persuaded him to assist her. No one else in her immediate circle seemed equipped to deal with her complete absence of willpower. The drink slipped past her tongue without protest, although the lack of a sugar hit left her unsatisfied. She drained it and poured another, not reaching again for the sugar bowl. "Tell me about the job. What went wrong?"

Rohan shrugged. "Nothing. I secured the hard drive containing the data. The mark handed it over without a fuss and assured me he'd made no copies. I set off home, and the client phoned me in a temper. Hackers threatened to release their database to the media in batches unless he makes payments to a bitcoin wallet. That means either the mark lied to me or someone else took a copy."

Emma wrinkled her nose. "What's on the hard drive?"

Rohan held his mug in both hands, his forearms resting against the table. His blond fringe bounced against his eyelashes. "The dating profiles of over two million people."

"So?" Emma narrowed her eyes. "Aren't those things public, anyway? Don't you need to swipe left or right or something?"

"Sort of." He raised his eyebrows. "But it's a bummer if you're married and logged onto a dating website, isn't it?"

Emma cocked her head. "Oh. Wow. The divorce courts will fill up fast as soon as people scroll through the names. Do I need to see if yours is there?"

He made a sound like a grunt. Rohan rarely sought escape from the actual world in facsimiles. He dealt in facts and figures, risks and actualities. He possessed no internal dialogue to comfort or disturb him. Scrolling numerics and formulae dictated his next move amid ordered sums of probability. Emma couldn't imagine anyone less likely to join a dating website to cheat on her.

"What did the mark say?" She grimaced at the gravity of her sugarless tea. "He must have taken a copy of the database. Did you go back to him?"

"Yes." Rohan glanced at the knuckles of his right hand. "I did." The unbroken skin harboured a faint blush. "He said he didn't make copies. I believed him. Eventually."

Emma frowned. "So, someone else at the firm sold or gave away the information? That's the company's issue, isn't it? You got back what you agreed to retrieve."

Rohan's eyes flickered with an inner light. "It's my problem now."

"Oh." Emma considered her next sentence. "What happens if you can't find the person at the root of it? Do you refund your fee?"

"It's not that simple. Failure damages my reputation. It's about more than finances. There are always others nipping at my heels in this business. The client didn't go out to tender and get quotes from other actuaries. They came directly to me based on my success rate."

"Where do you start?" Curiosity budded in Emma's brain. She yearned to understand Rohan's mental processes and become more than his wife and bed partner. "Can I help?

Rohan stared at her, and his glazed irises returned to their striking blueness. She tensed, waiting for him to destroy her illusions of partnership. His answer caused her body to jerk in surprise. "Yes." His eyes narrowed, and he gave a slow nod. "But I don't know how yet."

"Okay." Emma leaned forward, enthusiasm ticking in her breast. Her lips parted with ready questions, but the kitchen door opened and arrested her thoughts. Disappointment brought her crashing down to earth with a sickening thud.

"I wanna cuddle Stephie." Nicky bounced across the room in his pyjama bottoms. The shirt flapped open to his lean chest. Action Man dangled from his fingers, the bungee cord flapping around his legs. The kitchen door creaked as the slight bowing of the wall and tightness of the hinges closed it by slow, painful degrees.

Emma held out her arms and Nicky bounced towards her. "She's sleeping." A grunt escaped her lips as he clambered into her lap.

"That baby's always sleeping." He twisted his lips into a pout. "When is she gonna skateboard with me? And play soldiers and stuff?" He bobbed his head forward and back like a marionette. "She just nods at me. Her head's gonna fall off her neck."

"Her muscles need to get stronger. It might take a few years before she can play games with you." Emma wrinkled her nose at the faded red line snaking around Nicky's thin wrist. "Why didn't the paint come off in the shower? Did you use soap?"

"Yeah." Nicky inspected the streak and gave a nonchalant shrug. He closed his eyes in an expression of pure satisfaction. "I'm gonna love my book character costume. You're amazing, Mum. *The Cock with the Crimson* Comb is gonna win."

A knock on the swaying door heralded Christopher. He edged into the room after giving Rohan a sideways glance. "Hey guys." Damp hair stuck to his forehead and his chocolate irises darted their nervous gaze from Emma to Rohan and then back again.

"Harley Man." Nicky tipped his face like a blossoming flower and smiled at him. He added a cute wave which sent Action Man's bungee cord bobbing.

"Hey champ. How was school today?" Christopher stepped across the room and lifted the kettle. He weighed it in his hand before leaning towards the tap and adding more water.

"Okay." Nicky didn't sound sure. "Please, can I ride on your Harley again?" Christopher's spine stiffened, and he didn't respond. He moved with uncharacteristic woodenness as he waited for Emma to challenge him. She pushed her tongue against the roof of her mouth to stop herself rising to the bait. Picking a fight with the Irishman in front of Rohan seemed ill advised. Nicky's eyes widened and his lips tugged down to show his bottom teeth. "Oops," he breathed.

Christopher turned with a mug of coffee in his hand. Amusement danced in his irises. Emma glared at him and gave a slow shake of her head, which told him she'd discuss his babysitting activities another time. Nicky shifted his body in her lap. The action strained the tight skin across her scar, and she winced. He leaned close enough for her to smell the toothpaste on his breath. "I just went for the teeniest tiniest ride," he whispered. "When you went to the hospital. It wasn't Harley Man's fault. I made him do it."

"Did you?" Emma's tone sounded sickly sweet. She avoided Christopher's gaze. Instead, she struggled with the surge of grief which seized hold of her stomach and clenched at Nicky's reference to her operation. "Did you finish your homework?"

"Yep." Nicky nodded and pressed his cheek against her chest. "Please, can you tuck me in my bed and sit with me for a while?"

"I'd love to." Emma tuned into her son's inner plea and cupped his face in her hands. She rested her chin on top of his head and closed her eyes. Peace surrounded them for a moment. The door creaked in the breeze, accompanied by Rohan's gentle tapping on his phone. Stephie snored in her pram near the window.

Then Christopher cleared his throat. Emma tensed. "No luck yet on finding that other copy," he said. Emma glanced up to notice him run a hand through his hair.

Rohan exhaled and leaned back in his chair. The phone dropped the short distance from his fingers to the table. "Did the company give you access to their servers? They didn't want to, but I saw no other solution."

"Aye, they did." Christopher's enthusiasm grew as the men's relationship moved onto safer ground. "It could have been anyone. Their server has more back doors than a tart's boudoir." His eyes widened, and he winced at the unfortunate choice of language. Nicky's lips parted with the inevitable question, and Emma placed her hand over his mouth.

"Bedtime," she cooed. "What story shall we read?"

Nicky's nose wrinkled in disgust. "Mum!" he protested. He ducked sideways and her stomach complained. "Read *The Cock with the Crimson Comb.* I need to make sure I can act like him. All day."

Emma smiled through the pain and counted her blessings. "How wonderful for your teacher," she mused.

Segments

Rebekka Emmaline Duchovny. Emma's fingers stroked the fragile paper, the ink blotted over the swirl beneath the registrar's signature. She'd cried over the birth certificate many times, but the tear which smudged the identity of the official had stained the document decades ago. The base colours of the black ink had bled into the weave of the paper to reveal forest green and ochre. Emma covered the signature with her index finger as though hiding its nakedness. Its misery parallelled hers. Like the ink, she'd been broken down by the discovery of her adoption, her understanding spread thin and insubstantial across the sum of her life.

She blew out a sigh which seemed to originate near the soles of her feet. "Emma," she whispered. Her adoptive parents had used the first half of her middle name. The record showed she'd been too young to notice the switch. Emma's gaze slid to her sleeping daughter. She'd been two weeks older than Stephie when her birth mother gave her up to the barren clerics from Lincolnshire. Emma wondered what Rebecca Harrington thought as she cradled the little girl in her arms for the first time. Precious memories of the gentle vicar's wife filled her mind, leaving no doubt that she'd loved and wanted her. She hadn't planned to leave her baby motherless for a second time.

Emma's lashes grazed her cheek as she stared at her writhing fingers. The discovery of the documents hidden in her father's bureau had thrown her into a pit of confusion. Her name and her origins had been stripped of their certainty. Nothing was as she'd believed. Her world had rocked from side to side and then came Stephie's traumatic birth. Emma wafted a hand in front of her face as though to disperse the black fog which hung there. Only the truth would banish it. Hunting her ancestry should have been an archivist's dream if secrecy hadn't shrouded it with the potential for terrible disappointment.

Rohan's crutches clicked against the bathroom tiles as he manoeuvred himself from the shower. He'd offered many times to help her find the older brother listed on the adoption record. But Emma had signed up to an ancestry website and paid for the DNA test with a secret credit card, the urge for subterfuge providing a comforting warmth. She hugged the knowledge to herself like a diamond hidden in her chest. She needed to control the process. Finding her identity and her sibling had become a marker for the return of her independence. Letting Rohan take over would highlight yet another failure in her long and miserable list. He'd involve Christopher, and she rebelled against the Irishman's involvement. He already knew too much about her to risk volunteering more leverage.

At the sound of Rohan's crutches moving towards the door, Emma snatched up the birth certificate and bent it along its timeworn folds. She tucked it into the yellowed envelope where she'd found it and slipped it inside the hard backed novel on her bedside table. Her fingers trembled as she pushed a long curl behind her ear. The syllables of her proper name reverberated in her head like a distant echo. *Rebekka Emmaline Duchovny.*

She jumped and blew out a tense breath as the bathroom door creaked. Rohan emerged from the steam like a muscular Adonis, mist swirling around his head and arcing from his wide shoulders like a heat haze. Emma lifted her hand and jabbed her index finger at a switch next to the light. "You forgot to turn the extractor fan on again," she said, her tone flat.

"Prosti." Rohan followed the apology by turning on his crutches and flicking the button. A whirring commenced as the fan vibrated its obedience and he pulled the door closed behind him. He clicked across the floorboards, his towel hanging low over his hips. Emma doubted she would ever get used to the gap beneath the fabric where his right shin should take his weight. Sometimes, she still saw it there, its angular bone showing through the skin and downy blond hair catching the light.

"Do you know if anyone checked the post?" She kept her tone bright as she leaned back against her pillow. She drew her legs beneath her as though bracing herself for impact.

"I followed the van home." Rohan peered in the crib and his irises sparkled like diamonds at the sight of the sleeping child. With pale skin untouched by the sun and tufted highlights in her hair, Stephie resembled a cherub from an oil painting. Rohan sat on the bed near Emma's feet and leaned his crutches against the mattress. He inspected their position with his brows knitted into a line before adjusting them to form the hypotenuse of a neat scalene triangle. "He didn't stop today."

Emma's shoulders slumped. She'd intercepted the initial DNA testing kit weeks ago by pushing the pram down the driveway at the time the postal service delivered. Her house mates met the pretext of wanting fresh air and exercise with collective relief, especially when she'd feigned cheerfulness and waved away their offers to accompany her. Posting her vial of spit to the ancestry company had proved more difficult and meant confiding in Freda. Waiting for the results got harder with each passing week.

Rohan leaned sideways to snag Emma's left ankle, and he tugged her leg out straight before resting her foot in his lap.

His long fingers rubbed at the sore space beneath her arch. The roughness of his damp towel pressed against her heel and she closed her eyes and allowed herself to relax. "Thank you." She inhaled through her nose and released the breath. "Have you seen Freda since you got home?"

"Da." Rohan nodded. His white, blond fringe bounced against his eyelashes as he glanced up at her. "I saw her downstairs while you were up here changing Stephie's nappy. She said she would nip to her apartment to fetch something and arrive back in time for dinner. But she's using Ray like her personal chauffeur. I'm not sure how he feels about that."

Emma groaned. "Sorry. She has this horrible knack for diverting the conversation away from herself when I ask questions. I still don't know what's happened at the residential community, but she seems to have moved in here permanently." Emma held her breath as Rohan's deft fingers moved over a sore spot she hadn't noticed. "I don't mind her living here. She just seems so unhappy."

"Maybe she's fallen out with someone at the apartments?" Rohan framed the question and lifted an eyebrow.

Emma pursed her lips and her eyes widened. "Oh. Does your father still have a room there?"

Rohan shrugged and didn't glance up at Emma. "Who knows?" he mused. Lines appeared in his jaw as he gritted his teeth, and she sensed the dark cloud billowing over both their heads. "Why?" His fingers stilled over her foot.

"About that," she began. "I woke up in the middle of the night and found him here."

"Here? In the house?" Rohan's eyes narrowed to slits, making his aquiline nose more prominent.

Emma swallowed. "In our bedroom, actually." She tensed, studying Rohan's reaction with interest. "Christopher said he walked in through the front gate and let himself in with a key. He's investigating how."

Rohan made a sound resembling a growl. His fingers resumed their massaging. "He'll find no clue. I understand nothing about that man. Never have and never will. He knows things he shouldn't and appears at the most inopportune moments. I often wonder if he had me chipped like a dog. If there is a device capable of location tracking and equipped with a camera and microphone, he acquired it and inserted it into my body at birth."

Emma widened her eyes and blinked. Her face contorted into a grimace. "I can think of some moments I'd rather he didn't witness." Her nose wrinkled in distaste. "Is such technology possible?"

Rohan's lip quirked upwards on one side. He used his knuckles on the top of Emma's foot, massaging the small bones and tendons leading to her toes. "Anything is possible. Many times, I've asked Hack to use his equipment to check me for bugs. He finds nothing apart from a reason to mock me."

"I bet he enjoys that." Emma tilted her head back on her shoulders with a sigh. She stared at the plaster molding, which covered the ceiling in a pattern of geometric petals. "I woke up to find your father sitting on the bed. He scared me." Her brow furrowed and she lifted her head to stare at Rohan. "He asked about your finances. He mentioned you'd sold the manor in Scotland and the London house. Why didn't you tell me?"

Emma narrowed her eyes as Rohan's chin flattened into a stress tell. "Is that all he said, or is there more?"

She wiggled her foot in his hands to force him to look at her. "Do you have money worries?"

"Nyet." Rohan's body language relaxed as Emma studied his movements. His shoulders lost their tension and his fingers resumed their gentle work. He appeared relieved, and that reaction bothered Emma more than the alternative.

Rohan blew out through his nose. "I don't use the London house anymore." An inner peace radiated from his azure irises. He didn't need it because he came home. To her. "I sold it to another accountant. Falkirk Manor has been a money pit during its restoration, especially after Hack's debacle with the explosion. I've signed a contract with Historic Environment Scotland for them to manage it on a thirty-year charter. They'll perform basic maintenance and run tours. Any profits will go back into the property. I figured a thirty-year lease would make it Nicky's problem." He looked up at Emma and his fingers twitched over her bare toes. "I would have spoken to you about my decisions, but you've had things on your mind." He blinked and his smile resurrected a dimple in his right cheek. "You look better today." The massage coasted over her shin. "I'm glad."

"I feel better." The admission cemented Emma's painful crawl back to normality. "I'm not yet okay with everything that happened, but I'm getting there." Her eyelashes flickered as her gaze followed the lines and angles of the tattoo on Rohan's shoulder. She saw the tendons and sinews lengthen across his collar bone as he bowed his head in a graceful nod of acceptance and gratitude. The ornate cross moved in line with the solid plate of deltoid muscle.

"I'll speak to Winston." Rohan chewed on the inside of his cheek. "I'll make him respect our privacy." He added nothing further, not elaborating on how he intended to force his father to do as he asked.

Smiling, Emma waggled her foot in his lap in a silent demand for more massaging. Rohan tickled the sole instead and she squirmed against her pillow, a giggle escaping her lips. She tried to free her ankle from his grip and twisted her body sideways as he used his nails to intensify the sensation. The laughter died in her chest at the sight of the book resting on her bedside table. The birth certificate housed between the first two pages seemed to call to her, demanding her attention like a burn searing her chest. Glancing up, Emma realised her mistake as Rohan's gaze slid to the book and then back to her.

"We're alone." Emma twisted her lips into a coquettish smile.

Rohan blinked, his lashes grazing his damp fringe as he dragged his attention from the book. The lure of Emma's raw sexuality distracted him enough for conflict to bud in the furrows of his forehead. Emma tugged her ankle free of his grip. His fingers opened, removing the warmth of his contact with her soft skin. Desperate to complete the distraction, she held out her arms, knowing he wouldn't resist the opportunity to continue healing their relationship. Rohan cocked his head as he considered the sleeping baby in the crib. Stephie's eyes remained closed, her tiny thumb moving as she clamped it between her lips. Her eyelashes flickered, her body plumbing the depths of sleep.

He pushed himself upright and balanced on one leg. The towel slipped from his waist with little persuasion, its damp folds making a gentle sigh as it slithered to the rug. Hard muscle ridged his stomach, the shadows from the overhead lights kissing them into sharp relief. He nudged his way onto the bed next to Emma and she held her breath as the book pitched from the bedside table and onto the rug with a dull thud. Rohan ignored it, turning on his side to face her. He raised his hand and gentle fingers coasted across her cheek and over the fold of her lips. His scent surrounded her in a haze of security. The citrus shower gel mingled with the musky sage of his pheromones. Emma turned on her side and slid her leg across his thighs. Her soft skin found resistance against his shower-dampness and she hooked her calf behind his left knee. She inhaled, drawing safety and familiarity into her lungs as his fingers slipped beneath the skirt of her light dress and found the hem of her underwear.

The pads of Rohan's fingers warmed her. The nail of his index finger scraped against her thigh as he sought the softness beneath her underwear. Emma's breathing quickened, her lips parting to accept his kiss. His chest muscle quivered beneath her open palm, the connection between them flaring with heat and promise. Her stomach twinged and she ignored its warning, tuning in to Rohan's naked body pressed against the flimsy fabric of her dress. He sighed, the sound laden with anticipation. Emma's teeth grazed his lower lip before life intruded and thwarted their plans.

Rohan's groan followed the sharp rap which shook the bedroom door. Christopher Dolan's lyrical accent cut through the ensuing silence. "You in there, Emma?" A note of triumph lifted his sentence at the end. "Freda rang me because she says yer not answering yer phone. She only wants you. It seems she's got herself into a spot of trouble. "

"Thanks." Emma held her breath and imagined Christopher's elation at ruining her moment with Rohan. She wrapped her arms around her husband's neck and pressed her lips against his, desperate to rekindle the passion stampeded beneath Christopher's heavy foot. Stephie's tired wail called time on her efforts.

"It's not fair." Emma draped herself over Rohan's shoulder and pushed her face against his neck. Closing her eyes, she pretended it was just the two of them.

Rohan's powerful arms slid around her to form a protective cage. His breath warmed the soft skin beneath her ear. "It's always like this for us, isn't it? Stolen kisses and clandestine meetings."

Emma nodded against his shoulder. "At least we're not ducking and diving to avoid your mother." She winced as the words slipped free. Alanya had made her life a living hell, but Rohan had loved her. "Sorry," she whispered.

The knocking came again, and Stephie let out a wail of shock. Emma groaned.

"I'll change her dirty zad." Rohan jerked his head towards the door. "You see what he wants."

Perpendicular

"What's so important?" Emma slipped from the room, closing the door behind her. "Has something happened to Freda?" An angry squeal carried from inside as Rohan released Stephie from the damp nappy. "I need to feed the baby."

"No, Freda is fine. Have you told him?" Christopher narrowed his eyes. "Rohan. Have you informed him about the flash drive?"

"No." Emma blinked and her hair swished against her shoulder blades as she shook her head. "But I can if it's related to this latest job."

"Don't." Christopher paused and gnawed on his lower lip. "It's nothing to do with that mess. This is something else."

Emma glanced at the bedroom door and winced. "He has incredible hearing. Unless you want to share this information, we should speak about it later."

"Okay." Christopher walked backwards before turning. "Kitchen. Tonight. Text me."

Emma sent Nicky back to bed for the third time that evening. She stood under the skylight which ran along part of the hallway. The walls of the upper floor rose either side of it like weathered brown arms. Stars twinkled as evening settled over the house. The heat of the last few days had diminished as autumn ushered out the short-lived British summer. A chill drifted past her bare knees. She let herself into the room and shut the door with a click.

"Want me to feed her?"

"I'm not sure." Rohan wrinkled his nose as he considered the miniature dilemma thrashing on the bed. "I changed her nappy and tried to soothe her. What does it mean when she brings her knees into her chest and wails?"

Stephie obliged with an ear-splitting cry, which ended with a guttural grunt. She thrashed her fists on the change mat and her angry face expressed more than speech.

Emma stripped out of her dress at speed and hauled on clean underwear and a set of mismatched pyjamas. "Colic. It's my fault. Ray added onions to the mince at dinner. It doesn't agree with her." She climbed onto the bed and walked across it on her knees. "Poor baby. It's belly ache. Her tummy is telling her she's hungry, but she isn't."

"How do you cure it?" Rohan leaned against the pillows, a furrow marring his brow. He hoisted Stephie, his powerful biceps forming a sharp contrast against his daughter's delicate frame. Her tiny crown nestled in his cupped palms, her body spread along his forearms. The wail halted long enough for her to draw in a breath filled with hiccoughs.

"It's wind trapped in her belly." Emma's lips turned down in a sad expression as Stephie's gaze landed on her face. Her tone gentled. "Poor girl. You've been so good compared to your brother." She reached out and placed her index finger in the baby's tiny palm, rewarded by the firm grip which clasped it. "Granny Lucya put onions in everything. I didn't realise back then that my food affected my breast milk. Nicky suffered from dreadful colic."

Rohan's muscles flexed as he bounced his daughter in a gentle motion. A dusting of tears glittered on Stephie's cheeks as she stopped crying. Emma sat on her haunches and smiled at her husband. "That's working." Ridged veins stood out beneath the skin, covering his arms like dark shadows. "I give it five minutes before your muscles turn to jelly."

"Pah." Rohan gave her the side eye and scoffed. His abdominal muscles tensed as he dipped forward to take Stephie's weight.

Emma sighed. "Lucya fed Nicky weak chamomile tea with cooled water from the kettle. She said it settled the air bubbles." She slithered backwards off the bed. "Will you manage while I run downstairs to make up a bottle? I'll dump it in ice to cool it quicker."

"We're fine." Rohan's soothing tone filled Emma's heart with reassurance. Already smitten with his daughter, he appeared as a man in love, keeping the motion gentle and steady. Stephie lay back in his arms, her legs giving a sporadic thrash as the fragile workings of her tiny stomach contracted in spasms of pain. Her chest hitched as her cries reduced to an occasional grizzle.

"I'll be as quick as I can," Emma promised. She left the mattress and padded across the rug.

"Take your phone." Rohan jerked his chin at the device discarded on the bedside cabinet. "I'll text if I need you. I can't carry her and use my crutches. It'll take too long to fix my leg back on if she's distressed."

"Okay." Emma dashed around the bed and snatched up her phone. Frantic fingers pushed it into the top pocket of her pyjama shirt. "I'll run."

She closed the door and jogged along the hallway. The old floorboards creaked beneath her step and she corrected herself, shifting closer to the wall to avoid disturbing Nicky. Vera Lynn warbled a faint but familiar tune from wartime Britain as Emma passed Freda's room. She paused and frowned. But another wail from Stephie sent her dashing down the first dogleg of the angular staircase. She wondered if she'd missed an important anniversary relating to Freda's deceased husband. "Tomorrow," she promised herself. "I'll speak to her tomorrow."

A light glowed from under the kitchen door and Emma blasted in like a tornado. Christopher's chair scraped on the tiles as he jerked backwards in shock. "I told you to text me!" he complained. His black eyebrows drew together in a line of irritation.

"I'm here to make a bottle for Stephie." She winced and rubbed her stomach. Part sympathy with her daughter and part response to the tugging of her scar. "Let's talk about whatever it is another time." She strode across the tiles, the surface cold against her bare feet. The empty kettle elicited her groan of frustration. Emma held it under the tap to fill and set it to boil. She washed her hands and stared at an unopened box containing a steriliser. "I don't understand how to work this," she admitted. "I should have looked at it before I needed to use it."

Christopher rose and his trainers squeaked against the floor. He leaned over Emma to reach for the box and lifted it above her. "We'll work it out." He pulled a pen knife from his jeans pocket and slit the tape along the cardboard seam. The kettle hummed in the corner as Emma fidgeted. She watched his deft fingers pull out the packaging to expose a bowl with a plastic lid. He lifted it free in one hand and pulled out a bottle wrapped in shrink wrap. "Open this." He thrust the bottle at her. "You'll need scissors."

Emma turned away, searching three drawers before she found a pair. She hacked at the plastic and almost slit open her thumb. By the time she'd released the bottle and a single teat, Christopher had unwrapped the steriliser and read the label. "You place water inside and then microwave the bottles. It says it takes a couple of minutes."

"Thank goodness!" Emma gulped. "I worried it was one of those twenty-four-hour things."

Christopher shook his head. "They haven't used those since we came off the ark."

"Funny guy." Emma held out the bottle. "Do I microwave it all together or sterilise it in pieces?"

He placed everything on the kitchen table. He rolled his eyes and held out a hand for the bottle. "Are you giving her boiling water?" he demanded as the kettle switched itself off with a loud click.

Emma's eyes widened. "Chamomile tea. I'll make it while you do that."

Christopher assembled the steriliser with the bottle inside before Emma found the tea bags. His lips curved upwards in a smirk as he shut the microwave door and programmed the timer. He leaned against a cabinet and folded his arms. "I've discovered who wrote the information on that flash drive," he announced. "And I've worked out Frederik's involvement. I just don't understand why he's given it to us."

Emma poured hot water into a teapot and slotted the lid into place. She touched the rounded china side as though expecting it to have already begun cooling. A frown drew her brows together, and she yanked her finger away, pressing it against the palm of her other hand.

"To me, actually." Emma stuffed her hand in her pocket and touched her phone. "Why not Rohan?"

Christopher's smile spread to split his face in an evil grin. "Oh, it's safe to say your husband will want no part in this."

Empty Set

E mma sank into a chair. "Is it launch codes? He'd love those. There are lots of people he'd like to put a bomb under."

Christopher's smile widened. "You're on the right track."

Emma leaned forward, tension moving through her body. "I was joking!"

"Well, unfortunately, I'm not." Christopher leaned back in the chair and wiped the smirk from his lips. "Did you ever meet Frederik's son from his first marriage?" He paused a moment as Emma trawled through her memories of Susan's wedding day. Rohan's late attendance and the shock of seeing him again obscured any mental images of the rest of the event. Emma focused her gaze back on Christopher and shook her head. "Many people were there. Susan never mentioned a son, and I don't recall seeing a child in the wedding party."

"He's eighteen and nondescript. But he attended the wedding." Christopher raised an eyebrow and Emma's mind took her back to that day. Her borrowed shoes pinched her toes, her dress too small, and her confidence shot.

"Harley Man," she murmured. Nicky's fantasy hero had turned out to be the handsome Irishman. Emma bit back the ready comment about how good he looked in his leathers, not wanting to provide mixed messages.

He smiled again. "The very same." Then his expression grew serious. "Frederik asked me to speak to his son a year ago. He's a computer geek like me, but Frederik felt concerned that he pursued no purpose. The kid dropped out of school, slept all day and gamed or programmed all night." Christopher raised an eyebrow. "I didn't see the problem myself, but Frederik rescued me out of the crap enough times to warrant a favour."

"So, where is this going?" Emma rose and touched the side of the teapot. "Has this brewed enough?"

"No." Christopher followed her across the kitchen and lifted the lid on the teapot. "What are you trying to do?"

"I'm making chamomile tea to stop Stephie's colic."

"Brew it a bit longer but dilute it in the bottle."

Emma's shoulders relaxed. "I love how you know everything," she mused. "You're a walking encyclopaedia."

"I come from a big family." Christopher hauled a teaspoon from the drawer and stubbed it around in the teapot to agitate the chamomile. "Me mammy kept breeding to get eight more like me."

"So, Frederik wanted me to give the flash drive to you. I've done that." Emma leaned her hip against the counter and ignored his personal reference.

Christopher moved on without breaking his stride. "It's not that simple. His son mixed with some dubious characters online and I warned Frederik. The kid didn't have a paid job, so he got his money from somewhere." He held his hands up in front of him and Emma tensed. "I have a confession. I phoned Frederik earlier today."

She gasped. "Why would you do that? If he'd wanted your involvement, he'd have asked for it."

Christopher shrugged off her protest. "The flash drive arrived in the post at his home a few days ago, along with a note written in his son's handwriting. He asked Frederik to keep it safe. He explained the data was his insurance policy, he'd got into difficulty and done something stupid. Frederik tried to phone him, but the call went to voicemail. He didn't risk leaving a message. The kid's landlady hasn't seen him since last weekend, but all his belongings are still in his bedsit. Frederik got her to check, and she believes his laptop is missing."

"Rohan can find him." Emma snatched the teaspoon from Christopher's fingers and dug in the teapot. "Are the bottles ready yet?"

"Wash your hands again." He gave her the soap and they fought to get their fingers under the stream of hot water. Then Christopher strode towards the microwave, throwing his next sentence over his shoulder. "Oh, Rohan will definitely find him. Frederik's stupid son hacked a government database. Rohan has a standing contract with them to eliminate any risks they can't negate through official channels. Frederik's son just became a risk."

Emma accepted the warm bottle from his outstretched hand. She watched as he dumped ice into a jug and jerked his head towards the bottle. "Put that in the ice and pour a little tea into it. Add some of what's left in the kettle and it should cool quite fast. You want it tepid but not too hot or cold."

Emma obeyed. Tea slopped over the ice as she poured, giving the peaked diamonds a yellow tinge. "I don't understand why Frederik gave me the flash drive," she concluded. "Am I meant to dissuade Rohan from taking this job?"

Christopher grunted. "Rohan won't turn a government contract down, Emma. Why would he ruin a relationship like that? It's built on trust because of his time in the army. Medals and an injury got him that gig. No one else gets a look in with them. He won't turn it down, that's certain."

Emma shrugged. "What's my role?"

Christopher added water from the kettle and waited as she fumbled with a teat and lid. He inspected the weak mixture, gave it a shake and dumped it back into the ice. He leaned back against the counter and cocked his head. "Your role is to find Frederik's son before Rohan does."

Equals

"How?" The bottle clinked against the side of the jug as Emma tested the temperature. She took a step back from Christopher.

"I'll help you." His fingers closed around her shoulder. "But you can't tell Rohan."

Emma wrenched free and spun on her heel. "No. We made a promise to each other. No more secrets. I won't do it."

Christopher shrugged. He reached into the bowl and picked up the bottle. It hissed as he shook it, and a fine spray of liquid spattered the inside of the lid. "Still too hot. Give it a couple more minutes."

Emma groaned and clapped her palms over her ears. "I'm not doing it, Chris. Tell Frederik to get someone else."

He smirked as she met his gaze, one dark eyebrow raised in question. "I'm surprised at you, Emma." He took a step towards her, stopping just outside the range of her bare feet and the swift kick he saw framed in her eyes. "If you think the actuaries are dangerous, imagine who Frederik might set up against Rohan. He's a covert operative. I'm sure the people he could summon would make your husband disappear down a very deep hole."

"So, why doesn't Frederik find his own son?" Emma lurched for the bottle and snatched off the lid. Hot liquid spurted from the teat and Christopher ducked sideways.

"He tried."

A sneer marred Emma's features. She slammed the lid onto the bottle. "Perhaps he's not as great as you make him sound. I'll pass."

"You can't do that." Christopher's tone held a warning. His pupils grew to obscure his chocolate irises. "I know who he'll ask and they'll take out Rohan." He jabbed a finger at her face. "It'll be your fault."

Emma stamped from the kitchen without giving a reply. Despite the chill in the corridor, her dressing gown overheated her and she tugged at the cord to loosen it. Her heartbeat hammered in her ears as she digested Christopher's threat. She used the back stairs to the first floor, utilising the moonlight shining through the skylight to navigate back to her bedroom. Silence surrounded her as she passed Freda's door. The urgent cries from Stephie no longer issued from the master bedroom at the end of the hall. Emma stopped and pressed her ear against Nicky's wall. A faint glow filtered from beneath the door and she took a deep breath before turning the handle.

It moved without sound, but her gentle push met with resistance. The hinge had acquired an unusual elasticity, pressing itself closed despite her efforts. Emma gritted her teeth and shoved it, fitting her face through the narrow gap. It gave her a sideways view of Nicky's bed. The sheets flew upwards and torchlight played over his startled face to give him a ghoulish appearance. "Sorry," he hissed. The light stream bounced around the room to the staccato beat of footsteps. "I need to shut the door a second," he whispered.

Emma removed her face from the gap and released the handle. The door shut with a sharp click which echoed around the hallway. Scrabbling came from the other side of the door, followed by a twang. Then Nicky's face appeared. "Come in," he whispered. His lips twisted into a pout as Emma stepped over the threshold and watched him close the door behind her.

"You set up booby traps?" Her eyes narrowed. "Why?" Her mind flew to Winston's night wanderings and her fingers tensed around the bottle.

Action Man's bungee cord dangled from Nicky's fingers. "Because I was being naughty." He stood on one leg and pressed the sole of one bare foot over the instep of the other.

"What were you doing?" Emma leaned forward and took the torch from Nicky's fingers. The light flashed in her eyes for a second and created a series of dark floaters. She shone the beam on the rumpled bed and took a step towards it. A digital display cast a green hue from beneath the sheets. "A calculator?" She shook her head and drew her shoulders up to her ears. "Why are you still awake?"

"Look." Nicky's skinny stature brimmed with sudden enthusiasm. He bounced towards the bed and snatched the calculator from the mattress. His teeth shone white against the torchlight. "I've been learning my times tables. Dad gave me this calculator. I work it out and memorise the answer. It's quicker than doing it in my head. I'm up to one hundred and eight."

"A hundred and eight? Wow. Well done. Twelve times twelve is one hundred and eight."

Nicky snorted, the sound guttural and dismissive. "No! The one hundred and eight times table. I've done all the others up to that one."

Emma swallowed. No suitable reply presented itself. Like father, like son. Nicky reached out his hand and reclaimed the torch. "The naughty bit was nicking Harley Man's torch. He left it in the tunnel to the folly. I'm borrowing it until I can get my own." He gave an excited bounce followed by another. "Me and Daddy have a competition. Every time I win, he gives me a pound. When he wins, I give him a hug." Nicky's blond brows furrowed, a white line in the torch's glow. "He feels really loved, but I'm still poor. I'll never get a torch."

Emma released a sigh. "Right. Nick, tired people don't learn so well. You need your sleep so your brain can grow. Otherwise it'll fill with school stuff and there won't be room for extra maths." Nicky's eyes widened to freaky white orbs. Emma jerked her head at the torch. "And please give that back to Christopher. He's probably looking for it. I'm sure there's a spare around somewhere."

"Okay." Nicky tipped his face up for a kiss. His cool lips acted as a balm against Emma's cheek. "Is that bottle for Stephie?"

"Yeah." Emma held the sheets high while Nicky shimmied beneath them. "She got belly ache." She waited while Nicky turned off the calculator's green display and handed it to her. It clattered as she laid it on his bedside table. "How do I set up the elastic thing on the door?" she asked, turning to leave.

Nicky leaned up on one elbow. A grin split his face in half. "Slip the bungee cord around the door handle and fit Action Man's armpit over that picture hook on the wall." He cocked his head and aimed the torch towards the door. Emma's shadow obscured the light as she worked one handed to retrieve the action figure from where Nicky dropped it. She followed her son's instructions. The elastic looped over the door handle, but the narrow crack proved too tight for her to reach the wall hook. Nicky padded across the room and his fingers brushed hers as he took Action Man and wedged him over the hook at Emma's eye level. "Thanks Mum," he whispered. "You're the best." He blew her an exaggerated kiss before the torque of the elastic closed the door between them.

"Yep," Emma mused to herself as she tested the temperature of the bottle against her cheek. "And Winston will get more than he bargained for if he tries to sit on your bed."

She opened her bedroom door with calculated slowness to avoid the squeak of the hinge. Rohan still lay on the bed, the sheet covering him below the waist. His head tilted back against the pillows at an awkward angle. The thick plate of chest muscles rose and fell in a gentle beat. Stephie lounged across his forearms, her head still cradled in his palms. Her closed eyelids fluttered in sleep and her rosebud lips moved as though chewing. Rohan's arms had sunk to rest against his bent knee, twisting his torso in a painful arc.

Emma gazed upon the touching scene of a father soothing his distressed child. He appeared less confident and less formidable. Sleep and adoration for his infant daughter rendered a more vulnerable image of Rohan, one the world never saw. The rush of love which flooded Emma's chest sent a gasp into her lungs. Even the subtle noise woke him, and Rohan jumped.

His muscles tensed as he assessed his daughter's precariousness, and he jerked his arms towards his body. Stephie's hands splayed wide, and she gave a reflexive cry.

"It's okay." Emma hurried around the bed and took her flailing daughter. She cradled her in her left arm and knocked the lid off the bottle before shaking a bead of the chamomile tea onto her wrist. It left a tepid trail across her skin as gravity pulled it sideways to plunge onto the rug. Stephie fought the teat, not used to the different sucking action required to release the liquid. She grizzled and beat her fists until the first flush of the weak tea dribbled into her mouth. Then she silenced. Her brow furrowed at the distinct taste but she drank, slipping into a steady rhythm.

Rohan groaned and leaned back against the pillows, lifting his arms into a long stretch. Emma sat on the mattress and gave him a smile. "You did good," she soothed. "You got her to sleep. I'm sorry I woke you."

"What's the time?" Rohan turned his head and lifted his wrist to read his watch. He grunted at its analogue hands.

"It took a while to brew the tea and set up the bottle steriliser." Emma smiled as Stephie used her tongue to reject the teat and block her mouth. She set the bottle on the bedside table and lifted her over her shoulder. The baby gave a tired sigh and burped. Her slender legs dangled free against Emma's chest, no longer writhing in a palsy of pain.

Emma sighed and met her husband's sultry gaze. "Should I risk putting her in the crib?"

Rohan shrugged. He stifled a yawn with his hand. "Damned if you do and damned if you don't."

Emma swallowed, his words an accidental summary of her discussion with Christopher. She rose and laid her daughter in the crib, turning her on her right side to avoid compressing her stomach, and propping her up with rolled blankets. Stephie grunted and rooted for her thumb.

Emma tugged the sheet from Rohan's waist and climbed in next to him. He edged towards the centre of the wide bed as she slid onto the mattress and pulled the sheet over them both. He reached for her and tucked her head against his shoulder, his biceps creating a firm pillow beneath her cheek. Her fingers coasted across his hard stomach and she made her decision.

She'd find Frederik's son.

And ensure Rohan fired his chief operative.

A Prime Number

E mma waited for inspiration all the next day, realising as she put Nicky to bed that she needed to create her own. She made a phone call and started forming a plan while listening for Rohan to arrive home from his London office. When the lounge door opened, she looked up with an expectant smile which disappeared in less time than it took her visitor to join her.

"What ails you, Emma?" Winston settled on the seat opposite, the lack of invitation causing him no discomfort. His slender fingers smoothed creases from the fabric of his trousers, and he adjusted his shiny shoes until his feet perfectly aligned with the edge of the rug.

"Why are you here?" Emma dropped Ray's old brown jumper on the sofa next to her. A trail of brown thread snaked from the head of a darning needle to the feather in her hand. The half formed Cock With the Crimson Comb sagged against the cushion. "This house is as secure as Fort Knox, but you stroll in as though entering a church. Tell me how you're doing it."

Winston smiled and tipped the brow of an imaginary hat. "A church. I appreciate your assumption I'd survive without a metal stake through my heart." He leaned against the cushion and rested his forearm along the ridge of the seat. His posture appeared casual, but his feet remained planted. His fingers twitched at a loose thread on his trouser leg and his left eyebrow quirked. He looked so much like Rohan, it silenced Emma. "If I divulge my loophole to you, then you'll make sure that idiot Irishman closes it." Winston lifted his right hand and tapped his bottom lip with a manicured index finger. Behind his azure irises worked a superior, calculating mind.

Altering his body to sit square in the chair, he pressed his palms together as though praying but balanced them between his thighs instead. His irises flared as a casual glance at his feet revealed they'd moved. Winston cocked his head and clicked his heels. When he met Emma's gaze, a sense of understanding passed between them. She wondered if he'd allowed her to witness his compulsion in a peculiar truce offering.

Emma cleared her throat. "My husband says you mean us no harm. My primary consideration with the loophole is that someone else might exploit it." Despite her best efforts, her gaze slid over the porcelain of the baby girl snoozing on the sofa beside her.

A flicker of concern crossed Winston's lined forehead, and he blinked. "This ambiguity will open only to me. You have my assurance." Emma swallowed down a lump of relief and lingering misgiving. She didn't like Winston's sudden appearances, but his determination told her that as soon as she closed one door, he'd prise open another. Even with the mystery shrouding Rohan's father, she sensed his affection for his grandchildren in the fierceness of his certainty. "Your babies have nothing to fear from me."

"I hope not."

The delicate tendrils of trust thickened with Winston's convincing nod. His shoulders relaxed and some of his former cockiness returned. He checked his feet once more before allowing the self-satisfied smirk to commandeer his lips. "So, Emma, back to my first question, what ails you?"

Emma sighed. Her head shook from side to side in response to her internal wrangling. "I'm not sure you'd understand," she concluded.

"Try me." Winston's stare fixed on her face, the hardness of his stare stripping away her confusion and leaving her vulnerable.

She released a breath laden with exasperation. "I don't know where to start." Her eyelashes fluttered, and she winced. "I should talk to Rohan, not you. This isn't appropriate."

"I have no agenda." Winston spread his hands wide as though imitating an ordained priest inviting confession.

"You do." Emma's voice rose. "Why do you come here? What's in this for you?"

Winston tipped forward. His spine remained straight, but his torso dipped. "My only concern is the fortune of my son and the legacy he creates for his children." He popped upright like a released spring. "That's all I've ever wanted." The kink in his left eyebrow revealed his amusement. "I've learnt not to give directions to Alexei unless I wish him to do the exact opposite."

Despite herself, Emma smiled.

Winston jerked his head at her, a question in his eyes. His words were little more than the follow-up to his assumption. "You're in good health now, yes? And my granddaughter thrives." He cocked his head to the side like a quizzical bird. "Yet something eats away at you. It churns through your mind when you're quiet and still. What is it that bothers you? Perhaps I can help."

Emma inhaled through her nose. "Do you have nothing better to do than spy on me?" She blanched as Winston's affable grin twitched the corners of his mouth. He measured his elbows to rest square on his thighs. Sincerity added a gravelled quality to his tone.

"Yes." He tilted his head, soft white hair coiffed to perfection, so the fringe kissed the top of his left eyebrow. "I have much to occupy myself, but I can assist you, Emma. It's in my interests to prove myself worthy of your confidence."

Emma bit back a sarcastic laugh. "You murdered an innocent man outside my gate and imprisoned my husband. You bound your own son into a financial agreement, which forced him to take jobs that put his life at risk. Yet, you want me to trust you?"

Winston appeared to deflate. For an unguarded millisecond, he became a fragile, vulnerable old man. Then his composure flicked the mask over his expression and he straightened his shoulders. "Your choice." He shrugged. With a last glance at his parallel shiny shoes, he stood in a fluid movement unfettered by the rigours of age. Emma's heart pumped a staccato beat through her ears.

She lifted a hand as Winston turned towards the door. "Wait!" Adrenaline surged through her veins and her hands trembled. She hid the weakness by clasping them in her lap and hiding them in the folds of her skirt. Winston narrowed his eyes and inclined his head in a regal expression of forbearance. Then he settled back into the armchair and paused for Emma to collect her words into a sensible sentence. Against everything she believed, she resigned herself to fate and accepted a deal with the devil.

Duplication

"Alanya killed my father." Emma choked on the revelation. It didn't matter how often she repeated the unproven fact, it still nursed the power to shock her. To his credit, Winston gave no response. Emma's fingers writhed in her lap as though disconnected from her wrists. She barely felt the skirt fabric that sifted through them over and over as she fought the urge to tear something apart. "She kept us away from him and I didn't see him for the last month of his life." A glazed, faraway look misted Emma's eyes as she re-entered the pit in her heart where she kept all painful things. "I used to sit on the floor of the hallway outside his bedroom." The memories flooded back to her, hearing from a distance her high, girlish voice reading stories and telling him about her day through the wooden door. She remembered the smell of the floral polish which

Alanya used on the floorboards, her stepmother's fastidious cleaning a silent clue to her mental sickness. Anton loved to slide along the hallway and pitch down the long banister on his stomach. His giggles returned to Emma's ears, and she smiled at his remembered antics. Anton possessed the ability to turn every negative thing into a joke.

"Emma?" Winston's gentle prodding rocked the silence, letting her understand she'd stopped talking and receded into the forgotten space in her mind.

"Sorry," she whispered. "I only wanted to hold his hand." She closed her eyes and pictured Rodney Harrington's smiling blue eyes and the soft sideburns he nurtured either side of his face. His woolly white hair made him resemble a sheep, and Emma remembered the scent of cold tar soap associated with it. "Alanya refused. She said he didn't want to see me." Her stepmother's harsh Russian accent cut through her memory like a klaxon, low and jarring. Emma ground her teeth to stop the scream bursting from her chest. "I believe she poisoned him, though I never proved it." Her fingers jerked as though reaching out for one last time to touch her father's swollen hand. She'd seen him once through the door as Alanya exited, his face unrecognisable and his fingers like sausages. The scent of diarrhoea and vomit had choked her.

"How can I help?" Winston's soft voice pressed on the locked gate in Emma's mind. He hadn't asked what she wanted from him or what she expected him to do. He sensed he couldn't fix her sadness or provide any respite. Alanya's death took her crimes to the grave with her, unpunished. Yet he still looked for an olive branch amid the weeds.

Emma stared at her fingers. "Rodney Harrington wasn't my father." She let the statement hang in the air before Winston acknowledged it with a blink. "I found my birth certificate."

"And you're looking for answers?"

The almost inaudible sound escaped Emma's lips as a snort. She didn't bother asking how Winston knew even her most guarded secret. She suspected it explained Freda's perpetual unhappiness and reluctance to return home. He'd forced her betrayal. It was an issue for another time. "Yes." Silence clamoured around her single word answer. The conjured sights and scents of the man she'd known as a loving father surrounded her in the air as a tribute to Rodney Harrington's effervescence. The swish of his brush smoothing his hair. His ready cackle of laughter. The crinkles at the corners of his eyes from a lifetime of smiling. The scent of soap and Aramis aftershave. The hollowness his death left in her soul.

Winston rose, the susurrations of his expensive trousers making Emma jump. Her eyes widened and reality snatched her back at the moment her remembered father reached out his fingers to stroke her hair. Anger flared in her eyes for a second and then abated. Winston bent his body in a subtle bow. "I'll find you the answers." He turned and stole towards the door, his soles making no sound against the floorboards.

"But at what cost?" Emma's question sounded jarring and ungrateful. She spread her hands as grief drove its hard prongs into her heart. There seemed no end to its ability to take away from her the things she held dearest. Her mother, her father, Lucya, Anton, even the future children she should have bore. Her gaze stroked the sleeping face of her daughter, and she hardened her jaw and resolved to fight. She'd allowed passivity to force her into a chair and keep her there. The eyes which flicked back to Winston and held his gaze with a fire behind the irises were no longer cowed and defeated.

Winston inclined his head, one hand resting over the brass doorknob. "You're the key to everything, Emma Oskar. You hold my fate in your hands. Only you can decide whether to unlock the door."

Rohan's father slipped from the room without a sound. His shoes made no echo along the corridor. No one rushed into the lounge after seeing the intruder on the cameras. Rohan inherited his father's ghost like qualities and Emma studied the pattern on her skirt without seeing the vibrant flowers dancing along the hem. A warmth settled over her shoulders like a blanket applied to a sleeper. "What door?" she whispered to herself. "What key?" Her lips curved upwards as she realised Winston hadn't asked for information about her real parentage. He'd get nowhere without a name.

Right Angles

An early morning sunshine dappled the yellow paint on Emma's car as she wedged a bag of food behind her driver's seat. She slammed the door and turned to face her husband.

"You're sure this is a good idea, da?" Rohan settled Stephie into her baby seat and stepped back to close the door. A tiny dot of blood along his jaw revealed an accident with his razor, but his immaculate shirt and trousers showed the image he'd rather project.

"Yes." Emma frowned and projected false confidence to cover her lie. "Susan is expecting me. I'll drop you at the station on my way to Lincoln. Will you catch the late train home or stay in London?"

"I'm just checking into the office. Maureen's found a lead on the dating website issue." Rohan jerked his head towards the house. "I already asked Ray to take me to the station."

"Okay. Give Maureen my love, won't you?" Emma's features softened at the thought of Rohan's feisty assistant. "Didn't she talk about retiring soon?" She threw her handbag onto the back seat and clicked the door shut. Stephie's eyes fluttered closed, and she rooted for her thumb.

Rohan's irises flashed an icy blue. "No. I won't let her." His shoulders moved in a visible shudder. "I wouldn't condemn myself to relying only on the Irishman."

"Oh. You still don't trust him?" Emma stopped moving towards the driver's door and waited. A frisson of alarm travelled through her muscles. "Why?

Rohan snorted. "Because I commanded men just like him in the army. Their self-interest will always outweigh their usefulness as team players. Learning who not to trust is the reason I stayed alive." His blond brows knitted and he glanced down at the prosthetic leg hidden beneath his trousers. "Just about, anyway."

Emma reached for the door handle, her touch too light to do much more than stroke the chrome surface. "Rohan?" She turned to face him, her tone light and her eyes over bright as Winston's inference returned to her as something shady, a secret between them. "How did you become a captain so fast? Don't most people need to stay in the service for at least a decade to reach that rank?" She swallowed, wondering about the other work Winston mentioned, which she knew nothing about.

Rohan's expression never changed. He maintained his classic blank stare, but Emma noticed the left corner of his top lip move enough to register a reluctant smile. "You know the answer to your own question." His gaze bore into her face. "They moved me from soldier to officer training within the first six weeks when they saw my potential. I did everything they asked and more. I speak five languages and am in the novel position of representing a few Russian-born men who believe in democracy. What do you want me to say?" His eyes narrowed and his overt hostility to her prying made Emma anxious.

"It's just a question." She held her hands up in self-defence and fought the instinct to sever their emotional connection. They'd promised each other to disallow secrets in their marriage, yet every day brought more subterfuge. Sentences of condemnation rolled through her mind and she yanked the car door open with force. The handle slipped from her fingers and forced her to repeat the action. She pulled again, the strain tugging at the scar tissue across her stomach.

A hand appeared in front of her face and held the car door shut. Rohan placed his body in the way, blocking her grasping fingers and bowing his head to speak so quietly, she stilled to hear.

"You know why," he whispered. His breath caused her fringe to flutter. "And I can no longer return to Russia because of it."

His answer stripped away her anger. Emma pursed her lips to prevent the three letter word escaping. He'd spied on his homeland and received stripes on his epaulets as a thank you. Until someone blew his body and his unit to smithereens.

Emma winced and the rolling sentences filled with righteous indignation faded from her mind. "Thank you," she whispered in return. His honesty had cost him, forcing him to risk another small foothold in their relationship. His trust invited rejection, and Emma ground her teeth against Winston's divisiveness.

Rohan stepped back from the vehicle and pulled the driver's door open for her. Emma slipped into the gap between his body and the car. "Can we talk later?" she asked. Rohan's brow knitted, and she shook her head and waved aside his alarm. "Not about what you just told me. Other things."

"Problems?" Rohan cocked his head to one side and tried to read her face. Emma dropped her gaze to make the task more difficult. If she told him why she wanted to talk, he might insist she stayed and dealt with it then. Rohan disliked unfinished business.

"No. Not between us. External things really." She stumbled over the sentence, desperate to know why he'd cried the night of her surgery but baulking at saying the words. Perhaps the two hour drive or the opportunity to speak to Susan about it might give her clarity. She stood on tiptoe to press a kiss over his lips. With her thumb, she wiped the imprint of her lip gloss from his mouth. "Later, yeah?"

"Da." Rohan nodded and stepped away from the car. He dug his hands into his trouser pockets and walked towards the sweeping front steps of the manor house.

Emma started the engine of her yellow car and spat gravel from behind her as she released the handbrake. Stephie yawned in the passenger seat and her eyelids shuttered closed.

The drive to Lincoln gave Emma time for contemplation. She drove east, heading for the main A1 and remembering her inbound journey on the same road the previous year. So much had changed. She'd climbed into Rohan's car with such reluctance, fleeing a poverty from which she seemed unable to crawl. Time had stretched to create an illusion of more than a year's worth of difference.

Emma observed the other motorists accompanying her onto the dual carriageway. Only the journey connected them as they stared ahead, weaving through the traffic to their destinations. They all sped past her, hurrying to their appointments as though nothing else mattered. Emma sighed and relaxed her spine against the seat. She had all day to make the trip and return home. Everyone thought she'd arranged the visit with Susan, but she hadn't. A quick call the night before had uncovered the information she needed. She'd asked for the new address on the pretext of sending a card and discovered Susan moved into her bungalow that morning. Her friend mentioned she hadn't yet fathomed out the bus route with her guide dog. Emma had commiserated and made the plan in her head.

She crossed her fingers and hoped she found Susan at home. Alone.

Allaine phoned to let Emma know she'd dropped Nicky and Kaylee at school and taken Freda to the Baptist coffee shop for her volunteer waitressing shift.

"How did she seem to you?" Emma lifted her voice for the benefit of the inbuilt microphone. She caught sight of herself in the rear-view mirror and smoothed away the reflected frown.

"Subdued." Allaine's voice crackled. "Something is wrong, but I'm not the person she'd tell. Why don't you set Nicky on her?"

"Good idea." Emma's mind drifted to plausible scenarios where she could involve her son without abusing his peaceful nature. "What's your plan for the rest of the day?"

Allaine paused before releasing a sigh. "I have a job interview."

"Really?" Emma's tone brightened. "I didn't know you planned to return to work."

"Yeah. I can't rely on Will's payments to survive. And I've imposed on your hospitality for months now. It's just part time and fits in with school hours. I'd like to pay rent once we've finished moving into the apartment over the stables."

"You know there's no pressure from me." Emma jammed her foot onto the brake as a truck cut in front of her on the dual carriageway. She released a hiss of alarm. "Sorry. Someone just cut me up like I didn't exist."

"Well, take care. I hope the visit with your friend is awesome. It's nice to see you returning to normal after having Stephie."

Emma's lips tightened into a line. No one ever mentioned the emergency surgery, as though afraid it might plunge her back into the dark space in her mind again. She sighed as Allaine ended the call, wishing everyone would stop tiptoeing around it. "I'm not made of china," she grumbled to her sleeping daughter. "Pretending it didn't happen doesn't lessen the pain."

Vector

The roads around Lincoln city hadn't changed. Guilt made Emma consider stopping by her former home on the council estate in the northernmost suburb. Despite the harshness of their circumstances, the women there had banded together to provide comfort, support and childcare for each other. Emma swallowed at the memory of Nicky's friend, Mo, wondering what happened to him in the intervening months. She missed them with a physical ache which twisted in her gut at the thought of facing Fat Brian and asking for entry onto the estate. He controlled the forgotten patch of concrete and brick with an iron fist. He'd want something in exchange for safe passage, and Emma shivered. If he learnt she'd fallen on her feet, he would dig his hooks back into her life and demand repayment for imagined assistance. His mind would run riot with all the reasons she owed him.

She ignored the ring road which encircled the city in a wall of exhaust fumes and followed the signs for the village of Saxilby. The artery through the western suburbs took her close to the signpost for the estate, and she gripped the steering wheel and released herself from its pull. They'd owned nothing and left nothing when they abandoned their former life with its hardships and regret. "Leave it at that," she whispered to herself.

Emma followed the A57 arterial road as it flanked a straight piece of the canal. Susan gave her an address on Mill Lane, and the car's satellite navigation system alerted her to the right turn. One-storey houses stood on both sides of the street. The post-war bungalow styles varied little from one home to the next, but each radiated its own character through paint colour or landscaping. Emma slowed the vehicle, her gaze sweeping the front gates, so she could look for the number of Susan's new house. The style of houses changed, other eras creeping into their architecture. She looked for a bus stop but couldn't find one.

"You have now reached your destination," the robotic female voice of the satellite navigation informed her.

"Where?" Emma protested. She peered at the dwellings on either side of the road and shook her head in disbelief. "These are two-storey houses. Susan wouldn't buy somewhere with stairs!" She raised her voice as though the robotic sounding software cared.

"Turn around where possible," it replied as Emma let the car roll for another hundred metres.

Finally, she pulled over in frustration before the houses became older, rural styles with fields encroaching onto the residential scene. She tapped the gear stick and regretted her impetuous decision to make the four hour round trip to satisfy her curiosity. What did it matter to her if Susan's stepson found himself on the wrong side of Rohan's business contract? She groaned and acknowledged it mattered a lot.

After instructing her to turn around again, the satellite navigation took a vow of silence and abandoned her. With a huff of exasperation, Emma switched off the screen. Stephie stirred in her baby seat, heightening the sense of urgency. A glance at the dashboard clock showed her due a feed.

Emma performed a hasty three-point turn on the lane and retraced her journey to the row of bungalows. "Twelve!" She almost shouted the number, elated to have discovered the numbering pattern of the street. Odd numbers to her right and even to her left. She set off at a slow crawl, avoiding the vehicles parked on the road. A slender pensioner with a stooped spine stopped on the pavement to let her poodle sniff the base of a street lamp, and Emma dropped the passenger window. "Excuse me!" she called.

Wary enough to remain on the grass verge, the pedestrian lost her suspicious edge when she saw the sleeping baby through the window. She took a step closer to see what Emma wanted. "Yes?" Her tone sounded terse, and she missed the poodle squatting to relieve itself.

"I'm looking for number eight Mill Street," Emma called. She leaned sideways and her hair tickled Stephie's nose. The child gave a snort of irritation and scratched at her face. "Damn! Sorry." Emma looked up with a frown. "My friend just moved here. I can't find her new house." She jabbed her finger at the street behind them. "I found number twelve but not number eight."

"Oh." The woman's face relaxed, losing its lined appearance. "Susan?"

"Yes!" Emma's expression lit from within, her excitement palpable. "My sat nav took me towards the end of the road, but they're two-storey houses and she wouldn't buy one of those." She bit the inside of her cheek to stop her saying too much, but the woman picked up the baton with obvious enthusiasm.

"You're right, because of her sight." She waved an arm to encompass the surrounding bungalows. "I met her husband last week, but Susan arrived yesterday." She glanced behind her and her nose wrinkled at the poodle's activity. "Thomas adores Jay." Her chest swelled as though the dog held the role as favoured child in her household. She released a hearty chuckle like the sound of rattling chains. "He's smitten with him."

"Aren't we all?" Emma nodded, her appreciation for the retired guide dog genuine. "Why can't I find number eight?"

"Because it's behind number twelve." She turned to point at a driveway hidden between two bungalows. "No one can ever find it. I'm always having to give directions."

"Thank you!" Emma released her held breath. The irony amused her. Frederik picked the one house on the street guaranteed not to get passing visitors. She leaned sideways to address the woman. "Is there room for my car or should I leave it on the road?"

"Just drive to the end of the lane. They only have the one car and it's a big enough turning circle in front of their garage for you to park." The woman produced a green bag from a plastic bone tied to the poodle's leash. She bobbed out of sight to collect the stinky parcel left by her dog. It ignored her, tugging on the leash and keen to inspect the next tuft of verge.

"Thank you." Emma flicked the switch to close Stephie's window. She indicated left and turned down the narrow driveway, keeping the vehicle centred between the high wooden fences on either side. It felt like a fortress, the sounds of children playing muted by the fences and dense bushes behind them. She smiled to herself. Frederik hadn't banked on the interest of his rural neighbours. The driveway swept around to the left to stop in front of a navy garage door.

A bungalow stood at right angles to the double width garage, its windows tilted open and net curtains blowing through the gaps like bridesmaids' dresses at a wedding. Emma halted her car, pulling on the handbrake and pushing the gear lever into park. She held her breath as the garage door rolled up with a motorised clank and grind. A pair of male feet appeared before the door revealed a muscular torso and then a head.

Emma took her time, giving Frederik a moment for the shock to fade from his expression and to get control of his temper.

Unexpected Patterns

"What the hell are you doing here?" Frederik's fists balled even before Emma climbed from her vehicle. He dropped the box he carried and barrelled towards her. Jangling crockery and breaking china tinkled in his wake as the cardboard spewed open on the concrete.

Emma shut her car door with a click, at pains not to wake Stephie. She made the mistake of laughing. "What are you doing here?" she countered. "Why aren't you at work?"

"You need to leave!" His fingers clasped her shoulder, their grip tight enough to send an arc of pain blossoming into her neck. She gasped before Rohan's training kicked in and her mind switched to autopilot. A reflex action sent the heel of her left hand cutting through the air. The impact of it hitting Frederik's nose reverberated through the muscles of Emma's arm. She took a step backwards and twisted her body to release his hold on her shoulder, but she needn't have bothered. Frederik let go and dipped forward with a groan. Expletives bubbled through the blood gushing from his nostrils.

"You left me no choice." An uncharacteristic hardness resonated through Emma's tone. Frederik squatted on the concrete, blood dripping onto the grey slab. He pinched the bridge of his nose between finger and thumb, his words halting and muffled.

"No choice about what?" he demanded. "Turning up at my home unannounced or smacking me in the nose?"

"Both." Emma leaned against her vehicle and forced her body into a more relaxed stance. She sensed Frederik regretted his hasty welcome. She surveyed the open garage, and the boxes piled to ceiling height. Her nose wrinkled. "That looks dangerous, especially when your wife is blind."

"Do you think I don't know that?" Frederik rose with fury, his irises sparkling. "My son promised to help, and he's missing. How much longer can I keep lying to my wife?"

"Emma released a heavy sigh. "Don't. My relationship with Rohan is founded on secrets and lies. They take over and ruin everything if you let them."

Frederik's shoulders slumped and he wiped his nose on the cuff of his shirt, leaving a trail of blood across the pale fabric. "In that case, if you told him about this, you signed my son's death warrant." His gaze tracked to Emma's passenger seat as Stephie woke with a grumble and waved her arms. The yellow of her cardigan matched the colour of the car, and Emma blinked at the unintentional match. She side stepped Frederik's assumption about Rohan, pained by the memory of the trust in her husband's smile as he'd waved her off on her journey. Emma frowned as Stephie's wails became plaintive.

"May I at least come in to feed her?" she asked. Frederik gave a shrug of indifference and turned towards the house.

Emma retrieved the baby and the bag containing nappies, wipes and other paraphernalia which had sneaked back onto her list of essential items. She struggled to lock the car, anger burgeoning at his easy abandonment of her on the driveway. A woof echoed from inside the house as Frederik entered. Emma tensed as the enormous white retriever slipped past him and bounded towards her with a lolloping gait. She dropped the bag onto the concrete with a thud and clasped both arms around her daughter. Visions of the dog jumping at her with his giant paws made her hold her breath. But this was Jay.

He slid to a halt in front of her, his jaws parted in a doggy grin. The tasselled white sail behind him hit the floor with a flopping action as he sat. His bottom wiggled from left to right, the tail's wag hauling it in both directions. Emma released an audible sigh. "Jay," she whispered. "I always forget what a gentleman you are." She pressed Stephie against her and stroked the dog's crown. The sensation of his soft fur against her skin reminded her of a different life. Nicky scaled her legs the first time she'd met Susan and Jay. Her son had been older but wary of dogs. Emma smiled. "You worked your magic on Nicky, didn't you?"

"Jay?" Susan's light voice wavered as a strain crept into it. "Jay, where are you?" The dog bounced to his feet and trotted towards the front door. He looked over his shoulder at Emma, his invitation more gracious than Frederik's. She followed his plumed tail up a makeshift wooden ramp and into a wide hallway, pausing for her vision to adjust after the bright sunshine.

"Susan?" She spoke to his mistress, and Susan stilled. Jay licked her thumb and pushed his snout beneath her outstretched palm as though to reassure her of his presence.

"Emma?" Susan adjusted her spectacles and tilted her head, surveying Emma through the partial sight of her right eye. She lifted her voice in surprise. "Frederik! Emma's here. What a wonderful surprise."

Frederik grunted over the sound of running water, and Emma forced her face into an impassive expression. "I couldn't stay away," she said, sticking to the safety of the truth. "You're so much closer now. It's a hop up the motorway."

"Oh, I'm so happy." Susan's hand wavered as she covered her mouth. She walked the fingers of her other hand along Jay's neck until they closed around his collar. "Take me to

Emma," she commanded, a hitch in her throat. "Watch out for things on the floor." The dog walked at a snail's pace, each step calculated for Susan's speed and ability. His furry brows knitted in seriousness as he navigated an abandoned drawer and its disgorged contents. Susan held out her hand and Emma took it, clasping with a tight grip. She leaned forward to kiss her friend's cheek.

"I brought someone to see you," she whispered.

"The baby?" Susan's lips parted in a grin. She cocked her head, able to discern Emma's outline against the sunlight streaming through the doorway. Her fingers found Stephie's slender spine and she stroked the yellow cardigan with delight shining in her smile. "I can't believe you've come." Her tone wavered and she flapped a hand at the room behind her. "It's all such a mess. Frederik promised it wouldn't be like this."

Emma frowned at the strain in her voice. "Well, I'm here now," she announced, her tone soothing. "I'll feed Stephie and change her nappy, then we'll find a chair for you to sit in and you can be on babysitting duty." Emma cast a cursory glance around the lounge as Susan shuffled forward with the help of the dog. "Your husband and I can get this cleared up in no time." Frederik reappeared and leaned against the jutting corner into the lounge. He raised an eyebrow at her, trying but failing to mask the dismay and misery lurking beneath his irritated frown. Emma relented, reading the pain in his soulful blue eyes. "It'll be okay," she declared. "We'll work out how to make everything better."

The Equation of Friendship

S tephie fed with enthusiasm and didn't complain when Emma handed her to Susan after a nappy change. She lay in Susan's arms, her hands clasped together as though praying and a wet tongue charting the curve of her own knuckles.

"She's so tiny." Susan's body swayed from side to side as she rocked her. "They grow so fast."

Emma glanced up from her task. Frederik had found the cupboard belonging to the lone drawer and hunted down its mates in the garage. Emma had separated the detritus from the floor into piles and started filling the drawers. "You still own a lot of stationery, I see." She smiled and slid another packet of coloured paper into the widest drawer. "Do you intend to start a shop?"

"Funny." Susan's mouth quirked into her first genuine smile since Emma arrived. "That's one of my weaknesses. I love the smell of paper and I can see a little of the brighter colours if I take them to the light."

Emma stood up straight and inhaled. "I know what you mean." She crawled across the floor on her hands and knees and retrieved a stapler and pencil sharpener from beneath the sofa. "It looks as if a stationery shop exploded in your lounge." She glanced up to find Jay watching her. His ears pricked at the stapler in her palm and his tail thumped against the carpet.

Susan cuddled Stephie closer and released a dramatic sigh. "I wanted to use the bathroom, but Jay got confused. He's still not sure where everything is. He brought me things he thought might please me."

Emma smiled at the dog and his lower jaw dropped so it appeared he returned her smile. His tail thumped again. Emma rose to put the errant stationery into the top drawer with other similar objects.

"I felt so excited about the move." Susan stroked Stephie's downy crown with a gentle finger. "It's turned into a disaster. Frederik's son helped me pack most things a few weeks ago, and the removers shifted it all down here. But Regan promised to help at this end, so I could find my way around before putting things where I wanted them."

Emma winced. She doubted the effectiveness of a geeky teenager but didn't share her thoughts. He might have loved staging ornaments and battling stationery. "What happened?" Her lips twisted as she probed Susan's understanding of the situation.

"He got busy at work." Frederik's tone contained a growl of warning. "And couldn't make it." His irises flashed like ice as he glared at Emma. The force of his anger caused her to sway on her knees. Sweat covered his forehead and glued his mousy fringe flat. A pink stain at the cuff betrayed his respect for Susan. She wouldn't have noticed the blood, but he'd cleaned it, anyway. He stood in the doorway, fists balled and his biceps straining through his shirt. Emma swallowed at the latent threat in his stance. She knew what he was capable of, what all of his band of mercenaries could inflict. She held her breath.

It came to her in a rush of understanding. She was the threat. One wrong word could undo all Frederik's attempts to forge a normal life outside of his role for Rohan. She didn't doubt he loved Susan because she saw it in his eyes.

Emma forced her muscles to relax. She reached for Jay and ruffled his ears. Stephie gave a happy squeak and kicked her legs against Susan's forearms. Emma kept Frederik in her peripheral vision, recognising when his fists released their tension and his expression lost its chill.

Susan spoke first. "Jay can take me to the kitchen and I'll make us all a nice cold drink." The tiny smile at the corner of her lips made Emma rethink her friend's complete oblivion. She stroked Stephie's soft toes. "Shall we give you to Mummy?"

Jay snapped to attention, rising and dusting Emma's cheek with his tail. He stood before Susan's chair, his ears alert and his dutiful heart willing. Emma reclaimed her daughter and took a step back while Susan rose and placed her palm on Jay's head. "Let's give this another go, shall we?" She spoke to him like a child. "Kitchen, Jay. Let's go." Jay glanced at Frederik, worry in the dent between his eyebrows.

"I'll give you a hand." Frederik strode across the room and took Susan's arm, flanking her like a rear-guard. It dismissed Emma from their trifecta with as much precision as a knife cut.

"Jay. Let's go." Susan's voice continued her instruction until the hallway took them out of sight. Emma watched her daughter's rosy cheeks part in a yawn as Susan's praise echoed from a distant room. "Kitchen, Jay, good boy!" A happy snuff relayed his pleasure at succeeding, despite Frederik's assistance.

Emma sighed and pushed the drawer closed one-handed. "This wasn't one of my better ideas," she whispered to Stephie. She lifted the child to her shoulder and closed her eyes to savour the way Stephie snuggled against her and issued a sleepy murmur. Her warm breath coasted over Emma's neck and disappeared into her hair.

"No. It wasn't."

She jumped and Stephie hissed with shock. She snagged a lock of Emma's hair in her tiny fist and tugged. Then she turned her face towards Emma's shoulder and released a settling sigh, her turmoil disappearing as fast as it began. "I'm sorry." Emma used her foot to continue forming a walkway to the front door. "I'll make my excuses and leave soon. Visiting seemed a good way to find out the truth. Christopher speaks in riddles and I've no time for puzzles."

"Okay." Frederik blew out a breath. "But while you're here, you can make yourself useful."

"Yes, Sir!" Emma touched her temple with her index finger in a mock salute. Frederik narrowed his eyes in response, not impressed at all.

Susan found three glasses and a bottle of orange juice and they drank in the kitchen. Stephie slept in her baby seat between them, her head lolled sideways and her nose twitching. Emma surveyed a stack of boxes in one corner and pulled out a row of empty drawers. She rocked the seat with her foot. "What if I clear a surface and then open one box at a time?" she suggested. "It's pointless me putting all your cutlery and serving spoons in a drawer when it's not where you want it to stay."

"That would be good." Susan tilted her head to narrow the aperture in her right eye. She pointed to a counter behind Frederik. "The oven and hob are there, the sink is behind me and the fridge is to the left of the oven." She issued a definitive nod and released a happy sigh. "Just open the box, tell me roughly what it contains, and then I'll sort it out for myself." She dipped to peer at her feet. "There's nothing in here that I might trip over, is there?"

"No." Emma finished the last of her juice and sat the glass in the sink. "Do you want me to wash these before I continue clearing the floor of the lounge?"

"I'm fine." Susan dismissed her with a wave. "Just open the first box for me. Oh, Frederik, can you double check these drawers are clean before I put things into them?"

"They should be." Frederik pulled out one drawer and then another. "I know it's hard to believe, but the house looked spotless before we moved in here."

Susan laughed, but Emma didn't. Before inheriting Wingate Hall, she'd never owned more than a suitcase each for her and Nicky. Anton had stored the best pieces of furniture with a company tasked with restoring them. He'd scheduled an auction for everything else before he died, but delays meant it happened months later. The items returned piece by piece, filling the house by degrees. She couldn't imagine having enough stuff to mess up more than a couple of square metres.

Frederik lifted down the first packing box and withdrew a penknife from his jeans pocket. He flicked the blade open one handed and slit the tape from end to end. Emma observed the deftness of his actions and accepted defeat. He hadn't expected the nosebleed. She wouldn't catch him on the back foot again.

"Saucepans." Emma peered into the box, steering clear of Frederik and his knife. She glanced around the kitchen. "You have heaps of storage. I can't see anything sharp." Her gaze flicked to the penknife. Frederik ran a careful thumb along the blade. "Not in the box, anyway." Her stomach gave a painful twinge and exhaustion snatched at the escaping tendrils of energy. Her mission seemed ridiculous. Frederik had asked for her aid but somehow forgotten that fact in the dynamic since her arrival. She gave him a smile which didn't reach her eyes. "I'll help for an hour and then I'll drive home."

Stephie lolled in her baby seat as Emma snatched its carrying handle and hoisted it into the air. She flounced from the kitchen and set to work in the master bedroom. Jay followed her, slumping down next to the child with a grunt. Susan had straightened the bed with crisp hospital corners, but loose drawers and haphazard boxes made walking around the bed an impossible task. "You must feel exhausted," Emma told the dog. "A visit to the bathroom is like navigating land mines." Jay yawned in response.

"Hardly." Frederik lurked in the doorway and Emma ignored him. She straightened a tallboy and fitted the drawers with more difficulty than she'd anticipated. Swapping the top one for a thinner one in the middle seemed to work. She pushed the dressing table against the wall and snagged the empty drawers from its marble surface. They slid into place with ease. Emma navigated the baby seat and dog to retrieve one by the ensuite. Frederik's fingers closed around her wrist as she passed him. "Don't tell Susan."

She heard the command in his tone and a surge of defiance rose into her chest. A red mist descended and she let her other hand take the weight of the drawer. The sharp edge of the wood hit the side of Frederik's knee with a heavy thud, and his lips parted in pain. "Shit!" he hissed, but he released Emma's wrist.

"Everything okay in there?" Susan's voice carried along the hallway and Jay gave a whine of reply. He got to his feet and his shaggy body padded towards her location.

"Fine." Emma's tone sounded overly bright, and she shoved Frederik out of her way. She lowered her voice to a volume just outside Susan's incredible range of hearing. "But if your husband comes at me one more time, it won't be." She dropped the drawer onto the bedspread, wincing at the crack along one edge. Her sigh communicated frustration and tiredness. "You came to me, remember Frederik? I don't need this."

"Okay." He pushed the door closed but didn't turn the handle. "I'm sorry." He held up one hand in placation while the other rubbed the side of his knee. "I told Christopher everything I knew. Regan posted the flash drive before he went missing. It arrived here the day he should have caught the bus to the other house to help Susan finish packing. He's done something stupid and I need to find him before Rohan does."

"So, he posted it to this address?"

Frederik nodded. "Yeah." The muscles of his face tightened as he thought through Emma's question. "Yeah. Here. Not to our old address or to the motel I stayed at before we completed the contract on this place. He sent it here."

"Was that a risk?" Emma cocked her head. "What if the other people moving out had taken it?"

Frederik tapped an index finger against his chin. Swelling burgeoned beneath his eyes from Emma's earlier hit. He shook his head. "Nobody lived here. A trust owned it and we bought it right after it cleared probate."

Emma sank onto the bed as her mind churned through options and possibilities. "So, what makes here a safer bet than the old house or your motel?" Her mind shifted to her own difficulties getting her DNA test kit past a household of nosey lodgers. She dismissed the old address for the same reason. "Susan might have opened any mail arriving at your old place." Emma narrowed her eyes. "Why not send it to the motel? Nobody there cares what you receive through the post, do they?"

"I don't know." Frederik shrugged. He lifted the drawer from the bed and fitted it into its slot. The crack in the wood disappeared inside the cupboard. "But he took a risk posting it here. The sale almost didn't go through to completion. The lawyer discovered issues with a boundary fence at the rear of the property after Regan went missing. He couldn't know if that got resolved."

"But he knew the property remained empty?"

Frederik nodded. He used his pen knife to slit wide a box and hauled out a patterned skirt and matching jacket. Emma rose and snatched the items from him, opening the wardrobe and slipping them onto hangers. "Will all of Susan's clothes fit in here?" she mused.

"No." Frederik smiled. "I'll use the one in the next room." He passed Emma a dress and then a pair of trousers.

"I can do this." She flapped a hand in dismissal. "Find your own boxes and take them next door then. I'll feel like I've achieved something if Susan can climb into bed tonight without breaking her neck."

"Hack said he'd assist you." Frederik frowned as he peered at the next box. He found the massive 'F' which Susan had scrawled onto its surface in black marker pen.

Emma shook her head and hung another two dresses on the rail. "I don't think he can. Rohan can spot a liar at ten paces, particularly when it's Christopher. Their history makes that whole scenario hazardous." She rolled her eyes and added, "Especially as I have to live with both of them."

"So, you won't help me?" Frederik's tone conveyed his despair. His blue eyes sparkled with an icy chill. Emma wondered if he considered forcing her compliance. A bloody nose, a bruised leg and the thought of crossing Rohan made the idea risky, but she knew how desperation often drove idiocy.

"We don't need Christopher." Emma's fingers pushed spaghetti straps onto a hanger and the dress swished as she fed it into the wardrobe's greedy mouth. "I think I know where Regan's hiding."

Radical Deductions

"He's here."

Frederik looked around the bedroom, his jaw hanging open enough to look comical. "Where?"

"Well, obviously not in this room, but somewhere nearby. There are risks attached to every single place he could have posted that flash drive, including here. What makes this location different is that he could watch it somehow. Do you still have the envelope it arrived in?"

Frederik groaned. "No! You can see the mess we're in. I burnt it in the fireplace. And the note which came with it."

"But it definitely arrived via the mail? He didn't hand deliver it?"

He closed his eyes. "I saw a postmark. Durham. He mailed it near the old house. It had a label on the front of it."

"A tracking sticker? I don't suppose you remember the number or the date of posting?" Emma reached the bottom of her box and gave a grunt of satisfaction. She lifted it, tearing the tape from underneath and then folding it flat. Frederik's box remained full, a trouser leg spewing over the side as though trying to escape.

Frederik cocked his head. "Not the number. Sorry. But there's an odd thing about the date of posting." His voice held the strain of frustration. "I found the envelope on the morning the sale completed. It sat on the kitchen counter as if someone put it there." He blinked. "The postmark showed the date as almost two weeks earlier, so I assumed it just took a while to reach its destination. It wasn't there when I did a last inspection with the real estate agent the day before we paid for the house. I assumed he came back later, bumped into the courier, signed for the package and left it on the counter for me."

"So, it took two weeks when it should have arrived much faster?" Emma pointed to a fresh box and waited for Frederik to slit the tape. Bras and knickers popped up for air and Emma frowned. "Put that one on the bedside table," she ordered. "Susan can sort her own underwear." Frederik obeyed and fetched a box from the other side of the room. He slipped his knife beneath the tape and flipped it open with the same wrist action as slitting someone's throat.

Emma suppressed an involuntary shiver. She reached for the new crop of dresses and the silky fabrics soothed her anxiety. Reality crowded back into her psyche. Frederik needed her more than she needed him. For now.

"Focus on the tracking sticker." She scrabbled in the pile and sorted the dresses from the trousers. Her brain processed scenarios and possibilities even as her busy fingers filled the wardrobe.

"Okay." Frederik stopped folding jeans and creating a neat pile on the mattress. "It came in a plastic envelope with one of those courier stickers." He groaned and tilted his head back, closing his eyes. "Why did I burn it?"

Emma shrugged. "Fear. Worry for Regan." She pursed her lips to avoid introducing the more obvious conclusion. Rohan and Christopher disposed of evidence with enough regularity for it to become a reflex action. She dropped an evening gown and it slithered into a puddle of silk. "We need to find that tracking number."

Emma retrieved her phone from her bag in the lounge. She checked on Susan and found her humming to herself and sorting cutlery on the draining board. Susan turned to her at the sound of her steps. "How is it going?"

"Good." Emma added a lightness into her tone. "You have a wardrobe which is almost full. I've left your undies for you to sort. We're making a walkway around the bed. Two boxes down and another fifty to go."

Susan smiled. She closed her eyes and let the sunshine filter through the kitchen window to kiss her upturned cheeks. "I like it here," she announced. "I think things will be okay."

"Just okay?" Emma stiffened. Susan's words held an undertone she couldn't decipher.

"Yep." Susan shuffled a knife around a collection of dessert spoons. "Okay will do for now."

Not wanting to risk a phone call within her hearing, Emma went out to the car on a pretext of fetching something. She sat in the front seat and phoned the post office service number. "Hi, I posted a small parcel to my friend on the last Monday of August. How can I check if it arrived? I've lost the tracking number."

"What address did you write on the package?" The advisor sounded dour and unhappy with her life choices. Emma gave Susan's address and Frederik's surname. The clicking of keys formed the background of the call. "I can see that our service delivered a tracked parcel to that address on the first of this month. Is the recipient saying it didn't arrive? I can lodge a claim if you're the sender."

"Thanks." Emma held her breath. "I might need you to do that for me, but I thought I paid for someone to sign for it?" Her teeth ground hard enough to send shooting pains into her temples. "I didn't want it left at the property without a signature."

"Yes, that's correct. They did. The signature looks like *S Sandoval*." The advisor continued, bored out of her mind.

"Would you like me to lodge the claim? I see you took out additional insurance."

"It's okay. That's my friend." Emma's furrowed brow and confused expression stared back at her in the rear-view mirror. "I'll see if I can contact him again. Perhaps he forgot." Emma ended the call and stayed in the car for a moment. Her index finger tapped a beat on the steering wheel.

She found Frederik clanking around in the bedroom next door to the master. He unpacked his boxes and rearranged furniture. Emma returned to Susan's wardrobe and used the activity of folding sweaters and fitting them onto shelves to calm her thoughts. She tried not to run through the mystery over and over, keen not to muddy her existing conclusions with speculation.

After two more boxes, she groaned and slumped onto the bed. Her fingers worked at a knot building near the base of her spine. She jumped as Frederik appeared in the doorway. "What's up?" he demanded.

Emma relayed her conversation with the advisor. Then dealt the blow she hadn't expected to deliver. "Apparently S Sandoval signed for it on Wednesday of last week. That flash drive came here and then spent time in someone else's possession."

"No way!" he breathed, the sound a muted hiss.

Emma arched her spine before giving in and laying back against the mattress. "Okay, so what are you thinking?"

Frederik leaned against the wall and squeezed the bridge of his nose between thumb and forefinger. "We didn't finish completing the sale on this place until last Friday. So, how the bloody hell did my wife sign for a parcel at this house on the Wednesday of the previous week?"

"That sounds like quite a dilemma." Susan stepped into the room, one hand resting on Jay's soft crown. She cocked her head towards Frederik and a graceful smile flitted across her lips. "So, who wants to explain it?"

Constant

Frederik's expletive caused Susan to wince. Her brow furrowed, and she wrinkled her nose. He released a gargantuan sigh and sank onto the bed. "Fantastic!" he spat. A painful resignation leaked from his tone.

Susan looked from the sound of her husband's voice and back to Emma. She pushed her glasses up her nose with her index finger and squinted. "I can see your outline, Emma," she declared. "You're standing in front of the window. You should know by now that staying quiet won't save you."

Despite herself, Emma smirked like a naughty child. "How much did you hear?" she asked. A giggle laced her voice. Frederik closed his eyes and his head shook from side to side as though he'd imagined she might deny everything. Emma spoke to him before facing Susan's ready barrage of questions. "Your wife has supersonic hearing. I don't think you have as many secrets from her as you believe." She blinked and rolled her eyes to emphasise her judgement. "You're an idiot if you think you can hide things from her just because she's blind."

"Thank you for that." Susan's gaze hadn't moved from Emma's outline. She considered shifting just to fox her, but stopped herself. Nicky would have done it, but she needed to remember she wasn't seven years old. As an echo of her thoughts, Susan frowned and jabbed a finger in her direction. "Don't be silly, Emma. You're not five."

Emma's shoulders slumped with the sigh she released, and she glanced at her sleeping daughter. Much of Frederik's anxiety seemed understandable when faced with the fear of losing a child. "Regan is missing," she said. "He posted something to Frederik and he passed it to me. We need to find him." She glanced across at Frederik's bowed head and received no help. "Before someone else does."

Jay flopped onto the carpet at Susan's feet. A long grunt emanated from his doggy lips as he made himself comfortable. Emma joined him, kneeling next to his blond head and running her fingers through his soft coat. Susan shuffled forward with her left hand outstretched and Frederik jerked to life. He held out his hand, their fingers connecting as he helped her to sit next to him. Susan pressed her palms over her knees. "I heard you mention my name. How am I involved?"

Frederik cleared his throat. "Your maiden name is on the tracking receipt for the parcel Regan sent. Obviously you didn't sign for it."

"Because I can't see?" Susan's tone held a note of warning, and Frederik sighed.

"No. Because you weren't here. We didn't own the property until ten days later."

"But we had keys, remember? The owners let us fit new carpet once the solicitor approved all the paperwork for the sale."

Frederik recoiled and he closed his eyes. Emma's fingers coasted over Jay's crown as she observed a commander floundering in the face of personal adversity. The insipid thought crept into her brain that perhaps her disappearance seven years ago had distracted Rohan enough to get him and his platoon blown to smithereens. She pushed the guilt reflex away and grabbed a handful of the soft ruff around Jay's neck. He didn't move, grateful for her petting and attention. "Did Regan know you had keys?" Emma asked. She concentrated on the downy swirls of hair which wrapped Jay's body in a pattern of concentric curls. "Could he have taken a copy?"

Frederik shook his head, but Susan gave a definitive nod. "Oh, yes. He helped me with the packing at the end of last month. Frederik started his new job and I couldn't manage alone. Regan spent two days with me."

"But didn't Frederik have the keys down here?" Emma cocked her head, her gaze misty as she ran through scenarios in her mind.

Frederik heaved out a sigh. "I got another set cut without the agent knowing. I travelled home and back a couple of times a week and didn't want them getting lost. We intended to change the locks after the purchase, anyway. I guess Regan might have copied the original keys if he ran out on another errand."

"Which means he posted the flash drive to this house, tracked it, let himself in to wait for it, and then signed the receipt."

"But the carpet fitters came in here the day after someone took delivery of the package." Frederik's frustration showed in the tapping of his foot on the carpet. "I let them into the house. There was no package! It wasn't here."

"Exactly." Emma waved her hand towards the door and Jay lifted his head in a silent protest. His pink tongue chased her moving fingers and she settled them back on his head. "He let himself back in here again after he knew you'd completed the settlement." She frowned and stared at the ceiling. "For some reason, he couldn't risk keeping the flash drive between the date he posted it and when it arrived here. So, he put it in transit and then picked it up at the end of its journey."

"Does it matter why?" Frederik's tone sounded ragged with fear. "I just want to find Regan and keep him safe."

"I understand and we will." Emma shot him a conciliatory smile. "I promise."

"What did he do?" Susan rested a hand over Frederik's muscular thigh and waited for him to squeeze her fingers. "And who's looking for him, apart from us?"

Frederik's expression softened at her inclusion of herself in their shared dilemma, and he lifted her hand to kiss her fingers. "Someone who mustn't find him," he whispered.

Emma's teeth ground in her jaw. More secrets. She swallowed and steeled herself to honour her friendship with Susan. "Rohan. We don't want Rohan to find him first."

"Ah." The fact that Susan accepted the answer proved Emma's point. She knew more than Frederik gave her credit for. His eyes widened and his complexion lost its ruddiness.

"Oh shit!" he breathed.

Definition

Susan released a heavy sigh. "Thank goodness it's out in the open now."

"How long have you known?" Defeat hung on Frederik's lowered chin as his gaze raked the carpet. "I didn't want you involved."

Susan snorted. "I'm blind, not stupid. There aren't many situations as a security manager which demand your attention for days on end and with immediate effect. You disappear at a moment's notice and return bruised and battered. Anything involving students would make the news and yet it never has." She twisted her lips into a pout. "I also know about the hiding space at the back of the airing cupboard at the old house. The cabinet isn't deep enough and the shelves are too short."

"You never went in that cupboard." Frederik's brow creased into a frown and he turned to face her. "We kept nothing in there."

Emma pursed her lips and focussed on Jay. He rolled onto his side and kicked her with his back paw to indicate he wanted a belly rub. He closed his eyes as she smoothed the longer curls across his ribcage.

"And you didn't think that was weird?" Susan spread her hands in question. "An airing cupboard I couldn't use. Is it the reason you insisted I moved in with you after we married?"

Frederik shrugged. He tipped back onto the mattress and pillowed his hands behind his head. "No, I didn't think it was weird and yes, it's why I couldn't move in with you. I think you might have noticed me creating an armoury in the back of one of your wardrobes."

Susan groaned. "Bloody hell, Fred! I loved that house. It was purpose built for me. All you needed to do was ask!"

"I'm sorry." He shot upright using his stomach muscles. He fixed an arm around Susan's shoulders and leaned sideways to kiss her temple. "I'll tell you everything, but first, I need to find Regan before Rohan does."

Susan squeezed the bridge of her nose between finger and thumb. "Okay. So, what do we know?"

The weight in Emma's heart lifted as Susan added her quick brain to the mystery. She contributed to their sparse information, fleshing out her and Regan's movements across the two-day period. "He seemed upset," she admitted. "I didn't press for details but he intimated a friendship had gone a little sour." She closed her eyes, frowning as she sifted through their interaction. "We ran out of milk and bread on the second day. I asked him to nip to the supermarket while I continued packing, but he became difficult at the thought of catching the bus. The man next door always drove into town around eleven o'clock, so I phoned him and asked if Regan could get a ride with him."

"So, he might know if Regan visited a key cutting store." Emma brightened. "Would he tell you?"

"Yes." Susan nodded. "Jay." She turned her head in the dog's direction, but he'd already bounded to his feet. "Phone," she said, her tone commanding but kind. "Fetch."

Jay trotted away, bashing Frederik's knees with his tail as he left. His feet padded along the hall carpet and he checked each room on his way through the house. A snort of disgust heralded each lack of success until he reappeared with Susan's large mobile phone in his mouth. He dropped it into her lap and waited for his reward, her vocal appreciation and a ruffle of the fur on his chest.

Susan used her voice to unlock the screen and commanded the processor to, "Phone Norman."

"Phoning Norman," a robotic female voice stated before the ringing activated.

The old man's wavering voice communicated his sadness at Susan's leaving through the phone's speakers. His voice sounded tinny. "The new neighbours have five kids and three dogs," he complained. "And I miss your casseroles already."

Susan commiserated with him, but led the discussion around to Regan's visit. "I loved the bread he bought," she said. "Can you remember which store he got it from? I'd love Fred to try it and wanted to get a few loaves down here. Was it Tesco's or Sainsbury's?"

"I went to Tesco's, but he didn't come with me." Norman gave a guttural cough and the conversation paused. "He used one of those fancy bakeries near the precinct. I told him to meet me in the car park but he arrived twenty minutes late." Norman's tone held an accusatory note, as though he blamed Susan for Regan's tardiness. "He looked very sweaty, like he'd run. I didn't complain to you, my dear, because you had so much on your plate already." Self-righteousness bolstered Norman's wavering voice. "How is the new place working out for you?"

Frederik rose and jerked his head towards the door. Emma clambered to her feet and followed, hoisting her daughter's baby seat into her arms on the way. Jay seemed unsure about leaving Susan alone and he stood in the doorway, his tail swishing from side to side like a nervous truce flag.

"Dude!" Frederik protested. He stroked the soft blond snout and edged past the dog. "He's like the fun police."

Emma glanced back at Jay as she followed Frederik along the hall and into the sunny kitchen. "He wanted you to stay and divulge more of your secrets." Her tone held a note of mirth and she corrected herself. The man's son was missing.

Frederik snorted. "You heard my wife. I have no secrets."

She sighed and set Stephie's baby seat on an armchair just beyond the archway into the dining room. The child rooted for her thumb and settled when her lips closed around it. "How long do calls to Norman usually take?" she asked. "We need to work out where Regan is before I drive home. I don't want to leave it too late."

Frederik winced. "He enjoys talking to her, and she's too nice. Five minutes or five hours. I don't know."

"Okay." Emma gave a definitive nod. "Let's grab some lunch and one of us might have a bright idea after we've eaten."

He opened the fridge and released a groan. "That's where I meant to go just before you arrived. The supermarket." He closed the door with more force than necessary.

Emma raised a hand to halt his ready tirade of blame, suspecting he'd aim most of it towards her. "It's fine. I didn't expect you to have everything sorted already. There are sandwiches in my car and some cake Allaine made. My keys are by the door if you want to fetch it."

Frederik retrieved the bag of food from behind Emma's driver's seat. He lifted it onto the counter and unzipped the lid. The freezer packs had kept the food chilled, and he stuck his face inside to enjoy the cooler air. "This is amazing!" he gushed. His eager fingers hauled out packets of sandwiches, cake, a carton of salad and a bag of apples. He set a bottle of cola on the counter for a moment, having lifted it from where it had fallen on its side beneath a quiche. "I'm starving," he admitted. "This house moving lark is harder than any deployment."

"Tell me about it." Susan stepped into the kitchen, her hand resting on Jay's dutiful head. His tongue lolled at the scent of food, even though his training wouldn't allow him to beg.

"Emma brought lunch." Frederik's voice held a note of giddiness.

"Then we'll work out where Regan is." Emma saw Susan's nod of agreement before obeying her direction in finding plates.

Scientific

"So, Regan went somewhere else while Norman shopped in Tesco's." Emma licked the last crumbs of cake from her fingers. She'd worked out his hiding place an hour ago and fought the urge to drive around there and haul him out into the open. Frederik had dismissed her conclusion with surprising ease, needing to chew over the evidence.

Susan nodded. "He came back with bread and cakes, but not the milk or cheese. He said Norman hurried him and I know how difficult he can be, so I didn't question it. Perhaps I should have and he wouldn't be in such a mess."

Emma glossed over Susan's need to blame herself and concentrated on the facts. "Regan had the flash drive and knew where he wanted to hide it. It makes sense because he couldn't risk dumping it into your packing in case something went wrong. He posted the flash drive to this house and then tracked its journey. That means he needed to be here to sign for it when it arrived."

"He doesn't drive, but he might have caught the bus. Or got a taxi." Susan pushed her glasses up her nose with her index finger. "But how could he guarantee that Frederik wouldn't be at the house, or someone else?"

"Did he know the time-line for the sale?" Emma reached for an apple. She avoided a brown bruise spreading across one side and bit into the flesh. Juice burst onto her tongue.

"Yes." Susan gave a definitive nod. "He asked a lot of questions about it. There were issues with the carpet company bringing the date forward. He heard me speaking to the solicitor about early access to the property. The original owner's children wanted the sale closed as fast as possible, so they agreed. Regan knew Frederik intended to let the fitters into the house and pop back later to sign off the job."

Frederik ran his fingers through his fringe. "Regan took a risk by coming here at all. I visited most days. Why didn't I run into him?"

"Because he's smart." Emma waved her apple and finished her mouthful. "Where did you go when you weren't here? Did you work at all?"

Frederik shrugged. "Yes, until the start of last week. I took the time off to deal with the sale of our place and the purchase of this. In between popping out here, I stayed in my motel room on the phone."

"What about nipping out to the hardware store to buy things for the new house?" Emma's gaze misted as she remembered the ease of moving into Wingate Hall. "Could Regan have bugged your phone?" The question popped free and Frederik blinked.

"What?"

Emma shrugged. "Well, he's into tech. And whatever is on that flash drive is sensitive enough to send him into hiding. If the government contracted Rohan to find him, then it's something high end and expensive."

"No." Frederik gave a decisive shake of his head.

"Regan and Frederik weren't in Durham at the same time," Susan explained. "Unless he's attached something previously and hasn't used it until now." She turned towards her husband. He hadn't stopped shaking his head.

"Not possible!" Exasperation gave way to exhaustion. "I'm not stupid enough to let that happen, even at home."

Emma shrugged. "You didn't know Susan had found your armoury." She wiped apple juice from her chin. "Okay, so you're certain Regan didn't plant something on you. That means he must have watched you in person. He doesn't drive or own a car which indicates he stayed close. Very close."

Frederik inhaled at the same moment Emma dropped her apple core onto the carpet. She lurched for it and scooped it into her palm. "Did Regan know which motel you stayed at?" she asked.

"No," Frederik replied. "Why would he?"

"Because I told him." Susan's voice held guilt mixed with the uptick of excitement. "He asked me and I thought it was a strange question."

Vertical

"Regan, it's Emma Harrington!" She used her maiden name in case he'd heard of Rohan via Frederik and made the connection. Her fingers rapped on the door of the motel room and she took a step back to wait in the corridor. She heard no movement at first, then the faint shuffle of fabric brushed against the door. The light changed in the peephole, darkening as someone put their eye to it and then moved. Emma imagined Regan panicking on the other side. "Just let me in to speak to you," she said, keeping her tone soft. The distorted flicker of light patterns from the peephole gave her hope that he'd seen and at least read her lips.

A metal security chain rattled against the wood and then scraped free. Every slight sound seemed amplified in the corridor. Emma tuned in to her surroundings, assessing potential danger beneath the jarring strains of television programmes and the muted chatter of multiple voices. She'd counted the rooms on the way to this one, honouring Rohan's painstaking training. Going through the motions at the time to please him, she'd wondered why she might ever need such skills. But she stood in the dim light from the overhead bulb and faced a door the same as all the others, while knowing the rooms on either side sat empty and without threat. The receptionist hadn't questioned the fake identification from Her Majesty's Customs and Excises. Frederik had handed it to Emma with the assurance that few people knew what their ID cards looked like, anyway. She had no choice but to believe him. The receptionist had dipped forward to cast a cursory glance at the faded photo of a dull, brown-haired woman. Emma had smiled through the unintended insult and hoped she didn't appear quite as vanilla as the random stock image.

"Your father sent me." Emma raised her voice, growing impatient with the delay. Something clattered against a door near the lifts and she tensed. It whipped open to the sound of raised female voices and the wheels of a suitcase bumped into the corridor. Every muscle in Emma's body stiffened in readiness to defend herself. An earlier text from Christopher informed her that Rohan had accepted the terms of his latest government contract. The price was high, and he'd initiated Christopher's search for Regan. He would expect immediate results.

A woman jabbed at the button to call the lift. An overnight suitcase stood behind her, listing on a damaged wheel. The door creaked shut on its closer and she frowned, regret in her sad expression. She glanced back once at Emma without seeing as the lift doors parted like the dark mouth of an ethereal creature. Her heels clicked against the tiles as she stepped inside and hauled her suitcase over the metal lip. Emma noted her scruffy clothing and the dejected air shivering over her. Nothing about the woman presented a threat, but Frederik had warned her to take extra care.

The lift doors closed and the digital display above it signalled the woman's descent. Emma jumped as the door to the room she'd exited opened with force and another woman ran into the corridor. She stopped to survey Emma before seeing the numbered display show G for ground. "No!" she hissed. Her fingers jabbed at the call button and she paused a moment, staring up at it as though willing it to change. When nothing happened, she bolted for the door to the stairs.

Emma groaned and tapped the toe of her sandal against the muddy brown carpet. The ache in her breasts charted time with as much accuracy as any clock. She'd left Stephie sleeping with Susan, but knew she had less than an hour before the next feed. The rapping of her knuckles against the door marked a mental decision to quit. Light moved behind the peephole and Emma glared at it. "You're rubbish at this!" she snapped to the unseen observer. She dragged her phone from her handbag and dialled a number, beginning her tirade before the other person spoke. "He won't answer the door, Susan. I can't do anymore than this. Sorry."

A heavy metal lock clicked, and the door squeaked open enough to create a shaft of sunlight at Emma's feet. She held her breath as a mousy fringe and a pair of blue eyes peeked through the narrow aperture. "Susan sent you?" The male voice cracked with teenage strains and the eyelid blinked.

Emma released a sigh. "No, the Easter bunny. Would you like to speak to him?" She held out her hand and thin fingers with knobbly knuckles reached through the gap to snatch the phone. Then the door slammed in her face. "Fantastic!" Emma gritted her teeth and stared at the fake knots in the wood.

The builders of the motel used pre-cast concrete and identical fittings to create a grey, indifferent appearance. It walked the line between decent and passable, providing a temporary stop for wayfarers travelling through Lincoln. Not opulent enough to steal customers from the Bailgate area, but not trashy enough to encourage those running from the law. It was middle of the road. Perfect for a man taking up a new job at the university while buying a house a few miles away. Perfect for his son to hide in the room next door and observe his father's movements.

Emma jumped as the door opened again. This time, the gap widened enough for her to squeeze through it. She turned to face the frightened teenager who slammed it shut behind her. "What are you doing?" she sighed. She used the same voice she kept for Nicky in his moments of pure idiocy, meant to force reflection while conveying despair.

Regan handed back her phone in shaking fingers. "Susan vouched for you." He ran his hands through his hair and then tamped it back into a draping curtain over one eye. He had changed little since Susan's wedding, remaining a grey man with forgettable facial features and a strange sense of translucence. Unlike Frederik with his bulging muscles and larger-than-life personality, Regan made the perfect ghost. "I needed to run." He spoke without moving his lips much, the sound issuing from behind crooked teeth which made him self conscious. Emma tried not to react to the male scent overpowering the small room. The ensuite bathroom looked unused, the towels in their regimental positions on the shelf above the sink and a lone hand cloth over the rail. Rumpled sheets betrayed poor sleeping habits, and Regan's clothes reeked of sweat. But the desk in the corner oozed order and care. A laptop sat square in the centre with a hard drive parallel to the keyboard. Someone had placed it there with deliberation.

Emma took a step towards the window and peered from behind the partly drawn curtain. Frederik sat in the car park in Susan's car. From above, Emma watched his hands flex on the steering wheel as though itching to thump someone. "Your dad is worried sick," she stated.

"Is he out there?" Regan's eyes widened, and he shook his head. "He'll lead them back to me! Why is he here?"

Emma shrugged. "You have worse problems than the government. There's a contract on your head now and you don't want to know who has it."

"To kill me?" Regan's colour faded like water down a plughole. He slumped onto the bed and dipped at the waist. The heels of his hands covered his eyes.

Emma tutted. She wrinkled her nose at the thought of sitting next to him. Instead, she leaned her back against the wall nearest the door and released a sigh of exasperation. "No. To retrieve the data you stole. Rohan makes agreements rather than pushing people through upstairs windows. But I believe it's happened."

"Rohan? What kind of agreement?" Regan's words caught in his throat. "I know Rohan through Dad." A tear streaked through the greyness of his cheek. "Will his agreement make me move away and never see Susan again?"

"I'm not sure," Emma mused. "But you wouldn't want to break it."

Regan groaned. "I just want to go home. I wish I'd never tried to do the right thing."

Inclusive

"It started as a joke." Regan's hand shook as he poured boiling water onto a tea bag in the cup he'd designated for Emma. She inspected the rim and hoped it wasn't second-hand. When he thumped the kettle back onto its stand and reached for a tiny pot of long-life milk, Emma shook her head.

"I don't see many people laughing."

"Yeah, well." Regan didn't finish his sentence. He watched her fingers as she took the mug of tea and peered inside it at the strange, floating bits dancing around its surface.

"Try to calm down and tell me everything you know." She tilted her wrist to inspect her watch. "I must leave in fifteen minutes."

Regan's eyes widened. Terror turned his lips down in an unnatural likeness to a trout. "Why?" He bounced towards the door and ignored Emma's warning about calming himself. "What's happening in fifteen minutes?"

She gritted her teeth, giving her smile a manic quality. "I have a ten-minute drive back to the bungalow in Saxilby, by which time my daughter approaches hysteria for her overdue feed."

"Oh." Regan exhaled, and his backside contacted the mattress. "Okay." He sat, rigid as a plank of wood, with his praying hands trapped between his thighs to disguise their perpetual tremor.

Emma held onto the mug, but didn't sip the tea. She'd watched Regan make it, but actually drinking it seemed like a rookie mistake. If she wasn't already nervous enough to vomit, the floaty bits discouraged her. "How did this start, what did you download and who else knows you did it?" She fired out the questions Frederik most wanted answered. And then one of her own. "Who else knows you're here in this room?"

Regan swallowed and began his sorry tale. "I sniffed around the grey web for a joke with my friends. They got bored, but I didn't. I discovered I could make money tweaking gaming programs. A guy working for a big company made some stupid mistakes, and I found them while beta testing. He asked me to correct them and then let the company think he fixed the code. I don't think he really knew what he was doing."

Emma cleared her throat. "Regan, I don't mean to sound rude, but we don't have time to pick through your life history. When did you do that for him, and how is it relevant to what's happening now?"

Regan's head bobbed on his neck as though he'd lost control of it. "It kinda is relevant. I've done jobs for him on and off since I was fourteen. Just gaming stuff mainly. He got paid well and he passed a decent chunk on to me in bitcoin."

"Fourteen?" Emma released a groan of disbelief. She thought of her own wily son and mentally praised Christopher's belt and braces approach to the Internet at Wingate Hall. Nicky wouldn't get through the extensive firewall he'd set up, not without Christopher knowing. "Keep going," she sighed.

"He helped me navigate the grey web at first. Then he introduced me to a forum he ran. After a while, he started sending me different tasks and wanting me to figure out the program bugs. They weren't games anymore, but complicated algorithms for digital automation. I enjoyed it. The grey web is full of tutorials and dead drops of information." Regan's head bobbed again, and a fire sparked behind his irises. He looked more alive in that minute than in the preceding five.

"Grey web?" Emma frowned. "Do you mean the dark web?" Pride flickered in her chest at having retained some of Christopher's semi interesting tech chatter.

"No." Regan crushed her illusion. "The grey web is open to everyone. I'm careful there because it's the place where a lot of the downloadable material contains malware." He blinked and read her expression. "You know what malware is, hey?"

"Yes!" Emma's fingers clenched around the mug. "Just skip to the bit where you got yourself into trouble."

"I did odd jobs for the other people on the forum, and the original guy helped me get a special browser and anonymization software. I set myself up on the dark web as Spike and it kinda went from there."

"Grey web. Dark web. Right." Emma set her mug on the dressing table. "Then what?"

Regan hissed through his teeth. "At the start of last month, I came across an anonymous cache of breached accounts just left there. A quick sniff around showed it held over twenty thousand passwords belonging to government departments. Immigration, a directory of all the passwords for accounts in the British embassies, customs, army logistics and loads of others. Just sitting there waiting for collection."

"So, you collected it?" Emma's eyes narrowed. "What did you think would happen?"

Regan swallowed. "I just needed to get rid of the army ones." His shoulders straightened and his tone held belligerence. "My dad still has mates in the army. I didn't care about any of the others, but I don't want someone messing with my dad's people."

"What's on the flash drive?" She frowned, wondering why Christopher had struggled to remove an encryption constructed by a teenager. The smirk spread across her lips, but Regan didn't notice. He ran long fingers through his lank hair.

"Whoever dumped the cache withdrew without leaving a trace. I took a copy of everything in the dead drop, deleted the army files, and replaced the whole thing." His face crumpled. "I was so pleased with myself, I took a couple of screenshots of the process, so I could look back over what I'd done. That's when they saw me."

"When who saw you?" Emma closed her eyes as she processed the components of Regan's story.

"The government." He gulped. "I asked a question on a forum. I uploaded a screenshot of the code. The next thing I knew, my computer suffered a brute force attack. I couldn't shut it down or reboot it. Then I got a text." He thumped the side of his head with his knuckles. "The guy I work for sent the message. He said the secret service were coming for me and to get rid of the evidence." His hands trembled as he wiped his nose against his wrist. "They'll think I hacked the government sites and left the original cache for someone else to collect. I've gone over and over it in my mind and I must have left some kind of thumb print on the changed file."

"It sounds more like the forum contained someone who reported back to them. Why is the flash drive so important?" Emma glanced through the gap in the curtains. Frederik's car door opened and she groaned. "Your father is panicking." Frederik's boots hit the car park surface, and he paused as though contemplating his next move. "He's coming now."

Regan made a sound like an extended groan and his body tensed. He dipped forward and back in a rocking motion. "I downloaded the cache so I could delete the army information. Then I used the new data to overlay the original file and added a bug that wipes someone's computer if they try to download it. The flash drive is the only working copy."

Emma nodded. "So, it contains everything except the army stuff?"

"Yeah." Regan nodded. His eyes glittered with tears. "I thought I took enough care. If the modified file contained a print leading to me, then I can't work out how. Only the original creator would think to look at the time stamp and the code. And it means they'd have to risk touching it again."

Emma frowned. "You went to extreme lengths to protect yourself and then boasted about it on a forum. Why are you surprised?" Regan hung his head and she experienced a moment of empathy. "So, why keep a copy?"

"Insurance." He shrugged. "It's what they do in the movies. I thought they'd understand I changed the files because it didn't contain the army data. They'd see I wasn't the author." Despite his dire circumstances, his trembling lips quirked into a smile. "I wanted the guys in the group to see how well I did."

Emma swallowed the ready comment about pride. Regan's desire to celebrate his cleverness had landed him in deep trouble. She sensed he didn't need her to labour the point. "I'm sure they're desperate to congratulate you." Still, sarcasm oozed from her voice. She inhaled and caught sight of Frederik standing and leaning on the roof of the vehicle. "I need to leave," she said, her tone urgent. "The flash drive is safe. Stay here and don't open the door for anyone else. Stop using Susan's maiden name because that's the first thing they'll check."

Regan blanched. "Sorry. I needed to track the flash drive and make sure Dad got it. I hoped he'd know what to do. The text message gave me a grid reference to go to, but I ignored it and made my own plan. I put the flash drive into the postal service because I knew it would take it off the grid until I could get somewhere safe."

Emma cocked her head. "Who sent that text? Do you have a name? A phone number?"

Regan snorted, the sound filled with disgust. "No one uses their proper name. He doesn't even know who I am. It came as an SMS text, so I can't trace it. He spoofed the sender's display number."

"Okay. Emma heard the doubt in her voice. "You haven't heard from him since?"

Regan cocked his head. "I flushed my SIM card down the toilet. He can't contact me. Then, I hid out here and nobody found me, so I figured I could collect the package from the mail carrier and hide it until Dad took possession of the house."

"Hide it?" Emma stilled. "Where did you hide it?"

Regan's next statement displayed cunning. "In plain sight. There's an old lady with a poodle next to Dad's new place. I knocked on her door and said I attended the local college and needed work experience. She wanted her lawn cut, so I did it for free. I hid the flash drive in a plant pot in her garden. A week later, I went back and thanked her for helping me and she invited me in for coffee. I pretended to check the lawn, retrieved the package and left." He grinned. "See. I'm like a secret agent."

Emma sighed. "You picked the nosiest person on the street. I don't think MI6 are planning to head hunt you soon." At the mention of MI6, Regan paled. She forged ahead, the pressing need to return to Stephie greater than her desire to soothe Regan. "You're not using a credit card, are you?" She waved her hand in the air to indicate the motel room.

Regan wrinkled his nose. "I got it from a guy on the grey web. No one can trace it back to me."

"No more web!" Emma exclaimed. "Just lay low and stop drawing attention to yourself." She hauled an envelope of cash from her handbag and placed it into Regan's lap. "That's what I'm supposed to say to you, anyway. Your father sent this. Order room service and don't go outside, no matter what happens." She jerked her head towards the laptop. "How do you know they're not watching that credit card?"

Regan inhaled. "Trust me, they aren't."

Emma groaned. She couldn't bear to ask any more questions. Regan rose as her fingers closed around the door handle. The envelope of cash tumbled onto the rumpled bedspread. A bare toe poked through a hole in his striped sock. He represented a paradox; a child with a holey sock playing dangerous, adult games. "How did you find me?"

Emma turned, a slow smile breaking out across her face. The heaviness of the last few months shifted and for a moment, strength flooded through her bones. "I'm the Actuary's wife," she whispered.

Convex

The drive home seemed much longer than her earlier trip. Tiredness gnawed at her bones and made her eyelids heavy. She stopped at the first set of motorway services and lumped the baby seat into the bathroom with her. Then she left her car keys on the cistern and went back for them. When Stephie woke to the sound of a woman using the hand dryer, she cried for another feed. Emma admitted defeat, bought a hot chocolate and fed her daughter under a blanket, which she wrapped around them both. She picked a corner table in the cafe and watched vehicles zoom south along the dual carriageway. An articulated lorry eased from the slip road and into the traffic, drawing honks of annoyance from the cars switching to the other lane.

Stephie's fingers closed around the blanket and she attempted to yank it free. Emma kept hold of it, aware of other patrons staring at her across the crowded cafe. "You're playing now," she told her. Her knuckles showed beneath the blanket, preserving her dignity as she fastened her buttons. Stephie grinned as the cover flopped back over her nose. Emma played boo with her while finishing the dregs of her hot chocolate and left.

"I'm almost home." She checked the roundabout and listened to the clattering of Susan sorting crockery in the kitchen as Frederik answered her call.

He sighed. "Hey, thanks for today. I didn't know who else to turn to, but I never imagined you'd actually prove useful. I can admit when I'm wrong."

"Thank you." Emma smiled to herself and pushed aside the veiled insult. "I'll get the package back from the person I gave it to and see if there's room for negotiation. Stay away from the place we visited today."

Frederik's voice held a warning growl. "You can't tell me what to do."

"I'm not." Emma depressed the indicator switch and turned left. The clicking ceased as the steering wheel righted itself. "I'm asking. Kind of."

Frederik sighed. "Fine! What's happening with the lamb?" He avoided using his son's name over the airwaves. "Can't you take it back to the farm?"

"Nothing will happen tonight." Emma picked her words with care. "And no. It wouldn't survive the journey. I need to consult with someone with a bit more experience."

Frederik silenced. They'd endured the same argument before she drove away, and his fears hadn't lessened in the intervening hour. "Not the vet, Emma. He'll euthanise him."

"A different vet then." She frowned. He knew better than to have this conversation with her over the phone. "I need to answer another call," she lied. She pressed the button on the steering wheel to kill the discussion. She couldn't ask Rohan for help for fear of compromising him. Frederik hadn't trusted Christopher enough to hand him the flash drive without engaging her as an unwilling participant. But she feared her own limited knowledge would stop her fixing the situation.

Emma tapped her fingers against the steering wheel. Stephie grumbled in her baby seat, but her eyelids remained closed. The motion of the vehicle helped to shift the gas accumulating in her tiny plumbing system. Emma sighed and concentrated on the drumming of the wheels on the road. The ringing of her phone through the car's speakers made her jump, and she shot a fearful look at her daughter. Stephie growled and squirmed but didn't wake. "Hey." She pressed the button to answer, seeing Christopher's number flash onto the dashboard screen. "I'm not far away now. Just driving through Corby."

"Wasted trip?" His tone held antagonism and a hint of mockery.

She ground her teeth but stopped herself before the motion generated a headache. She breathed out and eased the tension in her face muscles, figuring Allaine told him where she'd gone. "No. I emptied about ten boxes. Susan's never met Stephie, so we enjoyed a lovely day." Emma pursed her lips and allowed herself a smile. Susan seemed less harried when they said their goodbyes, able to stop worrying about Regan and no longer at odds with Frederik over his secret occupation.

"So, you didn't go to check out Frederik's story?" The mocking tone continued. Christopher assumed she'd failed. She hated how much that irritated her, but it did.

"We talked." She slowed behind a tractor and paused. "That flash drive has more importance than we realised."

"Yeah." He made it sound trivial. "It's account numbers, usernames, and passwords for government agencies. I'm guessing they want it destroyed. A damaging leak is the last thing they need. Whoever set up the original dead drop is invisible, but the eejit who messed with it left enough skin to lead them straight to him. That's why Frederik's son went into hiding. He suspected they'd come for him."

"Maybe."

"I knew you wouldn't find him." Emma had wanted to drag out her victory as long as possible to make Christopher suffer. But he didn't give her the chance. "Ah well. No harm, no foul." He laughed. "Maybe leave it to the professionals next time. I'll find Frederik's idiot son." He gave an exaggerated yawn. "If I get a moment in between all my other jobs. Oh, and if Rohan doesn't find him first." A rustling intruded on the conversation as he placed the phone nearer his lips to whisper. "What's it worth if I find the son and tell you first?"

Emma opened her mouth to put him straight, but he ended the call without saying goodbye. "Idiot!" she exclaimed. Her palms slammed against the steering wheel and pain ricocheted through the delicate bones. "We'll show him!" she snarled. She glanced sideways at her sleeping daughter, including Stephie in her misguided mission. Christopher wouldn't apologise even when she proved him wrong. "It's best I don't give him a head start on Regan," she admitted out loud. "I'm not helping him." She worried at her lower lip and cringed. It didn't seem fair to send her husband on a wild goose chase. A solution presented itself on the rural road which skirted Market Harborough. But it involved stealth, deception, and betrayal.

In her new scenario, the person who stood to lose the most was her.

Percentage

"What will I use for a beak?" Nicky pranced into Emma's bedroom, wearing the crimson crest. A length of elastic wound around his head to keep it secure.

"I'm not sure yet." She laid Stephie in her crib before leaning backwards to stretch the muscles either side of her spine. "Oh, but Susan sent some mustard tights for your chicken's legs."

"Cockerel's legs." Nicky wagged a finger at her. "Can I try on the feathery body?"

"No!" Emma's reply sounded sharper than she'd intended. She avoided glancing across at its hiding place beyond the secret panel in her wardrobe. Her son's head contained a mental map of all the tunnels built into the old house, and the cockerel's flimsy body wouldn't survive too much action before the big day. She hoped her stitching would last the full six hours. "Give that to me, please." Emma took the crest from her son's blond head and smoothed out the dented cardboard spikes. "You've squashed it. What's the point of all that hard work if you ruin it before the book character competition, anyway?" She laid it on the dressing table.

"Sorry." Nicky bounced onto Emma's bed. "Can I see the feathery body, please?" He dragged out the end of the sentence and clasped his hands over his heart. His wide blue irises sparkled in the rays of the fading sun. "Just a teensy weensy peek?"

"No peeking. It's a surprise." Emma slumped across Rohan's side of the bed and hoisted her feet onto the mattress. The journey tired her more than she'd expected. Nicky crawled towards her, slowing his pace as he reached her side and bending to rest his cheek against her thighs.

"Does this hurt, Mummy?" he asked, an appeal in his voice.

"No, baby. I'm almost better." She reached out and stroked his cheek. The door opened with a creak and Emma tensed. A black nose pressed through the gap, followed by brown eyes and a wagging tail. "What are you doing upstairs?" she chided. He sat in the doorway and thumped his tail on the floorboards. His gaze moved from Nicky to her and back again.

"Farrell hoped you'd invite us to visit Susan and Jay." Nicky sat up and his lips curved down into a pout. "So did I."

Emma released a slow breath. "Did he? Well, they moved into a new house that is half the distance away from their old one. So, we can drive up to see them in the holidays, if you want?"

"Yeah!" Nicky blinked and nodded. "What about Farrell?"

"I'm not sure." Emma avoided following her son's impassioned gaze towards the dog. "We need to wait for an invitation, don't we?"

Lines appeared across Nicky's forehead and he stared at the bedspread. His thinking pose reminded her of Anton, and Emma allowed the moment of sadness to peek from the gilded box in her heart. The hidden grief pushed on the lid and its tendrils crept over the edge. "Right mister!" She slammed the thoughts of Anton back under control and jammed her fingers beneath Nicky's armpits. His giggles escaped until he clapped a hand over his mouth.

"Don't wake the baby!" he hissed. He glanced over his shoulder at the crib. Emma glimpsed into his soul. He got so little of her time or attention of late. It increased the importance of the cockerel costume she spent her evenings creating. And upped the stakes.

"Okay." She forced brightness into her reply and twinkled her fingers. "Tickle battle in your bedroom instead?"

Nicky fled, and Farrell followed. Emma set the baby monitor and carried the receiver next door. She chased Nicky around the room until she caught him, tickling the most vulnerable spots until he begged her to stop. They collapsed onto his double bed and Nicky snuggled against her ribs. "Harley Man is up to something." His statement caught her unawares and she cringed.

"Don't worry about it," she soothed. "Grown up stuff." Her mind flicked to Regan's issue, and she sighed.

Nicky leaned up on one elbow. "Why doesn't Daddy like Harley Man?" He watched her expression as though searching for clues in what she didn't say.

Emma shrugged. "They have a long history, Nick. From before we came along." She leaned her head against his pillow and closed her eyes, not wanting to reveal the truth. Christopher once betrayed Rohan, involved her in his dangerous scheme, and wheedled his way into their home. The answer demanded too much energy, something she lacked nowadays.

Nicky humphed and rested his head against her shoulder. "Does this hurt?"

"No. I promise, I'll be totally mended soon." Emma wrapped her arms around him and kissed his crown.

She didn't mean to fall asleep. Nicky snored, the pressure of his temple against her shoulder creating a painful tingle. Emma woke with a moment of confusion before releasing a groan of dismay. The evening had disappeared from around her, darkness filling the space between the curtains. A faint glow shone from the hallway, a triangular shaft of light crossing the rug and driving shadows into the corners. She lifted Nicky's head, pausing as he grunted and rolled onto his side. His school shirt hung adrift at the waist and his trousers twisted as he turned. Emma's fingers itched to free him from the uniform, but she didn't want to wake him. He owned an older set, which she kept for emergencies. He could wear it for a day while she laundered the one he'd slept in.

Her stomach twinged as Emma slipped from the bed. The baby monitor glowed with a faint green light on the bedside table, and she snatched it up and stuffed it into her pocket. She avoided the floorboards which creaked near the door, circumnavigating them and reaching the hall without causing a sound. The dog padded after her, and Emma waited until he'd sneaked past. He stared up at her, his tongue lolling and his tail swishing from side to side. No other sound disturbed the house. "Come on you," she said to Farrell. "Let's check on Stephie and settle you in the kitchen."

Her daughter slept with a thumb in her mouth and the other hand tucked under her cheek. Emma pulled the soft blanket over her shoulders and envied her relaxed expression. "Half your luck," she whispered. The clock showed the time as after midnight and she frowned at the sight of her phone lying on the floor next to the crib. She bent to retrieve it, wincing as she rose. She'd missed two calls from Rohan and a text.

'I've another job to do before I come home,' it said. *'Hope it went well today with Susan. Speak tomorrow.'*

Emma twisted her lips and whispered to the dog, "And we know what that other job is, don't we?" Sleep removed some of the weight, but it settled back into her chest like a block of iron. She jerked her head towards the hall and Farrell left ahead of her. She tapped the baby monitor in her pocket and closed the bedroom door. Making a mug of hot chocolate added itself to the task of settling Farrell for the night.

Emma padded down the rear stairs and along the main corridor of the lower floor. Loneliness nipped at the edges of her psyche as the ghosts belonging to the fabric of the manor taunted her with her isolation. Emma ignored them, unafraid of their secrets contained within walls built a millennium ago. Many other feet had trodden the same floorboards over the years, countless lost generations and hordes of servants. All nameless, all forgotten.

Christopher stood by the kitchen sink, staring out into the darkness. His laptop sat open on the table. "Hey." He spoke to her reflection in the window, without turning.

"I want a drink." Emma frowned at her statement. Owning the property meant she needed to give no explanation. It irritated her how she justified herself to Rohan's employee. She blinked away the tired rambling of her brain, reminding herself of Christopher's status as a friend. An annoying one.

Emma boiled milk in the microwave and added cocoa powder to her mug while she waited for the familiar ping.

Christopher returned to his laptop and tapped into a black screen containing screeds of indecipherable code.

"Is that from the flash drive?" She rubbed her eyes and watched the container of milk spin as it heated.

"Na." He lifted a glass of whiskey to his lips and sipped. Ice clinked against the crystal. "I got rid of that."

Emma's fingers froze on the microwave door handle. She spun to face him. "What?"

Christopher pursed his lips. "You didn't need it."

Emma hauled the microwave open. Her hand shook as she pulled the jug free. A wrinkled skin collected in the centre and she cast around for a spoon to remove it before dumping the contents into her mug. "Frederik gave it to me." Her voice shook with emotions she needed time to label. Milk splashed onto her hand as she tipped it into the mug. A piece of the skin dropped from the spoon and descended to the bottom of her hot chocolate. Emma lifted her drink, her grip unsteady. "How did you get rid of it?"

Christopher sighed and steepled his fingers in front of his face. Tiredness cast dark shadows beneath his eyes. "Does it matter?" He framed the question as rhetorical, inflaming Emma's temper further. It did. It mattered a lot. She'd intended to give it to Rohan. The flash drive was the actual risk. That's what the government wanted. She hadn't pursued the solution any further than that yet, knowing it left Regan still in danger but hoping for an element of negotiation. Fury transformed her muscles to wood and her body shook with the effort of not throwing the boiling liquid over Christopher.

"You've ruined everything!" Her growled statement caused him to jerk backwards.

"I don't think so." He shrugged, not caring that he'd detonated her carefully crafted solution. His index finger lifted and he jabbed it at his laptop screen. "I must get on with this. The dating site just suffered another big leak of names, only this one includes phone numbers and email addresses. Rohan wants me to reverse hack the dead drop." His long lashes swept across his hazel irises, hiding them from view for a millisecond. "Sorry. Tech talk."

The molecules in the room clanged with the dismissal. Emma stared down at her bare feet, the mug tilting in her grip. When she looked up again, Christopher resumed his tapping on the keyboard, his eyes darting left and right as he searched out something only he understood. Farrell clambered into his bed by the Aga and sank into its folds with a sigh. He rested his nose on his paws and stared up at her. Embarrassment bloomed as a flare along her skin and she strode across the kitchen as though escaping a bomb blast. The shrapnel of Christopher's arrogance dug into her spine as she closed the door behind her and slunk upstairs to bed.

Quadrants

Emma sat on a bench in the park outside the school the next morning, keeping an eye on Farrell as he gambolled from one side to the other. His keen nose swept for exciting scents in the undergrowth before his body surged in the other direction. A black lab tried to add himself to the game, lurching after Farrell's retreating tail. Its rounded belly lolled beneath stumpy legs as the distance grew between them. Farrell ignored him, more interested in the wonderful smells and the exhilaration of following them. His working cocker body arced in graceful movements, his spaniel paws hammering the ground in staccato beats. The lab admitted failure and trotted towards its mistress. The leash dangled from her wrist and she chatted to the owner of a pug which squatted in the grass.

Rohan had arrived home late and crawled into bed, still wearing his prosthetic leg. He slept on his back to avoid moving and Emma laid awake listening to his tired breathing, her hand resting on his chest. She fell asleep counting his heartbeats and fretted she'd detected a slight difference in the timing between each gentle thud.

The school bell rang and Emma imagined her son lining up with his class. He'd grown tall and wiry in the last year. She hated to admit that better food and living conditions might have helped the change. He'd settled beneath Rohan's care and tutelage, gaining in confidence and throwing his shoulders back to match his father's imposing frame.

She sighed and used her data to bring up an internet website. She clicked on the number displayed and waited for the call to connect. An automated response gave way to operatic music inappropriate for customers on hold. She pulled the phone away from her ear until a muted click preceded a voice filled with feigned enthusiasm. "Hello, you're through to the customer services department of TrackYourAncestry.co.uk and you're speaking with Barbara. How can I help you today?" Emma's lips parted with her rehearsed sentence, but the representative didn't give her long enough to speak. "Just to advise you that this conversation may be recorded for training and referred to as TrackYourAncestry.co.uk deems necessary. Your continuation with this phone call implies acceptance of these terms."

"Okay, thanks," Emma began. She drew a breath, but it proved a mistake.

"We do not sell or make your personal information available to third parties but may from time to time contact you with offers, deals and other items we deem of interest."

Emma waited, wondering if she'd finished reading the script or taken a break. A keyboard tapped in the background as though the owner of the fingers would rather jab someone to death. "Hello, are you there, caller?"

Emma huffed out a breath. "Yes. I'm here. Would you like my account number?" She turned on the bench to eyeball Farrell. He'd collected a pack of other dogs, keen to play his exhausting, silent game. He surged ahead of them, oblivious. The owner of a greyhound pushed a pram and shouted at it to come to her. Her frantic manner and accompanying screech meant it treated her to a bout of selective deafness. The woman glared across at Emma as though losing her dog wasn't her own fault. Emma ignored her and read her account number off the letter she'd crumpled into her pocket.

Barbara's keys tapped as she mouth-breathed into the phone. "I see we sent out the DNA kit at the end of July. Didn't you receive it? That's quite common. I can send out another, but after that, you must pay again or find a safer place to take delivery." She tutted in the background. "There's a note here from one of our sales team. They tried to contact you on the phone number listed and the person who answered said they'd pass on a message."

Emma released a groan. "I don't know who they talked to, but nobody mentioned it to me." She closed her eyes and hoped they hadn't used her personal data to find the landline when she failed to answer the secret number. She gnawed on her lower lip and gave herself a shake. Someone would have said something. "Look the test arrived, I took it and sent it back two days later. My friend ran it straight to the post office."

"Did you track it?" Barbara's keys tapped in the background with the speed of a court transcriber.

"No!" Exasperation laced Emma's tone. She'd asked Freda to add tracking but couldn't complain when the ninety-one-year-old apologised for forgetting that part of the process.

Barbara released a sigh. "It does state in the brochure that TrackYourAncestry.co.uk accepts no liability implied or otherwise for untracked samples travelling through the British postal service. We advise tracking, especially in areas where the post is unreliable. These areas include parts of Cornwall, rural Yorkshire and all of Scotland. You would have been offered insurance cover when you signed up to the website. That would have covered your sample for all types of loss except public riots or acts of God."

"It's a bottle of spit." Emma's chest tightened, and she blew out a controlled yoga breath. She'd signed up using her phone data, and the screen hadn't shown her an insurance option. The greyhound ran around Farrell in wide arcs, taking an eager boxer and a muzzled rottweiler with it. A white and tan spaniel kept pace with Farrell, a Yorkshire terrier bringing up the surprise rear. Its paws hit the ground with a rocking horse motion as it bounced along behind them, a blue bow wobbling between its ears. "So, you don't have my sample yet?" A growl of frustration entered her tone and her fingers gripped the arm of the bench. "Please, can you post another sample kit?"

"As you've admitted receiving the first kit, I'm unable to send you a replacement. If you'd like to pay for one, I can take your credit card details over the phone."

Emma gave a fake smile and moved sideways on the bench as a woman in a business suit inspected the lichen crusted seat. She winced and perched on the very edge, squatting to avoid the bird poop. "No thank you," Emma told the representative. "I'm not somewhere I can read that out to you." The business woman glanced sideways and her eyes widened. Emma admitted defeat and ended the call with, "Thanks for your help. I'll order another one later today." She hung up on Barbara's careful reading of a closing script, gaining a snapshot of herself as an entitled millennial. Her fingers trembled as she slipped her phone back into her handbag. A tut escaped her lips as she faced reality and knew she couldn't go through the deception with the DNA sample kit all over again.

Emma rose and brushed the back of her dress, releasing a sprinkling of crusty green lichen which tumbled to the dirt. She checked her watch and frowned, knowing Stephie would wake for her next feed soon. Allaine offered to mind her for an hour so Emma could spend a little time with Nicky on the journey to school. Her ex-husband got custody of Kaylee two nights a week and it left her at a loose end in the mornings when she would usually need to rush. Emma pressed her index finger and thumb together and slipped them between her lips. The shrill whistle she emitted made the woman next to her jump. "Thanks for the warning," she grumbled.

"Sorry." Emma waited for Farrell to change trajectory. He ran towards her, his shambling gang falling far behind as he sped like an arrow. His sleek black ears splayed behind him and his lips widened in a doggy smile of pure pleasure. Emma paused to allow the other dog owners to retrieve their pets, then she walked towards the road to collect her car with horrible thoughts about the post office playing through her mind.

Power

Emma brooded on the situation as she drove into town. She braced herself for a visit to her least favourite store to find something resembling a chicken's beak. Grey clouds rolled across the sky to obscure the sun in short bursts of warning. She left Farrell in the car with both the driver and passenger windows lowered. She browsed the aisles with little hope.

It seemed like a gift from God when she spotted the perfect appendage for her son's costume. She reached up, her fingers scrabbling on a top shelf to reach a yellow beak sitting alone amid feather boas and sparkly cowboy hats.

"We need a chat." The words hissed against her temple, the man sidling close as though bumping her by accident. Pain blossomed beneath her ribs as he dug something sharp against her stomach.

Anger flared in Emma's breast that she'd left herself so unguarded. She froze, wincing as a sting like a paper cut reached her brain.

"Nice and slow." The man's voice held an eerie calm, its cadence unhurried. Emma glanced to her right and released the breath making her lungs ache.

"What do you want?" She lowered her arm, the beak's flimsy elastic looped over her fingers. "I know it's the last one, but you can't have it." Headlines scrolled through her mind. *'Woman stabbed over plastic cockerel beak.'* Her shoulders slumped at the realisation *The Cock with the Crimson Comb* would be the death of her. Bloody Vladimir, whatever-his-name was. Bloody Russia too. Emma kept the mask dangling from her hand and counted her blessings she'd left Stephie at home with Allaine. The absence of all her special people infused her with confidence.

"Turn nice and slow and pretend we're friends."

The blade dug into Emma's side with more intention. A trickling sensation against her skin heralded blood. Rohan's tutelage in her memory overwhelmed the man's instructions. His training had continued through her pregnancy until her bulging stomach made it risky. Then he'd taught her the theory. Emma's lips moved as she murmured her husband's treasured words like a mantra. "I am my hero. I don't need rescuing."

"What?" The knife dug harder into her side, the point sharp as it cut through a thin layer of skin and fat. The scent of garlic on the stranger's warm breath made her recoil. "Are you wearing a wire?" Startled green eyes blinked in Emma's peripheral vision, and she turned with exaggerated slowness to examine their owner.

"I might be." She curved her lips into a tight smile. "Get your little pen knife out of my ribs." She gripped the mask's elastic, closing her fingers around the fragile thread. Her son would have his moment as *The Cock with the Crimson Comb*, even if it killed her.

He shook his head. A shock of ginger curls wobbled against his ears. Scruffy jeans and a tee shirt with a gaming emblem drowned his skinny body in fabric. Thin fingers with knotty joints clasped the knife. He cast his gaze over her light summer dress and grinned. "You're not wired. But I know who you are. Let's walk out of here together and discuss our mutual friend."

Emma's body stiffened as he tugged at her wrist. Her feet remained planted. The knife dug in enough to make her blink. "What mutual friend?" The thin elastic from the chicken mask trembled in her left hand. The oddness of the situation communicated itself to her brain and progressed beyond her possession of the chicken's beak.

"Come with me and you'll find out." The man shifted his stance, glancing down at Emma's waist. He withdrew the knife from her ribs and winced. "You bleed easy," he said. His indifferent tone made the red stain on her yellow dress the least of her problems. A nick in the soft fabric sent a flicker of temper into her eyes.

"I hate this shop." Emma spat the words with conviction. She'd ventured back for the mask, having exhausted all other options in the small town. "I'll shop online in future." She slipped the elastic over her left wrist and reached for her handbag. The strap sank from her shoulder to her forearm, removing any hope of reaching her mobile phone and sending an SOS to Rohan. The man shook his head and raised a bushy red eyebrow.

"Let's not do this here," he advised. Emma glanced down as the dull metal blade aimed for her stomach. The scar along the elastic of her underwear tingled as though to remind her of its vulnerability.

"Screw you," she hissed.

"What?" The single word sounded like a croak but ended in a grunt as Emma moved. She shifted her legs back in an ungainly hop before dipping forward and blocking the man's forearm with the hard edge of her right wrist. Her bag strap slipped into the way and tangled with the knife, but she ignored it, using her left hand to strengthen the block. The handbag bumped against her shins as she crossed her arms to wrap the man's forearm up and back into a painful arc. His head dipped forward as she hugged his elbow to her chest and pressed either side of the joint to straighten it beyond its limit. The chicken beak survived the first part of the manoeuvre but gave an unhealthy crack and crumpled beneath the pressure of his elbow against her stomach. Pain blossomed in a rush as the sharp plastic edge dug into the tender skin. Emma gritted her teeth, using the leverage of his compromised upper arm to drive him onto the ground. He grunted as the joint stretched, but to his credit, he didn't complain.

Emma ripped the knife from his hand, the trembling of the stretched tendons making the action easy. She threw it along the aisle and then halted. Fragments of the ruined mask rained down on the man's back, the ultimate insult being the slithering of the elastic from Emma's wrist and its negligible impact amid the wreckage. Rage blinded her. Her desire to be an exemplary mother seemed always hampered by her Andreyev connections. Her thigh muscles tightened as her rational mind fought to prevent her sealing his fate with a knee to the side of the head. He didn't deserve prime viewing of her fifth best underwear. Every muscle in Emma's body shook with temper.

The man laid on his side with his arm stretched behind him in the air, an expression of resignation on his face. Emma twisted the joint further and leaned forward to vent her anger over his head. "That was the last mask!" she screeched. Any semblance of the graceful Krav Maga moves disappeared as the frustrated mother emerged. Only the appearance of the two security guards thwarted her desire to rip his head from his neck.

"Oh no. It's her again." Pete screeched to a halt at the end of the aisle, his rubber-soled shoes squawking against the tiles. His skinny sidekick's lips peeled back from his teeth as he recognised Emma. "Just get the cops." Pete took a step back, shaking his head.

"I'll deal with her." Matt straightened his waistband with a purposeful hoisting action and approached Emma with decisive steps. "What seems to be the trouble here?" he demanded, a waver in his voice.

"He wrecked the last chicken mask!" Emma spoke from between gritted teeth, her body arched forward over her captive.

"I'm sure there's another in the stock room." Matt waved his arms in front of his face before his gaze took in the knife lying on its side a few metres away from the prone man. His eyes widened, and he swore before glaring at Emma. "What did you do?" His voice rose at the end of his question. "You can't stab someone over a chicken mask!"

"He stabbed me!" A mute appeal met the snarl on Emma's face. She pressed on the man's upper arm and he groaned and bent his face towards the tiled floor.

Matt noticed the streak of red on Emma's dress and panicked. He looked to Pete for help. "What do I do?" he appealed. "Call the cops!" But he'd distracted Emma enough for the man to utilise his minimal advantage. Rage had made her forget her training. She didn't move to safety or secure him enough to prevent him flipping backwards over her left thigh and landing next to her with gymnastic precision. He gave her a hard shove which sent her cannoning into the shelf, collapsing her right arm. The structure shook and fancy-dress costumes rained down on her head in a rustling rainbow of tinsel and glitz.

"Tell our friend hello from me," he hissed. "I won that auction and paid. This is your first warning." Emma listened to the squeak of his training shoes against the tiles as he bolted and Pete's panicked tones as he dialled the emergency number.

Coefficient

Emma sat on the familiar chair in the security office. She fumed and pressed a hand to her side where the knife blade nicked her skin. "I don't need an ambulance," she growled, naked fury in her voice. She huffed and fumed like a wild bull as humiliation added itself to the mix. Not only had she lost Nicky's chicken mask, she'd let her attacker escape, acquired a stomach wound and a bruise the size of Britain on her right arm.

"That scary Russian guy is here." Matt's eyes resembled saucers in his pale face as he skidded to a halt in front of the door. "He doesn't look happy." He swallowed and glanced back along the corridor. "I need to do something important." Running footsteps indicated his intention to avoid Rohan.

"Emma?" Rohan's bulk filled the doorway, storm clouds scudding through his glittering irises. "What happened?" His customary threat survey took in the blood on her dress and the ice pack covering her arm.

"Please, can we go home?" She rose and her handbag spewed its contents onto the floor. Pete glanced at her purse and lipstick, but made no attempt to help retrieve the items. Rohan bent in front of her, folding his giant frame to peer into her face.

"Are you okay?" His question sounded superfluous, but Emma sensed it probed beyond the blood and bruises.

"Yeah. Just angry." She frowned and her voice rose. "He attacked me and the chicken mask broke." Her eyes filled with tears of fury. They tumbled over her curled eyelashes and bounced off her yellow dress.

"Matt said there's one in the stockroom." Pete fled in a squeak of rubber soles and disappeared into the corridor. Emma gave a disgusting sniff and wiped her nose on the heel of her left hand.

"They won't come back," she concluded. "They're too afraid of you."

"Did they call the cops?" Rohan's blond brows knitted. "Do you need to give a statement?"

"I don't know. And no." Emma shook her head. "Can we leave?" She got to her feet and wrinkled her nose at the mess on the floor.

"Da." Rohan bent his left knee and kept his prosthetic straight. He used his impeccable balance to dip forward and retrieve her belongings from the stained carpet. Her lipstick looked insignificant in his large hands and he fumbled stuffing everything back into her small bag. "You need a bigger purse," he stated, catching her phone as it made a break for it.

Emma closed her eyes and shook her head. The smarting sensation from her right arm spread to include her neck. "I don't. Everything else goes in the big bag I carry around with Stephie. That's my no-baby bag." She laid the ice pack on the desk and sent silent thanks to Matt for providing it.

"Okay." Rohan gripped the strap in his giant fist and her pathetic bag dangled against his thigh. He held out his arm to her. "You will explain what happened on the way home. I'll get Hack to break into the security footage and use the recognition software to find the man who attacked you."

Emma slipped her left hand through his elbow and shook her head. "It was a silly fight," she conceded. "We both wanted the same thing." To dismiss Rohan's obvious concern, Emma forced a smile onto her lips. "Hey, I used the Krav Maga on him."

He blinked, and Emma sensed his brain working behind his azure irises as he conjured up the expected compliment. "Well done," he managed. "I'm proud of you." Her chest lost its tension when he didn't pick apart her tactics. Properly executed Krav Maga wouldn't have ended with an escaped assailant and injuries like hers.

They walked through the shop and Emma reinforced her earlier decision to never return. They'd just reached the sliding doors when a shout behind them made Rohan halt.

"No, let's leave," she hissed. "I don't want a fuss." She closed her eyes and gritted her teeth, refusing to engage as Rohan's body turned beneath her grip.

She heard him say, "Spasibo. Thank you." He continued walking, taking her with him. Emma opened her eyes as the bright sunlight outside warmed her eyelids. The automatic doors swished closed behind them. She glanced down at Rohan's hand and blinked at the sight of the chicken mask dangling from his fingers.

"Where did you get that?" Her expression lit from inside as delight mixed with relief.

"Security guard." Rohan's brow creased, and he squinted against the sunshine. He pulled a pair of sunglasses from his shirt pocket and slipped them onto his regal nose. The chicken mask bounced against his cheek.

"What's wrong?" Emma's feet ground to a halt in the last second before she stepped off the curb. "What's happened?"

Rohan stopped to face her. His nose wrinkled and the action pulled his upper lip higher. "I need to return to London. It's not a great time to leave you again."

"Problems?" Emma shifted her shoulder beneath the spreading ache, grateful to discover the pain involved her upper arm and not the joint. Another thought occurred to her and her eyes widened. "Please tell me you'll be home to see your son prance around as *The Cock with the Crimson* bloody *Comb*?"

Rohan snorted. "I don't remember expletives in the title, but yes, I'll make sure I'm home to witness Nikolai in yellow tights." He dangled the mask from his fingers. "And a beak which you were allegedly willing to die for." He blinked at the sight of a police car pulling up in a reserved parking spot in front of the store. His eyebrow curved upwards, and he looked hard at Emma. "You sure you want to just leave?"

"Yes." She steadied herself with a determined breath and clutched Rohan's arm to cross the car park. Farrell perched on the passenger seat with his head sticking through the open window. Guilt infused his panic at the sight of them, and he shot into the foot well and sat on his tail. A cool breeze nipped at Emma's bare legs and she glanced at the greying sky. Autumn threatened from behind the veneer of warmth.

Rohan questioned her on the way to Wingate Hall, but without conviction. Three phone calls interrupted their conversation. Her antics had stopped him packing for London and guilt formed a hard knot in her chest. Ray informed Rohan he'd driven his car back from town and left it in front of the house. Maureen phoned from the London office to check in regarding the dating site breach. Emma remained silent as Maureen detailed a name and location for the origin of the latest release. Someone sent a journalist an email with a list of over ten thousand account holders. She'd published it online. "Breadcrumbs," Rohan said with a sigh.

"Is that good or bad?" Emma frowned at the blood stain on her dress. It dried in the heat, becoming brown and crusty.

"They're leading me where I need to go." Rohan tapped his fingers on the steering wheel and peered through the driver's window. He looked for a space to pull into the traffic heading south. His blond fringe fluttered in the breeze from the passing vehicles, exposing a scar over his temple caused by flying shrapnel. Emma reached her painful arm across the handbrake and rested her palm on his thigh. Life flooded through him, vibrant and real. She sighed and leaned her head against the seat until Rohan depressed the gas pedal and joined the traffic.

"Do you know who leaked the rest of the data?" she asked. She turned her head and squinted at him.

"Yeah." A sly grin slid across Rohan's face. "The mark is more than a disgruntled employee. He's also the discarded lover of the company's chair. She finished their relationship and he didn't appreciate it. He understood her married status but didn't realise she'd used the database to find other dates. I paid him cash for the data and he assured me he didn't own copies. I made it clear I would pay him a visit he wouldn't like if I discovered otherwise."

"He lied?"

"No." Rohan shook his head. "But he's also married. His wife found the hard drive and took copies after discovering his infidelity. She's released the data to journalists, hackers, and anyone who shows an interest. He claims he didn't realise that when I paid the ransom."

"Wow!" Emma winced. "Sweet revenge on a cheating husband and his mistress. Perfect." She smiled. "Why don't you leave them to destroy each other?"

"A member of the board paid me to neutralise the risk. Now the truth is out and the financial investor has suspended the company chair. I don't want my reputation and abilities put in doubt, so I've agreed to act for the company and double my fee for the inconvenience."

Emma frowned. "You're going to visit the wife?" She gnawed on her lower lip, not sure she liked the idea. Rohan pressed his hand over hers and squeezed her fingers.

"I'm taking Maureen. She's better equipped to deal with hysterical females."

"Because she's a woman?" Emma recoiled. Her upper arm twinged, and she leaned forward to ease the pain.

"No!" Rohan's face creased into a mask of horror. "Because she's bloody terrifying."

Isosceles

Ray left the Mercedes on the driveway in front of the main door. Rohan parked Emma's car behind it and disappeared upstairs to finish packing his overnight bag. He wanted to examine the wound on her side but she refused. He shook his head and didn't press her. Little more than a trickle of blood stained her dress. The cut smarted, but nothing like the pain of childbirth, which created a recent enough comparison. Her right arm ached from the elbow upward in growing throbs, and she avoided moving it as she walked along the corridor to the kitchen. The empty room greeted her, and she frowned, checking the lounge and finding only silence in the sunlit room.

Ray fiddled with a screw in the banister of the rear staircase and stood aside to let her pass him.

"Is Allaine upstairs?" Emma's voice held a feigned lightness. Farrell wagged his tail and padded along the corridor towards the kitchen and his water dish.

Ray frowned. "No." He twisted the handle of his screwdriver to make a clicking sound. Then he popped off the tip and replaced it with one from his pocket. "I saw her walking towards her apartment with the baby. Is the captain ready to go to the station yet?"

"Not quite. He's just packing." Emma's shoulders slumped at the prospect of another night alone. And another day without having their difficult conversation. "I wish he didn't have to keep leaving." The comment slipped free and she pursed her lips to stop more confidences spilling. She shot a sideways glance at Ray and found him regarding her with a raised eyebrow.

"Everything okay?" He cocked his head as though it might give him extra sensory power. "It's none of my business, but if you want to talk, I'm always here."

"Thank you." Emma sank onto the third step and gathered the fabric of her dress behind her knees. The action hid the blood stain. She leaned forward so her body rested along her thighs. "I have a lot on my mind."

"Yeah." Ray pulled a brass screw from his pocket and clasped it between his lips. He concentrated on fitting the end of the screwdriver into a flat headed screw already in place. His muscles flexed and his knuckles protruded as he twisted the handle. Emma appreciated his silence and lack of criticism. He'd known more sadness in his lifetime than she could imagine bearing. With a proven track record of loyalty, he created a bubble of safety around her in Rohan's absence.

"Someone asked for my help recently." Emma lifted her index finger and traced the delicate swirls a wood turner made when he created the spindles for the staircase. This part of the mansion dated back to six centuries earlier, but the man's craft still spoke his name. "I let them down by allowing someone else to destroy a thing they entrusted into my care."

Ray popped the screw from between his lips and jabbed it into the next hole. "So, you didn't destroy it?"

Emma's shoulders relaxed. He hadn't asked what it was she'd lost, focussing on the main issue. The fact she lost it at all. "No. Someone else did. But I could have used it to help them out of their situation."

Ray tightened the second screw and gave the banister rail a shove. It remained fixed, and the crow's feet at the corners of his eyes crinkled into a smile of satisfaction. He glanced up at Emma. "Don't tell the conservation officer from the council I used newer screws, will you?" Mischief danced in his irises as glittery specks.

Emma knitted her brow and peered beneath the banister rail at his handiwork. "They look original to me."

"Not authentic enough for him." Ray put his hands on his hips and leaned forward, glaring at Emma from beneath his eyebrows. His voice changed to an accurate impression of the council's heritage representative. "It's an offence to destroy the provenance of a historical artifact, don't you know?"

Emma smiled and ran her index finger over the smooth wood which many hundreds of hands had gripped. Hundreds of hands. Hundreds of people weighed down by their cares as they trudged upstairs. Or others with a light, fleeting touch as they skipped to the upper levels of the house. Her eyes glazed as her archivist's mind sympathised with the council officer charged with protecting the history for future generations. Ray's light touch on her shoulder caused her to jerk and give a blink of alarm. "What's wrong, Emma?" His voice softened. "I can go back to the scrap yard and find older screws." He climbed up to her level and sank onto the step next to her. "Is that what you want?"

"No." She rested her chin on her forearms and clasped her knees. "The screws are fine. He's right about protecting our history, but he's not the one who'll break his neck when the banister gives out in the middle of the night. I will and I'll have a screaming Stephie in my arms."

Ray nodded. "Or the captain on his crutches."

"Yeah." Emma frowned. She turned to face him and their knees bumped together. "Can I ask you something?" She studied the lines of his face as his expression remained open and unguarded. He'd once used his skills as an army medic to stitch a knife wound to her neck, using household supplies while she bled onto the kitchen table. His son worked as a local detective, yet Ray never betrayed Rohan's undercover role as the Actuary.

Ray shrugged, his expression guileless. "Yeah."

"Did you ever meet Frederik?"

Ray's left eyebrow quirked upwards, and he gave a slow nod. "He visited with his wife in the spring, didn't he? You drove her for lunch at Foxton locks while Rohan showed him the property." His eyebrow gave a waggle as though of its own accord, and Ray tapped the side of his nose. "But actually they hid in the folly and geeked out over the tech."

Emma nodded and released a sigh. The day had seemed so full of hope. Susan marvelled over Emma's pregnancy, and they'd chatted and laughed as Nicky skipped ahead with Farrell. Jay stayed in his harness with great reluctance, so they'd stopped at Farndon Fields on the way home, so the dogs could chase each other on the open field. They'd proved a handful together and both had forgotten their obedience training when the time came to climb back into the car. Her lips parted in an empty smile. "It seems so long ago, but it's just a few months. Too much has happened." Her fingers twitched, wanting to caress the sore spot over her panty elastic where the obstetrician carved a long line through muscle and fat to save her life. She swallowed and to her surprise, Ray slipped an arm around her shoulders and pulled her close. He rested his cheek on the top of her head. Emma gritted her teeth as warning tears pricked her eyes. Ray's silence and refusal to use handy platitudes touched a raw space in her heart. She had Nicky and Stephie, but he didn't speak the obvious consolations. Gratitude persuaded the tears to plop onto her dress.

"It's normal to grieve a future you'll never have," he whispered. "I understand. For a while, it's as though there's no path for you because someone dumped rubble on the one you'd taken." He pressed a kiss to the top of her head. "And so, you sit there for a while and then you pick a different direction."

Emma sniffed and nodded against his shoulder. "I think that's what I'm doing, trying to find my path again. But I keep getting pulled back to stare at the old one and everything seems impossible."

"I know." Ray squeezed her against him. "But it's like those screws I just fitted. They're not the originals, but they do the job. The council guy will know by looking at them, but no one else will notice. He's trained to hunt for anomalies and we're not. You're doing great at pretending it doesn't hurt. But everyone who loves you can see it does."

Emma held her breath. She'd heard his words and sensed the warmth as they hit home. But his wisdom had stretched beyond his original intention. She'd been pretending, and it came as a shock to realise she'd done a poor job of covering up her grief. But his words dislodged more than that fact. She'd missed something important. Ray was right, she didn't have the correct training and so she'd ignored the signs.

Emma jerked upright and wiped her eyes on the back of her wrist. She inhaled and fixed a smile on her face. "Thanks Ray." She planted a kiss on his rough cheek and he released her with surprise in his eyes. "You've really helped." She rose, straightened her spine and skipped down the three steps to the tiled floor of the corridor. "I need to feed Stephie. See you later."

She waved over her shoulder, not wanting to acknowledge Ray's knitted brow or the anxiety making his irises sparkle like azure.

"Damn it!" she cursed as she jogged towards the front doors. "How could I be so naïve?" A light rain speckled the driveway as she stepped outside and turned right. She followed the path towards Allaine's apartment over the stables, careful to watch her footing while texting her revelation to the one person who would understand.

'It's not about the flash drive.'

He replied with a single exclamation mark and Emma smiled to herself. She winced as her aching breasts told her even before she arrived that Stephie was calling.

Scalene

She found Allaine in her apartment. She looked up at her as Emma entered. "Hey, girl. You might have missed Rohan. He drove off with Ray while you were out."

Emma pursed her lips. "Yeah. He met me in town and we came back together. London's calling, so he's packing to leave." Stephie cooed and blew bubbles, but cranked up to more demanding levels when she scented her mother.

"Sit in the rocking chair by the window if you want." Allaine waved towards a wooden framed seat situated by double doors leading to a veranda. Emma took her grumbling daughter and settled back against the floral cushion.

"Are you happy up here?" Stephie thrashed her arms and legs with growing impatience as Emma released the buttons at the front of her dress.

"For sure. I'm so grateful to you and Rohan for letting us stay." Allaine pottered around in the adjoining kitchen and mugs clanked as she pulled them from the dishwasher.

Emma rocked as Stephie fed with enthusiasm. "You've helped me out more than I had any right to expect." She smiled across at her. "You were my first friend in Market Harborough. I wouldn't trust anyone else to babysit Stephie for more than a few hours."

Water trickled as Allaine finished making their drinks. She walked across the rug and placed Emma's on a side table. "It's hot," she warned. "Maybe wait a few minutes."

She sank onto the sofa and slipped off her shoes before pulling her bare feet onto the cushions. Emma closed her eyes against the warmth of the sunshine spilling onto her face. "Tell me about your interview?" She opened one eye to observe Allaine's expression. "You mentioned it went okay, but I want the gory details."

Allaine drew her knees up to her stomach. She wrapped her arms around her shins before answering. "I didn't get the job." She rested her chin on her knees, making her wiry body as small as possible. "It's stupid to think I'd walk back into the job market like I didn't just take a two decade sabbatical."

Emma picked through her usual sentences of commiseration and abandoned them all. She lifted Stephie into her arms and rose, moving across to sit next to Allaine. "I'm sad that happened," she said. "Please understand you're fine to stay here as long as you want."

"But I wanted to pay you some rent." A fat tear rolled down Allaine's cheek. She brushed it away with a jabbing motion, not caring that she scratched her face in the process. "You've been kind enough to renovate this place and let us live here. I wanted to pull my weight."

Emma bumped her shoulder against Allaine's and shook her head. "I understand. It feels like charity, and that's not always as good for the soul as people might believe. I get it, Allaine. But right now, I'd rather you were here than not here." She twisted her lips. "I said you were my first friend, but the truth is, you're my only friend."

Allaine blinked and wiped her nose on her sleeve. "You're always surrounded by people." She frowned. "Ray, Freda, Christopher."

Emma raised an eyebrow. "And I love them all. But I wouldn't tell Ray my nipples hurt from breastfeeding and I couldn't tell Freda because everyone at the Baptist coffee shop would know by tomorrow."

Allaine pursed her lips and fought the smile wanting to break free. "I'm sure Christopher would express sympathy."

Emma frowned and her expression clouded. She concentrated on the baby lying like a lead weight in her arms. Stephie's hands hung limp, and she slept, satiated and full. Her rounded tummy protruded from between the buttons of her lace cardigan. Allaine slipped her arm around Emma's shoulders. "Sorry. I didn't mean to suggest anything inappropriate. It's impossible to understand your relationship with him." She sniffed and released her legs into a more relaxed posture. "You're the last person I should punish for my mess."

Emma sighed, the long exhale seeming to deflate her. "Yeah. Christopher." She said his name with more conflict than she intended to reveal. She lifted one of Stephie's hands and it slithered free and flopped over her stomach. The baby stirred but didn't wake. Emma smiled and wished she could relax with such abandon. She turned to Allaine, a frown lining her brow. "Please, can I leave Stephie with you for a little longer? There's something I need to do."

"Sure." Allaine leaned sideways to collect the bundle and regarded Emma with narrowed eyes. "Is everything okay?"

Emma nodded and extracted herself from the sofa. When she rose, Allaine blinked. "What happened to your arm?" she demanded. "And is that blood on your dress? Why didn't you say something?"

Emma glanced down at the spreading bruise and inhaled. The sleeveless yellow dress contrasted with the black and purple to create a dramatic effect. "It's not as bad as it looks," she said. Her arm ached when she lifted it, the line from the shelf stark and angry against the darkening skin. "I fell in the shop earlier. Ray dropped Rohan there so he could drive me home." She forced her lips into a smile and held up her other fist in victory. "But I secured the last chicken mask in the town, so it was worth the hassle."

Allaine frowned and didn't look sure. "Kaylee is going as the police officer character from 'Daddy I Worry About You' by Clarke Paris. She's borrowing some of Will's uniform." Her expression darkened and she clasped Stephie closer. "He's taking her to school that day, so I won't see her until afterwards." Pain radiated from her blue irises and the wave of her hand lacked energy.

"I can take a photo of Nicky and Kaylee together, if you'd like?" Emma didn't suggest Allaine gate-crash Will's moment with his daughter. She ached for her, but they'd made their choice and nothing she suggested would change the outcome.

Allaine nodded and the light of hope reappeared in her eyes. She jerked her head towards the stairs. "Hurry, Mummy. Or your daughter will wake and gripe for the rest of her feed before you get back here."

"Okay." Emma let herself out of the apartment and traversed the veranda. She passed Ray's identical lodging and clattered down the wooden steps to the cobbled stable yard. The loose boxes stood open and empty, their doors pulled back on their hinges. But the buildings remembered the busy scrape of shod hooves on the cobbles and the occasional neigh of an impatient horse. Their whisper caused the hairs to stand up on Emma's arms as she followed the concave drainage pipe set between the stones to the end of the yard. Then she turned right and braced herself for trouble.

Equivalent

I vy covered the outside of the folly on its south side, ragged brown tendrils clinging to the brick in a last bid for salvation. Ray spent hours liberating the building from its clutches, sawing and poisoning the hardy roots in a never-ending battle to conclude its reign. Emma wrinkled her nose at the resulting devastation from the war of man against vegetation. The ivy had shrouded the folly in its embrace for over a century, wreaking havoc to the stone and cement beneath the cover of its evergreen leaves. Once Ray destroyed the ivy, he would need to repair the structure. Rust flaked off the balustrade and dotted Emma's fingers as she climbed the ten steps up to the entrance.

She paused and took a deep breath before hammering on the wooden front door. Christopher's Jeep sat on gravel to her left. The sun's rays glinted off the chrome of his Harley, parked in a shed beyond it. The open roll door and the metallic clicking betrayed Christopher's recent arrival. She narrowed her eyes and glared up at the camera drilled into the lintel. "I know you're there!" she snarled. "Don't make me fetch my key!"

Creaks and dull thuds echoed from inside the building. Emma counted Christopher's footsteps as he followed the staircase around the outer wall of the interior, giving a brief pause as he turned another dogleg and continued. The front door opened with a whoosh and he greeted her at the same time as brushing his black fringe from his eyes. "What's wrong?" His bike leathers hugged his body as though painted onto him at birth. His chocolate irises lit up with a sparkle as he stood aside to admit her.

"Nothing is wrong." Emma frowned at the snippiness of her tone and moderated her frustration. "Ray said he'd almost won the battle with the ivy. Allaine is looking after Stephie for a few minutes, so I've walked across to admire it for myself.

"What happened to your arm?" Christopher's eyes darkened to the colour of coals and he reached out to touch the bruise. He cocked his head as though hoping he'd discovered the flaw in her marriage before biting his tongue to prevent himself from saying it out loud. "I'd like to see the other guy." His unblinking gaze studied every tell-tale nerve in Emma's face. He'd watched over her for long enough to learn the signs of distress or desperation. Emma smiled and blocked his view of the turmoil in her heart.

She shrugged. "You wouldn't. He escaped, but without the chicken mask he picked a fight over." She kept her tone light and surveyed the results of an expensive renovation. "Show me what Anton's money paid for."

"Oh. Okay." Christopher dropped his gaze and Emma pushed away the disappointment the action conveyed. He cleared his throat and waved an arm around the expansive downstairs vault. "Ray's a pretty decent builder for a medic."

Emma nodded and spun on her heels. She clasped her hands behind her back and ignored the tug of her sore biceps. Christopher hissed and snatched at her wrist. "There's blood on your dress!" He jerked his head towards the wound she'd forgotten. Emma tuned in to the faint sting and shook her head.

"It's nothing."

"What aren't you telling me?"

She closed her eyes while her brain scrabbled behind them for an answer. Her haste to get to Stephie stopped her changing her dress or examining the knife cut. She settled on an excuse and replied through gritted teeth. "A man pushed me in the store and I burst a stitch. I don't want to talk about it."

Christopher gave a shallow nod and released her wrist. "If you're sure." He took a step away from her, as though her mention of the hysterectomy conjured a wall between them.

The awkwardness in his stance and the way he backed off filled Emma with both relief and regret.

"Is Ray planning to plaster the walls?" She pointed at a scaffolding platform set up at the far end of the room. Wheels fixed to the corners made it mobile.

Christopher shrugged. "I'm not sure. We're still working out how to stop that council surveyor gaining access." He drew his lips back in a sardonic smile. "The upstairs doesn't exactly reflect the period of construction."

Emma winced. "I hoped he'd dropped that. Folly architectural traditions made them objects of decoration to demonstrate the affluence of the land owner. I guess they're still covered by local building regulations." She glanced at her watch and flapped her hand. "Okay, show me the rest."

The downstairs comprised a lounge, kitchen and dining area. Bare concrete made up the floor surface with a rug placed in front of an open fire. Ray had worked hard on the brick walls, removing the decayed lath and plaster caused by a roof leak and sanding them smooth. Emma stroked the wall as she mounted the staircase to the upper level. His clever repointing of the brick proved seamless, the new cement invisible against the original. The archivist in her brightened, convincing her they hadn't desecrated it in the name of necessity.

The staircase finished at a gap in the mezzanine floor installed by Lord Ayers in the 1960s. A heavy pile carpet dulled the sound of their footsteps as they stepped across its gunmetal grey surface. The floor contained two rooms and Emma glanced into the first. Christopher hissed from his position behind her. "I would have tidied up if I'd known you wanted to see it." He swallowed mid-sentence, betraying his discomfort with her unexpected presence. He skirted her in the doorway and picked up discarded clothes from the floor, tossing them onto the unmade bed and hauling the bedspread over the heap. Emma inhaled a mingled scent of sweat and fresh paint and wrinkled her nose. A single bulb burned in the centre of the ceiling, the tiny window near the roof line useless as a source of light.

"Your poor mother would be ashamed," she mused, withdrawing her head and shoulders from the room. She kept her tone jovial, but the barb remained. Christopher spread his messiness to the main house and the kitchen he frequented far too often. The one downstairs in the folly appeared immaculate. Unused.

Emma stepped into the second room and halted. Christopher's scattergun approach to life ended at the doorway. A floor to ceiling glass wall halved the room. An air conditioning unit whirred behind it. Server racks stood shoulder to shoulder, flashing lights indicating the online sentience of the machines stacked within them. Three keyboards and five monitors rested on a wooden workbench which faced the servers. A split screen showcased four angles of the front gates and the road beyond, flickering as the view switched to widen and shorten the aperture. Emma inhaled and released the held breath. "It's quite impressive," she acknowledged. She kept her gaze on the security screen, watching as it switched view and waiting to see if it revealed the interior of Wingate Hall. Christopher read her mind and gave a tight smile.

"I didn't put cameras inside the house." He sounded resigned, and Emma sensed his disappointment. He exhaled in a snort of derision. "Rohan sweeps for bugs and cameras, anyway. It would be a waste of time bothering."

Emma nodded. She hadn't known that. But it wasn't the reason she'd walked across the field or risked putting herself anywhere near the horny Irishman's bedroom. "I want the flash drive," she said. A cursory scan of the desk showed numerous devices, but not the one she wanted.

"I got rid of it." Annoyance flashed in his eyes and he circumnavigated her to slump into his office chair. "The stuff on it was a waste of time." His leathers squeaked against the fabric as he leaned forward. The exaggerated breath of frustration disturbed the only piece of paper on the desk. It appeared lonesome and obsolete amid all the technology which clicked, flickered and whirred around it.

"You're lying." Emma exhaled in a rush. She'd resisted telling Christopher about finding Regan and battled a constant guilt at her subterfuge. His sense of superiority stood between them like a wall, preventing her from confiding in him for the first time in more than a year. He'd mocked her, demonstrating his lack of belief in her skills. She clamped her teeth down over her bottom lip, fighting the urge to scream at him.

The uneven plaster and whitewashed walls contrasted with the flush of Christopher's cheeks. His fingers tapped on the nearest keyboard, bringing up a dark screen filled with code. He added an underscore and removed it, his gaze falling onto the slip of paper before flicking up to meet Emma's watchful stare. "You've seen the folly now." His tapping continued. "Is there anything else?"

Emma held out her hand. She tightened the tendons in her arm and wrist to mask her shaking. "Flash drive." She snarled the word, sick of his one-upmanship. "I hate how you've set me up to fail." Her words cut through the air like a knife. "I thought better of you. Is it so bad that Frederik came to me instead of you?"

Christopher's jaw gritted, creating a line through his cheek. Suppressed laughter sparkled behind his irises as arrogance rolled off him as a nauseating stench. "Fine!" he snapped. He reached across the desk and plucked the flash drive from the nearest USB port, holding it between thumb and forefinger. "Remember this when it's too late," he jibed. "All I've ever done is protect you, Em."

She crossed the floor and held out her hand, closing her fingers around the metallic rectangle as he dropped it into her palm. Her lips parted to warn him not to lie to her again, but sealed shut against the futility of it. He would. He just did. She hadn't had the benefit of his extensive training or his years of experience. But she knew a liar when she met one, as false as the screws in the banister rail.

Emma whirled from the room and retraced her steps to the front door. But she paused with her hand on the doorknob as curiosity burgeoned. Her footsteps tapped across the concrete floor to where she remembered emerging from the tunnel months earlier. Ray disguised the aperture with an ornate set of crafted oak cupboards which covered the entire wall. He'd taken trouble to create an authentic replica of those at the main house, bevelling the edges and giving them an aged appearance. Emma stepped back and surveyed his handiwork. She figured she'd need to open each door to find the entrance to the tunnels. A key in the one at the end betrayed the location, but also showed Christopher's intention to maintain his privacy. He could stampede through her home at his leisure, but guarded against anyone doing likewise. "Typical!" Emma hissed to herself.

She poked her head into a bathroom next to the front door and nodded with approval. Ray had outdone himself with the level of craftsmanship he'd put into the space. A claw footed bath sat beneath a layer of dust, testament to Christopher's lack of interest in a candlelit soak. But the wet tiles surrounding the overhead shower and the steady drip from the plastic curtain revealed his preference.

"Are you imagining me slippery and naked?" His voice tickled her ear at the same time as his chest bumped her shoulder. She jumped, and he laughed. The flash drive fell from her hand and skittered into the puddle from the shower.

"No!" Emma scowled, drawing her features into a look filled with more anger than denial. She bent to retrieve the flash drive and wiped it on her skirt. The scar tissue ached and set off the sting from the knife blade. "Now, see what you did!" she protested, focusing her energy on drying the device.

Christopher's black lashes fluttered and mischief back lit his smile. Emma glanced up at him and tears prickled behind her eyelids. The Irishman was her Achilles heel. In that moment, she both loved and hated him with equal passion. The sob escaped her throat, surprising her as much as it did him. Emma pressed her fingers over her lips to hold in the ones building up behind it. Christopher's leathers squeaked as he wrapped his arms around her and pulled her against his chest.

Emma rested her forehead against his shoulder and collected her thoughts and emotions into a pile manageable enough to stow back in her box of grief and regrets. "I'm fine," she whispered. Lifting the hem of her dress, she used the fabric to wipe her eyes. Black mascara left shades of grey in streaks across the material. Emma swallowed. "Thank you for the flash drive." She held it up between them and managed a watery smile. Christopher's lips twitched, and a line appeared and disappeared between his eyebrows. His mouth opened as though he wanted to say something, but he pursed his lips shut and fought the sentence back into submission.

"Take care out there," he growled after an awkward moment of silence. His soothing tone washed over Emma like summer rain.

"I will." She sniffed, wiped her nose across her wrist and stepped over the threshold of Christopher's lair. The door closed behind her with a click, and she imagined him calling up the camera app on his phone to watch her retreat. The corners of the flash drive dug into her palm, but her fingers refused the order to relax their wooden grip. A gentle breeze and the sun's tender kisses warmed her body and dismissed the icy tremors trickling up from her core. Emma scrubbed at her face to remove the tears, pausing at the bottom of Allaine's stairs to make herself presentable. She took a deep breath before jogging up the steps to the veranda and striding to Allaine's ranch slider. Stephie's head bumped against Allaine's shoulder as she entered the apartment.

"She woke up." Allaine turned to view Emma over Stephie's bouncing crown. "Maybe she's still hungry."

"Yeah." Emma manhandled her daughter from Allaine's arms and kissed her downy forehead. She dropped into baby-talk as she carried Stephie towards the kitchen. "That's what happens when we fall asleep in our brunch," she cooed. "You and I should walk to the house for round two and then you can sleep in your crib. What do you think to that?"

Emma killed the call, muted her phone and dropped it into her open handbag. Stephie gurgled against her collarbone, leaving a wet trail across the front of her yellow dress.

Constant

Emma stood on the gravel drive and watched Rohan's Mercedes retreat into the distance. He hadn't waited for her to get home and she couldn't shake the worry that she'd disappointed him. Stephie abandoned all hope for the second part of her feed and dropped to sleep over Emma's shoulder. Her warm breath caressed the soft skin of her mother's neck. An icy wind whipped up from the north, bringing with it the harbinger of a late autumn and a bitter winter. Emma shivered and hurried into the house.

The library of Wingate Hall held a special place in her heart. It provided a sanctuary for her and a place to think. The scent of aged paper and leather binding greeted her as she slipped inside and shut the solid oak door behind her with a click. She closed her eyes and absorbed the peace which came with standing amid the written accounts of witnesses to history. Anton purchased the Ayers' entire collection, perhaps hoping to one day delight her by showing her the floor to ceiling shelves loaded with books. Instead, he'd left it to her in his will and let her find it for herself. A reconditioned chaise sat to the right of the long sash window, sheltering from the damaging glare of stray, early morning sun rays. Emma settled her sleeping daughter on the rich sapphire fabric and surrounded her with cushions to stop her rolling. Stephie rooted for her thumb and gave a deep sigh.

Emma glanced at the fire she'd laid months before and not used. A chill followed her into the room, and she rubbed her arms to banish the goose flesh. She walked towards the mantle and the ready box of matches, wondering if starting a fire meant declaring the long summer finally defeated. "Soot and books don't mix," she mused, sliding the match box open and peering in at the regimental incendiaries nestled inside it. But she felt cold, and it wasn't yet time to activate the unwieldy central heating system, which would flood the radiators with scalding water and make the gas meter spin like an expensive windmill. Emma relented and lit the fire, finding the activity calming. The action of holding the flame in just the right spot and watching it lick against the paper and kindling invoked a primal need for survival. She knelt on the rug, the crackling of fledgling sparks creating a comforting aura of peace and security. Emma marvelled at the way the dance of the amber flames warmed her heart before the fire's glow even reached her skin. "Better already," she whispered.

She rose and tugged open the doors of an oak cupboard next to the window. She slid out the custom shelf Ray built into its carcass and booted up the computer hidden within its shadows. A monitor flickered to life and Emma pulled up the application she used for cataloguing the books. Her notebook wasn't where she'd left it, and she rolled her eyes. A search of the cabinet's drawers revealed it in the bottom beneath a pair of cotton gloves.

Three dusty tomes from The Complete Works of Shakespeare sat next to her keyboard and she pulled on the gloves before opening the cover of the first with care. The spine creaked, and she winced. A note fluttered free, the scrawled handwriting shaped in pencil on a torn square of acid-free paper.

'Hope these are the right ones. Love Nick.'

A smile touched Emma's lips. He'd climbed to the top of the ladder to fetch down the volumes for her. He scaled it like a monkey, showing no fear for his own safety and reminding her of Anton's zest for life. But he'd inherited his uncle's foolhardiness. He wasn't meant to climb without an adult present.

Emma crossed the room and stared up at the gap where the books had rested for decades. Perhaps longer. Nicky replaced the texts she'd already catalogued, and the end one leaned across the gap to touch the hard cover on the other side.

A book of receipts and invoices she'd found in the butler's pantry showed Freda's brother-in-law had renovated the library in the 1960s. He'd removed the hazardous Scheel's Green wallpaper with its arsenic colouring. The few spaces not covered by the original oak shelving wore a regal Tudor rose. The south facing aspect kept it shielded from direct sunshine after the initial morning glow. Emma glanced at the fireplace as the phurnacite in the grate heated and a piece of charred kindling slid onto the hearth.

"So much for archival conditions." She frowned and returned to the books. Her careful fingers lifted the hard cover and she examined the date embossed on the first leaf. "1714," she whispered. "Second edition of The Complete Works of William Shakespeare, London, by J. Tonson in the Strand." The shape of the lettering and the copperplate engravings enthralled her. Emma lost herself in her work, detailing the book's attributes and recording any damage to it. She allocated a number to it, photographed the front cover on her phone and emailed it to herself. Her busy fingers wrote the number in pencil on a sheet of acid free paper and tucked it inside a small oven bag. It slipped between the cover and fly leaf, and she moved the heavy volume aside to deal with the next one. A dehumidifier hummed in the corner to fight against mildew. The fire wouldn't help, but she couldn't bear working in a fridge.

Emma didn't hear the door open behind her.

"What is your plan?"

She jumped and released a squeak of fright, hating how desperate that sounded. Her hands were fists by the time she'd spun around, but she dropped them with an exasperated sigh at the sight of Winston gazing at a set of Encyclopedia Britannica at waist height. She relaxed her shoulders and turned back to her computer monitor. "Nothing with those. They're only worth about two hundred pounds, but Nicky likes them. I'll catalogue them and perhaps move them to a different shelf."

Winston jerked his head towards the cupboard next to Emma, which housed a scanner. "That's an expensive device. What will you do with it?"

Emma frowned and gritted her teeth. "I'm making digital copies of the books without damaging them. The delicate ones will go to a London museum and they'll photograph them from a cradle to protect the spines." She kept her back to Winston, not wanting to feed his demand for drama. "I'm attempting to preserve a little history for my son and besides, I don't remember inviting you here." Her fingers paused over the keyboard as she darted a glance at the closed cupboard door, realising he'd snooped to discover the scanner. She released the held breath and continued tapping in a description of water damage on the rear cover. Winston moved around the room in her peripheral vision, stopping to peer at Stephie.

Stealth and maternal instinct put Emma next to him in three strides. She held up her hand in warning to him not to touch her daughter. He flattened his lips into an insincere smile and took a calculated step away from the chaise. "I mean you no harm, Emma," he said. He continued speaking as he examined the books on a different shelf. "You asked for help with your ancestry issue." His blue irises flashed as his eyelids narrowed to slits. "Don't you remember?"

Emma swallowed. "So?" She edged closer until gauging it would take him more time to reach Stephie than her. "What did you discover?" Her heart set up a dizzying tattoo in her chest, sending blood to pound across her eardrums.

Winston pushed his hands into his trouser pockets and took his weight on his right leg. His posture appeared casual, but Emma detected weakness in his left side. She gritted her teeth and decided where she'd kick him if he ventured any closer to his granddaughter. "I discovered you'd behaved with more than a little foolishness." His smile clashed with his words.

"What?" Emma frowned. "Rohan knows about my adoption." She injected scorn into her voice. "We don't keep secrets from each other." She bit her lip to stop herself adding the word, *anymore*.

"But he doesn't know you went looking for your family, does he?" Victory back lit Winston's eyes as he sensed himself holding the upper hand. His smile disappeared, replaced by disdain. "I'll guess he doesn't realise you joined an ancestry site or provided your DNA to strangers."

Emma swallowed and found herself in the last place she wanted to be, on the wrong side of Winston. She stuck her chin in the air. "Rohan won't mind. Anyway, I don't need your help," she spat. "It's sorted."

Winston gave a snuff of sarcastic laughter. "I don't think so." He lowered his head to view her over the top of his spectacles. "Do you know how stupid it is to entrust your genetic code to an organisation which is subject to laws and regulations?" He lifted a fine boned index finger and jabbed it at her. "You'd no control over that sample from the moment it left your hands. Utter stupidity."

Emma gaped. Any semblance of a sensible retort abandoned her, retreating to the back of her mind and hiding there. She closed her eyes to avoid looking at him and managed a whispered conclusion. "You intercepted my sample, didn't you?"

"I most definitely did!" A hint of Slavic flavour crept from behind the impeccable image of the English gentleman. "And you're wrong. Alexei would mind very much. We don't enter this world with many assets, Emma. But we guard those which belong to us." He pulled the thin spit container from his jacket pocket and held it out to her.

Emma blinked. "You didn't use it?" She took a step forward, disappointment creating a heady disregard for manners or safety. "You said you'd help me, but you've stood in the way of me trying to help myself." Her gloved fingers trembled as she reached for the vial in his outstretched hand. It took all her self-control not to snatch it and beat him around the head with it, imagining the plastic casing shattering and her precious DNA dribbling onto the rug. Emma jumped as his fingers snapped shut at the last second. With the skill and precision of a tennis player, Winston Wright flicked his wrist, and the container spun loose. It moved in a gentle arc, too fast for her to intercept its fateful trajectory. She inhaled as the fire swallowed her sample, the plastic hitting the coal with a dull tap before melting and spreading its contents across the super-heated phurnacite.

"Get out!" Her croaking voice held determination. "Get out and don't come back again." She lifted a shaking hand and pointed towards the door. The white cotton glove shivered against her skin.

"You're too hasty." Winston dug his hands into his jacket pockets and pursed his lips. The tilt of his head increased his air of arrogance.

"I don't care." Exhaustion gripped Emma's chest in its knotty fingers and twisted. She tried to push her shoulders back against its bite and failed. "We're doing just fine without your interference, thank you. Show yourself out and don't return unless you've rung the bell at the gate and waited for permission."

Stephie snuffled against the cushions, the reminder of her presence giving Emma clarity. She jabbed her index finger at the door, realising the mistake she'd made in ever confiding in the wily geriatric.

"As you wish." Winston turned and Emma fancied she saw a stoop creep into his spine. As he reached the end of the chaise, he pulled a folded piece of paper from his left pocket. It slipped free with a gentle action. Winston dropped it onto the cushion and kept walking. He didn't look back as he left the library and closed the door behind him.

The paper sat on the cushion like a triangular paper roof, its apex pointing at the ceiling in an accusation. Emma's steps faltered as she edged towards it, her nerve endings frayed and sending tingles of conflicting pain to her brain. She bent from the waist, her spine rigid. The paper shook against her cotton clad fingers, the folds behaving like a troublesome child as they refused to open at her touch. A rip split the silence, jarring and loud. Emma peered down at the familiar name and the date of birth, her next breath lodged in her chest. She released it with a whoosh at the second number scrawled after a hyphen from the first.

The date of her brother's death.

Zero

E mma sat on the hearthrug and hugged her knees to her chest. The Shakespearean masterpiece rested over her keyboard, creating a nonsensical entry of its own until it ran out of characters in the description field. She tugged off the cotton gloves and let them fall beside her, watching as the hollow shells of fabric lost their sense of aliveness. They created an allegory for her heart, shocked and empty. "How can I grieve someone I never knew?" she breathed. She pressed her eye sockets against her knees and touched the gnawing ache in her soul with the fragile tendrils of her mind. Unbearable pain radiated outward in an arc to consume her sense of self. The tears on her cheeks dried under the ministration of the fire's warmth, leaving her as empty as a husk. When Stephie woke for the rest of her feed, beating her tiny fists against the world, Emma fed her with mechanical movements void of emotion. She changed the baby's nappy afterwards and pinned the ends of her vest together over one shoulder. Stephie lay on the rug, kicking her legs and thrilled with the lack of restriction. She thrashed her arms as though flying. Emma scooted her away from the fire's reach and hauled an old fireguard in front of the flames. The eerie numbness returned, shrouding her like a cloak and segregating her from her surroundings.

She reached for the fallen slip of paper, Winston's crabbed scrawl sitting above the printed lines as though afraid of commitment. She'd never seen his handwriting, but sensed his personality within the spiky lettering. A dissident's English. However that looked.

Emma smoothed her index finger across the date of her brother's death and closed her eyes. It was Nicky's birthday, and the day Rohan's platoon lost their lives in Helmand Province. She wondered if Winston understood the horrible significance. He'd scrawled *Meningitis* as the cause of death, writing it smaller, as though afraid to give it the same prominence as the other details.

Emma rose, sensing she'd regret her haste, but doing it anyway. She pulled back the fireguard and dropped the paper onto the hot coals. It flared like a phoenix taking flight before curling and blackening at the command of the heat. "This didn't happen," she hissed through gritted teeth, burying the knowledge and its associated emotions in her Pandora's box of terrible things.

Finding her father's note in the bureau with the birth certificate upended her world and cast her into confusion. It left her questioning her perception of herself and the life she'd struggled to build. Meeting her brother might have coloured in some gaps in her understanding, making her feel less like a package passed from hand to hand. Or they could have at least felt that way together.

"Idiot!" Emma gasped. She reached towards the fire, wishing she'd stalled her haste long enough to absorb the impact of the note before destroying it. Winston's assistance achieved nothing, providing her with no extra information about her brother. Had his new parents changed his name like hers, or did he keep it? Did he know about her or ever try to find her? His death raised more questions than it soothed, and Emma wrestled with the ball of frustration in her chest. The note provided no closure, but opened up a wider cavern of mystery which needed solving. She sniffed and used the hem of her dress to wipe her eyes. Stephie snoozed on the rug and she bundled her into a clean nappy and left her to sleep. Then she returned to her cataloguing, safeguarding the past for her son's future.

A knock on the door heralded Allaine. Deep lines creased her forehead. "Here you are," she said, her tone strained. "Is your phone on silent?"

"It should still vibrate." Emma dug in the pocket of her cardigan and frowned at missed calls showing on the screen. "Oh, sorry. It didn't." She turned from the keyboard to regard her friend. "Did you take Freda to the cafe?" She frowned and covered her mouth with her hand. "Did I say I'd do it?"

Allaine ventured into the room and left the door ajar. A draught followed her across the rug. "This is about Freda," she said, noticing the sleeping baby and lowering her voice. Her blue irises held the sparkle of alarm. "She collapsed at the coffee shop and is asking for you. Christopher intercepted the call to the house phone when you didn't answer it. I guess you wouldn't hear it in here."

Emma's eyes widened, and she froze. A harbinger of loss floated in front of her face, misting her vision and masking the hope in her future. "Not her too," she whispered. Her chest hitched as grief lodged there like a hard lump.

"What?" Allaine fixed her hands over Emma's shoulders and gave her a light shake. "What do you mean? Has someone else died?"

"No, no." Emma ducked from her grasp and turned back to the keyboard. She saved her work and shut down the computer. "I'll go to her now. Is she at the Cottage Hospital near the Catholic church?"

"No." Allaine winced. "The ambulance took her to Leicester Royal Infirmary."

The colour drained from Emma's face. "This is serious. I sensed there was something wrong with her, but she wouldn't give me a straight answer." She groaned. "I meant to set Nicky on her but didn't. This is my fault." She rubbed at her swollen eyes and berated herself. "This can't go on, I need to get my act together."

"Emma, stop!" Allaine blocked her path as she closed the doors to the cabinet. "This isn't on you!" She jerked her head towards the baby. "Ray will drive you to the hospital and I'll push Stephie around the grounds in the pram. Then you needn't worry about being too far away from her when she wakes for a feed. Come on."

Emma watched as Allaine dipped and collected the baby from the rug. Stephie's arms and legs flopped like a doll's as she stayed asleep. Allaine cradled her against her chest. She gave Emma the same look she bestowed on Kaylee when the child dragged her feet, jerking her head towards the door. Emma nodded and forced herself to move forward, the heels of her sandals striking the wooden floorboards without commitment.

Ray met them in the lobby, securing the front doors before hopping behind the steering wheel of Emma's yellow car. Allaine fixed the baby into the back with Emma before jumping into the passenger seat.

Emma pulled her phone from her cardigan pocket and frowned at it. The missed calls blinked on the screen until she deleted them without examining each number. A text from Rohan offered consolation.

'*I love you*,' he'd written. '*Talk soon*.'

Her gaze slid sideways to her daughter's flickering eyelids and she straightened her lips into a hard line. She sent up arrow prayers for poor Freda's health before her mind turned to Allaine's comment about the landline. Christopher Dolan's stranglehold on the technology and communications in the house had reached beyond her realisation. Her fingers shook as she stroked them over the screen of her cell phone. Rohan had known. And he'd warned her, but she didn't want to hear it. Emma heaved in a sigh of gratitude for the moment. Thank goodness he'd intercepted the call from the landline this time, and bought her valuable extra time with Freda. But what else had he gleaned from calls she hadn't answered?

Format

"How do you feel?" Emma took Freda's fragile hand in hers. Age spots accentuated the paper thinness of her skin.

"Like a hundred-year-old woman." Freda's pencilled brows narrowed to a line. Hours earlier, her failing eyesight caused her to draw the left one higher, giving her a startled appearance.

Emma snuffed out a laugh filled with relief. A return to sarcasm heralded her improving health. "You are almost a hundred," she replied.

Freda waved her other hand, a cannula poking from a ridged blue vein. A strip of sticking plaster kept it in place despite her flapping motion. "Rudeness doesn't suit you, my dear." She fluttered her pale eyelashes. Forgotten blobs of brown mascara turned them into jointed spider's legs. Thin lips pursed into a line and formed a portcullis behind which she hid her genuine feelings. Emma relinquished her hold and let Freda's hand rest on the white sheet.

Rising, she walked across to the window and focussed on the view from the towering building. Leicester Royal Infirmary hummed, vibrations from turbines and generators turning it into a living thing with breath and movement. Emma watched a blackbird land on the roof below her. It settled its feet on a metal chimney which arced into the sky before curling downward like a short-sighted reader peering at a book. A curious beak pecked at the brick before acknowledging its futility. Opening its wings, it soared into the sky and a white line of excrement spattered the roof like a rejection.

Emma turned around in time to see Freda swipe at her eyes. Tears glittered on her wrinkled cheeks and the back of her wrist. Emma said nothing, moving to the visitor's chair and taking a seat. Then she waited.

When Freda wiped her nose on the bedsheet, Emma leaned over and pulled a tissue from the box on the side table. She handed it to her without comment. The old lady sighed. "That's one of the things I've always loved about you." Her guttural sniff punctuated the sentence. "You don't probe."

Emma twisted her lips and clamped her teeth over her tongue to avoid ruining the compliment. It seemed academic to admit she probed her husband and son like a Home Office interrogator behind closed doors. She accepted the praise with good grace and silence. Emma gazed at a poster on the wall as Freda blew her nose into the tissue in a lengthy and disgusting evacuation. "You and Rohan are so kind to me." Her tone held an emotional thickness. "I've taken advantage of your hospitality and you haven't once complained." Emma wondered whether to correct her, but decided against destroying the illusion. Freda's voice grew stronger. "It's difficult to admit you need help." Emma lurched for another tissue to stop her using the snotty one to dab her eyes. "I've spent my entire life flexing my independence, especially after darling John died. It's painful to acknowledge the things you can no longer do."

Emma blew out a breath and nodded. "Yeah. I hear you. Our lives share an incredible parallel right now."

"They do." Freda reached across and gripped her hand. "But you have Rohan."

Emma squeezed her eyes shut and let her thoughts drift to the previous year. She'd been penniless and alone with her son, forging a half life for them both against the odds. She twisted her lips and tipped her head. "I have this illusion of myself drowning, trying to keep Nicky above water and failing. But it's not true." Her eyelashes fluttered and a smile spread across her face. "There was always someone looking out for us. Anton, Lucya, Dolan and now Rohan. But there's also Ray, Allaine and you." Emma stroked the back of Freda's hand with her thumb and a warm sensation bloomed from her stomach and spread into her chest. "And

God. Nicky's always telling me he was there, even at my worst times." She lifted Freda's delicate fingers to her lips and placed a kiss over them. "And you're not alone either. You have us, don't you?"

Freda's eyelashes fluttered against her cheek. Her head lolled sideways on the pillow and gentle breaths puffed from her mouth. Her bottom set of false teeth slipped forward to give her a dramatic under bite. Emma's eyes widened and she held her breath. Freda looked so still and pale against the stark white hospital sheets. "No, no, no," Emma breathed, pleading with age and inevitability.

Then Freda's eyes popped open, and she sucked her dentures back into place. "You thought I'd died, didn't you?" A smirk spread across her face. "Admit it, you thought I'd pegged it."

Emma groaned and released her wrinkled fingers. "Not funny," she bit.

Freda waggled her mismatched eyebrows and amusement accentuated the creases either side of her lips. Her sparkling irises looked as though they belonged to a much younger woman. "That's cheered me right up, dear." She used her flimsy arm muscles to push herself upright in the bed. "Can I go home now?"

"My home or your home?" Emma cocked her head and waited for the reply.

Freda's brow furrowed and she paused. Her thin chest rose and fell as she considered her answer before bobbing her silver head in a definitive nod. "My home." She tilted her chin so her nose stuck higher in the air. "You're right, Emma. Independence is a lonely illusion. And a little too empty for my liking." She patted the sheets with her bony fingers and flopped back against the pillow. "Perhaps you'll allow that handsome young driver of yours to drop me at my apartment?"

Emma blinked before realising Freda referred to Ray. "That's fine." Her eyes narrowed, and she winced. "But first, you need to convince the doctors to release you."

"I sense there's a second part to this condition." Freda sank against the pillow like a discarded marionette. She released a sigh long enough to shake the bed.

"I'm afraid so." Emma sat back in the visitor's chair and folded her arms. "I need to know what's upset you enough to have heart palpitations. Or who."

Coordinate

"Stupid body." Freda set her jaw and closed her eyes. Emma sensed avoidance in the tilt of her sagging chin. "I almost got away with it."

"With what?" Emma's eyes narrowed. "Come on, Freda. You're right. Rohan and I have shown you kindness. Now, show me some in return."

Freda squirmed. She flapped slender fingers at a passing nurse. "Young man, can you fetch me some drugs?"

"Huh?" The nurse halted, his blond curls bouncing as he stopped sharp. The rubber soles of his shoes squeaked against the tiles. "What sort of drugs?" A fluffy blond eyebrow disappeared into his fringe.

"I don't care," Freda grumbled. "Anything will do."

"For the pain?" The nurse approached the bed, sympathy already blossoming across his face.

"No!" Freda screwed up her features. "To euthanise me."

The man gasped and took a step backwards out of range of her grasping fingers. "I can't do that, Mrs Ayers." His voice wavered, and he shot a silent plea for assistance in Emma's direction.

She sighed and made a twirling motion with her index finger before tapping her temple. "Don't worry, nurse. It's the dementia talking," she soothed.

Freda sat up in the bed as though fired from a gun. She startled the poor man with her sudden energy. "There's nothing wrong with my mind!" she snapped.

Emma glared at her. "No, there isn't."

Freda buried her face in her hands, realising she'd blown it. She couldn't return to the wilting daisy act after that performance. The nurse retreated with a promise to speak to the doctor, although he didn't specify what direction the conversation might take. Or how fast the doctor would appear.

"I'll leave you alone." Emma rose. The soreness emanating from her bra warned her she needed to find Allaine and feed Stephie.

"Do you hate me?" Freda's plaintive voice made her wince.

"No!" Her reply sounded sharper than she intended. She inhaled and released the tension in her shoulders as she let the breath go free. "But avoiding telling me the truth isn't helping our relationship." She spread her arms and shrugged, looking around her at the hospital ward. "It's not conducive to your good health, either. I know you gave my DNA sample to Winston. The ancestry company didn't receive it. I phoned them."

"Winston?" Freda's brow furrowed into deep lines. "I didn't give Winston anything."

"Then what?" Emma's voice rose, driven by frustration and the urge to escape the clinical hospital ward. "What did you do that's so terrible?"

Freda's lips twisted and her eyes grew too round for her slender face. Her fingers writhed in her lap. "I might have had a minor accident." She flapped her hand. "Nothing to worry about yet."

"What kind of accident?" Emma whispered. "Tell me."

"A mishap with my mouth." Freda's thin fingers patted the blanket over her knees until it lay flat. "Marjory Ellis from the Historical Society made me do it. You can blame her."

"For what?" Emma's temper unleashed from her lips. The waistband of her dress had tightened across her stomach as the day progressed. A brown line remained where she'd scrubbed away the blood. She wished she'd relinquished her ban on sweatpants. Positivity sucked.

"I let her sell tickets to a garden party at Wingate Hall." Freda's words emerged in a rush and took her false teeth with them. She clapped a hand over her mouth and forced her bottom set back into place with her fingers. "She goaded me, Emma. Ridiculed me about being the bastard heir and I cracked."

Emma's jaw hung slack and no calming thoughts seemed able to retrieve her lower lip. The ramifications passed through her brain like sand on glass, misting her brain until no sensible answer worked itself free. Freda's frantic fingers smoothed across the blanket as though plucking a chicken. "This is terrible," she conceded. "There's no excuse for agreeing to it without your permission."

"No," Emma managed. "No."

"I'm sorry." Freda gulped. "I understand how much work goes into disguising what Rohan and Christopher do for a living just so Ray's son can visit."

Emma closed her eyes against the security and logistical nightmare unleashed upon them by an old lady's throwaway comment."

"When?" Emma whispered. "When is this garden party?"

Freda shifted in the bed as though biting ants invaded her underwear. She cleared her throat twice and her voice sounded reedy when she replied. "This Saturday. Marjory says they've sold a hundred and thirty tickets. There's so little known about Wingate Hall, the first hundred tickets went in less than a day." She sighed. "Will you ever forgive me?"

"I don't know what to do." Strain leaked from every syllable. Emma's heart hammered in her breast and her stomach roiled at the thought of telling Rohan and Christopher about Freda's latest disaster. "I need to find

Allaine and Stephie. I'll visit again tomorrow," she promised. The heels of her sandals clattered over the tiles as she leaned in to plant a kiss on Freda's forehead.

"With any luck, I might be dead by the weekend." Freda sounded hopeful. "Then you can cancel the garden party."

The Power of Two

Two days later, Emma's fingers shook against the mantel as she counted Rohan's long strides across the lounge. Visiting Freda in the hospital brought back painful memories of Stephie's birth. They needed to talk about more than Freda's inability to avoid a foolish dare and her ongoing feud with Marjorie.

"Why the cryptic text?" He lifted his head to smile at her, a frown clouding his light expression as he read the anxiety in her face. "What's wrong?" Dark circles ringed his eyes, evidence of his late drive home in the early hours. His limp seemed more pronounced and his Russian accent snuck into his speech.

Emma glanced down at the kindling and newspaper in a bucket next to the hearth. She contemplated busying herself and wondered if it might make the conversation easier. She'd dreaded it for so long, she'd built it into an insurmountable wall.

"Emma?" The sharpness of his tone made her jump, and the rehearsed sentence fluttered into the back of her brain. Retrieving the words seemed like an impossible task.

"Nicky said something." Her hands writhed like snakes. She touched her fringe and then her lip, not sure how to arrange her features.

"About what?" Rohan stopped before her and cocked his head. His eyes narrowed. "He can't get into the armoury. Ray helped me block the tunnel from the other side. It's all key coded now and wired into the house security system."

"Not that." Emma bent her knees and straightened them, unable to stand still anymore. "Nicky said something a while ago." The trembling of her bottom lip alarmed her. The muscle seemed beyond her limited control. "At the Baptist coffee shop." She blinked back dismay at herself. The location didn't matter.

"Emma, you're scaring me." Rohan's irises flared wide, cerulean blue sparkling with diamond highlights. Emma doubted anything ever frightened her husband, but for a moment he appeared haunted by terrible possibilities.

"Sorry, sorry." She wrapped her arms around herself and then let them fall to her sides. In desperation, she dropped to her knees and seized the poker, raking it through the ash in a frenzy of activity. "Nicky said you cried the night I had

Stephie. He said he climbed into our bed and you didn't see him."

"And?" Rohan ground out the word, defensiveness giving it hard edges which his accent turned into knife blades.

The poker rattled against the metal grate, sending the ash skittering through its gaps to collect in the tray beneath it. Emma leaned too far forward and overbalanced, recovering with a jerky movement. "It's not like you," she managed, closing her eyes and wishing she'd never started the horrible conversation.

"You think it's weakness?" His voice changed as he turned and walked towards the window.

"No. Not that." Emma dropped more kindling than she collected from the bucket, haste turning her fingers into unmanageable bananas. She dumped a handful into the grate before remembering the need for a fire lighter.

"What then?" Rohan dug his hands into his pockets, his outline silhouetted against the light.

Emma hissed as the second handful of kindling left a splinter in her palm. She dropped it onto the hearth with a clatter.

"Stop doing that." His touch on her shoulder made her jump. "Just say whatever is bothering you." He stepped back to let her rise from her knees. The action negated any refusal and she scrambled up to face him as though controlled by strings which he commanded. "What did Nikolai tell you?"

Emma swallowed. She peered at the splinter in her palm, watching a speck of blood ooze like a protective bubble. She wished her heart could do likewise.

"Emma." Rohan spoke her name again, impatience creeping into his tone.

She took a giant inhale and choked on it. Her voice sounded ragged. "You wanted more babies and I can't give them to you. That's why you cried." The words stuck in her throat and her hand instinctively moved over her stomach. The splinter left a faint trail of blood like pinpricks over the floral fabric. It blended in with the swirls of a rose. "I feel so guilty, like a failure."

She'd said it. Finally.

"Failure?" Rohan repeated the word which had haunted her since that night. His tongue negated its bite. "That's how you feel?" An element of wonder crept into his voice, as though he'd opened a cupboard containing lost things. "Oh, Emma!"

She looked away, not wanting to see the truth emblazoned on his face. When he seized her chin, she let out a squeak of fright. She turned to find him glaring at her. "I didn't cry for the children I'd never have! What do you think I am?" Hurt darkened Rohan's irises and his fingers dug into her cheeks. Frustration drove him to shake her chin as though attempting to vibrate sense into her. He forced her to maintain eye contact with him and she recognised the fury which made those he bounty hunted quail in their boots.

"You almost died! I cried at the thought of a life without you. That's what Nikolai heard." Rohan dropped his hands and his head sank into a stance of defeat. Emma tensed as he turned away from her. She held her breath, fearing he might leave her to stew in her self-pity. She blinked at the knowledge she'd believed him myopic enough to calculate her worth in offspring production.

"I'm sorry." She closed her eyes against his disappointment. "You said you wanted six children and a dog." Pressing her knuckles into her eye sockets, she waited for the click of the lounge door.

"Durak." The soft rebuke sounded close, and she released the breath straining her lungs. When she blinked, Rohan stood in front of her, his tie hanging loose and his collar undone. Reaching up, he pulled her fingers away from her face and closed them into his wide palm. "I love you more than anything, Emma. I wanted you to live and you almost didn't. You haemorrhaged. I've never seen so much blood, not even on the battlefield. It created puddles on the floor." He gave a shuddering sigh and shook his head. "The doctors forced me to leave. They shoved Stephie in my arms and wheeled you into surgery." His irises darkened and pain radiated outward from pupils like pinpricks. Then he sighed. "You've taken a throwaway comment I said at nineteen to tease you and wrapped it around my neck."

Warmth flooded Emma's breast, trickling along her spine and removing the chill which had settled without her realising. She heaved in a breath that contained hope and restitution. Bound up in her own suffering, she never considered the effects of that night on Rohan. She remembered the birth, her daughter's first cries and the sensation of her initial breast feed. Then the sound of liquid hitting the tiles, followed by shocked faces surrounding her and then nothingness. "I'm sorry for doubting you." Her neck sagged and her forehead touched Rohan's shirt. His arms enfolded her, holding her hard enough for it to restrict her movements. Emma didn't care. She closed her eyes and breathed in his familiar scent. No one else on the planet shared his same aura of musk and spice with a hint of sunshine. Except perhaps his children.

"I've made a mess of everything." She raised her forearms and pushed them around Rohan's waist. His solidity grounded her in safety and a sense of immovability despite external pressures.

He sighed. "I don't think so. Chaos is a perception." Emma lifted her head and tried to look into his eyes. He lowered his lips to kiss her forehead. "Not everyone will see your worth. Sometimes you first need to believe it's there for yourself."

Emma nodded, accepting his wisdom. The surgery had altered her self-image when it shouldn't have done. It saved her life, and from within the emotional minefield, she'd forgotten that. "So, what would the Actuary do about the mess I've made then?" Her voice held a note of sadness and regret.

Rohan's lips twitched as though he wanted to laugh, but stopped himself. "The Actuary would expect you to get out of it by yourself. You must be your own hero."

"Oh." Emma rested her forehead against his shirt. A button scratched her soft skin. Her shoulders slumped as Rohan placed his hands over hers.

"But your husband will help you fix things." He bent at the knees to look into her eyes. "If you ask him."

Algebra

R ohan settled on the sofa, and Emma nestled between his biceps and his chest. She drew her legs up onto the seat with a sigh. "Where do we start?" she asked.

"Are we good now?" His fingers traced an invisible pattern across her upper arm. "I'm unhappy you know I bawled my eyes out like a baby, but I'm disturbed you believed it was disappointment over some narcissistic breeding program." His tone hardened.

Emma nodded against his shirt, the susurrations filling her ears. "We're good," she concluded. "I don't think that now."

"Okay." Rohan pressed his lips to the top of her head and balanced his chin against her crown. "About the other thing, it's a shame Dolan wiped the flash drive. I'm glad you told me immediately and didn't keep it a secret, but you should have checked it before you threw it away."

Emma sat up at speed, indignation lining her face as she remembered his texted exclamation mark. The action caused Rohan to shift to accommodate her. "I saw it in his eyes. He'd wiped it." She tapped a beat against her thigh. "It's not about the flash drive. There's another angle to this, but I haven't found it yet." Their new spirit of openness dictated she tell him about the DNA test, but she couldn't do it. Maybe later, when life became simple again. "But the flash drive was the risk, wasn't it? If I'd given it to you in the first place instead of him, you'd have neutralised the problem?"

"Perhaps." Rohan's non-committal tone caused a flare of irritation to bud in Emma's chest. She liked things neat and baulked against him denying her closure. He frowned and pursed his lips. "You still should have checked it."

"I promise you, he wiped it!"

Emma imagined she saw the mental calculations spinning through Rohan's eyes as he weighed and rationalised probable outcomes. They'd had the same argument almost word for word when she arrived back from Allaine's. He jerked and blinked as though woken from a deep sleep. "Regan is also part of the risk. My government contact believes he hacked their site. Unless they incarcerate him, he could choose to repeat the process."

"He says he didn't and I believe him." Emma dug in on Regan's behalf, determined to convince her husband of his innocence. "He collected the information from a dead drop. The person who dumped it there left no thumb print."

Rohan released a heavy sigh. "I need to speak to him, Em."

She groaned and squirmed. "You'll do something to him. I can't risk it."

Rohan's bark of laughter echoed around the walls. "Define 'do something to him' please?"

"I'd rather not know how you neutralise risks." She dropped her gaze and her dark curls snaked against her shoulder. "Once was bad enough." She shivered at the thought of the clean up required after her first experience with the Actuary at the manor in Falkirk. Christopher had torched the place with the bodies still inside it. "What would you ask him if you met?"

Rohan rolled his eyes. "Fine!" he grumbled. "It's like that, is it?"

"Sorry, but yes." Emma held her ground and gritted her teeth against the twitch beneath her right eye. It betrayed her anxiety and the sense of being outclassed and outmanoeuvred. She rose and walked across to her father's bureau, lifting a notepad and pen from the top drawer. "You tell me the questions and I'll write them down and ask Regan." She scribbled on the pad with four pens before finding one that left more than scratches.

Rohan fired his questions faster than Emma could record them. She sensed he did it on purpose. "Slow down," she entreated him. "Repeat what you just said while I was still writing the one before it." She perched on the edge of the sofa with her right leg folded beneath her. Rohan smoothed his fingers across the hem of her dress and a sparkle entered his azure irises. "Stop!" She slapped his hand away and edged out of his reach.

He curved his lips into a smile, and he flicked a speck of dust from his trousers with a lazy action. "Maureen would have typed and encrypted that by now." He jerked his head towards the pad balanced across Emma's knees. She wrinkled her nose and sighed, not doubting the truth of his statement.

"Anything else, Captain Andreyev?" She forced her features into an expression of submission and fluttered her eyelashes.

Rohan laughed. "That's enough for today," he replied. "I'll make an assistant of you yet."

Emma blossomed beneath the compliment. He'd teased her, but within his ribbing she detected a flicker of hope. "Mr and Mrs Andreyev," she dared to suggest. "How does that sound? Like Mr and Mrs Smith."

Rohan's lips twitched, but he ignored the jest. Emma cocked her head and frowned. "Why did you call yourself the Actuary? I've always wondered."

He inhaled and his gaze tracked to the window. "I didn't."

She waited, but pressed him when he ventured nothing further. "So, who gave you that title?" She detected reluctance in his slow movements as he ran a hand through his hair. He seemed wrong footed for long enough to send concern to cover the light hearted question with a blanket of doom. She wished she hadn't asked. "A woman?" She whispered the words, dread snaking into her heart. He'd promised there'd been no one else during their period of estrangement. She'd believed him.

"No." His eyes glittered with a peculiar diamond quality. He reached out a hand and settled his palm over her bent knee. An electrical current spread along her leg to the foot trapped beneath her. "My brother thought it was funny. My first contract was for a friend of his. They worked in the theatre together and it's the name he gave me."

"What was the job?" Emma stared at the rug, allowing the colours to merge in her vision. Anton had left it for her, like most of the other furniture and fittings. She let her mind explore the box of sadness trapped in her heart and slammed the lid with a snap. The void of Anton's death seemed as much a yawning cavern of grief as it did the last time she dared delve into it.

The pain in Rohan's eyes mirrored hers. "A leading lady got herself entangled with a stage hand. There were photos which might have tainted her celebrity status and made it difficult for her to work in children's theatre."

"Oh." Emma pursed her lips. She wanted to ask him if he'd looked at the images, knowing she would exhibit far less restraint. She would promise herself just a little peek before digesting every scrap of evidence. He once told her he verified the data and then moved on, refusing to allow it to taint him.

She dropped the pad and pen onto the floorboards and leaned against the sofa. "It seems so unfair," she whispered.

"I have Anton's house and his dog, his money and his furniture. I'd trade it all just for an hour of him clowning around like a teenager."

"Da." Rohan slipped into Russian as he released a heavy sigh. "Remember that time he bitch slapped me?" His tone lightened, but his eyes remained lacklustre.

"Yes!" Emma exclaimed. "You had a crimson hand mark on your cheek. I don't recall why he did it."

"Da." He sighed. "I wanted to confess to Alanya about us and he stopped me. I was such a blind fool. Another hour in his company would allow me to inform him he was correct about everything. He'd love that."

Emma stiffened. He ceased calling her Mother after her death in a remand prison. She bit back all negative comments, not realising she'd also held her breath until her lungs spasmed in protest. She yearned to ask what other things Anton had been right about, but Rohan lifted his hand and snagged a stray curl from her ponytail. He twisted it between his thumb and forefinger. His eyelashes flickered as he allowed the activity to engross him. When he stopped and dropped his hand, his body language changed to one of dismissal. He edged forward on the cushion before standing. "Make your call and ask those questions." He stretched, his long arms striving for the ceiling metres beyond his fingertips. "Speak to him only." His raised eyebrow conveyed a note of warning. "Make sure you're not overheard."

"Okay." Emma smiled, the expression filled with genuine gratitude.

But Rohan hadn't finished. "Emma?" He relaxed and dug his hands into his trouser pockets. His feet faced the door. "We don't mention this again." She swallowed. It didn't seem a fantastic moment to ask him to talk to his son about a pressing issue. Nicky had rifled through her drawers and wardrobe for the cockerel's outfit, unable to wait for the big reveal. But she nodded and accepted her husband's unravelling of her other mess.

"Okay," she agreed.

Linear

Speaking to Regan seemed like such a simple thing in Emma's head. The reality proved very different.

"What do you mean he left?" Her voice rose to a screech as she spoke to the receptionist at the motel. She'd rung the number on the website and asked him to put her through to the landline in Regan's room.

"He checked out last night." The man gave an exaggerated sigh and Emma jerked at the sound of his energetic gum chewing in her ear.

"Where did he go?" Her right foot tapped an irritated beat against the floorboards. "Did he leave a forwarding address?"

The receptionist's patience snapped, and he hung up on her after snarling, "This is a motel, lady. Not the bloody post office!"

Emma swore into the empty connection and dragged the phone from her ear. Rohan had handed her the burner phone before sending her on her fruitless mission, telling her to use it away from the house.

So, she spent her Saturday morning sitting at a tiny table beyond what resembled a multicoloured padded cell. It qualified as a location away from the house, but didn't lend itself to concentration or dedicated sleuthing. Nicky and Kaylee raced past her, their mouths opened in perpetual squeals of excitement. The transformation occurred the second they shucked their shoes, and they'd been demon children ever since. Ball pits and plastic tunnels created a child's paradise and an adult's worst nightmare. Emma glanced down at her miracle baby, amazed she slept amid the din of hollering and screaming. A small boy in baggy pants raised his arms halfway down the slide and grabbed hold of an overhead beam. Emma held her breath as he hung there.

"Look at me, Aunty Becky!" he shouted. As a blonde woman looked up with horror in her eyes, he let go of the bar and plunged the six feet to the padded floor. A split lip and a bloody nose ended his outing. The aunt carried him into the lobby as the unfortunate mother wrestled five pairs of shoes onto the children of their joint families.

Emma sighed and stared at her phone. "Why Regan?" she hissed. "You had one job." She used her own phone to find Frederik's contact details and transferred them into the burner. It rang and rang, but he didn't answer. She repeated the exercise with Susan's, before realising they were ignoring the unrecognised number of the burner phone. In frustration, she jabbed out an abusive text to Frederik. Then she tried again.

"Regan's gone!" She gave him no opportunity to respond to her rude message when he rang, hoping they could gloss over it in the spirit of camaraderie.

Frederik gave a sigh which held his general sense of exasperation with her existence. "I know," he growled. "I moved him. This better be a burner phone you're calling from!"

"Hi, Emma." Susan's voice sounded distant, as though she sat across the room from the phone.

Emma's jaw hung slack. Nicky bounced up to her with Kaylee in tow. They stopped squealing long enough to demand fizzy drinks and chips. "No," Emma snapped. She held up her other hand to block their protests before shoving the phone over her ear. "We have food at home."

"Where are you?" Frederik paused and another group of screaming children pounded past her. "Are you back in the lunatic asylum?"

"Oh, haha," Emma grumbled. "Allaine drove to Leicester on an errand, and I'm not meant to use this phone anywhere near Christopher. Yes, it's a burner. So, I've come to this horrendous place with the children. I doubt I'll get them out of here alive and I'm never coming back again."

"Right. That implies we should tell Hack nothing about what we're doing from now on?"

"He works for Rohan." The spiky sentence contained the sum of Emma's frustration. "Isn't it obvious? He goes where the money is and right now, he earns that by handing Regan to the authorities. Besides, he's turned this into a competition and made it personal. So no, tell him less than nothing."

"That's not possible, is it? Nothing is nothing. Less than nothing doesn't exist." Frederik groaned and Emma figured Susan hit him. Or sent Jay to do it by proxy. She hoped it hurt.

"Where is Regan now?" She rocked the baby seat with her foot even though Stephie's eyelids remained sealed shut. Her lips twitched as she sucked her thumb in her sleep.

"I probably shouldn't tell you either."

Emma groaned. "Fine! He was safe where we left him, wasn't he?"

"He thinks not. The motel owner knocked on his door last night and suggested Regan found somewhere else to stay. He said too many people were asking questions about him and it wasn't good for business."

"Who?" Emma mused. "Did he say?"

"No, but it started with you. Maybe the Actuary?"

"Not Rohan." Emma wrinkled her nose as Nicky wedged himself into a transparent globe at the intersection between two tunnels. His mouth opened and closed and he pawed at the window like a trapped animal. She gave him a wave. He created a bottleneck in the flow of traffic and bodies piled up behind him. Faces pressed against the plastic as the log jam continued, then Nicky set off on his hands and knees again. Like water down a drain, the blockage cleared and Emma relaxed. But she'd missed part of Frederik's sentence. It took a prolonged second for her to catch up on his meaning. "Oh. Ohhh." She drew out the last sound and rocked Stephie harder. "He thinks someone else is after him?" She frowned and pondered the notion. "Not the government. They employed Rohan. So, who else? I wonder if it's connected to the guy who attacked me over the chicken beak."

"The chicken beak?"

Emma twisted her lips. "Yes. He asked me to say hello to our mutual friend. He said he'd won an auction. I think he wanted me as collateral."

"Geez!" Bristles scratched as Frederik rubbed his hand across his face. "This is a bloody mess." Exhaustion filtered through his sigh. "I had to bring Regan here. He used a fire escape at the motel and I drove around for a couple of hours before coming home. Susan came with me and we did a grocery shop at midnight." He yawned. "Do you realise there are entire armies of people who do their food shopping in the middle of the night?"

"No. I hadn't thought about it."

Frederik yawned again. "Well, there are. But I'm getting too old for this."

"So, Regan is with you?" Emma nodded. "Okay. Please, can you put him on? I have some questions for him."

A few clunks and a rattle plagued the connection before Regan's weak hello sounded, backed by a dull echo. Emma watched her son diving into the ball pit and cringed. "That's a toxic soup if ever I saw one," she murmured.

"What?"

"Nothing, sorry." Emma inhaled and withdrew her list from her handbag. She unfolded the paper filled with scrawl from her conversation with Rohan. "Right, think about these questions. You might not be able to answer them straight away, but do your best. If they trigger something else later, text or ring me on this number."

"Okay." A shuffling sounded in the background and Emma realised Frederik had remained in the room with his son. She tensed. "You're not on speaker, are you?"

"Yes, we're all here." Frederik's tinny voice echoed in Emma's ear.

"You weren't supposed to do that!" she grumbled. Rohan wouldn't want her as an assistant when she'd failed at the first two instructions. *Speak to him only and don't let anyone overhear.* Emma pictured the ruckus if she asked Regan to cut his father loose. He wouldn't do it. She battled onward, delaying the questioning to give him advice. "I don't think you're safe at your father's house. The guy who accosted me in town meant business. Someone like him might set up listening equipment at a nearby property." She raised a quizzical eyebrow. "That's if Christopher hasn't already. You need to remember who he works for and it's in his interests to find you and get paid." Emma allowed Regan to digest her revelation. Frederik cursed.

A barista delivered Emma's cappuccino, and she nodded to the girl in thanks. "Do you have any information on the person who first recruited you on the grey web? Are there any identifying markers, perhaps an identity or something attributable to him? You said you'd worked for a few people."

"Why do we need to rake over all that?" Frederik hissed. "How will that help what's happening now?"

"Okay, it's possible they're linked to the dead drop. Regan, you said you were sniffing around, but what sent you to that location of the dark web? It's a big place. Why did you go there?"

Regan cleared his throat before speaking. His voice held the drawl of someone who hadn't slept in a while. "I intercepted chatter about the dead drop in a forum. The hacker left it on the grey web, but the forum is on the dark web. No one wanted to touch it, just in case."

"In case of what?"

"The cops have spies on there. And the government. They leave stuff lying around that tracks right back to you when you're sniffing. It doesn't matter how much anonymization software you have. The right people can still find you. I don't have unlimited means to protect myself."

"Right." Emma bit down on the ready comment about not jumping out of planes with inadequate parachutes. She imagined Frederik suppressing a similar rebuke.

"What's the relevance of these questions?" Susan's gentle voice added the missing quality to the conversation and Emma released a heavy sigh.

"I'm trying to work out if the person who recruited Regan could have also set him up for a fall. On purpose."

Silence greeted her words and Emma frowned and pulled the phone away from her ear. The digital display showed the call was still active and she pressed the speaker harder against her face.

Frederik spoke first. "That would mean someone played a long game, Emma. Almost five years of drawing him in just to put him in the government's firing line. It makes no sense."

"Could this be about you, Frederik?" Emma asked with more force than she intended. "There's more to it than the flash drive." She watched her wilful son and his malleable sidekick trail a server carrying a plate of chips to another family.

"They smell nice," Nicky commented, shooting Emma a sideways glance through slitted eyes.

"Home time?" She mouthed the words guaranteed to send him skittering back into the ball pit.

"I don't know." Defeat and exhaustion laced Frederik's tone. "Every suggestion is a long shot. I don't have any answers and I've gone over this until I've driven myself mad."

"I hear ya." Emma softened her tone. She exhaled. "Regan needs to move somewhere safe. There's been some kind of auction, which means money has changed hands. Someone has paid a lot of bitcoin for data that valuable. The guy I tangled with carried a knife and the trouble is, Christopher wiped the flash drive." She rushed the last part of her explanation and air whooshed through the speaker as Frederik swore.

"He did what?"

Emma gulped and moved on through her instructions. "Regan needs to wait for the equipment, which will arrive at your place by courier later today. I'll reroute it from his room at the motel. And he needs to think about what triggered his desire to touch something nobody else wanted to go near." She paused, assessing his potential stupidity. "And Regan, you must do that without going back to the forum or to the conversation. Do you understand? I don't need verbatim, just a sense of what they said."

"What equipment?" Frederik's voice grew louder, as though he'd moved nearer the phone. "He's never fired a gun."

"Only because you didn't let me." Regan returned to the role of entitled teenager, a sullenness entering his tone. "I wanted you to teach me, but you refused."

"Computer equipment." Emma tapped her finger against her saucer and ignored the family spat. She took a sip of the cappuccino and closed her eyes. "A new laptop and some software." She put her lips closer to the microphone. "Do not under any circumstances use any of your existing tech. It might have tracking information hidden in the code." A smile broke across her lips. Her smattering of knowledge made her sound like a tech mogul. Unless Regan challenged her, which she hoped he wouldn't. "Regan, listen to me. This is important. Spike is dead to you, do you understand? You don't use that identity ever again. This is all too smooth for a coincidence. Wait for the equipment to arrive and then get the hell out of there. Use cash, no credit cards, no matter where you got them from."

"Credit cards?" Frederik's question held a growl of threat. "Where did you get a credit card?"

Static overlaid Regan's reply. Emma watched her son dive bomb Kaylee in the ball pit and decided it was time to leave before the attendant noticed. Frederik finished growling at Regan and returned to Christopher's destruction of the data. "Gotta go." She slurped the rest of her drink and burned her tongue while rising to her feet.

"This is not over," Frederik warned.

"Yep." Emma waved to Nicky and his face crumpled when he spotted her standing.

Kaylee trotted over to her and waited like an obedient puppy. "Is it lunchtime yet?" Her little voice piped over the din of marauding children. Emma glanced at her watch and gave a groan of defeat. Inheriting Anton's fortune hadn't changed her poverty driven outlook and the prices displayed on the chalk board above the barista's head made her wince.

"Baptist coffee shop," she said, reaching down to grab the handle of Stephie's baby seat. "Shoes on quick before I change my mind."

"What?" Two male voices and one female held concern. Emma groaned, having confused everyone, including herself. Reverting to her maternal responsibility left the call open and gave her mental whiplash.

"Not you guys." She spoke into the phone with a sigh. "I'm trying to manage children here and take care of Regan." She glanced down as shoe laces trailed like snakes from Nicky's trainers. She shook her head and waited until he bent to tie them well enough not to trip. "Wait for the equipment and then leave. No one can track you if you do as you're told." Sternness inflected her words. "I mean it, Regan. Break the rules and we're done. I have other things to get on with." She jerked her chin at Nicky again. "Do them up or you'll fall."

"Where did you get the equipment?" Suspicion sneaked through the phone and into Emma's ear.

"Frederik, it doesn't matter. Not from where you think it came from. I bought it online, a friend just drove an hour's round trip to fetch it and she's dropping it at the courier's depot as we speak. The package contains a link and an account number for legitimate anonymization software and not the open source rubbish. You'll also find a list of instructions and tasks I need Regan to complete. Does he understand?"

"Yes." Emma heard Regan's voice behind Frederik's.

She gave a nod of satisfaction. "Great. I'll text her the new address or she'll have it delivered to the motel. Don't get caught." She killed the call and texted Allaine. Her own phone and the burner went into her handbag. "Right, who wants Baptist coffee shop tea cakes and china teapots with tea?"

"Meeeee!" The children chorused at once. They waited for Emma to hoist her sleeping daughter's baby seat against her hip and make sure she'd left nothing. Kaylee bounced towards the outer door and heaved it open, but Nicky hung back with a frown on his brow.

"Come on, I thought you wanted food." Emma looked back and paused, his pensiveness spelling trouble. "What's wrong?"

Nicky pouted and his azure irises sparkled. He gave a shrug and followed her. "Right then on that phone call, you sounded just like Daddy."

Measurements

E mma jumped as a phone trilled from her handbag.
She'd driven to Leicester the following Monday to
choose wallpaper samples for the ballroom at Wingate Hall
after dropping the children at school. Rohan had driven
back to London before dawn and without telling her why.
She reached for her phone and frowned at the darkened
screen. Her eyes widened as she remembered the burner
phone still switched on in a hidden pocket and winced.
"Sorry, I need to take this," she said to the assistant. The man
nodded and left the book of wallpaper open on the table. He
moved away to give Emma privacy.

"Hey." She turned her back on the shop and pushed the
pram towards the window. "I'm in a public place," she
whispered.

"No worries." Regan's voice crackled over the connection. "They won't find me here in a hurry."

Emma grinned at Stephie and spun a yellow teddy dangling from the hood of the pram. Stephie gave a series of jerky blinks and smiled. She pressed her tiny hands to her lips and made popping sounds. "Where are you?" Emma lowered her voice to a whisper. "I shouldn't ask, but the curiosity is killing me."

Regan laughed. "Spain. I'm wallpapering for an elderly relative of Susan's. I'll come back when this is over."

"You can wallpaper?" Emma turned back to the giant book of period designs and gave a sigh. "Can you do mine afterwards? The man who decorated some of our rooms broke his leg skiing. He isn't available until next year and I'm on a schedule."

Regan gave a sharp inhale and lowered his voice. "I'd never tried it before today. YouTube clips are helpful. There are tutorials for most things."

Emma sighed and twisted her lips. She imagined herself clambering to the top of a scaffold and trying to unravel the correct length of wallpaper required for each run. "I should wait for my usual guy," she concluded. The trust Anton set up for renovating the manor released a set amount at intervals. He'd stipulated what he wanted each deposit used for and left copious notes and plans with his solicitor for Emma to follow. She sank onto a plush seat, made available for the rich customers who frequented the bespoke design studio, and rubbed a hand over her eyes. Reading the notes conjured up Anton's voice and his mannerisms as though he described his dreams for the house in person. She found the experience exhausting, the grief fresh with the completion of each room he would never enjoy.

She forced her mind back to the phone conversation, realising she disliked every design in the assistant's giant sample book. Regan still prattled on about types of paste and overlaps. "Always wallpaper towards the windows," he concluded. "Otherwise the light casts a shadow over the overlap and you get lines."

"Thanks, I will." Emma smiled at the assistant and nudged the pram wheel with her toe to keep Stephie moving. "What did you find out about our minor problem?"

Regan took a giant inhale, which sounded as a whoosh in Emma's ear. "You're not gonna like it," he replied.

She tensed and held her breath as Regan delivered a potted summary of his investigation. "You were right about the guy who helped me. I'm such an idiot. He scheduled an auction for the information. He believed I had the flash drive and sold it to the highest bidder. I figured the people looking for me at the motel were government personnel." He paused in thought. "Or a disgruntled buyer. It's him."

"Don't beat yourself up." Emma's laugh sounded fake. "That's my speciality, blaming myself for the world's problems."

"I did a little digging without going too deep. I've found a few references to his identity buried within other conversations because he got sloppier in the last year. He recently gave someone in the forum a phone number he'd contacted me on at the start. He must have switched back to that burner SIM card and forgotten he'd used it in our conversations. I also played with that other little piece of software you sent, and it performed a search on repeated numbers or keywords in specific conversations. People adopt habits without thinking about it." Regan exhaled. "I thought I'd done jobs for a few other customers, but they were the same individual. Him. He puts capital letters in weird places."

"Oh, wow." Emma's mind blanked. Fears for her own children rose to the fore. How could she keep her inquisitive son away from this stuff?

Regan continued. "I sniffed around that dead drop in the first place because he pointed it out in the forum. But the only other person in there at the time was another of his fake identities."

"You didn't go back to that forum, did you?" Emma's tone held a parental warning.

"No. I promise. I used the gear you sent and the identity in the note with the link to the anonymization and obfuscation software. But I stuck to the open forums, which I didn't need to re-join. He often spoke to other people in lots of the more casual chat rooms and because it's innocuous kinda stuff, nobody deletes the threads. But the closed group is static, and they'd notice someone new asking to join." He sighed. "I suspect there are only two members who are genuine people. Him and me. I've thought hard about the conversation and it was the army account numbers and passwords that interested me. Nothing else."

"So, you're sure he's the one who mentioned it because all the other personas are fake?"

"Positive."

Emma tapped her toes against the pram wheel. "Do you think he set you up? How could he know the army information would trigger your sense of loyalty?"

"It's a long shot." He cleared his throat. "I'll tell the Actuary but it's my only piece of leverage. Sorry. I found the auction thread. The same person sold the data, and I need Rohan to know it wasn't me. A guy called Mack4 bought it. You need to avoid him. I've noticed him in other forums buying and selling similar high tag items. He isn't messing around."

"Okay." Emma drew out the sound. Curiosity budded in her chest, accompanied by a yearning to know the identity of the person who'd find it amusing to groom a teenager and play a long game before wrecking his life. She opened her mouth to protest, but Regan continued speaking.

"Where did you get the links and account numbers for all that software? It's amazing stuff. Can I keep it when we're finished?"

Emma winced. "I can't tell you where it came from, and I don't know if you can keep it. I suspect not." Pride swelled her chest and she ached to praise Rohan's programming skills. He'd asked her not to share the knowledge.

"Damn." Regan gave an exaggerated sigh to convey his disappointment. "It makes the Onion browser look like a kid's tool. The trouble with my theory is it's conjecture based on a few repeated spelling mistakes. I didn't notice this guy's thumb print on anything related to the dead drop, but I can't go back and take screenshots."

"It's still there?" Emma's hand jerked against the pram handle. "Didn't the government take it down straight away?"

Regan snorted. "They're playing a game of wait and see. It's been out there a while, so why not leave it longer and catch anyone else touches it?" He exhaled. "I booby trapped it anyway."

"Fair enough." Emma spied a length of 1930s floral Damask vintage wallpaper hidden behind a stand of brochures and sample cards. She rose and pushed the pram towards it. Cream flowers spilled from an urn which followed a repeat after a two metre drop. The gold background evoked a sense of luxury. "This is it," she said, her voice brightening. "It's perfect."

"What?" Regan coughed into his phone and Emma pulled it away from her ear.

"Sorry." She traced a line of flowers and tuned back in to the conversation. "Perhaps he's cleverer than you believed. Which also makes him very dangerous. Are you ready to talk to Rohan yet?"

"Yeah." Regan sighed. "He can call me in a couple of hours. I'll text you a new number for him because I'm using this one for you and Dad. There's just one more wall to finish and I want to do a good job for her. Then I'll speak to Rohan."

"Done," Emma agreed. She smiled at the assistant and pointed to the Damask pattern. "I'll tell him." She paused and watched the man grab another tome containing samples and stagger to the tall table to thud it onto the surface. He leafed through the thick pages with lines of concentration marring his forehead. When he lowered his spectacles to the end of his nose, Emma got the message she needed to end the call. "Regan?" She allowed herself one more question, knowing he wouldn't risk telling her the identity of the conspiracy's author even if she begged him.

"Yeah?" His voice sounded upbeat and less weighed by worry.

"You're not in Spain, are you?"

"Na," he replied with a chuckle. "But I am wallpapering."

Abacus

"She did what?" Christopher spat the words, laughter forming their baseline. Emma arrived home after choosing the wallpaper and found him sitting at the kitchen table. She took the opportunity to break the news to him about the garden party. She'd visited Freda in the hospital and showed her the wallpaper sample, hoping to gain her approval. Rohan had agreed to the party, but with conditions.

Christopher shook his head and leaned back against the chair, arms folded as though he owned the place. "It's not happening," he growled. Emma bit down on a comment about his sense of entitlement. Her tongue hurt as her teeth subdued the ready vitriol threatening to bubble from her mouth. He cocked his head at her. "I hope you told her to get them uninvited." His laughter burst free and his chest heaved. "Can you imagine the nightmare of having strangers crawling all over this estate? Your husband has an armoury, for goodness' sake!"

"We're locking the rooms we don't want people to view. All the internal doors have keys. I've engaged a security company to patrol. Everything is organised."

"What?" Christopher spun to confront her and his eyes bugged. "You're going through with this?"

Emma gazed down at the infant in her arms, finding a purpose for the smile which broke free across her face. Stephie blinked and her lips parted in a gummy grin. "Yes, we are." Emma spoke to her daughter but included Christopher in the reply. She kept her tone light and used the special baby voice she reserved for Stephie. "It'll be fun as long as the weather behaves."

"The weather?" Christopher's complexion paled to a waxy hue. Stress broadened his Irish accent. "You're worried about the weather? I have a bloody control base in the folly."

Emma inhaled and gave him her full attention. "Then make sure no one gets in there. Ray will lock the tunnel from the butler's pantry at this end. Freda can run a few tours of the house without going into the bedrooms or revealing the tunnels. It will satisfy local curiosity and give us a dry run for locking everything down at short notice."

"Short notice!" Christopher's voice reached an unnerving high pitch and Stephie turned her head to track his outline. "You're allowing three days, Em. It's not enough."

"Then, get to work." Emma rose and pushed her chair away from her legs. Stephie lay in her arms, dribbling milk from the corner of her mouth and frowning at the air bubble wreaking havoc in her tiny digestive system.

"You can't do this." Christopher shook his head, convincing himself of his autonomy. "Rohan won't allow it. I won't let you."

Emma narrowed her eyes and fixed her steely gaze on his face. "This is my house and you're a guest in it." She ground her jaw against her cheek.

Christopher swallowed and his Adam's apple bobbed in his throat. "I'm just concerned about your safety."

She snorted. "Then where were you when a man attacked me in the Pound Shop?"

"What?" He took a step towards her. "Why didn't I hear about this?"

She breathed out a long breath filled with frustration. "It's something to do with Regan's disappearance. The man told me to say hello to our mutual friend." She sniffed, continuing the facade through a primeval sense of superiority. He'd dismissed her effectiveness, and she wasn't ready for him to know she'd found Regan. Twice.

Christopher gave a series of blinks and seemed lost for words. "But why come after you? What links you to Frederik's kid?" He turned away, genuine concern in the set of his shoulders. He shook his head from side to side before spinning to face her. "This is serious. Why would someone looking for Regan end up here?"

Emma shrugged. "I don't know how he found me but he attacked me in the store." She exhaled. "I'm not going there again. I have the chicken's beak for Nicky, but I need to stay away. Bad things happen to me in that shop."

Christopher strode across the floor and seized her shoulders. His grip caused her to hold Stephie tighter. "Bad people are looking for that stupid kid, Emma." He gave her a shake which rocked her back and forth on her heels. "They won't stop until they get what they want." He released her and spun in a circle to face the door and then the window. Sunlight poured over the draining board and cast shards over the table's oak surface. "You need to stay here until I work out who this guy is. I'll hack into the store's security footage. You visited Frederik. Maybe he followed you from there."

"No!" Emma backed towards the door, clutching her daughter against her chest. "I don't want you to interfere." Her fingers closed over the door knob.

"Interfere!" Christopher's cheeks flushed and his chocolate irises seemed to pop from their sockets. "This is what I do!" He stilled as Emma ignored him. She licked her lips and then cursed the stress tell which revealed her error. The door groaned as his hand landed over hers on the knob. He forced it closed and leaned on it. Her finger joints complained beneath his grip. His breath smelled of coffee and toothpaste, underscored by his familiar musky scent.

"This mystery guy caused the bruising on your arm and the blood on your dress, didn't he? You found the kid and said nothing." His voice contained a concrete element he'd never used on her. "You let someone follow you home." His fingers became a fist and he thumped against the wood. "Where is Regan? You need to tell me." The sound reverberated through the house. Emma sensed danger behind his anger and it threw her into confusion.

She lifted her chin and narrowed her eyes. "Yes, I found Regan. If you hadn't behaved like such a jerk, I would have shared the information." Her teeth ground in her jaw and Stephie tasted the disharmony in the air and released a grumble of misery. Emma hoisted her higher over her shoulder. "You still treat me like the pathetic single mother who Anton employed you to babysit." She lifted a finger and jabbed it into his chest. "He paid you cash. It wasn't all about empathy." Christopher's irises flashed with an eerie light, as though she'd stabbed him through the heart. Emma shook her head. "You won't let me become someone different, Chris." She swallowed and lowered her tone. "I'm not the same woman who couldn't pay the electricity bill. Nicky and I don't need Harley Man anymore." Pity entered her voice, and she dropped her cheek onto Stephie's shoulder. "You ridiculed my attempt to help Frederik and forged mistrust in our friendship. You did that, nobody else."

Christopher swallowed and his hand fell to his side. His fingers still balled into a fist despite his sagging chest. "You're saying you don't need me." He released the sentence as a whisper, a statement of fact. His bunched fingers rubbed across his forehead as though he'd lost control of them, and he pursed his lips and stepped away from her. "You don't know what you've done, Em," he whispered. "You've made a terrible mistake."

She held her breath as Christopher seized the knob and hauled the door open fast enough to make the hinges screech. His footsteps echoed along the corridor as he strode towards the butler's pantry and the tunnel leading to the folly. The laptop he'd abandoned on the table gave a muted chime and Emma frowned. She turned to face the email alert blinking on its screen.

Number Blind

"I can't contact Rohan." Emma's voice wobbled as she patted Stephie's back and clasped the phone under her chin. Farrell sighed in his bed next to the Aga. The silence of the house held no comfort, oppression bearing down with relentless speed to land on its unwitting roof. "He's not answering his calls."

Maureen's reassuring tones cut across the distance as though she stood at Emma's shoulder. Rohan's personal assistant gave her a sense of stability. "A person of interest arrived to meet with him. Can I help?"

Emma swallowed. "Is it the mark related to the government contract?" She closed her eyes and hoped Rohan's meeting involved a speedy conversation with Regan, no violence and a trip home. She planned her words with care before unleashing a tsunami of misery onto her household.

"Yes." Maureen dragged out the word, a question buried beneath it. "The meeting shouldn't take long. He'll check in with me as soon as it's finished. Can I help with something?"

Emma blew out a breath. "I've made a terrible error of judgement and put my family in danger." She gnawed on her bottom lip and lowered her voice. "I don't know how to fix it."

"Okay." Maureen's tone became clipped. She asked very few questions before forming a solution. She instructed Emma to open a video link on her phone so she could survey the email for herself. Clicking in the background betrayed the speed of her fingers as they hammered a keyboard and took screenshots. "Get out now," she demanded. "I've booked you into a hotel off the grid. Grab your children and go."

"But what about Allaine and Kaylee?" Emma winced against the whine in her voice. She'd caused this catastrophic mess.

"I've given you a suite. Get them now and leave!" Urgency entered her direction, and she morphed into the drill sergeant who'd once set terror in the hearts of soldiers. Emma groaned as the call ended and the white noise of silence engulfed her. Farrell blinked up at her from his bed, and he wagged the end of his tail.

"Leave no man behind," Emma breathed. She clicked her tongue and he rose with a grunt and padded across the kitchen. "Come on, boy." She pulled open the kitchen door and followed in Christopher's wake, turning towards the lobby instead of the butler's pantry.

Farrell stuck to her side as she half ran and half walked to Allaine's apartment. She clattered up the steps and past Ray's ranch slider. Guilt prickled in her chest for not thinking of his safety too. She hauled her phone from her pocket and sent Maureen a hurried text. Farrell sat on her foot with a sigh. Allaine hauled open her door as Emma received Maureen's reply.

"Want coffee?" Allaine's guileless expression pained her.

She wagged her phone in the air. "She spoke to Ray. He's staying until Ro gets here."

"What?" Allaine scrunched up her features. She gave a shake of her blonde head. "What's that about Ray?"

Emma heaved out a sigh and tension locked her shoulders. Stephie grumbled against her chest and drew up her legs in discomfort. "I need you to just trust me." She implored Allaine with her eyes. "We have to grab the children from school and leave. Now."

Allaine gaped, studying Emma's expression as though searching for a hidden joke. "Why?" She cocked her head to one side before waving her arm at the apartment behind her. "Where are we going? What do I need?"

"Nothing!" Emma dipped at the waist, hating the disruption she'd caused. "Lock up and leave now. Ray's guarding the house. We need to use your car because it's less distinctive than mine." For the first time, Emma recognised the stupidity of a bright yellow vehicle. It was all fun and games until someone got hurt. "Please can you take Stephie? I'll grab her baby seat and meet you back here."

Allaine's lips moved, but she made no sound as Emma handed over her daughter and fled down the stairs. Farrell padded behind her, his perceived urgency making his tail move in a jerky wag. She left him outside and sneaked through the front door to snatch her car key from the mantelpiece in the lobby. He bounced to his paws as she emerged and stood next to her while she unclipped Stephie's seat from the back of her vehicle. A heavy hand on her shoulder produced a blood curdling scream.

Whirling around, she found Ray standing behind her. She exhaled in a rush and glared at the dog. "Well, you failed at the first hurdle!" Her rebuke earned her a tentative tail wag and pricked ears.

"I'll take that." Ray collected the seat from her arms and turned on his heel. He glanced back at her as she fussed over locking her car. "You need to leave now, sweetheart," he urged. "Not in a week's time."

Emma exhaled and regretted surrounding herself with authoritative males. She trotted after him, the dog bounding next to her. Farrell lifted his head and swiped at her fingers with his tongue. "I didn't ask Maureen about the dog," she breathed. Ray's lengthy stride caused her to jog.

"Leave him with me."

"I can't!" Conflict budded in Emma's eyes as she gazed on Farrell's smiling lips. Her shoes skidded to a halt. "This is ridiculous! It's my home. I'm not leaving!"

Ray turned to her and his tanned features hardened into a mask of impatience. He stopped and matched her determined stance, his heavy boots grinding against the gravel. His biceps flexed as he cradled Stephie's baby seat. "Yes, you are," he growled. "Don't make me lock you in the car boot and drop you off in the middle of nowhere."

Emma tossed her dark curls. "You wouldn't dare." Her hands settled over her hips and she glared at him. "Rohan would kill you. Anyway, you'd need to suppress me first. Ro taught me Krav Maga."

Ray blew out a frustrated breath like the snort of an angry horse. "First, the captain would thank me. Not to mention I could suppress you in less time than you imagine without breaking a sweat." He jabbed his thumb into his chest. "And I've forgotten more hand-to-hand combat moves than you've ever known." He jerked his head towards the stables. "Now move!"

Emma twisted her face into a pout but followed him as he beat a course to Allaine's apartment. She met them on the balcony. "What's going on?" she demanded. Stephie grizzled in her arms.

"Car key." Ray held out his creased palm and tapped his foot until Allaine locked the ranch slider and dropped her keys into his hand. "Downstairs. Two minutes." He hefted the baby seat under one arm and jogged past his apartment and down the steps to the yard.

Allaine handed over the wriggling child. "I don't like this." A frantic edge entered her voice, driving it up an octave. "This isn't right, Emma. Tell me what's happened?"

"We'll walk and talk." She turned towards the stairs and hoisted Stephie over her shoulder. "You need to drive in case I have to feed her in the back seat. Nicky can sit in the front with Kaylee next to me."

Allaine groaned and her long legs carried her after Emma. "Fine! But I'm going nowhere without an explanation. We can't take the kids out of school with no good reason."

Emma's stilettos clattered down the wooden steps. She held onto the banister with one hand and cradled Stephie's nodding head with the other. Her daughter flopped over her shoulder as though created to fit. "I got into a fight with Christopher. He stormed out of the kitchen in a temper and left his laptop." Emma swallowed. "The screen hadn't timed out, and I heard a notification. I couldn't help myself." She looked back at her friend, asking for forgiveness instead of permission. "He's been fielding threats towards the family."

"What threats?" Allaine's cheeks flattened as a worried expression claimed her face. "Why didn't he say something?"

"I don't know." Emma picked up speed, following Ray towards Allaine's car. It nestled alongside the wall enclosing the stable yard. His bottom protruded from the rear door as he fixed Stephie's seat into position. "The email gave him one more hour to sort things out, or they'd come for his wife and kids."

"He doesn't have either!" Allaine's lips turned down in disbelief. She spun on the spot. "Where is he? I'm sure he can explain this."

Ray pursed his lips. "Hack left ten minutes ago. He took the bike." Grit moved beneath his boot soles as he stood back to let Emma thread Stephie into the baby seat.

"He's not answering his phone." The car's interior muffled her voice. "I tried him first. Then I rang Rohan and got Maureen." She clicked the buckles into place and withdrew her head as Stephie opened her mouth in a wide yawn. "Maureen said we need to get out. It's possible someone has mistaken me or you for Christopher's family."

Ray snorted. "He should be so lucky." He jerked his thumb towards the gate. "Just get going. I'm sure the captain gave you a burner phone. Use that to contact me or Maureen until this is over."

Emma nodded. On an impulse, she threw her arms around Ray and kissed his cheek. "It could be a giant mistake." She flattened her lower lip at the shake of Ray's head.

"I doubt it," he replied.

"Did you forward the email to Maureen then?" Allaine jangled her keys and opened the driver's door.

Emma frowned. "No. She told me not to do anything that someone could trace. I connected a video call on my phone and she looked at it for herself. She said she'd track the sender and asked me to mark it as unread in the inbox. Then she instructed me to leave."

Allaine settled into her seat and fired the ignition. Emma clambered into the rear and shot a final look back at Ray. Her feckless wave communicated more than words as she fastened her seatbelt.

Exponent

Emma turned to stare through the rear window as Farrell's black lips parted in a distressed bark. The lap belt compressed her scar and sent darts of pain into her groin and chest. The dog bounced beneath Ray's grip on his collar, twisting and turning to escape the man's strong fingers. Tears pricked behind Emma's eyelids as she watched his frantic struggle. She closed her eyes and faced the front of the car. "He thinks we're going to school without him." Betrayal loaded her voice.

"Well, we are." Allaine tossed her blonde head and the grinding of her jaw demonstrated her irritation. She headed along the driveway and the nearing gates grew in the windscreen. "So, he's right. Where are we going after we've got the children?"

Emma pulled her phone from her skirt pocket and peered at the screen. Her eyes widened. "I didn't pick up the burner phone." She twisted in her seat to look back at the house. "I need to get it."

"No." Allaine blew out an exasperated breath. "We'll collect the children and drive around for a while. I can text Maureen from mine and explain. It's unlikely anyone is interested in triangulating my phone signal."

She pressed the button on a remote attached to her sun visor. The gates to Wingate Hall creaked open to let them leave. Ray had replaced the mechanism, but it hadn't altered the gate's painful slowness. Allaine tapped her fingers on the steering wheel as she watched the Verdigris-stained metal inch into an opening wide enough for a vehicle.

Emma glanced behind her and panicked. "Farrell's coming!" Her voice rose to a wail. "We have to stop and let him come with us."

"Can we take dogs where we're going?" Allaine peered in her rear-view mirror.

"I don't know." With every blink of Emma's black lashes, the dog powered closer to the car. Ray chased him at a jog as though assuming they'd wait for him. "I'm not leaving him here to get blown up or shot." Emma unfastened the lap belt and stretched across the baby seat to open the passenger door. A panting Farrell scrambled into the footwell and sat on his bottom as usual. His tongue lolled sideways from his smiling lips.

"Drive!" Emma struggled to haul the door closed, the forward momentum of the vehicle assisting her. When it clicked, she snatched the lap belt and pulled it across her stomach. "What's Ray doing?"

Allaine edged through the gates and glanced in her rear-view mirror. She winced. "He threw his hands in the air and shouted something with swear words in it. I'm not stopping to ask him for a repeat."

Emma's belt gave a satisfying click, and she leaned back against the seat. Stephie sucked her thumb next to her, delicate eyelashes fluttering against her porcelain cheeks. The dark tufts of hair she'd arrived with showed signs of lightening to create another mirror image of her father.

Allaine turned right onto the rural road and headed north towards Market Harborough. "Did Maureen text you the location we need to get to?" She glanced back and Farrell wagged his tail. He sank to his stomach and rested his chin on Emma's foot.

"I'll check." Emma activated the phone screen and scrawled through a plethora of old texts. Her shoulders slumped. "She'll send everything to the burner phone. It's too risky to contact this one."

"Throw it out the window." Allaine stretched her hand behind the seat and nudged Emma's knee. "Do it now. It's a risk."

She groaned. "My world is on this phone. Emails, reminders, bank details, and all my contacts." She blew out a breath. "I'll turn it off and take out the SIM card."

"I don't think that makes much difference. Everything is trackable nowadays." Allaine reached the outskirts of the town and slowed in response to the signs lowering the speed limit. Traffic built behind and in front of them. She tutted. "You didn't shut that door properly. I just noticed the light flashing on the dashboard." She turned her head and frowned. "Can you close it without me stopping?"

Emma leaned across the baby seat and stretched. She groaned as her scar sent a blossoming ache across her stomach. Her scrabbling fingers pushed the handle and a view of the passing asphalt made her gasp. She shoved it again and then released it, hoping the pressure would force it closed. "Did that work?" She sat up and pressed a hand over the pain.

"No." Allaine's hair ruffled as she shook her head. "I'll pull over here. There's a lot of traffic." She checked her rear-view mirror before edging the vehicle alongside the curb. Cars streamed past them on their way into town. She hauled on the handbrake and covered her face with her palms. "This is stressful," she breathed. "I can't believe we're blindly running like this."

"I'll do it." Emma sighed and extracted her foot from beneath Farrell's chin. "I'll slide out the other side to avoid clambering over Stephie." The dog rose in response, his tail bumping the baby seat. "Stay!" She wagged her finger at him and slid across to the other door, checking the road behind before edging it open. Her heels clicked against the asphalt as she made the trip around the back of Allaine's car. Vehicles whooshed by, rocking theirs and sending air to snatch at the fabric of Emma's skirt. She pulled on the door handle and opened it, tutting as Farrell performed a complete spin in the footwell and whined for her to let him out again. "Wait. You can get out for a minute when we arrive at school," she promised. Farrell's brow knitted as she slammed the door against his protest.

A heavy utility vehicle pulled up behind Allaine's car, its diesel engine sending a rumbling vibration through the road. Emma ignored it, moving around the rear bumper with her gaze fixed on her passenger door. Her mind whirred with problems and solutions. They'd collect the children on the pretext of a family emergency, text Maureen from Allaine's phone, and go to the hotel she'd booked. Farrell turned his body to chart her progress, and Emma wrinkled her nose at him through the window. She wondered if she could persuade him to climb into a large suitcase to smuggle him into a hotel room.

Allaine's door opened at speed and she struggled to unwrap her right arm from her seatbelt. "Get in the car, Emma!" she shrieked. "Get in the car!"

Emma blinked as a black SUV split from the traffic and dived in front of Allaine's car bonnet. Its wing missed her open door by millimetres.

"Hello again." The diesel engine behind her had masked the opening of the driver's door and she jerked as a hand clamped over her wrist.

Quotient

Emma turned with exaggerated slowness, already recognising the bony finger joints encircling her wrist. Blood roared through her ears, directing her anxiety towards Stephie and the unlocked passenger doors.

"Go!" She screamed the word at the same time as spinning to face her assailant. Her peripheral vision revealed Allaine clambering back into the car and the engine revving. She used the heel of her hand to deliver a painful uppercut to his chin while pressing a sharp stiletto into the top of his training shoe. The cloth upper gave beneath her weight and her heel jolted as it divided the fine bones of his second and third toe.

But he wasn't alone. Emma's head yanked backwards with force as another attacker pulled her ponytail. She cried out in torment and anger and found herself staring at the azure sky.

Not a single cloud marred its face as it gazed down on her trial. Allaine's rear bumper banged her thigh as she shoved the car into reverse gear by accident. A stretching, tearing sensation bloomed from Emma's stomach. The man with the green eyes and unruly ginger hair withdrew his fist after the punch, grimacing with satisfaction as she crumpled to her knees clutching her scar. He hopped on one leg, his teeth bared from the injury she'd inflicted on his foot. Exhaust fumes filled her lungs, a testament to Allaine treading on the gas pedal. But the car didn't move forward, remaining stationary and burning oil which shrouded Emma in black vapour.

A sharp inhale accompanied another tug of Emma's hair and the second man disappeared. Her eyes watering and her fingers pressing on the bruise consuming her belly, she glanced up to catch the fear imprinted on her skinny assailant's features. He swallowed and took a step backwards, lifting his elbows to cover his face. Emma's laboured breathing doubled her forward, a pair of stout black shoes blocking her view. A dull thud signified a body falling to the road, and through her tears, she saw ginger curls scraping against the asphalt.

"Mrs Oskar?" A thick, Russian accent cut through the hum of her blood in her ears. A palm with chunky digits attached, appeared in front of her face. "Your father sent us on behalf of Alexei. Can you stand?"

"I don't know." She touched her crown with tentative fingers. Her hair tie came away, taking strands of mahogany curls with it. Allaine's frantic revving ceased and warm air rushed to fill the space vacated by the exhaust fumes. A car door slammed.

"Emma. Are you okay?" Tears littered Allaine's ragged speech. "They boxed me in and I couldn't move. I didn't want to leave you." Her breath hitched in her chest and she sank to her knees beside Emma. Her arm trembled across her shoulders as she tried to offer comfort.

"Stephie." Emma lifted her torso, and the pain remained constant. It didn't worsen as she rose. She accepted the stranger's outstretched hand and pushed one leg into position, readying herself to stand. The strain of using her muscles drove her to the ground again. "Where's Stephie?"

"She's fine, I promise." Allaine disappeared, returning seconds later with a watery smile on her lips. "She's sleeping. I can't believe she slept through all that." She lifted her mobile phone from her pocket and unlocked the screen. "You need an ambulance and I want the cops. If these men hadn't stopped to help, they'd have taken you."

"No ambulance. No cops." The man whom Winston had handpicked to save them reached out and snagged Allaine's phone. It disappeared inside his jacket. Emma looked up into eyes the colour of an icy lake, a chiselled jaw squaring the lower half of his face. He jerked his chin towards a second SUV parking close behind the assailants' vehicle. "We go now." He presented the sentence as a command with no room for negotiation.

Emma shook her head. "I need Stephie."

Soles ground against the loose grit embedded in the pavement, and footsteps moved around Allaine's car. The passenger door opened.

Allaine panicked. "Emma, who are these men? What about fetching the children from school?" Her fingers writhed in front of her and tears budded in her eyes. "You can't go with them. We need to tell Maureen."

The footsteps returned, followed by a whispered conversation in Russian. Emma caught the word *sobaka*. Dog.

"Wait!" She accepted the proffered hand again and forced herself to stand. Her abdomen throbbed enough to take her breath away and leave her with shallow puffs. "He's protecting her," she gasped. She used the boot of Allaine's car to support herself as she weaved her way around to Stephie. Farrell stood guard in the open doorway, his lips pulled back to reveal his incisors and four lethal canines. He looked so unlike the softer version of himself. It made Emma pause with her hand on the roof. "Good boy," she rasped. "We need to go now."

Farrell's mouth closed with a snap, and the glazed look in his eyes melted. His rigid tail moved in its regular swishing action. He bounced from the vehicle and sat on her foot, his floppy ears pulled back as though tied together.

"Come." Emma rested her hand on his head and hobbled towards the nearest fence. He moved with her but kept glancing at Allaine's car. Growling issued from low in his throat as the Russians lifted the sleeping baby from the car and placed her seat into the second sleek SUV. Allaine drifted next to Emma and kept her face in her hands.

"Someone will call the police." Her voice held a keening note. "The traffic is heavy. Someone will have seen what happened."

Emma nodded, pain snatching her explanation as she stammered disjointed words. "Rohan's father sent these men." She blew out a breath. "Trust them. They're taking us home."

Sirens sounded from far away, their plaintive wail like the onslaught of reality. The first man returned to Emma, not bothering to offer his hand this time but sweeping her into his arms. He settled her in the passenger seat with care and closed the door. Allaine jumped into the rear and clambered over Stephie, abandoning her vehicle to the probing of approaching police officers. Farrell bounced in after her and slumped into the foot well. With a whir, the SUV spun around in the traffic and headed south, away from Market Harborough. Emma cradled her stomach and dipped forward, able to peer into the side mirror. A second SUV set off in the other direction.

"What about those other men?" Allaine's voice caught as she craned her neck to stare through the tinted rear window.

Their driver grunted but offered no reply.

Emma sighed and leaned back against the seat. Her insides seemed less jellified as the minutes passed, and though she felt like a horse had kicked her between the legs, she credited the pain to bruising. She'd feared her stitches might have burst, but good sense informed her they'd dissolved weeks ago and the scar would hold. She released a long exhale. "I don't know and I don't care," she replied.

Take Away

Emma faced Christopher, her features set into hard lines. She'd grown weary of walking the line with the Irishman, tired of letting him push his agenda without regard for the consequences for her. "Leave me alone!" she snapped. Her fingers patted Stephie's delicate back as her daughter writhed against the wind trapped in her belly. She used her elbow to shove away the book she'd been reading.

"Why are you behaving like this?" Lines marred Christopher's tanned forehead. He took a step towards her. His arms opened as though he might cajole her as usual. His brow furrowed. "Why did Andreyev take you to the doctor's surgery? Are you sick?"

Emma's right hand strayed to her stomach. Just bruised and tender. She'd lied to the doctor about a fall, but the spreading purple marks from the imprint of knuckles had now flagged her as a risk. It formed another black mark against Christopher Dolan.

"Come on, babe. You can tell me what's wrong. We have a thing, remember?" His expression softened, and he narrowed the distance between them.

"There is no thing, between us, Christopher. I liked you once. But you betrayed Rohan, and by doing that, you put me in the firing line." She glanced down at Stephie's sweet face. "And I was pregnant the first time you did that."

"No, you know what happened there." Christopher's eyelids flickered for a moment and he dipped forward as though to suppress the truth. "It was a misunderstanding."

"It always is." Emma sighed. "You're on a mission to self-destruct and I don't see a way to stop it happening. You're a liability to me and my children." Her jaw set into a hard ridge against her cheek.

Realisation touched Christopher's expression, but then he jumped to the wrong conclusion. "You told Andreyev." His eyes widened for a split second before his chest appeared to deflate like a balloon. "You confessed I made a pass at you, didn't you?" His tone flattened, the volume reducing to a whisper.

Emma nodded. Rohan knew everything. She needed to stop Christopher using his own feelings to lord them over her like a shared secret. She watched misery dawn in the slow smile which spread across his lips in a reluctant admission of defeat. Her heart gave a pang of sympathy, but only for a second. The moment contained the bitterness of ash. "Rohan and I don't keep secrets from each other."

Christopher's snort of derision held a strangled quality. "Fine. So, what did he say?" He pressed on, their conversation going even further in the wrong direction and skirting the actual issue.

Emma sighed. "I can't repeat it." She lifted her right hand in a dismissive wave. "The Russian syllables are complicated."

Christopher ran both hands through his hair. Desperation shrouded him like a cloak. "I should watch my back for a while."

Emma shook her head. "Longer than a while."

He whipped around, his trainers catching against the expensive rug. "Are you enjoying this?"

"No." Emma sighed. "Not at all." She pushed Stephie over her shoulder and rose as the child squirmed, patting the raised bottom with her palm. Stephie gave a shriek of delight and her legs spasmed. Emma's gentle twirl increased the baby's enjoyment as her strengthening vision picked up the colours and light patterns through the window. Entranced, Stephie forgot about her bellyache.

Christopher swore and slumped into a dining chair. His fringe stood tall like a crest of black surf. "Sorry." His apology sounded hollow, pulled from a reluctant heart. "I enjoy living here. It's the first time I've felt part of a family since I left Ireland."

Emma wrinkled her nose. "You just had to accept my relationship with Rohan. It was the only condition."

Christopher leaned his forearms on the table. His fingers tapped an irritating tattoo. "You liked me though, didn't you? At the start. We could have got together if Rohan hadn't resurfaced."

"Oh, Christopher," Emma sighed. "I can't be the only woman to refuse you. We are where we are and I won't cheat on Rohan or my children. You should know that by now."

Christopher dipped forward and rubbed his eyes with the backs of his hands. He gave a nod of concession. "It's become a game, I guess. One I don't want to lose."

Stephie's gurgles extended into a groan. She followed it with a grunt of discomfort. Her tiny fists snagged a hank of Emma's hair and tugged to communicate her urgency. Colic surged and the grunt morphed into a grizzle. Emma bobbed her knees to grab her phone from the table. Her book tipped, the pages making a shushing sound before it plunged to the floor. She froze as the birth certificate fluttered free and landed a millisecond before the heavy book crushed it beneath its weight.

"What's that?" Christopher's brown irises glittered like gems.

Emma slipped the phone one handed into the front of her bra. Stephie's cries increased in pitch and the cool plastic case chaffed against her breasts. She dipped to retrieve the book, balancing the wriggling child with difficulty. Christopher moved lightning fast, his reflexes practised and deft. He squatted before her, gathering the dustcover with careful fingers and lifting the fragile birth certificate from beneath it. He smoothed the bent corner across his knee.

"Who's this?" His black eyebrows rose as he inspected the typed name.

Emma sighed and held out her hand. "Someone I used to know," she said, her tone wistful.

Christopher rose, and she sensed his gaze following her towards the door. Emma's body blocked his view of her shaking fingers on the door knob. "I'll try harder," he called after her. She turned with a smile to acknowledge his decision, but it was all too late. Christopher gave his characteristic nonchalant shrug. "Even I know when I've got a good thing going here." He flapped his hand in dismissal. "I'll behave from today." He performed a fake bow and pointed at her. "What did you do with that flash drive?" The blackness of calculation darkened his chocolate irises. "I need to borrow it back for a couple of days."

"No." Emma pulled the door towards her. "And by the way, Ray's waiting for you at the folly. He'll make sure you sabotage nothing as you leave the property." She retreated during Christopher's wail of protest. The corridor outside nursed a chill from the breeze ushering in a late autumn. She hoped the tired sun clung on for Freda's garden party at the weekend. It could do what it liked beyond that and disappear for its usual four months' sabbatical.

"Hey!" Christopher yanked the door open and Emma's shoulders tensed against his anticipated protest. He held up his right hand, the index finger pointed as though in question. She stopped, a frown settling over her brow as Stephie wiggled over her shoulder. A smile spread across his features like sunlight in a grove. "The answer is yes, by the way. You are the only woman who ever refused me."

Emma walked along the corridor, battling with conflicting emotions. He ignored her command to vacate the folly as though she hadn't spoken. Christopher Dolan hadn't just kissed the Blarney Stone. He'd eaten it whole.

Hexadecimal

H er hopes sank as Christopher followed her along the corridor leading to the lounge. He would make it into a battle because he couldn't contemplate losing. "What did you mean before?" A vein ticked in his neck as he considered she might have been serious. "You were joking, weren't you?" Affront filled his tone and increased his Irish lilt. "It wasn't funny."

Emma glanced at her watch. Rohan had given her an hour's grace before he waded in and threw the Irishman out himself. She sighed. "I was serious. You need to leave. Now."

Christopher rolled his eyes and followed her into the lounge. "Come on, Em! Are you sore because you couldn't find Frederik's kid? It's fine. I found his hiding place, but then I lost him again. He'll surface. Nobody hides from me for long."

Emma nodded. She patted her daughter's spine and pressed a kiss to her delicate temple. "I know they don't." Exhaustion nipped at her ankles and the pain in her stomach spread into her legs. "Don't treat me like an idiot."

"Just give me the flash drive." He winced. "I should have made a copy, but I didn't expect you to demand its return."

Emma snorted. "Because you assumed I'd believe you like I always do. I underestimated you. I felt so sure I understood you, but I missed the mark on every level because I'm not trained to spot liars."

"What are you talking about?" Christopher's tone held desperation. He dipped forward as he spoke and sweat beaded over his top lip.

"I worked out you'd lied about ditching it. But when you returned it with less fuss than I anticipated, I figured you wiped it." Emma inhaled. "So, I threw it in the bin."

"You what?" Christopher's body stiffened, and he stepped closer. "Is this a joke, Em?"

"No." Her chestnut curls bounced against her shoulder as she shook her head. "It's true." She turned aside to concentrate on her daughter. "Does that mean you can't fulfil the auction? What a shame. Has he already paid you? Do you think a wallet full of bitcoin will help you?"

"Who?" Christopher's lips peeled back in a snarl. "Has who paid me?"

"The guy who attacked me in the store the other day." Emma shifted Stephie into her arms and gazed on her porcelain features. Tufts of white hair mingled with the darker strands to create woven curls. Her eyelashes flickered as she blinked and pursed her lips. "He seemed angry, like a man who'd lost a fortune."

"Give me the flash drive, Em." Christopher held out his hand, the palm curved as though imagining the device nestling there.

Emma closed her eyes. "You created the cache, Chris. I'm sure you have other copies." She clicked her fingers. "Oh, yeah. You couldn't risk that, could you? There needed to be a single point of truth, and then you could direct everyone to Regan. Tell me, what makes a man sink low enough to recruit a child to do his dirty work?" She rocked her daughter and wished she hadn't volunteered to perform the horrible task. Circumstance forced her to do it with her vulnerable baby in her arms. The pendulum of the grandfather clock swung in her peripheral vision, marking time until Rohan appeared and finished the job for her.

Christopher's audible gulp betrayed his inner turmoil. "I don't understand."

Emma whirled to face him. "You've spent years grooming Regan as a hacker. Then you baited a hook too tasty for him to avoid and sat back to wait for the fun to start. You thought he'd delete the army files in situ. But he took a copy, changed it, and then added a virus to the original." Despite herself, she smiled. "He's smart, Chris. Beyond what you gave him credit for and he outwitted you. You didn't expect him to use the postal service or hide himself so well, but you guessed he'd go to his father for help. And who would Frederik turn to next? You. I wonder how well you hid your shock when you learned of the flash drive's existence. So, you suggested he planted it on me, needing it in your hands while pretending you'd done us all a favour. I suspect the auction was a means to capitalise on a happy accident." Her disbelief moved through disappointment and settled as disgust. "You knew I went shopping for Nicky's costume because we talked about it before I left. I bet you called the store and told the security guards I'd stolen something, so they'd detain me." She wanted to slump onto the window seat, but his proximity made the action inadvisable. "You knew Frederik wouldn't tell me you'd already spoken because it might jeopardise my help. I'd realise you both manipulated me. I understand his behaviour because he'd lost his son, but not yours. You're not the man I believed you were."

"And who did you think I was?" Christopher spread his hands out either side of him. It looked like a plea for the mercy Emma could no longer give him. "The guy on the bike who watched over you during your darkest times. The one who lived on the same property to fix up your husband's mistakes and cover them with clever technology? Or this one? The one just wishing you'd look at me long enough to see how much I love you."

Emma turned away from his beseeching brown irises. "You've broken my heart." She meant it. With trembling hands, she laid Stephie in her bouncy chair and watched her daughter look up at the ceiling as her eye muscles focused. The child pushed both hands into her mouth and gurgled. Emma's fingers writhed in front of her stomach, casting strange shadows across her skirt as the sunlight dodged their agonised movement. "I loved you," she admitted. "Until you searched my drawers and wardrobe for the flash drive. Until I realised you'd thrown me into the mix as collateral damage. I just never loved you the way you wanted." She spun to face him, her eyes flashing and her jaw showing as hard angles through her cheek. "You wear corruption like a badge of honour." A shudder began in her chest and radiated through her muscles until she struggled to control the tremor in her fingers. "I can't have you around my children, anymore."

Christopher's neck jerked and a frown line appeared between his eyes. "You don't mean that." His tone contained a half certainty, as though he believed he could talk her around to his way of thinking. "Anton made me your minder. He made me love you with all his ridiculous stories about the poor wee vicar's daughter." Christopher took a step forward, his arms outstretched. "Emma, I can't break my promise to him. I'm not leaving you."

"You can. And you are." Emma closed her eyes and when she opened them again, she found her inner vision clearer. "Just tell me what Frederik did to make you want to ruin his son's life."

Christopher's features sharpened into hard points and his tone became lacklustre and flat. "He told me to stay away from you. Years ago, before you even realised I existed."

For a moment, Emma's breathing stalled. Her heart hammered faster as her chest froze and she gave a series of rapid blinks. Christopher responded to her distress, risking four steps across the rug before stopping. Her voice wavered. "That's all?" Her lips parted in a smile which carried more misery than mirth. She pressed her palm to her chest to suppress the bubble of pain threatening to burst free. "If that's all it took to make you into an enemy, I can't imagine why I ever thought you were my friend."

"I am!" Christopher's protest held sincerity. "You can't see the mistake you're making."

Emma clapped her hands over her ears and turned away from him. A swarm of thoughts buzzed through her mind like distressed bees. "So, you hacked a government website and set Rohan against Frederik. Why? Did you think they'd kill each other, Christopher? Is that your idea of entertainment?"

He shrugged, the action casual and effortless. His arms hung limp by his sides, but his hands twitched. "One can hope."

"You shouldn't have involved me." She snapped her fingers and spun to face him. "Oh, I get it. To make me rely on you and cement our cosy little team. But you intended me to fail, didn't you, Chris? Then what? You'd console me on my uselessness and sell the flash drive to the highest bidder?"

Christopher released a deep sigh. Playfulness appeared from behind the spark in his eyes as his conscience took a holiday. "Doesn't matter anymore. You found him all by yourself and you hid him. Well done, Emma. You're an exceptional student." His palms closed together in a slow, antagonising clap. The applause showered her in sarcasm and not celebration. "Now, you just need to tell me where I went wrong. When did you realise what I'd done?"

She swallowed and paused to give herself time. Her tongue stuck to the roof of her mouth. "You're sloppier than you think you are," she managed. Stephie grizzled in her seat and Emma lifted her into her arms. Her daughter blinked azure irises against the sunshine pouring through the window onto her face. It lit her up like an angel. Emma gritted her teeth and turned to Christopher. "You need to leave. Now." She looked at the rug with its vibrant colours, red mixed with black and forest green. Her vision blurred until it became a mess of shades. She choked on the lump in her throat and it distorted her words. "In exactly ninety minutes, government operatives will arrive to collect you."

Christopher gaped. "What?"

Emma rehearsed her sentence before releasing the words into the air. "You hacked a secure government site and passed it off onto a child. Then, you auctioned it and didn't deliver. Everyone thinks you have the data and they're coming for you." She jerked her head at the door. "In less than an hour, Rohan will start walking from the house to the folly and he has no mercy for you. I suggest you meet Ray now and gather your belongings."

Christopher ran a hand over his jaw and shook his head. "No. You don't mean any of this." His chocolate irises darkened with pain. "You can't replace me!"

Emma closed her eyes and struggled with the final arrow in her quiver. She didn't want to use it, but his constant need to overpower her will left her no choice. "I already did," she whispered. "He's in the folly changing all the codes."

She didn't look up as the lounge door slammed hard enough to send a book tumbling off the nearest shelf. Emma stood like a statue in the centre of the room while her heart cracked right down the middle.

Binary

Emma's burner phone rang on the dressing table the next morning and she snatched it up as she paused for breath. She'd squeezed into her jeans, but not without difficulty. The zipper had made her eyes water, and she observed herself in the full-length mirror. The pressure of the denim compressed the bruising which had blossomed in purple welts from her groin to her ribs. It didn't help. "What?" Her tone held a bite as she aborted her mission and slipped the jeans down over her buttocks one-handed. She'd lost the baby weight, but the stomach wound wasn't yet ready for a fashion statement. Emma sat the device on the mattress and released herself from her discomfort. Frederik's number remained on the screen, but he kept silent. "Are you there?" she grunted as she wrestled her ankles from the cloistering fabric.

"Yeah." His dull tone forced her hands to still. He hadn't queried the soft grunts emanating from her lips as she wrestled with the bottom of the jeans and resorted to turning them inside out to extricate herself.

"What's wrong?" Emma stood in her bedroom in her bra and knickers. A child's fake engine noise from the hallway outside revealed a seven-year-old playing a lone game of bomber pilot with his Action Man. She took a deep breath and seized the phone, taking it with her into the walk-in-wardrobe.

"Regan is missing."

Emma gave a sharp inhale. "What are you talking about?" An eerie sense of deja vu slithered up her spine and set off a tremor of fear. She yanked a light cotton dress from a hanger and yanked it over her head. She switched the phone into her other hand to settle the fabric over her hips. "You lost him again?" Her voice rose at the end of the sentence and she winced against the accusation behind it. "Sorry." She pulled her lower lip beneath her teeth. The bouquet of fabric conditioner covered her, mixing with the musky scent of Rohan's aftershave. She lifted the sleeve of a white shirt hanging from the top rail and pressed it against her nose to reconnect with his essence.

"I need to speak to Rohan." Frederik cleared his throat and blew out a sharp breath. "But can you sound him out first? Explain what's happened and see if he knows anything about Regan's location. I don't want to compromise his position but I'm worried." He swallowed. "I doubt he'll ever let me work for him after this."

Emma groaned. She pushed her feet into flip flops and closed the wardrobe door behind her. "Nooo!" She dragged out the sound, reluctance in every fibre of her being. "I can't talk to him about it! He helped me once and made it clear we couldn't speak about it again. It's compromised him already."

"He helped you with Regan?"

"How?" Frederik's tone became clipped and business-like. "How, Emma?"

Stephie grumbled in her crib and tension settled in Emma's spine. A sense of finding herself caught between a rock and a hard place surfaced. She stamped like a child. The floorboards complained with a guttural creak, and the bomber pilot game ceased. Pattering footsteps headed along the hallway in her direction. Emma huffed out an exasperated breath. "This was not my problem," she hissed. "You seem to have forgotten that. And much as I'd love to think I could pull anonymization software and the necessary tech out of my ass, I needed his help."

Frederik swore. Not once, but many times. He added a few impressive consonant run-ons which sounded Swedish. Emma jabbed at the phone to take it off speaker and lifted it to her ear.

"There's no need to be so ungrateful!" she snarled before disconnecting. Her bedroom door squeaked and Nicky's face peeked through the gap. He kept his hands over his eyes.

"Are you rudey dudey?" he enquired.

"No. I'm dressed." Emma forced herself to smile.

"I heard a massive bang. Did you just drop Stephie on the floor?" His eyes popped wide and his gaze tracked to the crib. Unable to see his sister, his light steps skipped across the room. Action Man's bungee cord trailed along the rug behind him. Emma pursed her lips as any hope of Stephie going back to sleep faded with the arrival of her brother's clownish face peering down at her. She gave a squeak and created popping sounds with her mouth. Nicky laughed and a tiny, bare foot appeared over the edge of the blanket. He reached for the baby's toes and tickled them with gentle fingers. Leaning down to kiss them rewarded him with a kick to the chin. "Ouch!" He exaggerated his yelp and Stephie made a sound like tinkling bells.

"I need to feed her and then we'll drive to school." Emma organised the paraphernalia required for a swift nappy change and met Nicky by the crib. She hoisted the baby at the same time as flicking open the buttons at the front of her dress. "Where's Dad?"

"Do you want him?" Nicky twisted his lips and gazed back towards the wardrobe. "Were you looking for a gun?"

"No!" Emma widened her eyes in reprimand. "They aren't there. He moved them." She frowned. "Why would I need a gun to take you to school?"

"Dunno." Nicky shrugged. "And they are there. Otherwise, why did he block the tunnel and install an alarm panel?"

"Ask him." Emma abdicated responsibility for something over which she had no control. She cast an eye over her son's attempt to dress in his smart uniform. "Well done for getting your buttons straight this morning. Maybe tuck your shirt into your trousers."

Nicky's grin widened to display the gaps in his front teeth. "It's yesterday's shirt," he admitted. "You did them up straight the first time and I just slipped it over my head." He balanced on one leg and waved Action Man in the air. His nose tracked to his armpit. "It's not too stinky. Who's that new person in Harley Man's office? Is he staying forever?"

Emma's shoulders slumped. "No. He's helping for a few days. Someone else is arriving on Saturday."

"Is Harley Man coming back then?"

"Not at the moment. Please can you nip downstairs and tell Dad I need to see him before he goes to work?"

"Okay." Nicky leaned forward for a kiss, waiting until her lips touched his forehead. Then he trailed the bungee cord across the floor. The door clicked shut behind him and Emma listened to his footsteps patter along the hall. He skipped to the far end and his voice echoed as he bellowed down the back stairs, "Dad! Mum wants ya!"

Computational Weakness

"I thought we agreed not to discuss it." Rohan licked his lips and his shoulders tensed. "Don't you trust me?" He closed the door behind him.

"It's not that." Emma's fingers writhed in her lap. She focussed her gaze on Stephie's legs as they lifted and fell on the change mat. Her pink bottom held the colour of a pale rose as the sun's rays sneaked from between the curtains to kiss its delicate skin. "Regan is missing again. Frederik wanted me to ask for your help."

Rohan's brow furrowed into a set of hard lines. Emma dreaded his disappointment and quailed beneath its heady threat. Instead of chiding her, he sat next to her on the mattress and fixed his arm around her shoulders. "Emma,

I didn't contact you when Anton asked me to, but not for the selfish reasons you believed. You and the children are my single weak point."

"Oh." Emma closed her eyes and remembered her night of captivity when another actuary used her as collateral to force Rohan's hand. "Like at Falkirk?"

"Like at Falkirk." Rohan pressed a kiss to her temple. "There's a role for you in my work, Em, but this is not it. Frederik is using you to tap for information or compel me to take an action, which is contrary to my intention. Do you understand?"

"Yes." Emma closed her eyes as she nodded. "But his child is missing. He's trying to appeal to your better nature." She observed her daughter's flailing legs and put herself in Frederik's situation. "I would do the same."

"Da." Rohan inhaled. "Do you trust me?"

"Yes!" She turned to him, insulted by the question. Rohan's smile spread to his eyes as he stymied her. "Then let me do my job."

Emma swallowed. "What do I tell Frederik?"

Rohan's lips flattened and sadness shrouded his shoulders like a cloak. "Block his number."

She gaped. "I can't do that! Susan is my friend."

"Da." He nodded and released her from the embrace. When he rose, cool air rushed into the gap between them. "Then tell him I no longer need his services."

Rohan's footsteps receded along the hallway. Emma clutched her stomach and bent double so her forehead touched the mattress. Frederik's agony communicated itself to her in waves of nausea, which ascended from the soles of her feet to encompass her entire body. Rohan asked her if she trusted him, and she'd answered without thinking. "I did once," she whispered. Her eyelashes fluttered against the bedspread, her memories raw. Her adoration for her vibrant, Russian husband had consumed her, as naïve and foreboding as a field of poppies. Beautiful and deadly.

"Ohhhh." Emma rolled onto her side with a groan and watched her daughter's jerky arm movements. She reached out to tug the cloth nappy under the baby's bottom. "This is too hard," she breathed. "He's asking me to pick a team and stick to it." She sighed and flopped backwards on the bed. Stephie gurgled and blew bubbles, her growing cerebrum soaking up the details of her surroundings as her sight developed. She squawked and stared at something above her head which Emma couldn't see. "Are you looking at angels again, baby?" she whispered.

Her stomach muscles responded to her command to sit upright. They woke as though from slumber, the movement laboured and slow and infused with the familiar ache from her stitches. But it marked the start of an improvement which her body had begun even before she took up the mantle of recovery. The punch in the stomach hadn't helped, but it caused no permanent damage. Rohan's voice rumbled in the hallway as he chatted to Nicky about something relating to their shared love of mathematics. Emma strode across to the door and hauled it open.

Her boys stood beneath the glass roof half way along the hallway, the early morning sunshine lighting up the highlights in their hair. Nicky balanced on one leg, his eyes glazed as he worked out a complex equation in his brain. Rohan turned his gaze to regard Emma with a quirked eyebrow. "Would you like me to drive Nikolai to school?" he asked.

"Yes." Emma winced. "But first, we need a conversation."

Rohan frowned as though tempted to make an excuse. His jaw hardened, and he nodded down at his son. "You can have longer to work it out," he concluded. His fingers ruffled Nicky's blond hair. "It's a hard one."

"How much longer?" Nicky twisted his lips and gave a slow, appealing blink. "Can I tell you at school?"

"Da." Rohan's feet turned towards Emma and he set off walking.

"Dad?" Nicky's plea halted him. "Can you make Kaylee stop talking in the car then? She muddles my brain."

"No." Rohan resumed his uneven gait, the sleek trousers clinging to his thighs and his suit jacket squaring his firm shoulders. "Distractions come in many forms. Learn to use your concentration to disregard them."

"Okay." Nicky heaved out a breath. "What's your biggest distraction, Dad?" He skipped behind Rohan, until reaching in and throwing Action Man onto his bedroom rug. He slammed the door before waiting for an answer.

"Your mother." Rohan's expression didn't change as he reached the doorway and waited for Emma to step aside.

Nicky's whoop of laughter continued along the hallway, echoing against the high ceiling of the lobby as he skipped down the main staircase. Rohan stood at ease like a soldier, just inside the bedroom. His jaw flexed and he observed Emma through narrowed eyes. "You wish to talk me around to your way of thinking?" It sounded like a statement of fact, and Emma bridled.

"No." Her biting answer carried her across to the bed and she busied herself with covering Stephie's pink bottom with a clean nappy. "I'm asking for help with my dilemma." She inhaled and released the breath. "Frederik will call again, and it's not enough to just block his number." The fingers which stabbed the safety pin through the thick fabric shook with a mixture of anger and dismay. "Nor is it my job to fire him. Do your own dirty work." Emma fitted the rubber pants over Stephie's wiggling legs and fixed the poppers of her vest. She lifted the baby over her shoulder and patted her back. "When the Contessa's goons kidnapped me last year, Frederik came for me. I owe him."

Rohan stared at her, his gaze impassive. Then he shrugged and his hand closed around the door knob. "Fine. I'll fire him myself."

Emma's facial muscles tensed to the point of pain. "That's it?" She released a snort of derision. "That's the level of our teamwork, is it?"

He shrugged. "What do you want from me?"

Emma turned and hauled open a drawer one handed. She tugged out a blue cotton dress and laid Stephie on the bed to shrug it over the baby's head. The child grumbled as Emma fitted her waving arms through the gaps and hauled it down over her legs. "You ask for trust, while offering none. You expect me to change who I am while refusing to meet me even half way."

Rohan twisted the door knob and Emma's heart thudded in her breast. She waited for him to walk out on her, nursing her surprise when he didn't. His fingers released the door knob. "I understand." His shoulders relaxed. "I'm desperate for you to trust me, but didn't consider your point of view."

Emma's phone rang as though on cue, and she glanced at the number and sighed. "Help me?" she implored her husband. "Please?"

Analysis

"I trust you, Rohan." The phone vibrated across the bedspread as she uttered the statement and infused it with strength and commitment. She held his gaze, forcing herself not to blink first, though the effort made her eyes water. "But Frederik trusts me. I worked hard to earn that, and it cost me."

Rohan's slow nod offered an acknowledgement. He clasped his hands behind his back and stood at ease, lowering his centre of gravity and spreading the weight across his real leg and the prosthetic. "I understand. He's still fired, but you can tell him Regan is at a safe house, alive and unharmed. That's the end of this conversation."

Emma pursed her lips. "Frederik didn't hide him very well then?"

Rohan shrugged. "No matter. I created the anonymization and obfuscation software you asked him to load onto his new laptop. It contained a key logger which sent me his location."

Emma sank onto the bed next to Stephie. Her shoulders slumped and the words she wanted to say evaded her. "You set me up," she managed.

"No." Rohan shook his head. He relocated to the armchair opposite the TV they rarely used. "I said I'd help you fix things, but didn't explain how that might happen." He dipped forward, leaning his elbows on his thighs. "Remember how the Contessa followed my jobs, mopping up loose ends and capitalising however she could?"

"Yes." She released a loud breath and kissed her daughter's cheek. Stephie turned her face sideways against Emma's shoulder and her eyelashes fluttered closed. Tension created a strange atmosphere in the room, adding a dangerous electrical charge. Stephie whimpered as though it pained her.

"That's what happens." Rohan steepled his fingers and examined the white scars criss-crossing his knuckles. "I might secure a contract, but a dogfight ensues behind me as other actuaries pick up the crumbs and monetise the assets. A job isn't over until the final payment clears. Then everyone goes home and counts their cash or their losses until the next contract." He cocked his head and flattened his lips. "Regan was a loose asset and between you and Frederik, you hung him out to dry. I contacted him and we met at my office. You knew that."

Emma nodded. Her chest burned with the rebuke. "So, can I tell Frederik his son is okay?" She forced herself to meet Rohan's gaze. "I can at least say that?"

"Da." Rohan inclined his head. The action reminded her of Winston. "You can, Emma."

The dryness of her throat caused her sentence to crack in half. "I didn't know you'd rigged the software." Another piece of the Rohan Andreyev puzzle slotted into place, one she hadn't realised she needed. "It's more than a hobby, isn't it?"

He shrugged and rose from the chair. The air moved around him and his familiar, musky aftershave circled Emma like a warm blanket. "I couldn't rely on the Irishman for my safety. He has a split personality, the idiot and the criminal mastermind. I was never sure which version of him would show up on the day and besides, code follows numeric patterns. It's just sentences in another language and it fascinates me."

Emma pursed her lips to hide her smile. "Rohan Andreyev the hacker." Her chestnut irises glittered. "Will you teach me?"

"Maybe." Rohan's smirk spread and he captured his lower lip between his teeth.

Stephie sneezed, a delicate sound like a tiny, wet explosion. Emma rose as Nicky's footsteps thundered up the main staircase. "Dad!" he shouted. "I know the answer to your sum."

"I'll take the children to school." Rohan dug in his trouser pocket for his keys. He opened the door as Nicky barrelled inside, accompanied by Kaylee. "Then I'll drive to the station and leave the car there."

"Okay." Emma followed him, shooing out the children and snapping orders about shoes and lunches. She lifted her face for a kiss and enjoyed the electrical connection their contact created. Rohan's lips lingered over hers and she tilted her head, wanting more of him than either of them had time to give. "Thank you for trusting me," she whispered.

Rohan straightened his shoulders and nodded. He placed a kiss on Stephie's downy crown and ran an index finger beneath Emma's chin. "I admire your loyalty," he said. The heels of his shoes clicked along the hallway as he followed the children to the head of the stairs.

"It's a thousand." Nicky bounced next to his father, his backpack riding on his thin shoulders.

"A thousand," Kaylee repeated. Her ponytail swished from side to side as she ran to keep up with them. Her feet halted with such suddenness, her body dipped forward. "Why is it a thousand?" Confidence leached from her slender frame.

"I'll explain," Rohan promised. They descended the stairs together and his gentle tones rumbled to the lower levels.

"The square root of a million is a thousand because one million has six zeros. So, it's ten with the power of six."

Kaylee's chirpy voice interjected with tiny facts, and Rohan's affirmations drifted up to echo around the hallway. Emma pressed a kiss to her daughter's temple. "You have some catching up to do," she whispered. "But he won't leave you behind." She spoke the words and absorbed their truth. Rohan treated Kaylee no different from Nicky in encouraging her to love numbers. He'd shown her how to calculate the nine times table using her fingers and many other tricks. Her end of term reports demonstrated a shrinking fear of big numbers from her constant exposure to them.

Emma walked to the window and stared at the leafy side view of the garden. It offered a fresh perspective from the sweeping driveway and the expansive lawn. It intimidated her less, and she liked it.

Stephie lay down in her crib for a nap after a feed, and Emma took her two phones and the baby monitor to the laundry room at the other end of the hall. She set off the washing machine and wiped up a puddle of fabric conditioner before rescuing Freda's bloomers from the tumble dryer. Her burner phone rang as she folded Nicky's sports kit. "Hi Frederik." She put him on speaker so she could continue her task.

"Stop ignoring my calls!" His voice held a dangerous, ragged element. Helplessness and lack of sleep had created a cocktail of fury.

Emma weighed her loyalty and put it where she should have at the very start. "Regan is safe," she told him. She wrinkled her nose at a hole in the seam of Nicky's underpants. She parroted Rohan's words, "He's alive and unharmed."

"Where is he?" Frederik snarled. His acerbic tone set her teeth on edge, and her heart rate increased at the violence in his voice.

"I've told you he's fine," she bit back at him. "I don't know any more than that. Don't contact me again!" Her hands shook as she pulled a corset from the bottom of the washing machine and held it up to the light. She mentally added contortionist to the list of Freda's significant skills.

Frederik's hail of expletives split the airwaves, aimed both at her and at Rohan. Desperation exposed his manipulation of their friendship. The first time, she'd been a volunteer, but his cajoling and insistence pushed her to the edge of becoming an unwilling conscript. Emma inhaled and hoisted the phone. She jabbed the screen to take it off speaker and lifted the device to her ear. "That's enough!" she snapped. "Our association is over, Frederik." She swallowed as his anger stretched across the miles to lap at her consciousness like a vitriolic thread. "Your service with the Actuary is terminated as of today." Her tone hardened as confidence filtered through her words. "Don't contact me or Rohan again."

Her fingers shook as she pulled the cover of the burner phone apart. She released the SIM card and poked the tiny cardboard rectangle down the plug hole of the laundry sink.

"Hey."

Emma squealed and set the tap running too fast. Water spattered off the porcelain surface and soaked the front of her dress. She turned to find Rohan leaned against the door frame, his hair mussed from the wind and his tie hanging loose beneath his collar. His eyes glinted, and she sensed her angry conversation with Frederik had masked his steady tread. "Hi." Her voice wobbled and she darted a glance back at the plug hole. Liquid funnelled over the lip to carry the fragment of tech into the septic tank hidden under the front lawn. "I thought you planned to go to the station right after dropping the children." She used a stray towel to mop at the damp patches on her dress.

"My client rescheduled." Rohan stepped forward and teased the towel from her frantic fingers. He draped it over the side of the sink and his arms encircled her in a fluid movement. "I decided to come home and treat my wife to a late breakfast." His breath coasted over her soft neck as he placed butterfly kisses along her trapezius muscle. Her hair swished against her shoulders and he moved it aside for greater access. The hard edges of the washing machine dug into Emma's calves and she pressed herself against Rohan's strong body to counter its bite. The burner phone clattered to the floorboards with the sound of shattering plastic.

Emma dismissed the promise of cafe eggs and coffee in favour of something much more wholesome. She'd swapped relationship for partnership and craved time to compare the two.

Result

Nicky pranced around as *The Cock with the Crimson Comb*, his backside hanging through a hole in the yellow tights. The plastic chicken beak clung to his forehead like the horn of a unicorn, lifted there to allow him to breathe. He ran towards Emma and instinct made her turn her hip to take the blow. But he screeched to a halt in front of her on the gravel, and his lips turned down into a pout. "I'd never hurt you, Mummy." His shoulders collapsed forward to give him a concave chest. Kaylee arrived next to him, tripping at the last second and cannoning into Emma's hip. She laughed and rubbed at her nose. Her police officer's hat slipped off her head backwards and she spun to fetch it, stumbling over the curb and landing in a heap on Ray's neat lawn. Nicky shrugged. "Fair enough," he conceded. He rolled his eyes at his friend's giddy antics before reaching up to kiss his sister's bare foot.

Stephie's lips parted in a wide grin which encompassed her entire face. Nicky made a sniffing action on her toes and she blew out quick breaths of excitement. Emma smiled at her son. "She loves you," she said, reinforcing a sibling bond which would outlive her.

"I love her too." He took Stephie's hand and rubbed it across his damp fringe. His blonde hair poked from beneath the crimson crest and the misplaced beak. The baby squealed with delight.

Nicky bounced away with Kaylee, waiting as his friend fell over the legs of her father's trousers for the fifth time. Emma smiled and shook her head. A crash of thunder in the distance reminded the crowd on her lawn that the end of the party approached. The guests sat around on garden chairs, enjoying the last vestiges of a freak summer before the shortened autumn delivered them into the cruel hands of winter again.

Freda waved at Emma from her throne near the beer tent and Emma shielded her eyes and then waved. "Cooee!" She called and waggled her skinny arm. A tumbler containing ochre liquid slopped its contents across her skirt. She tipped sideways in her chair as though about to fall out of it. Emma held her breath as another elderly lady tried to sit her up straight and became entangled in Freda's flailing arms and the spreading whiskey. "Oh dear," Emma breathed.

"Hmmmn." A figure appeared next to her, shielding her from the rays of sunlight that made her squint. He cast Emma into shadow and stood as a soldier at ease, legs apart and his hands behind his back. The expensive suit he wore fitted him like a second skin, and he showed no sign of discomfort in the heat. A missing tie betrayed his only concession to a casual dress code. He jerked his blond head in Freda's direction. "I'm not carrying her upstairs." His arm touched Emma's and his voice rumbled through her body. Rohan brought his hands forward and twinkled his fingers. "She's an octopus when she's drunk."

Emma bit her lip to hide her smile and patted Stephie's back as her daughter settled over her shoulder. "You're the hottest guy here." She kept her comment casual.

Rohan's bark of laughter disturbed Stephie, and she popped her head up before butting her chin against Emma's neck. "I'm the only male under sixty, so I refuse to accept that as a compliment."

"Hold me." Emma moved nearer, and he slipped his arm around her shoulders. She relaxed beneath his embrace, their fragile connection strengthening with increased knowledge of each other. He'd die for her, but he wouldn't always instinctively know she needed a hug. She rested her head against his chest. "Ray's here. He's under fifty."

Rohan made a sound low in his throat. "And he's busy."

"Do you think your new guy will work out as well as his predecessor?" Emma pursed her lips and tried not to think of the Christopher she'd known. Handsome, funny, vulnerable Christopher had disappeared beneath the face of an enemy she sensed she'd meet again.

"Better." Rohan's mouth twitched as an old man carried a tumbler of whiskey from the tent and pushed his walking frame one-handed. "He does as he's told. Lachlan will stay for a few months after he arrives. I trust him to show the new tech the ropes. I know him from my army days."

"Is Lachlan a communications expert?" Emma tried to sound knowledgeable and failed.

"Bomb disposal. Then shifted into the intelligence service after they arrested him for hacking." Rohan's lips quirked. "Just as well they caught him."

"Because he proved dangerous?"

Rohan's blond fringe blew back from his forehead to reveal the fine scars across his skin. "Because he blew himself up. Bomb disposal wasn't his calling."

"Oh." Emma gulped. "Has he discovered all Christopher's little booby traps in the system yet?"

Rohan sighed. "Most of them. I suspect the new guy will find more."

"Christopher let Winston in, didn't he? I blamed Freda, but it was him."

"No. My father has men working for him with a level of skill Dolan can only dream of. He walked through the gate and into the house under his own directive." He released a sigh and shook his head. "I'm used to his appearances. This one day, he just lifted the flap on my tent and sat on the bunk next to me."

Emma frowned. "Well, that's easier than getting into a house teched out like a fortress."

Rohan's blond eyebrows rose. "Not in a war zone surrounded by British forces and terrorists."

"Oh." Emma's shoulders drooped. So, Winston would be a fixture of her life with Rohan. His rescue of her at a moment's notice had already proved his worth. She figured if his presence didn't bother Rohan, she would learn to live with it.

Stephie made a gurgling sound and spat up congealed milk onto her bib. She screwed her tiny features into an expression of disgust and closed her eyes. Emma mopped her daughter's face with the cloth she'd had the foresight to wear across her shoulder. "What happened about your government contract? They paid you up front to find Regan, but did you deliver?" Stephie pulled her knees up to her chest and released a wail as Emma ventured into dangerous territory with her questions.

Rohan held his hands out for his daughter, and Emma shifted Stephie into his arms. She lifted the cloth to lay it over his shoulder, but he shook his head. He cradled her along his forearms, her crown in his cupped hands. When he bounced her up and down in a gentle rocking motion, her fretting ceased. She squinted up at the sky and relaxed, the air bubbles in her tiny system moving instead of forming pockets of pain. "They paid half as a retainer and half on delivery of the risk." He smiled at Stephie and her bottom lip dropped to form a gummy grin. "And I delivered. I gave them the person who created the dead drop."

Emma swallowed. "Christopher. But they didn't catch him." A dart of anguish twisted in her chest. The memory of her last conversation with him would stay with her forever. His eyes had reflected love, regret and surprise laced with pain. He'd underestimated her and she'd betrayed him.

When Rohan didn't answer, Emma turned sideways to stare up at him. "They didn't catch him, did they?"

He inhaled, the sound hissing through his teeth. A crack of thunder rocked the earth and Stephie flung her arms out wide on either side of her. Nicky whooped as he performed his spiky chicken strut for the benefit of Freda and her cronies. Rohan looked down at Emma, his azure irises sparkling. A line appeared and disappeared in his forehead. "I don't want to lie to you." His tone held a gruff quality, and he lowered his pitch to a whisper. His Russian lilt loaded the words with staccato beats. "I collected the other half of my payment, Emma," he concluded. "And Regan is safe. Please leave it at that."

Emma broke eye contact with him. She stared at the grass beneath her sandals as a ball with the density of osmium settled in her stomach. The ramifications of Rohan's words proved endless. Christopher Dolan was incarcerated. Or dead.

"Mummy! Look at me!" Nicky clucked and waggled his arms. He stuck his backside out to give his cardboard tail feathers an opportunity to waggle. The spiky ends had bent where he forgot about them and sat down at a table to eat his scone. He performed his chicken strut to Kaylee's peals of laughter, the hole in his yellow tights big enough to reveal the fabric of his underpants.

"Whose child is that?" Rohan spoke through the side of his mouth and shook his head. He carried on his life as though he hadn't just dropped a bomb on Emma's.

"Yours," she whispered. She wondered how long it would take before Nicky started missing Christopher. Emma had pushed the pram across to the folly the previous day on the pretext of getting her colicky daughter to sleep. The shed next to the Gothic structure remained open, the door still up to reveal its contents. Christopher had taken his car in his haste, but the Harley Davidson he loved so much sat exactly where he'd left it.

Emma pursed her lips as the first spots of rain broke up the garden party. A local bus driver fired up the sixty seater he'd driven from Market Harborough and the sound of air brakes hissed over the rumbling thunder. Within minutes, the elderly guests had lumbered across the lawn to their van from the residential home and the other locals piled onto the courtesy bus. The various traders went to work on their marquees, causing the fabric to shudder and the legs to tilt. The cheerful scene had turned to destruction in seconds.

A guard, from the security company they'd hired to keep people from the areas off limits, hauled Freda to a standing position. Nicky and Kaylee attempted a combined effort to extract her bottom from the deckchair but it resisted. Rubbish littered the front lawn, and a napkin floated past Emma's feet. Ray appeared in her peripheral vision. He wore a fluorescent vest and carried a black rubbish bag.

"Let's go inside," Rohan said. He shifted Stephie over his shoulder and frowned down at Emma. He reached to cradle her cheek in his free hand and dipped to kiss her lips. "I love you, Mrs Andreyev," he whispered. "You have all of my heart."

The twisted knot in Emma's chest lessened its bite, and she rose on her toes for another. "I love you," she replied. A smile reached her eyes as she stared up at her husband. "And Stephie does too, even though she just puked on your suit jacket."

A taxi slid between the open gates and halted on the driveway. The departing guests stopped it progressing further along the narrow lane. The autumnal orange of the maple trees hid the passenger as he slid from the vehicle and slammed the door. Emma shielded her eyes against the glare of sunrays wrestling through angry clouds, unable to discern more than a skinny male wheeling a suitcase. "Who's that?" Her brow furrowed.

Rohan inspected his wristwatch and nodded with approval. "Right on time," he murmured. The thin man battled his bag up the long driveway, stopping to correct it as the wheels wedged themselves in the gravel. She glanced at Rohan, looking for answers and irritated by the slight lift of his upper lip. An energy exuded from him as though he struggled to suppress his laughter behind a severe mask. As the man reached the curve in front of the house and navigated the departing bus, Emma gave a sharp inhale of recognition.

"Regan!" She stepped forward and waved to him, causing him to alter his trajectory from the front door to their position at the edge of the lawn.

"Hey." He greeted Emma with a wide grin, but his pupils dilated as he eyed Rohan and shifted on his feet. "Mr Actuary." He swallowed and blinked at his mistake.

Rohan gave an upward lift of his chin and turned away, but Emma recognised the amused shake of his shoulders as he tried not to laugh. He took care with the steps while carrying his daughter, taking them one at a time and not wanting his irregular gait to disturb the bundle in his arms. Regan hauled his suitcase towards the stairs, creating ridges in the gravel with the wheels as though charting the first in his journey to a new life. He paused at the bottom, looking up at the arched front doors and the bank of windows above him as four storeys stared down with disinterest. Rohan passed through the open doors and Regan stopped to murmur to Emma. "Dad's upset," he whispered. "Will you speak to your husband about forgiving him?"

Emma paused, a sense of hopelessness landing on her head like a weight. She sighed and fixed a blank mask over her expression. "Do you understand why Rohan fired him?" The steadiness of her voice surprised her.

Regan nodded and then changed it to a shake, his greasy hair tapping against his collar. "Not really. Is it because I got into a mess and he tried to help me?"

"No." Sympathy radiated from the softness in Emma's brown irises, but her expression remained fixed. "It's because he manipulated me to get to Rohan."

"Oh." Regan stared at the gravel but jerked his gaze back to her as he gave a nervous swallow. "Oh. Like I just did."

"Yes." Emma narrowed her eyes and glared at the young man in front of her. "I suggest you don't do it again."

"I'm sorry." Regan's dejected nod conveyed his understanding. "Will you tell him?" He jerked his head towards the stairs. "Should I call the taxi to come back for me?"

Emma straightened her shoulders and stepped into her role as Rohan's latest operative. Nicky darted past them and only the sound of his tights finally ripping destroyed the illusion of a badass woman as she cringed in response. "I tell him everything," she said, her tone severe. "But I think you and I understand each other now, don't we?"

Regan nodded, his head performing the pecking action Nicky had spent all week practising. Emma opened her arm to indicate he should follow the children into the main house and he turned, his shoulders stooped and his skinny arms bumping the battered suitcase up the steps into his new home.

Can you help me?

I realise you might want to just skip this page because I'm asking for something.

And I hate to do it.

But if you could leave me a review, it would make my day.

My words don't sell my books, yours do.

Your opinion matters to the readers searching for their next read and who trust the most reliable recommendation of all: word of mouth.

Your word of mouth.

If you're prompted by your retailer to give a review, please consider doing that for me.

And let me know.

Email me, Message me, prod, Tweet or Insta me.

I'm interested in your thoughts, opinions and suggestions on how I can do better.

About the Author

K T Bowes worked in education for more than a decade, both in New Zealand and the United Kingdom and has been writing since she could first hold a pencil.

She graduated from Aberystwyth, a college of the University of Wales where she studied English and received a BA (Hons). And then she went in completely the opposite direction and trained to become a law enforcement officer in the Trading Standards department of local government.

While raising children, she worked part time wherever she could fit in extra duties.

That included, cleaner, gardener, dog walker, commissioned artist, teaching assistant, administrative assistant and archivist.

In 2006, she climbed on a long-haul flight with her family, a suitcase, and a heap of dreams for a life in New Zealand.

In 2017, her husband gave her permission to quit everything and write.

She believes in God, which is just as well because the situations she gets herself into often require divine assistance.

Surprisingly happily married despite her crazy escapades, K T Bowes still hankers after another parachute jump but hasn't convinced her husband to join in. Her four beautiful children are all now making their own way in the world and finally eating salad and vegetables.

She lives in the North Island of New Zealand between the Hakarimata Ranges and the Waikato River with a mad cat and often a few crazy horses. Horse riding is her passion but unfortunately she keeps falling off and breaking bones, so has gone back to road running instead. She can't be seen pacing the streets of Ngaruawahia because she runs in the dark, convinced people will laugh.

Often accompanied by one of her characters complaining about something, the author appears to have mental problems as she frequently answers back, which is another good reason for running under cover of darkness.

You can find her hanging out on social media in the following places.

Check in and say hello. Maybe suggest she gets back to writing and stops watching cat videos.

FACEBOOK

https://www.facebook.com/NZauthorKTBowes/

INSTAGRAM

https://www.instagram.com/k_t_bowes

Also by this Author

The Calculated Risk Series:

The Actuary

The Actuary's Wife

The Actuary in Trouble

The Heart of The Actuary

Troubled series for teens:

Free from the Tracks

Sophia's Dilemma

A Trail of Lies

Gone Phishing

Escaping the Back Country NZ Series:

Pirongia's Secret

Deleilah

Standalone novels:

Artifact

Demons on Her Shoulder

All Saints

Her Quiet Legacy

Humorous Cozy Mystery Series from New Zealand

Dead Straight

Bad Hair Day

Side Parting

The Boring Bit

The copyright is registered with the National Library of New Zealand, so there's no point anyone plagiarising or pirating any part of it.

Everyone will know.

Rohan will go after them.